THE DEAD NEVER DIE

CHRONICLES OF CAIN
BOOK 5

JOHN CORWIN

RAVEN HOUSE

ZOMBIE APOCALYPSE

They say no good deed goes unpunished, and Cain is living proof of it.

His quest to help the gorgon, Dusa, and his favorite bartender, Aura went terribly right and horrifically wrong. Now the sword Soultaker has claimed two more souls and added them to its undead army. Zeus and Mars tell Cain to fix the situation, or they'll erase him permanently along with everyone he cares about.

To free souls from Soultaker, Cain needs information from the original Thanatos, Greek god of death. But Thanatos vanished long ago, creating the office of the Grim Reaper which is now occupied by a man named Garrick.

Garrick agrees to help Cain find Thanatos, but before they get started, the other three horsemen, War, Pestilence, and Famine put Garrick in a coma so they can they seed the world with plagues, conflict, and starvation and start the apocalypse.

Without Death to free the souls of the humans dying from the chaos, their bodies are rising from the dead, killing more humans, and threatening the very fabric of fate itself.

Cain reluctantly accepts the mantle of Death so he can stop the zombie apocalypse and use the powers of his new office to find Thanatos. His journey will take him all over the world, to Hell, Hel, and beyond.

Dealing with one pantheon was nearly impossible. Now Cain

finds himself tangling with the Norse, Greeks, Christians, and of course, minions of the Elder Things. Cthulhu and Shub-Nuggerath were horrific enough, but this new entity is even worse.

But there's one thing Cain's enemies didn't count on. If there's an apocalypse, there will be no more mangoritas.

No more plastic pirate swords with fruit.

No more toothpick umbrellas.

The bad guys are about to find out the hard way that no one, not even a god comes between Cain and his mangoritas.

BOOKS BY JOHN CORWIN

Join the Overworld Conclave for all the news, memes and tentacles you could ever desire!

https://www.facebook.com/groups/overworldconclave

Or get your tentacles via email: www.johncorwin.net

Fan page: https://www.facebook.com/johncorwinauthor

CHRONICLES OF CAIN

To Kill a Unicorn

Enter Oblivion

Throne of Lies

At The Forest of Madness

The Dead Never Die

Shadow of Cthulhu

Cabal of Chaos

Monster Squad

THE OVERWORLD CHRONICLES

Sweet Blood of Mine

Dark Light of Mine

Fallen Angel of Mine

Dread Nemesis of Mine

Twisted Sister of Mine

Dearest Mother of Mine

Infernal Father of Mine

Sinister Seraphim of Mine

The Next Thing I Knew

Outsourced

1

M y adventure started with a salad.

It was a brunch salad, to be sure, covered in scrambled eggs, bacon, and slices of French toast. I never would have tried the thing if the Devil himself hadn't recommended it, but I had to admit it was fucking delicious. It was also a very unorthodox meal for me when kicking off a quest.

Lucifer was already four shots deep into his meal, while also sipping Clase Azul Reposado from a whiskey glass. "I'm so bloody excited I can hardly wait." He took a bite of his eggs Benedict and sighed in pleasure. "Great food and enough drama to keep me entertained for at least a week. What more could a lord of Hell ask for?"

I cleared my throat. "You do realize this is serious business, I hope? Loki and gang are tearing apart the fabric of existence, meaning no more humans for you to enjoy once the Elder Things conquer the divine realm."

"Oh, I don't think there's any danger of that." He scoffed. "That infernal father of mine claims he's omniscient, so I'd love to see him singlehandedly stop an outsider invasion."

"Infernal doesn't sound like the right word to describe your father." Convincing Lucifer to take anything seriously was like pulling teeth, so I took another tack. "What will you miss the most if Gaia is taken over by outsiders?"

"I think Earth is perfectly safe, but I would certainly miss a lovely woman I met not long ago. She's the only person I've met who easily resists my charms." His gaze went distant. "Yes, I would miss her the most. I wonder, do you think the outsiders have sex?"

Lucifer's nonchalance was maddening. My hand clenched around my whiskey glass so tight it shattered.

His amused gaze turned confused. "Why are you so uptight, Cain? Garrick will be here soon, and all this will be easily settled, I assure you."

Garrick was Death. Not lowercase death, but capital "D" Death. The Grim Mother Effing Reaper. Thanatos himself. Well, not exactly. Thanatos, a son of the night goddess, Nyx, had been the original Death, but he'd long since grown tired of the job and handed the job off to mortals. Garrick currently occupied the office of Death using the vestments of the office, the cloak, scythe, and a ghastly pale horse named Mortis, to carry out his duties.

Garrick had become an expert at reaping souls and delivering them to the appropriate afterlife, but I had a problem not even he could solve. Aura had murdered the goddess, Athena, with Soultaker by turning her briefly mortal so the sword could add her soul to the army of the undead trapped inside the sword. Athena's body still lived, but it was empty of consciousness.

Zeus had charged me with returning Athena's soul to her body. Mars had ensured my compliance by killing Layla with Soultaker, trapping her soul along with Athena's. They'd healed her body and taken it with them to the divine realm for safekeeping, or so they'd said.

Garrick might be an expert on handling souls, but he had no idea how to free one from Soultaker. Hephaestus had forged the weapon, but the magic that trapped the soul had been crafted by the original Thanatos. The original god of death, however, had vanished long ago and now we had to find him.

Tracking hard to find individuals was my specialty, but this went so far beyond my particular set of skills that I would have to rely heavily on Garrick's abilities.

"Cain, you're brooding again." Lucifer stabbed his eggs benedict with a fork and leaned back. "I told you I can't simply waltz into Hades without upsetting the natural order of things. My domain is Hell."

I calmly wiped my bloodied hand with a napkin and glared at him. "That's not why I'm brooding, and you know it."

A frantic waiter hurried over. "Sir you have glass stuck in your hand!" His face paled and he looked ready to faint.

Lucifer stood, pulled out another chair and helped the waiter sit down. "It will be all right, young man." He poured him a glass of water. "Here, drink this."

The waiter took it and sipped gratefully. "I'm so sorry. The sight of blood makes me weak in the knees." He looked away and shuddered.

"Quite all right." Lucifer sat down and put a hand on his shoulder. "Would you like some eggs?"

I plucked the glass shards from my hand and wrapped the cloth napkin around it. "Where the fuck is Garrick?"

Lucifer looked aghast. "Mind your manners, Cain. This poor chap is having an episode and all you care about is Garrick?"

I pounded my injured fist on the table, rattling the silverware, sending water glasses tumbling. The waiter yelped and jumped up as I rose to my feet. "Layla is fucking dead, Lucifer, and all you can think about is your gods damned brunch!"

The crowd on the restaurant patio went silent. Wide eyes and gawking stares locked onto me from all angles. I took a deep breath to quash my emotions and calmly dropped cash on the table. I unwrapped the bloodied napkin, dropped it on Lucifer's eggs bene-dict, then left.

"You didn't even eat your bacon salad," Lucifer called after me.

We were at a trendy eatery off Melrose Avenue in Hollywood, a place frequented by celebrities. A few paparazzi snapped photos of the scene, probably wondering if the infamous local celebrity, Lucifer, was in a lovers' spat. I cast a sigil and the electronics in their cameras sparked and smoked. Paparazzi cried out in surprise, throwing their burning electronics to the ground.

My submarine was parked in the Hollywood Reservoir and Lucifer had picked me up, so I went to the curb to call a taxi. I hadn't been standing there long when Lucifer appeared next to me, expression serious for once.

"I'm sorry, Cain. It's difficult for me to appreciate the severity of a situation unless it has directly impacted my life." He sighed. "One of my character flaws, I suppose."

I took a deep breath to keep my calm intact. "Did you call Garrick again?"

"I did, but it went to voicemail immediately." Lucifer shrugged. "That usually happens when he's not on Earth."

"Where else would he be?"

"He is technically mortal, so he requires sleep and relaxation." Lucifer looked up at the sunny blue sky. "His home is in Purgatory, I believe."

"Purgatory?" I shook my head. "Why wouldn't he live on Gaia?"

"It's Earth, not Gaia." Lucifer huffed. "The rules don't allow him to live on Earth. At least that's what he told me. Something about his presence affects mortals even if they don't know he's there. Purgatory is a part of the divine realm and separate from mortals."

I considered it. "The presence of Death must be chilling to mortals."

"Indeed."

I regarded my devilish companion. "Well, can you take us to his house?"

Lucifer's eyes flared. "I'd much rather not, Cain. You know I abhor the divine realm."

"Because you might run into dear old dad?"

"That or my siblings." He shuddered.

"From what little I know of the divine realm it's divided into parts. Isn't Heaven separate from Purgatory?"

"The offices of the Fates, Time, Death, and others are at the very center of everything." Lucifer patted his brow as if checking for sweat. "Just thinking about it makes my heart flutter."

I wasn't terribly familiar with Christian mythology, but I knew enough to guess at Lucifer's real problem. "You were banished from Heaven. Does that mean you can't return to the divine realm either?"

"Well, if you must get personal, yes I was kicked out." He dramatically spread his arms and turned his face to the sun. "I'm a fallen angel, forbidden from seeing my home ever again. If Father discovered I was anywhere near Heaven, he'd be quite upset."

"Well, Purgatory isn't Heaven." I snapped my fingers. "Problem solved."

"I understand your mortal mind can't comprehend the gravity of this situation, so I won't bother arguing it further."

I pressed my lips into a flat line. "You won't help me, then?"

Lucifer rubbed his hands together and grinned. "Of course, I'll help you. Two bloody fools leaping into the divine realm and possibly setting off Armageddon? What could possibly go wrong?"

"You just said exactly what could go wrong." I shook my head. "I give up trying to figure you out, Lucifer. One moment you're absolutely not going and now you're all in?"

"If truth be told, the tequila I drank for brunch is finally giving me a bit of liquid courage." He giggled. "That, and I also realized just how much fun sneaking around the divine realm like hooligans will be."

I wasn't sure if I should be frightened or relieved, so I opted for cautious optimism. "When can we leave?"

"I'll need to speak with Castiel first." Lucifer gave a sheepish look. "I promised I'd warn him if I decided to do anything apocalyptic. He thinks I've already set the end days in motion from previous indiscretions, but I wholeheartedly disagree."

One of the paparazzi whose camera apparently hadn't been affected by my earlier hex approached us. "Lucifer, what are your thoughts of the impending lockdown? Do you think Perdition can survive?"

Lucifer blinked as if suddenly realizing the man was there. "Lockdown? I have no bloody idea what you're talking about."

The paparazzi looked confused by Lucifer's confusion. "Don't you watch the news? There's a pandemic—a plague sweeping the world."

"I have little time for such trivial things, so why don't you be a good chap and explain it to me?"

I was just as confused. The nub life was peripheral to me, meaning I rarely paid attention to their news or anything else. The only times I'd cared were when I needed to track down someone for Eclipse, the bounty hunting and assassination agency I'd once worked for. Even so, I couldn't believe I'd missed hearing about a worldwide plague.

"The virus is everywhere," the man was saying. "They're making people stay at home to avoid spreading it. That means closing night-clubs, restaurants, and any place where people gather. It's affecting food production the most. They're predicting a worldwide shortage."

Lucifer's brow furrowed in concern. "What about alcohol production?"

The paparazzi blinked. Shrugged. "Yeah, probably that too."

"Bloody hell!" Lucifer gripped my arm. "We need to get to the liquor store this moment so I can stock up."

I freed my arm. "I don't care what you do as long as you get me to the divine realm first."

The paparazzi stared at both of us as if we were insane. "Are you on drugs?"

"I'll ask Ashatha to go to the store for me." Lucifer sighed. "Well, Cain, I suppose it's a good thing we've got this little adventure to keep us busy. At least I won't miss anything while we're in the divine realm."

The paparazzi somehow looked more confused. "Is that the name of another club?"

"Yes, my father's very exclusive club." Lucifer pointed to the cloud-less sky. "You humans think it's up there in the clouds."

"There aren't any clouds," the man said.

"Because Heaven gave up on LA." Lucifer touched the door handle on his Rolls Royce Dawn and it swung open from the back rather than the front like most cars. He motioned toward the passenger seat. "Well, come on, Cain. Let's get this party started, shall we?"

The paparazzi flinched as if waking from a dream. "No comment on the pandemic?"

"Drink early and often." Lucifer grinned. "For tomorrow the world may end."

I slid into the passenger seat and buckled in. Lucifer's driving wasn't for the faint of heart or even the strong of heart, for that matter.

He backed up without checking for traffic, then gunned the car down the road. He managed to get us back to Perdition quickly despite LA traffic, somehow weaving through the gaps between cars and hitting green lights with uncanny precision. It was enough to make me wonder if his aura actively affected the world around him, bending it to his will. Then again, he might just be a supernaturally skilled driver.

Castiel was reading a book on the balcony in Lucifer's penthouse when we stepped out of the elevator. He looked up, narrowed gaze sweeping across the two of us. "What's going on?"

"An adventure, brother." Lucifer poured himself a glass of whiskey. "We're going to the divine realm."

"The Hell you are." Castiel closed his novel and set it on the table. He rose in one quick motion, as if lifted by invisible strings. "That's far too close to Heaven, and you know it."

"But it's not Heaven, is it?" Lucifer sipped his whiskey. "I won't be breaking my exile."

Castiel scowled. "I'm going with you to make sure you stay out of trouble."

"Not a good idea." Lucifer stepped onto the balcony and stared out at the city. "We have an urgent matter to discuss with Garrick, but he hasn't been answering his calls."

Castiel frowned. "Who?"

"Death, brother."

"Ah, him." Castiel's frown deepened. "I remember his wife more than him."

Lucifer chuckled. "She's quite hard to forget."

My eyebrows arched. "Garrick is married? What kind of life does his spouse have?"

"A very interesting one, it turns out." Lucifer tapped his empty glass and went to the bar for a refill. "Brother, let this serve as notice that Cain and I will be popping over to Deaths' house for a visit. I ask simply that you remain here and cover for me."

"Cover for you?" Castiel scoffed. "That didn't work out so well the last time."

"Yes, but it certainly made the night memorable for the patrons, or so I hear." Lucifer downed a glass of whiskey in one shot. "In any case, we should get going now, Cain."

Castiel sighed long and hard. "I'll pray for you, brother. I have a feeling this won't end well."

Lucifer set down his glass and waved at the city past the balcony. "World's already ending, or hadn't you heard? There's a pandemic."

"A pandemic?" Castiel's brow furrowed. "First I've heard of it."

"For people living in the mortal world, we're awfully disconnected from it," I said.

"Plagues don't affect us." Castiel shrugged. "I pray Father isn't killing off the humans again."

"Well, he promised not to," Lucifer said.

"By flood." Castiel shook his head. "He's been absent from mortal affairs for so long, I doubt this is his doing."

I leaned against the grand piano in the middle of the loft. "There's a world full of people constantly getting sick and infected with new diseases. Pandemics just happen."

Lucifer nodded. "Quite right. It might also be why Garrick isn't answering our calls. He might be too busy collecting souls."

"I'm not so sure." Castiel had clicked on the television and was watching the news, lips curled in disgust. The image showed rows upon rows of cots with sick patients moaning and crying out in pain.

"Their bodies are beyond saving, doctors are telling us, but these people refuse to die." A reporter with a mask on stood at the scene. "Their lungs are ruptured, hearts no longer beating, but these people still seem to be alive. It's a phenomenon medical experts can't explain."

A man in a white lab coat appeared on screen. "They have no pulse, no vital signs at all, but somehow, they're still alive." He shuddered. "I've never seen anything like it."

The image switched to what appeared to be grainy security camera footage of a makeshift morgue. Black body bags were piled in one corner of a room. Several of them were flailing violently.

The reporter continued. "Now there are reports that some of these bodies are reanimating. This scene unfolded in a morgue in Jakarta, India. Frightened workers refuse to enter the morgue and with good reason."

"What in the bloody Hell is going on?" Lucifer poured himself another drink. "This can mean only one thing."

Castiel nodded. "Death hasn't been collecting souls. The souls are trapped in dead bodies."

I watched the newscast as they showed twitching bodies flopping off cots. "What does that mean?"

"Zombies, Cain." Lucifer tossed back another shot. "This is how you get zombies."

2

"Zombies?" I scoffed. "The only way you get zombies is when necromancers reanimate dead flesh."

"Usually, yes, but that's not what this is." Lucifer took a swig straight from the bottle and offered it to me. "I fear something foul has befallen Garrick. We need to find him now. There are far greater implications for the living and the dead when the primary collector of souls isn't on the job."

I took the proffered bottle and took a healthy swig of my own. I'd need a lot more than one bottle to quell the dread knotting my stomach. "If Death isn't collecting souls, does that mean we'll have a zombie apocalypse on our hands?"

"Let's just say it will make for interesting headlines." Lucifer took a deep breath and rubbed his hands together. "I'm nervous, brother." He laughed nervously as if to underscore that. "It's been far too long since I've gone into the divine realm."

Castiel nodded grimly. "You should be far more than nervous, Lucifer. Some of our siblings won't take kindly to you entering the divine realm."

"Naturally, brother." Lucifer brushed lint off his expensive suit. "I'm not concerned about them, so much as my attire. I haven't kept up with divine fashions for quite some time." He wrapped an arm around my waist and winked. "Enjoy the ride, Cain."

I blinked. "Huh?" Hera had taken us into the divine realm with a portal. The last thing I was expecting was the rustle of feathers and magnificent white wings unfurling from Lucifer's back. We launched straight up off the balcony and shot skyward so fast, it should have turned my internal organs to paste.

Thanks to the wonders of magic, I felt only slight disorientation.

The world blurred into shadow, the city skyline morphing into a chaotic landscape of obsidian plains and canyons. A new skyline formed in the distance—massive monolithic towers framed against a giant red sun that sat low on the horizon.

That should have been enough to hold my attention, but my gaze was drawn toward something else, a speck on the dark landscape. I couldn't look away as it grew larger, coming into focus.

It was a wooden two-story house. Light from the windows shone on the patchy grass in the yard. The laughter of children echoed in the cold night. A baby's cries cut through the laughter. Heavy objects thudded against wooden floorboards and the house went quiet.

"No," I hissed. "I never heard laughter. I never heard babies. I wouldn't have done it!"

Something tightened around my waist. I flinched and looked into glowing red eyes set against a face with red skin. "Almost there, Cain. Apologies, but this is the most direct route."

A shadowy figure in my peripheral vision drew my gaze from the demon. The figure walked around the house, staff in hand. It looked straight at me, black, soulless eyes boring beneath my flesh. There was no emotion on that face, just a grim set to the jaw and deadly calm demeanor. I'd seen that look a thousand times after completing an assigned job.

Because the face was mine.

The lights in the house flickered out. Windows exploded as countless black wraiths flooded out of the house and into my body, each one a dagger of ice burrowing straight into my very core. I gritted my teeth and roared defiance as they wrapped themselves around my insides.

"I didn't know!" I shouted. "I didn't know!"

Golden sunlight assaulted my eyes. The hellish landscape was gone, replaced by verdant green, rolling hills, and the susurrus of a gentle breeze through trees. The grip on my waist loosened and I stumbled to my knees. I winced at the brightness and shielded my eyes with a hand.

Lucifer knelt next to me, grinning madly. "Goodness, Cain. You have some vicious demons, don't you?"

I blinked a few times as realization hit me. "We were in Hell."

He nodded. "You're not a believer, but I suppose the psychological effects are bound to affect anyone who enters my domain."

I blew out a breath to quell my rising gorge. "That was pure hell."

"Naturally. Humans are exceptional at punishing themselves." Lucifer's grin widened. "We do, of course, still employ normal torture. It's the only way to properly punish vicious and psychopathic souls since many of them have zero remorse or guilt."

To say I was disappointed in myself was a gross understatement. Hell was the ultimate mind trap and none of my training had prepared me for it. Had not Lucifer carried me out of that place, I would never have escaped it on my own.

"Don't look so down, Cain." Lucifer patted me on the back. "The deeper the guilt, the harder it is to forgive yourself and find redemption."

"I couldn't resist it." I took a calming breath. "It completely over-powered me."

His grin flattened into a more sympathetic expression. "Very few ever find forgiveness within themselves. Oh, they might overcome that first obstacle eventually, but most people have deep guilt about many things in their lives. Working through every dark stain on your soul takes even the strongest people centuries. Most are doomed to an endless, eternal cycle of self-flagellation."

"Because they lack the ability to forgive themselves."

He nodded. "Precisely. Very few humans possess the willpower to overcome the scars on their souls. Why do you think they're so miser-able even while alive?"

I didn't like the idea that I was no better than normal humans. I was trained in psychological warfare. A well-honed weapon. Torvin used to point me in a direction and let me go. He thought I was an inferior human, but even he knew I'd perform my duty, no questions asked. At least until that fateful night when I'd murdered a house full of innocents and been haunted by their ghosts. Their influence had slowly changed me into something else.

Thanatos had relieved me of those souls, so I no longer heard their voices in my head. They'd forgiven me, but I'd never forgiven myself. If I died and ended up in Hell, it seemed I was doomed to relive that moment for the rest of eternity.

I took a deep breath "Why can't I forgive myself?"

Lucifer chuckled. "Humans are masters at self-rationalization. They make themselves feel good about what they did and why they did it. But all they're really doing is suppressing guilt any way they can."

"I feel terrible about what I did."

He nodded. "Of course, you do. But feeling bad about something isn't even close to forgiving yourself for doing it. That takes a forti-tude of spirit very few have."

And apparently, I didn't have it. When I thought about it, I didn't even know where to start when it came to forgiving myself. "You mentioned psychopaths earlier. If they don't feel remorse or shame for their sins, wouldn't they qualify for Heaven?"

"Heavens no, Cain." Lucifer smirked. "It's our duty to make them find that shame so they can understand their wrongs if possible. We assign our best torturers to those sorts."

I grimaced. "What a wonderful system."

He shrugged. "It is what it is."

"You just let these people suffer in a cycle of self-induced agony and anxiety without actually trying to help them redeem themselves, no matter how small the sin?"

Lucifer bit his lower lip. "When you put it like that, it does sound rather awful."

"Well, maybe it is." Then again, what did I know? The gods didn't care about logic. Religion was mostly fear-driven, designed to make people cower before their makers or suffer the consequences. Hell was a consequence most would suffer while Heaven was a reward a miniscule number of people could realistically earn.

I was certain the Christian god didn't care about populating Heaven so much as he wanted to control everyone while they were alive.

Quacking ducks pulled me from my reverie and directed my attention toward a small yellow cottage on the shore of a crystal-clear pond where the fowl darted across the water. Squeaking squirrels chased each other around the trunk of a massive oak in the front yard while a large red cardinal watched from the branches above.

I frowned and looked around in confusion. "Where are we?"

"Garrick's house." Gravel crunched beneath Lucifer's expensive shoes as he walked the path toward the house.

"This is where Death lives?" I shook my head in confusion. "I was expecting something more Gothic."

"It isn't always like this," Lucifer said. "Garrick has changed it many times over the years."

"I thought you didn't come here often."

"He's shown me pictures." Lucifer walked to the front door and knocked. "Even Death likes to show off his home."

The door opened almost immediately. A ghostly pale man stood on the other side. "Ah, Lucifer, Yuki will not be pleased to see you."

"I expected as much, Gerald." Lucifer looked him up and down. "I see Purgatory is treating you adequately."

Gerald sighed. "It's preferrable to an eternity of torture."

"I can always take you down for the nickel tour if you'd like to get a feel for it."

The man shook his head somberly. "I'm perfectly okay here."

"As it should be." Lucifer stepped inside.

I followed, unable to stop staring at the man. "Are you dead?"

"Yes."

"Gerald is one of many whose souls attain a perfect balance between what some people ignorantly call good and evil." Lucifer rolled his eyes. "It just means they essentially did nothing in life that they deeply regret, nor did they do anything impressively productive to push them over the threshold required for Heaven."

"I'm agnostic," Gerald said. "Or was."

Lucifer snickered. "Naturally."

I looked back out the door at the perfect weather and beautiful scenery. "Purgatory looks nicer than I thought it would."

"Well, it is in the divine realm," Lucifer said. "It's located between Heaven and Hell and is next door to Limbo."

Somehow that made perfect sense to my mortal mind. The divine realm was vast, full of the human Elder Gods on one side and Elder Things on the other. Mount Olympus, Asgard, and other mythical realms existed in the divine realm, somehow neighboring each other but infinitely far apart. An eternal war raged here, and the various human pantheons were not faring well against the Elder Things.

I turned my attention on the house and wasn't surprised to see it was much larger on the inside than the outside. A young Asian woman looked worriedly down from an upstairs balcony, her lips curled up in disgust. "Lucifer?"

He waved. "Hello, Yuki."

She visibly shrank back. "Get out of my house, you monster!"

Lucifer turned to me and shrugged. "Not everyone is accepting of me."

"Who is she?"

"Garrick's girlfriend-slash-wife." Lucifer sighed. "Yuki, my dear, Garrick is no longer collecting the dead. I am here to see what's wrong." He turned to me and conspiratorially whispered, "She doesn't like me much."

"No, really?" I decided to try my luck. "I'm Cain, an acquaintance of Garrick's. Is he okay?"

Fists clenched, face tight with anger, she took deep breaths and reigned in her emotions. "I have called out to Fate and Time, but neither of them responded. It's as if they abandoned us."

Lucifer grinned broadly and spread his arms. "Well, we're here, darling. Just tell us what's wrong and we'll get Garrick right as rain in no time."

I frowned. "Is he alive?"

Yuki motioned toward the stairs. "Come up and I'll show you."

We climbed the stairs and followed Yuki into a large master suite. Garrick lay on his back, eyes closed, arms folded over his chest. I put a finger to his neck and felt a slow pulse. "He's sleeping."

She shook her head. "He's comatose and has been so for days."

Lucifer's grin vanished. "Impossible. His office protects him from such maladies."

"Garrick dropped me off on Earth so I could visit my family and friends for the weekend." She took his hand and pressed it to her heart. "Mortis came to pick me up a day late. He was alone, which was very unusual. Mortis was stomping his hooves and neighing. He was upset. Distraught, even."

Lucifer frowned. "What does a half dead horse get upset about?"

"It usually has something to do with someone threatening Garrick." She glared at Lucifer. "Like the times you tried to get him to participate in an orgy or take drugs."

"Darling, that's not threatening at all." Lucifer held up his hands in surrender. "I just want the poor boy to enjoy himself. No need to let your jealousy project foul intentions onto me."

"Jealousy?" Yuki's voice rose threateningly. "You actively try to corrupt him!"

I snapped my fingers to get their attention. "Let's worry about trivial things later. What we really need to figure out is why Garrick is comatose." I slapped him gently on the cheeks, but his eyes didn't so much as blink.

"Fate or Time could probably diagnose him, but I've been unable to reach them, probably because I'm just a nobody." Yuki wiped tears from her cheeks. "What's the use of having such powerful acquaintances if they won't help?"

I pursed my lips. "Is this the same Fate who cuts the threads of mortals?"

"Yes." Yuki's lip trembled. "I'd hoped she could find Garrick's thread and examine it to see what happened."

"Make sense." Lucifer tapped a finger on his chin. "This might seem mundane, but have you considered taking him to a human hospital?"

I summoned my staff and used the true sight scope. Garrick's aura was muted, but I didn't see anything magical affecting him. There were no sigils, glyphs, runes, or other signs indicating someone had cursed, hexed, or bound him. Considering I could see even god-level magic with my upgraded scope, it seemed plausible that an ordinary malady might be affecting him.

"Maybe that's a good next step." I lowered my scope and was about to banish the staff when something nagged at the back of my mind. I couldn't specifically say what it was, but years of honing my skills allowed me to notice something subconsciously without actively realizing what it was. I just had to lock onto whatever small detail had triggered my instincts.

I put the scope back to my eye and scanned Garrick's body. A freckle on his forehead drew my attention almost immediately. To the uninitiated, something so small might seem meaningless. To those trained in detective work and the medical field, tiny things often yielded the cause of sickness or death for the afflicted.

I lowered the scope and quickly realized why the freckle caught my attention. Garrick didn't have any blemishes on his forehead. I magnified the freckle and discovered it was no freckle at all, but a tiny spot of dark energies focused on his forehead right above the cognitive centers of his brain.

Lucifer tried to look through the scope. "What do you see, Cain?"

"Garrick is bound by high-level magic." I gave Lucifer the staff and shook my head. "I've never seen anything like it before."

"Goodness." Lucifer peered through the scope for a moment. He handed me the staff and leaned over Garrick, peering at the spot on his forehead. "This magic feels familiar, but I can't quite place it."

I grunted. "God level?"

He shook his head. "The gods wouldn't dare tamper with Death. His absence would disrupt the order of things. This magic is something quite different."

Yuki put a hand on my staff. "Can I look?"

I handed it to her. "Knock yourself out."

She looked through it and flinched. "He's glowing!"

"That's his aura." I aimed the scope at the mysterious binding on the forehead and magnified it for her. "That's what's affecting him."

Yuki stared at it for several minutes before handing back my staff. "How does your scope work?"

I shrugged. "Hephaestus built the oblivion staffs so their inner workings are way above my understanding."

"It'd be nice if you could remove the scope instead of having to hold the entire staff."

"They weren't exactly made for something like this." They were made for killing but mentioning that seemed counterproductive. "Well, maybe a god can undo it."

"I already asked a god." Yuki scowled. "War brought Hermes to look at Garrick, and Hermes said there was nothing he or any other god could do." She clenched a fist and seemed to resist banging it against a wall. "He said it was against the rules."

If the gods couldn't help, I had no idea where to start. For all intents and purposes, Death was comatose, and the dead or dying on Earth would be in agony until their souls were released.

3

That was when I realized something was off about her statement. "War?" I frowned. "Are you talking about Mars?"

She shook her head. "War is one of the horsemen."

My eyebrows rose. "You're saying War, Famine, and Pestilence are physical entities?"

Her brow furrowed in disbelief. "You're standing in the room with Death and still ask that question?"

I shrugged. "Just seems weird. Especially since Mars is basically War."

"Mars is Greek. War is Christian." Yuki shook her head. "You should study Revelations."

Lucifer laughed. "Cain was raised by the fae and taught the gods were dead. You really mustn't blame him for his lack of knowledge about Christian entities."

I might not know much, but some of the dots she'd presented weren't connecting. "Why would War, a Christian entity, bring Hermes, a Greek god, to see Death?"

Lucifer scoffed. "Because my father most certainly wouldn't deign to help."

Yuki scowled. "I prayed to God, but he doesn't seem to care. I don't care which pantheon answers my call, as long as they can help."

Another thought hit me. "Isn't the original Thanatos a Greek god too?"

"He is, or rather, was." Lucifer shrugged. "His persona as Death incarnate was coopted by several religions. Unlike War, who became a separate incarnation from Mars, Thanatos remained the same entity for Christianity as well."

I had no idea which god, if any, could help Garrick, but I knew of at least one individual who might be able to divine the cause of his curse. The only question was how to bring him here. Alternatively, taking Garrick to him might be the better course of action. This house obviously wasn't safe.

A few questions were in order. "Did you find Garrick in bed like this?"

Yuki blinked and looked at me. "No, he was in his old apartment on Earth."

It was my turn to blink in confusion. "What in the hell was he doing there?"

Her gaze went distant. "Garrick never wanted to be Death. He was manipulated into taking the mantle and forced to keep it to protect me. Free time is rare for him, but when he has time to kill, he likes to go to his old home, play video games, watch sports, or have beers with his best friends. When he does that, he usually sends Mortis away."

I tapped a finger on my chin. "Might be a dumb question, but can the horse talk?"

She shook her head. "As far as I know, Mortis, while much more intelligent than a normal horse, can't talk."

"So, you found Garrick in his apartment."

"Mortis did," she said. "He found me and took me there. I slung Garrick over Mortis, and we brought him here."

The fact that the attack happened there meant the perpetrator had intentionally waited for Garrick to go there. "How safe is this place from an attack?"

Yuki's eyes flared. "You're calling it an attack?"

I nodded. "Garrick was cursed while in his mortal state. That's why I need to know how safe his body is here."

"Very safe." She cleared her throat uneasily. "There are Nephilim tasked with protecting this realm, and even angels. A necromancer once sent minions to attack us. Garrick destroyed several of them and then the Nephilim appeared and finished them off."

I wanted to ask how a necromancer managed to send minions into the divine realm, but that was a question for another time. "How proficient is Garrick at protecting himself?"

"Extremely while wearing the vestments of Death. Without them, he's unfortunately average and clumsy." Yuki sighed. "I've tried training him, but he's not naturally gifted."

It seemed safe to bring my contact here, provided he agreed to come. "Will Mortis take me to fetch someone who might be able to identify the curse?"

Yuki flinched. "Oh, I don't know. He's extremely particular."

"Can we ask him?" I spread my hands imploringly. "Not to make this about me, but in addition to stopping a zombie apocalypse, I really need Garrick's help."

"You need him to bring Athena back to life." She sighed. "He mentioned you needed to find the original Thanatos for that task."

"I do."

"He asked the other horsemen and put out feelers to Hades, but nothing ever came of it."

I shrugged. "If anyone can find the original Death, it's gotta be the current office holder."

"Maybe." She watched me thoughtfully. "I'll get Mortis, but he might not respond well to you trying to ride him."

"I'm willing to find out."

"Then I'll ask him." Yuki left the room.

I turned to Lucifer. "You've been oddly quiet."

Gaze distant, he seemed lost in thought then abruptly looked up at me. "Oh, yes. I've got a lot on my mind."

"Really?" I tried to read his facial expressions, but he was hard to judge. "Like what?"

"Well, for starters, we need a stand-in for Death. Whoever cursed him has put the mortal world on a very slippery slope toward the end days."

I frowned. "Zombie apocalypse?"

Lucifer nodded somberly. "When the dead can't rise, they will inherit the Earth."

I couldn't tell if he was being serious or not. "For real?"

"Yes, Cain, for real." Lucifer scowled. "This is going to be a bloody mess. Not just because of the zombies, but because the dead naturally attract the dead, meaning restless ghosts will join the throng, affecting living humans even more severely. It would be disastrous physically and psychologically."

I knew first-hand the effects ghosts had on the psyche, but I didn't understand how the zombies would pose much of a threat. "The zombies are just bodies with souls trapped inside. What can they actually do to hurt anyone?"

"The last time this happened, the original Thanatos had decided to stop doing his job." Lucifer scoffed. "There were fewer humans, and most of them back in those days died in armed conflicts which falls outside of Death's purview. But a plague in a small town killed off most of the inhabitants. The survivors had to contend with bodies bursting from shallow graves. The zombies craved—"

I saw where this was going. "Brains?"

Lucifer chuckled. "They craved life, Cain. The warmth of living bodies drew them like moths to flame. Unlike the crude zombies raised by necromancers, these aren't simply reanimated meat-puppets. They have souls which are slowly being driven insane as their bodies decay." He paused, eyes flashing dramatically. "The survivors were attacked and torn limb from limb by frenzied zombies. Since their souls could not leave without Death, they in turn became zombies, some of them little more than walking skeletons with tattered flesh hanging from their bones."

I held up a hand. "I get the idea, though I don't understand how they could walk without muscles, or why zombies would eat flesh when their stomachs aren't working anymore."

"Magic provides locomotion. As for eating, well, they simply stuff the meat down their throats where it rots. As their insides continue to rot, holes form in their bodies, allowing the rotted meats to pour out in a liquid soup."

"Well, now I'm hungry." I'd seen worse, but the last thing I felt like encountering was an army of zombies with liquified rot pouring out of their bodies. The stench would be unbearable. "How long do we have until the dead start attacking the living?"

"It took about a week for the first zombies to walk." Lucifer shrugged. "Then again, no one was actually measuring much of anything back then. We had to track down Thanatos before the situation truly spun out of control. He agreed to appoint a successor and created the vestments which grant his powers to whoever wears them."

"In other words, anyone can be Death."

Lucifer laughed. "Oh, heavens no. It takes a person of stout fortitude to bear the vestments of the Grim Reaper. The unworthy will go mad." He shook his head. "Since the successor must be human, it took quite some time for a worthy candidate to be found. The occupant of the office will be immortal so long as they hold the office, and mortal once they leave it."

I frowned. "The vestments make them immortal, not the job."

Lucifer nodded. "Yes, precisely."

"You can quit just like any other job?"

"Not until a worthy replacement is found." He looked down at Garrick. "Death has an innate ability to find those who are able to take on the job."

I grunted thoughtfully. "The vestments are the cloak and scythe?"

"And the horse, and a few trinkets."

"Do they make Death invulnerable to attack?" I asked.

He waggled a hand. "Not directly, though they do offer some protection." Lucifer pursed his lips. "Immortality does not equate unkillable. The office holder of Death can be killed with enough force."

"Makes sense," I said. Though I'd located the source of Garrick's coma, I wondered if there might be physical trauma. I lifted his right hand and examined the fingernails and palms. His hands were soft and uncalloused. There was no blood or tissue under his fingernails indicating a struggle. The same went for his other hand.

His head bore no evidence of injury, nor did any other part of his body aside from bruising around one of his biceps. It looked as if someone had gripped him tightly, leaving a faint imprint of two fingers. Even if I had an FBI crime lab lift fingerprints from those bruises, I highly doubted they'd lead to anything.

Then again, nothing ventured, nothing gained. If Mortis agreed to let me ride him, then maybe he'd be okay with a pit stop at Sanctuary. I had a room full of forensic tools that were invaluable when trying to track down difficult targets for Eclipse.

"Find anything useful?" Lucifer said.

"Just this bruise." I traced it with a finger, then noticed faint bruising around Garrick's right ankle. I moved to the end of the bed and knelt to examine his feet, especially the areas between the toes.

Lucifer grimaced. "What on earth are you doing that for?"

I found what I was looking for between the second and third toes of the right foot. It was almost unnoticeable, even to trained eyes, but I'd learned a lot from my time in a coroner's office during my first years on Gaia. I pointed to the tiny red mark. "It's a needle prick."

His lips curled with distaste. "A needle? You're saying something as mundane as a syringe took down Death?"

"Whoever did this didn't want to kill him." I imagined the perpetrators sneaking in behind Garrick, grabbing him, and then injecting him with a syringe. "They wanted to subdue him so they could put the curse on him. Why they didn't simply kill him, I don't know."

Lucifer shook his head. "If Garrick was alone in his apartment without the vestments or Mortis, then they could have possibly killed him outright. But there's a rule that whoever kills Death must become him."

"They have no choice whatsoever in the decision?"

"Correct." Lucifer shrugged. "Since only a mortal human can become Death, I'm not sure what would happen if a god or other deity killed Death. It would make for an interesting paradox."

"Magical paradoxes usually create a feedback loop that doesn't end well for the parties involved." I'd seen the results of conflicting wishes granted by the same fae godmother. She and the two elves involved had died violently and taken out a large portion of a small town in the process. The amount of magical power involved in that had been relatively low, so I couldn't even imagine what it would be like if a god or deity killed Death. The magical feedback loop would be enormously dangerous.

Lucifer walked to the bedroom door and looked up and down the hallway. "Where did Yuki get off to? Surely Mortis wouldn't have wandered far." He left, presumably to track her down.

I continued looking for clues, but nothing else stood out to my trained eye. I left the room and went downstairs. The front door hung ajar. I assumed Lucifer had done it, but given Garrick's current condition, I wasn't taking any chances. Whoever did that to him might have decided to pay his home a visit.

Crouching, I crept to the door, put my back to the frame, and peeked outside. Lucifer stood in the front yard with Yuki who was waving her hands imploringly toward Mortis. The horse stomped a skeletal foot and his glowing green eyes locked onto me.

Yuki glanced at the house and frowned.

She didn't see me, but the pale horse did. I had a feeling Mortis was probably one of the most powerful vestments of Death and his gaze made me distinctly uncomfortable. I stepped outside and joined the group on the front lawn.

I cleared my throat. "Not going well?"

Yuki sighed. "Mortis will take you."

"Then what was the bloody holdup?" Lucifer said. "We've been waiting all this time."

"Nothing." Yuki glanced sideways at Mortis. The horse stomped a foot and blew dark mist from its nostrils.

"What aren't you telling me?" I backed up a step.

"It took some time to convince him." Yuki huffed. "Can you please go get the person you think can help?"

I nodded and met Mortis's green gaze. "Uh, how do I tell him where to go?"

"Climb on his back and he'll take you." Yuki winced. "Brace yourself. His method of traveling is a little unsettling."

"Good thing I ate a light brunch." I gripped the saddle horn, put a foot in a stirrup, and swung the other leg over. The saddle was black, but otherwise ordinary. "Someone missed a real opportunity to have a metal skull on the saddle horn and some spikes on the stirrups."

Confused by the aside, Yuki's eyebrows did the mamba. "What?"

"Nothing." I looked down and noticed reins in my hands where there'd been none before. I thought about where I wanted to go and wondered how to convey that to Mortis. "How—"

We lurched forward so fast, I should've rolled off Mortis's ass and onto the ground. The world blurred around us, phasing to a black obsidian plain. At first, I thought we were back in Hell and braced myself for the mind trap of self-torture. The night sky was brilliant, the stars like dust against a violet nebula. We seemed to be on another world entirely, one without life of any kind, and yet I had no trouble breathing.

That was when I noticed how deathly silent it was. Mortis's hooves sparked soundlessly on the rocky ground. "Where are we?" The words hung in the air, echoing strangely.

I tried to direct a mental question to Mortis. *What in the hell is happening?*

The next instant, the world twisted sideways beneath us, three dimensions reduced to only two, rotating until Mortis galloped along the paper-thin edge. It abruptly flipped open like a popup book, but the imagery was starkly different—green and bustling with human activity. It sprang into three dimensions and Mortis's hooves clopped along the asphalt of a busy road.

A large moving truck was less than ten feet away and speeding right at us. I reflexively tried to spring straight up and out of the saddle for a last-chance effort at landing on the truck's roof, but Mortis deftly dodged around the truck, leaping over cars and effortlessly weaving through traffic until we stopped in front of the house.

It still looked much the same as I'd last seen it, though a newer compact car graced the driveway. Symbols etched into the driveway told any member of the supernatural community that this house was protected by the local mage guild and its knights. I was happy to see Fitzroy Simmons had put the money I'd given him to use, though I hated the idea of supporting the Mage Guild in any capacity.

Mortis trotted up the driveway and stopped at the front door.

I swung my leg over his rump to get off and was assaulted by a fit of dizziness just as my foot touched the ground. Holding onto the saddle horn, I paused to recover my wits. The saddle seemed to have absorbed most of the side-effects of traveling, but it apparently caught up to the rider once they disembarked.

Taking a deep breath, I released the saddle horn and walked to the door. I'd had to enter Fitz's backyard during my last and only visit to his house since vampires had been watching and waiting for me. I had no such worries this time, thankfully. I swung the coconut-shaped knocker against the door.

A moment passed then I heard a soft exclamation from the other side of the door. It swung open and Fitz stood on the other side, eyes blazing with anger.

4

Fitz took a deep breath. "What are you doing here, Cain?" He looked behind me. "The last time I saw you, vampires broke into my house and tortured me for information!"

I pointed a thumb over my shoulder toward the guild markings on his driveway. "Hopefully, that's not an issue anymore."

He scoffed. "Those are just for show. I used the money you gave me to hire personal security services. You'd better believe the vampires came back for me after I returned home. Thankfully, they left me alone when they found out I hired the Van Helsing Group."

"Smart move." Van Helsing had been a monster hunter until the monsters became more civilized along with the rest of the world. Since then, the company had turned from monster hunting to protective services against those who broke the rules. "Did the Mage Guild turn you down?"

Fitz shook his head. "I couldn't stand the thought of giving those miscreants any money." He looked around suspiciously, then stepped outside and closed the door behind him. "Why are you here, Cain?" He peered at my face and frowned. "The veins are gone." His eyes widened. "Did you eat a unicorn heart?"

"No, but it's a long story." I considered how to tell him what I needed, then thought, *fuck it.* Might as well hit him with everything. "I need you to come to Purgatory with me on Death's horse to see if you can figure out who cursed Death and find out whether you can help him."

"There's something wrong with Death?" Fitz held up a finger. "Ah, that would explain so much!"

I frowned, disappointed that he hadn't been remotely surprised. Then again, he was a witch doctor and kept a keen eye on strange happenings. "You're fine with everything I just said?"

"This is an honor, Cain!" He opened the front door. "Tell me what you know so I can decide what to bring with me." He hurried inside, motioning me to follow.

I followed him through the house, into the backyard, and down into a large cellar, telling him the little I knew about the situation. Fitz plucked several jars from his shelves, nodding as I spoke.

"We'll need to go by my place so I can get my forensic tools," I told him.

"No need." Fitz picked up a large duffel bag and handed it to me. "This is my mobile crime lab."

"Mobile crime lab?" I shook my head. "I thought you were a witch doctor."

"That's my specialty, yes." He shrugged. "But I was once a detective here in Seattle. After a time, I couldn't take the bureaucracy anymore and became a private detective."

"A private detective witch doctor?" It was hard to wrap my mind around. "Is that an actual thing?"

"Are you not familiar with the wizard detective in Chicago?" Fitz sighed. "I was an ordinary young man in law enforcement long ago, a corrupt person who took bribes and looked the other way. But when I was nearly killed, a witch doctor took mercy on me. He taught me Obeah, helped me become a better man. I moved here to escape my enemies and joined the local police. When I heard about the wizard detective in Chicago, it gave me this idea. I realized I could make more of a difference by being independent of the police."

"Do you advertise in the yellow pages too?"

He nodded. "Of course. They're online now, though."

I grunted. "You need a hat and a leather duster to make it official."

He frowned. "Why would I wear a hat?"

I peered inside the duffel bag. "Is this everything?"

Fitz examined the contents and nodded. "Did you say we're riding on *the* pale horse?"

"Yep." I followed him back upstairs and motioned him to the driveway where Mortis stood patiently, green eyes blazing. "He's right there."

Fitz frowned and looked past the big horse in front of him. "I don't see anything."

I pointed to Mortis. "He's right in front of your face."

Fitz put his hands out like a blind man feeling his way through an unknown house. Despite being right next to Mortis, he managed to completely miss touching him, as if repelled by an invisible force.

The horse snorted as if amused. Dark mist plumed into Fitz's face, but the man didn't seem aware of it.

I sighed. "Really, Mortis? Fitz might be able to help us, so it'd be nice if you revealed yourself to him."

Mortis neighed, stomped a foot and then blew another plume of mist into Fitz's face.

Fitz gasped and stumbled back, wide-eyed. "That is truly high-level glamour!"

"Yeah, it has to be." I looked at the duffel bags and wondered how hard it'd be to carry these things and double up on the horse.

Mortis apparently read my mind. He stomped a hoof and a fancy black chariot coalesced into being behind him. It had only two wheels like a war chariot but with a wide cushy seat and cargo straps.

"That is amazing!" Fitz tentatively held out a hand as if to touch Mortis, then thought better of it when the horse stomped a hoof.

I strapped my duffel into the back of the chariot and Fitz did the same. Then we sat down. Before I could give instructions, Mortis galloped down the driveway at full speed. The world flattened into a pancake, turned sideways, and flipped back into three dimensions as we entered the twilight world.

Eyes wide, Fitz looked around. "What is this place? Is it the space between realms or something else entirely?"

An instant later, we were suddenly back in Garrick's front yard. I remained seated for a moment. Dizziness washed over me as it had the last time. Fitz swooned with the same effects. If I'd had as much to drink for brunch as Lucifer, I'd have hurled by now.

Lucifer rose from a chair on the front porch and clapped his hands. "You're back!"

Yuki jumped up from the chair next to him and looked Fitz up and down. "This is the person who can help?"

"Or at least diagnose," I said.

Fitz nodded at Lucifer and Yuki. "I am Fitz, a practice of Obeah and other arts. I diagnosed Cain's curse of Cthulhu, so perhaps I can divine what ails Death."

"His name is Garrick," Yuki said. "Death is just his job."

"And I'm Lucifer." Lucifer grinned as if anticipating fear or surprise.

Fitz nodded. "I thought as much. You have the aura of a fallen angel, but it was too powerful for you to be anyone but the king of Hell."

For once, Lucifer looked speechless. He cleared his throat. "I'm rather disappointed in your reaction." He paused. "Though I should probably be quite pleased. Not many mortals recognize me."

Fitz tapped a finger to his temple. "I used my true sight to see your aura. It unfortunately can't see through high-level glamour, so I can't see your true face."

Lucifer stroked his own face lovingly. "This is my true face. My devil face is merely another facet of me."

I scoffed. "That makes no sense."

Lucifer scoffed back. "On the contrary, Cain. It makes perfect sense."

"Fitz, please come with me." Yuki hurried inside.

Fitz and I grabbed the duffel bags and went upstairs to Garrick's room. Fitz almost instantly locked his gaze on Garrick's forehead. "Oh, my. That's a powerful binding."

I felt a little jealous that he'd spotted it faster than me. Then again, he had a true sight spell on command, and I relied on my staff. "We need to find out who did it and how to unbind it because the world is going to hell in a handbasket in a hurry."

Lucifer shook his head. "Technically, the world isn't going to Hell or Heaven. At least not until Death is back in action."

"I have been working overtime to bind the undead so they won't kill the living," Fitz said as he unpacked jars from his duffel bag. "Unfortunately, the virus plaguing the world is killing people too quickly. The elderly and infirm are the first to die. I've not had enough time to study the virus to see if there's a magical cure or treatment." He looked up at the rest of us. "I'm well aware about what happens if Death isn't doing his job."

I nodded. "What about the Morrigan. Can't she fill in for him?"

"She gathers only those slain in battle." Fitz shook his head. "Now, there are other pantheons with their own versions of soul collectors. Unfortunately, Christianity spans the globe, meaning a large percentage of the world population relies on Death to do his duty. The viral pandemic will quickly lead to an apocalypse."

Yuki put a hand on his shoulder. "Can you help Garrick?"

Fitz took a deep breath and slowly let it out as he examined the binding on Garrick's forehead. "I must first determine the source of the curse. If it's god level like the one that afflicted Cain, then no, I won't be able to cure it."

"Let's hope it doesn't involve eating a unicorn heart," I muttered.

I glanced out the window and saw Mortis staring up at us, stomping a foot and blowing dark mist from his nostrils. He was clearly agitated, like a stallion standing outside a barn full of mares in heat.

Lucifer joined me at the window. "Mortis is drawn to the dead and dying. The sheer volume must be driving him mad."

I looked back at him. "There must be another deity who can fill in for the time being."

"I'm afraid not." Lucifer headed toward the bedroom door. "I could use a drink. Might as well join me while we wait."

Yuki hovered anxiously over Fitz, too preoccupied to notice as we left the room.

Lucifer took a glass from a shelf and produced a flask from a leather holster beneath his designer jacket. He poured three fingers for me then drank directly from the flask.

I took a sip and savored the smoky flavor. Lucifer reached over and nudged the bottom of the glass. "Bottoms up, Cain."

I tossed the rest back and held out the glass again. "Shame to waste such good whiskey on shots."

"It's a cognac, actually." Lucifer refilled the glass. "I can understand the mistake."

I shrugged. "I'm more of a mangorita kind of guy. Get me some sliced fruit, plastic pirate swords, and tiny umbrellas and I'm a happy man."

Lucifer barked a laugh. "I'd certainly love to party with you some day." He looked me up and down. "Ashatha has expressed the desire more than a few times as well."

I grunted. "I'm not much of a party animal." I downed the cognac and set down the glass, suddenly feeling as antsy as Mortis as I considered the path that brought me to this point in time.

I'd made a bargain with the gods—ridding the Shalthaes Woodlands of the minions of Shub-Nuggurath in exchange for Athena removing her curses from the bloodlines of the gorgon, Dusa, and Aura. At the last minute, the batshit insane Aura from dimension Beta had kidnapped Aura from Alpha, switched places with her, and murdered Athena right in front of us with Soultaker. Mars then killed Layla, condemning her soul into the blade as extra incentive for me to find a way to save Athena.

I'd spoken to Hephaestus. He'd told me that the magic used to forge Soultaker came from the original Thanatos. Finding him was the key to possibly saving the souls from the sword. I didn't stand a chance of finding him without Garrick, the current office holder of Death. Even with him, I might not find Thanatos since he hadn't been heard from in centuries.

I left Lucifer and went outside.

Mortis stomped his foot and snorted, as if warning me not to come closer, then galloped away, vanishing in a blur. Part of me wished I could do the same. I didn't necessarily owe anyone anything. If roles were reversed, Layla would probably leave me trapped inside the sword. My meddling in divine affairs had gotten us here, after all. At what point should I simply say, "Not my problem" and walk away?

Now seemed like an ideal time. Lucifer could deal with Garrick or ask for help from higher up the divine chain. Once Fitz arrived at a diagnosis, he and I could head back to Gaia and let the gods deal with it. When Garrick recovered and caught up with his grim duties, then we could start a search for the original Thanatos.

I found a spot under a tree, sat down, and took a nap to pass the time.

Footsteps woke me. I looked up and saw Fitz and Yuki exiting the house. Lucifer sat on the front porch, flask in hand. Fitz spoke to Lucifer. The Devil's eyes pinched with concern, then he hopped up and threw his flask to the ground.

"I should have bloody known it!" Lucifer stormed off the porch and over to me. "The three horsemen are up to no good, Cain."

I rose to my feet and stretched. "Can you back all the way up and tell me what Fitz told you?"

Fitz was already approaching. "The binding on Garrick is a complex weave of three distinct energies. Two of them reminded me of residual magic I'd found in a remote community in Washington where half the population died from food poisoning and a variant of the bubonic plague."

I held up a hand. "Did you say the bubonic plague?"

He nodded. "Dark magic is very much alive and well even in this day and age. I suspected a warlock or dark shaman was behind the deaths, but instead I found residual magic that was far too powerful to have been directly wielded by a human magic user."

Fitz's gaze became distant as his mind went to the past. "I discovered that this was the fourth remote town to suffer such an incident. The others happened in Australia, Europe, and China, all within the last few months."

Lucifer huffed. "Long story short, it would seem Famine and Pestilence have been playing with lives."

I frowned. "You're telling me Famine and Pestilence put this curse on Garrick?"

Fitz nodded. "The third binding energy is most likely that of War."

I took a moment to consider this new information. "Are Famine and Pestilence allowed to go around murdering entire populations?"

Lucifer shook his head. "They should be following the grand plan laid out by my father. Some years back, Famine was quite upset that human scientists kept finding ways to avert starvation through genetic modification of food sources. Pestilence was convinced the sheer number of humans was growing too large for the Earth to sustain and requested a grand culling. War, however, was quite pleased with the status quo since more humans means more armed conflicts."

I tried to make sense of this in context with Garrick's current condition, but the pieces of the puzzle didn't quite fit. "If you're going to start killing off humans, why take Death out of the equation?"

Yuki gasped. "It's been so long that I almost forgot an incident that happened several months ago. Garrick came home upset because the other horsemen approached him and wanted to ride. Just out of the blue they decided it was time to start the apocalypse."

"Bloody fools." Lucifer pulled a flask from the other side of his suit coat and took a swig. "War, Pestilence, and Famine have wanted to end the world for decades. Garrick once admitted that when he was new, they tried to convince him that it was time to ride. Thankfully, that crisis was averted."

I still didn't understand why they would put Garrick in a coma since they needed him. They were the four horsemen of the apocalypse, not the three. In order to bring about the end, they needed the fourth member to ride with them. I turned to Fitz. "Can you remove the curse?"

He shook his head. "This curse is far above my level. Perhaps an angel can unbind them."

Lucifer sighed. "I could make a few calls, but if Father hasn't sent anyone to heal Garrick, then this must be part of his marvelous plan." He abruptly laughed. "Oh, who am I kidding? Father hasn't been paying attention to anything for eons. If he knows about this, he probably doesn't even care."

"Make the calls then, Lucifer." I was ready to go to Voltaire's and drink mangoritas until this crisis was over.

"I'll be back in a moment." Lucifer's brilliant white wings unfurled. He shot into the sky, vanishing an instant later. Hardly a moment had passed when he and Castiel landed before us in a flash of wings, causing Fitz and Yuki to recoil in surprise.

Castiel went inside without saying a word and came out moments later. "It can't be done, brother. Only those who cursed him can unbind it."

"Are you certain?" Lucifer tsked. "There was a time when you could heal any malady."

"You know good and well that even I can't affect some magic." The other angel shook his head. "There is only one solution. We must find someone else to take on the mantle of Death."

5

"No!" Yuki stepped in front of Castiel. "The only way another can take on the mantle is if Garrick gives it up to a worthy successor or is killed. He can't very well give it up, and I won't let you kill him."

"I believe there's a clause in the contract that refers to Death being incapacitated." Castiel frowned. "Heaven above, Lucifer. If what you told me is correct, I think I know what the horsemen are up to."

Lucifer's eyes flared. "Do tell, brother."

"One moment." Castiel turned to Yuki. "I need to read the Death contract."

She narrowed her eyes. "It's on the black slate on the wall in his office."

"Let me be sure of my reasoning before jumping to conclusions." Castiel strode toward the house, the rest of us following to find out what he was thinking.

The office was the first room on the right past the foyer. The black slate in question was a slab of stone hanging on the wall. Castiel waved a hand over it and the tiny symbols engraved in it glowed to life, casting a three-dimensional version into the air before us.

Castiel scrolled down the dense text and stopped after a time.

Brow furrowed, he read the text and nodded. "Yes, there is a clause for incapacitation, in which case Death can be replaced by a candidate worthy of the vestments." He turned to Yuki. "Where are his vestments?"

Her eyes flared. "I have no idea. Garrick usually keeps them close by unless he's going to his old apartment to relax."

I looked away from the text. "Then he left them here?"

"In his closet." Yuki ran upstairs and the rest of us followed. She threw open the door to a walk-in closet. Most of the racks held contemporary clothing, but what really caught my eye was the six-foot skeleton standing in the center.

"It's not here." She walked around the skeleton. "He usually tosses the cloak over the bone rack when he wants to take some time off."

Lucifer stroked the skull. "I must have one of these for my closet."

The bone rack was certainly an eye-catching addition to an otherwise ordinary closet. "I don't suppose the skull is housing a spirit of intellect, is it? Does he call it Bob?"

Yuki frowned. "I don't understand."

"This settles it." Castiel looked grimly at the empty rack. "The other horsemen intend to find a replacement for Death so they can usher in the apocalypse."

"And I only recently found a reliable source for Macallan aged scotch." Lucifer huffed. "I really don't have the patience to endure the end of the world."

I shook my head. "Can the horsemen even incite the apocalypse without the Antichrist?" I looked at Lucifer. "Do you have any kids we should know about?"

"I've never had the desire or need to spread my progeny across the world." He rolled his eyes. "And I don't understand why people seem to think the Antichrist is the offspring of the devil. It's complete nonsense and an attack on my good name."

Castiel laughed. "Good name my angelic ass."

Fitz snorted.

I held out my hands helplessly. "Then who's the Antichrist?"

"I certainly wouldn't know," Lucifer said. "It could be any number of bad actors in the world."

"Only Father would know," Castiel said. "But I've seen none of the signs that he exists."

Lucifer smirked. "In any case, any one of the four horsemen could wreak havoc and throw off the natural order."

I grunted. "The absence of Death is already doing that."

"Precisely. A zombie apocalypse would eventually flood the afterlife with insane souls, and no one wants that." Lucifer shuddered. "Dealing with sane human souls is already bad enough."

I left the closet and stared at Garrick's comatose form for a moment. "I guess this is in God's hands now."

"Pray it isn't." Lucifer grimaced. "Father hasn't lifted a finger to intervene in centuries. I don't expect him to change."

"You don't know that," Castiel said. "He works in mysterious ways."

Lucifer's eyes flashed dangerously. "Does, he, brother? Is that why he threw me from my homeland, condemning me to an eternity of torturing souls?"

Castiel tried to speak. "Lucifer—"

"Don't protect him, brother! There is no mystery in Father's ways." Lucifer shivered. "Only brutality."

I didn't want to get into the middle of a family argument. The comfort of home and a nice sandwich was calling out to me. "Lucifer, can you take me back to my submarine? I'm going to wait this out until it's sorted."

Fitz looked at me as if I was crazy. "You have a submarine?"

"Yeah." I shrugged. "It's a long story."

He shook his head and turned to the others. "I'm afraid I've done all I can. Will the horse return me home?"

Yuki sat in the desk chair, eyes red from crying. "I feel so hopeless. If an angel can't help Garrick, then no one can."

I didn't like the situation any better than she did but listening to Lucifer and Castiel bickering was giving me a headache. I just wanted to get out of this place and back home. I headed downstairs and out of the front door.

Fitz followed me outside. "You seem different, Cain."

I raised an eyebrow. "Last time I saw you I was half dead from Cthulhu's curse. I'm better now."

He shook his head. "You seem much colder. More certain."

"More certain?"

"You were conflicted from the ghosts haunting you." Fitz nodded as if agreeing with himself. "I assume they are gone?"

I nodded. "Garrick took them. Apparently, I satisfied them with my actions, and they were able to move on."

"Ah, yes. You are back to being you and you alone." His eyes narrowed. "You are moving back to your true center."

I shrugged. "I've got kids now. Not sure I'll ever get back to being my old self again."

"Kids?" Fitz smiled. "I would love to hear what happened after I saw you the first time, but especially how you now own a submarine."

"It's not a nub submarine. I stole it from the mechanists." I looked around and saw no sign of Mortis. I assumed Yuki would have to call him and I didn't feel like going back inside. I told Fitz the abbreviated version of my path to the cure and how I'd eventually forced Cthulhu to release Hannah.

"How remarkable!" Fitz clasped his hands together in thanksgiving. "I'm quite happy to hear you didn't sacrifice the unicorn."

Yuki and the others made their way outside. As if on cue, Mortis galloped into view, a pair of black saddlebags hanging at his sides. He hadn't had them earlier but considering he could conjure a chariot out of nowhere, saddlebags were probably no problem for him.

He stopped in front of me, pawed the ground with a hoof, and blasted mist in my face. Then he turned sideways, presenting a saddlebag.

I began to climb onto his back, but he bucked sideways, nearly taking my arms off. "What the fuck?" I flexed my fingers to make sure they still worked.

Mortis pawed the ground again and snorted, then turned slowly sideways and turned his head toward the saddlebag.

"He wants you to look in the bag," Yuki said.

I was almost afraid to see what kind of horrors this half-dead horse had in his saddlebag, but I lifted the flap and looked. The bag was stuffed with black cloth. I pulled it out, and it unfurled into the Grim Reaper's cloak.

Yuki's eyes widened. "His vestments!"

"Well, that's good news, I guess." I held them out to her, but Mortis stomped a hoof and got in my way. He neighed softly, sending chills down my spine. No words were spoken, but his intent suddenly became clear. "Oh, hell no."

Yuki gasped. "You want him to wear them?"

Lucifer burst into laughter. Castiel frowned.

Fitz nodded. "Garrick suspected something would happen so he picked a successor and hid his vestments. Cain, he means for you—"

I held up a hand. "I know that Fitz. I'm not a complete moron."

"Of course, he chose you, Cain." Lucifer shook his head. "You've wielded the most powerful weapons in existence. You understand that with great power comes great responsibility."

I groaned. "Thanks, Uncle Ben."

"What makes this man fit to assume Garrick's role?" Yuki said. "I know nothing about him."

"I'm not taking the job." I draped the cloak over Mortis's back. "Lucifer, can you take me home? I'm done with this."

"Absolutely not, Cain." Lucifer grinned brightly. "Can't you see that this is perfect? With Death's abilities, you'll be able to comb the realms for Thanatos on your own."

I opened my mouth to reject the idea and paused because he was right. First, I'd have to zip around the world to clean up the mess Death's absence had made, then I'd be free to start my search for Thanatos. It wasn't a win-win situation, but it sounded a lot easier than waiting around for Garrick to recover.

I pursed my lips and thought. "What's to stop the other horsemen from cursing me into a coma and stealing the vestments?"

"You will stop them," Lucifer said. "Garrick was but an ordinary mortal without the vestments of Death. You, however, are something quite different."

His reasoning was sound, but I needed to understand a few things about the job before I accepted it. "This won't be permanent. I'm not looking for a new career."

"As Death, you'll have a much better chance of convincing the other horsemen to remove the curse from Garrick." Yuki looked pleadingly at me. "Then he can take over again."

"And if I can't get them to do it?" I dreaded the idea of being trapped in such a heavy role. "What then?"

"Then we find a suitable replacement." Lucifer squeezed Yuki's shoulder as if to comfort her, but she recoiled instantly.

"Don't touch me, Devil."

Lucifer made a sad face. "Come now, deary. You're hurting my feelings."

Castiel rolled his eyes. I got the feeling he rolled his eyes a lot while listening to Lucifer.

Thinking long and hard about my next steps was the smart move, but I wasn't feeling particularly smart. It was almost as if someone plotted this path for me, lured me here, and backed me into a corner. But who would stand to gain anything from me taking on the mantle of Death?

If this was somehow engineered by the gods of chaos, then they were dumber than I thought. I'd already driven Shub-Nuggerath from Feary and possibly given the other gods a much-needed power boost in the divine realm.

It was entirely possible that I was overthinking this. In fact, that made the most sense. Taking on the job of Death would give me access to places I could have never dreamed of. Mortis could get me just about anywhere in minutes, meaning I could track down Thanatos without waiting for someone to help me. Another thought occurred to me, one that might mean I didn't even have to worry about finding Thanatos.

The more I worked over the pros and cons, the more I liked it. There was a good chance it would end in disaster, but it was worth a try.

I turned to the others. "Can someone tell me what I'm supposed to do?"

"Garrick had to learn a great deal on his own and it was a miserable experience." Yuki looked at me hopefully. "He wrote a manual to help his successor."

"A manual?" Lucifer frowned. "How quaint."

Yuki scoffed. "It's not a particularly intuitive job, Devil."

I held out my hand. "Where is the manual?"

"It's only visible to the wearer of the cloak," Yuki said. "I don't understand much more than that."

"Fine." I picked up the cloak and rummaged through it, but if there were pockets or hidden folds in the cloth, I couldn't find them. "Where is it?"

Yuki looked worried, as if I might change my mind. "I think you have to put on the cloak first and accept the job."

I was starting to feel like a cornered rat again, but it made sense that Garrick would safeguard the proprietary secrets of the job. "How did he figure out what he was doing in the first place?"

"A lot of trial and error with minimal help from the other deities." Yuki scowled. "I was just getting to know him at the time, both of us caught up in a game neither of us understood, much less knew the rules to. He had to learn fast, or I would have died."

I felt like I was stalling even though I'd made my decision. Time was wasting and I needed to clear a massive backlog of the dead before doing anything else. Steeling myself, I slid my arms into the sleeves, and pulled the cloak around me. My hands still looked the same. "Am I Death now?"

"Not yet." Yuki took my hand. "Come with me." She looked at Lucifer and Castiel. "Stay here."

Lucifer put up his hands in surrender. "As you say, my dear."

Castiel nodded in consent.

Yuki took me inside the house and upstairs to the bed where Garrick lay. "Take his hand."

I did. A jolt of icy energy ran up my arm and down my spine. "What the hell was that?"

"The cloak discovering that the office holder is incapacitated, and a new candidate is ready."

Dark mist enshrouded my vision. A faint whispering reached my ears. *You have been chosen. Do you accept the burden until such time as the owner of the vestments can do their duty again?* The smart answer would have been no. But I hadn't done much of anything considered smart since deciding to help Aura and Dusa get rid of their curses.

I took a deep breath and nodded. "I accept."

The chill deepened, penetrating every last part of my body right down to the bones. The cold was so absolute that I couldn't move. It might have lasted only an instant, but it felt like an eternity. Using all my willpower, I moved my arms and watched in horror as the flesh from my hands disintegrated to dust. I looked at the wall mirror as the flesh peeled from my face, dropping like old scabs until nothing was left but a grinning skull.

The cold was gone. I felt normal again. But the mirror told me I was anything but. The old Cain was gone.

I had become Death.

6

When I rubbed my fingers together, I felt bone. If my hands were truly nothing but bone, I shouldn't have felt anything. I'd thought that Death's shroud used glamour, but it obviously used something much different. Glamour was just high-level illusion, meaning I'd still feel my flesh.

Yuki took my hand. "Garrick did that a lot."

I blinked, but the skull in the mirror simply stared with gaping black holes. "He did what a lot?"

"Stared at himself in the mirror." She reached up and tugged on the hood, but it didn't move. "No one else except for you can remove the cloak. At least no one as powerful or less powerful than you. He never asked a god to try to remove it."

A faint tug on my consciousness pulled my gaze one way and then another.

Yuki noticed. "You feel the draw of death. Garrick said it felt like instinct. He would feel it and Mortis would take him there seconds before the person died."

"That's how it works? I just sit around and wait on someone to die?"

"More or less." She touched the cloak. "You should now be able to feel a pocket inside the cloak. That's where he hid the manual and the other tools of Death."

I reached inside the cloak and felt my bare ribcage, which was a little unsettling since I was still breathing, and my heart still beat in my chest. Just next to my ribcage my fingers found a fold in the cloth. It opened and I reached into the hidden pocket. There were several objects inside. I pulled out the first one, a metal wrist band with a white orb suspended above it. I had no idea what it was, but it fit perfectly over my wrist, so I put it on.

The next object was an ordinary computer tablet like the kind nubs used. I pressed the center button and it prompted me for a fingerprint. I walked to Garrick, picked up his hand, and put his thumb on it. The screen displayed an error.

Incorrect fingerprint.

Yuki shook her head. "Use your finger."

"But—"

"Just do it."

I put my bony thumb on the reader and it worked. "How in the hell did he get this thing to accept a bone as a fingerprint?"

She shrugged. "I suggest you read the manual before getting on Mortis."

"I don't have time to sit around reading." I looked at the last object, a small glossy black ball. "What's this?"

Yuki gripped my arm. "Read the manual, Cain!"

"I'll read it on the way." I strode out of the room, my thick black leather boots pounding on the hardwood floors. I stopped and looked down at my shoes, because I definitely hadn't been wearing these before donning the cloak. The toes were tarnished metal shaped like skulls. I pulled open the cloak and was relieved to see that I was wearing pants. A Death boner would've been a psychological shock to anyone. The pants were black, of course. A black shirt covered my ribcage, but when I touched it, I felt bare bone.

Death it seemed, was metal as fuck.

There was no making sense of how the cloak worked, so I hurried out of the house and to Mortis.

Fitz watched me with wide eyes. "Goodness, you look frightening."

"I think he looks fabulous!" Lucifer was giddy with excitement. "Ready for your first day on the job, Cain?"

I shook my head. "Not really, but I'd better get it over with."

Castiel put a hand on my shoulder. "Good luck, Cain." He closed his eyes. "Father in Heaven, please watch over this man."

Lucifer scoffed. "Oh, please, Castiel. The odds of Father watching over anyone are about as astronomical as him inviting me home for dinner."

"Lucifer, this isn't helpful." Castiel sighed. His wings unfurled and in an instant and he blurred away into the sky.

Lucifer gripped me in a hug and kissed my cheek before I had a chance to react. He sighed in contentment. "I would love to get you in bed with this cloak on."

"Yeah?" I waited patiently for him to release me. "I guess Death always has a boner."

Lucifer backed away, grinning lasciviously. "That's what I'm counting on, Cain." His wings unfurled. "Please visit soon. I can't wait to hear how your day was."

I sighed. "Honey, I'm home. Today was a real killer."

Lucifer burst into laughter and launched into the sky, vanishing seconds later.

Fitz looked uncertainly at me. "Will you give me a ride home, Cain?"

I nodded. "Sure."

Yuki stood on the porch watching me with concern. "Cain, you'll regret it if you get on Mortis without at least skimming the rules."

I clenched my bony fists and groaned. "Fine!" I hated reading instructions, but she obviously knew what she was talking about. I pulled out the tablet and turned it on. There was only one icon on the screen labeled *Death Manual v802.c.* I opened it. The table of contents was short, but the sections it led to were several pages each.

"This is gonna take hours to read," I muttered. I started skimming. The bracelet thing was called the death beacon. I read up on it, then skipped a few paragraphs to the one about soul collection. The black ball was the soul catcher. I read the instructions on it and figured that was good enough.

Yuki stood next to me. "Good luck, Cain."

Fitz climbed onto Mortis ahead of me.

"Thanks." I put a foot in a stirrup and swung my leg over the saddle. "I'm—"

The horse galloped ahead before I could even finish the thought. There wasn't the least bit of a jarring effect as I'd experienced the first time. I suspected it was due to my new cloak. We entered the dark realm. It collapsed beneath us as before. Two-dimensional houses popped up and Mortis stopped in Fitz's driveway. The shaman hopped off, staggering drunkenly.

"Oh, goodness. That was quite—"

I didn't hear what else he had to say because Mortis galloped away again, cutting through the dark realm once again. We emerged and cardboard cutouts of skyscrapers sprang up and expanded into three dimensions an instant later. It was like being inside a kid's popup book if the popup book was a nightmarish fever dream.

Mortis's hooves sparked against asphalt. The faint tug I'd felt earlier strengthened as the dead called out to me. Tangles of electrical wires ran overhead. Lights flickered in windows. Fires burned in alleyways. A group of screaming people ran past, oblivious to the specter of Death looming nearby.

I glanced at the globe on the bracelet. It was no longer white, but blue and green—a small replica of Gaia. It zoomed in and flattened into a map as I rode. I didn't even have to look at the map to know I was in Rome, Italy—the heart of the Catholic Church.

Crimson blips appeared, some scattered here and there. Then I saw something that made my blood run cold. I pulled back on the reins and Mortis stopped, dark mist puffing from his nostrils. The entire area of the map ahead was red. Not because it was supposed to be shaded that way, but because there were so many crimson blips that they all ran together.

According to Garrick's manual the recently deceased were

supposed to be green. The longer the soul remained in the corpse, the more the color began to shift toward the deep red that now dominated the map. I pulled out the manual and skimmed that part once more to confirm what I already knew. Crimson was the worst. It meant the souls had hit critical and gone batshit insane.

It meant the undead had risen.

I looked down the street and saw what had sent the other people screaming and running. The area was overrun with shambling, rotting corpses. "Nothing to worry about," I told myself. "I'm Death now."

I loosened the reins and Mortis trotted forward, the echoes of his hooves mingling with the wails of the undead. The zombies groaned and screamed, some of them clawing at each other as if trying to end their misery. Dozens of unmoving bodies lay in the streets, bright blood running from gruesome wounds. It seemed they'd recently been killed by the zombies.

"Finally!" A middle-aged woman stormed out of the shadows. "The loom is breaking, thanks to you!"

I stopped Mortis and looked down at her with confusion. It occurred to me in the back of my mind that she probably couldn't see my expressions since my face was a skull. That was when I realized that she shouldn't even be able to see me at all. "Who are you?"

She stepped closer, eyes narrowed. "Don't play games with me, Garrick. You stopped collecting the dead! I tried to enter your domain, but without your express permission, I couldn't pay you a visit in person." She huffed. "If this is in retaliation for our decision not to intervene in your argument with War, then it was the most foolish thing you could have done."

Rather than reveal my identity, I decided to play twenty questions. "How did you find me?"

"I've been keeping my fingers on the threads and sensed something big was about to happen here. I assumed it would be due to you." She abruptly stopped talking and tilted her head slightly. "There's something different about you. You've always been headstrong, but I don't sense the same kind of emotion in your voice that you normally have." She flicked her fingers, and a web shot toward my face. I reflexively drew my staff to defend myself.

But instead of my staff, I found a great scythe in my hand. It slashed through the webs and they fell to the ground, glowing faintly.

The woman grunted. "You are not Garrick."

I lowered my hood and felt flesh creeping back up the bone. "No, I'm not."

Her mouth dropped open. "This is worse than I thought. Where is he? What happened? Who are you?"

"I'm Cain." I glanced down the road and noticed that the shambling horde of zombies seemed to be fixed on my location. Arms outstretched, they lumbered in our direction. "Garrick was incapacitated by the other three horsemen."

"Incapacitated? That's impossible!" She stared at me, aghast.

"What's your name?" I asked.

"I am Ithia."

Her comment about a loom and the webs connected the dots to something Yuki had said earlier. "You're Fate."

She nodded.

The raucous mob of shrieking zombies was getting close enough to make hearing difficult. "We need to talk." I slid off Mortis. "But first, I need to take care of the undead before their shouting gives me a headache."

Hoping I knew what I was doing, I pulled the hood over my head and walked toward the undead swarm. Intermingled with the screams, the groans, the shouts, I heard words I understood all too well even though I didn't speak a lick of Italian.

"Help!"

"Kill me!"

"Mercy, Father!"

They'd lost their minds, but those who still had vocal chords were crying out for relief. Their bodies were weeping blood and pus. Their skin was jaundiced and peeling. Guts spilled out of some where the post-mortem sutures had torn through rotten flesh. It was a horrible sight, but I'd seen worse.

The first zombie reached me, hands extended as if I might welcome it home. I reached out and my hand passed through the flesh and touched something rough and woolen. I gripped it and pulled. With a deafening shriek, the body collapsed. A shadowy human-shaped thing writhed in my skeletal hand as if trying to get free.

Ithia gasped. "Hold on tight, Cain! Don't let it escape or that wraith will torment the living until they go insane."

I was surprised by how strong the damned thing was. The soul bucked and writhed one moment, then wriggled like an eel the next. I pulled out the black ball and pressed it to the soul. With a ghostly sigh, it swirled like smoke and vanished inside.

"Holy shit." I backed away from the encroaching horde. "Are they all going to be like that?"

"The souls are insane, Cain." Fate wiped tears from her eyes. "You will have to wrestle each one of them into the afterlife."

"Just fucking great." A zombie lunged at me. The body slumped against me and slid to the ground. The soul streaked skyward. I snagged it at the last instant, barely hanging onto the shadowy leg. I touched the soul catcher to the shadowy mass, and it vanished in a vortex of mist. The entirety of the horde was almost on me. If just a touch from me was all it took to release their souls, then there was no way I could let them get near me. I needed to do this one-on-one.

"Can I just touch this soul catcher to the bodies and vacuum out the souls?"

Fate shrugged. "I don't know. I've only seen Garrick deal with newly dead souls, and it looked nothing like this."

Mortis stomped a hoof and watched me, as if waiting to see what stupid thing I did next. I wondered if there was anything in the instruction manual about dealing with an undead horde. I could probably ride Mortis a safe distance away and read up on it, but the longer I took, the more of the living this horde would take with them.

"The threads of those who die are cut. Their part in the tapestry is done." Fate shook her head. "But now the dead are killing people whose threads should not be cut. Because of this the loom is breaking and fate will soon be rudderless!"

"We make our own fates." I climbed onto Mortis. "This is going to be messy."

Ithia scowled. "You're a fool to think you have any control over destiny."

I drew the scythe and guided Mortis toward a straggling zombie. A quick slice, and the head separated from the neck. The body instantly dropped to the ground, quivering, but not moving. "I wasn't sure if that would work." I watched the body twitch for a moment, to make sure it didn't get back up.

There was no logical reason that cutting off the head should prevent it from walking. After all, most of these decaying bodies barely had the musculature to keep going. But deep down inside these insane souls, some small shred of sanity prevailed, telling them that it was impossible to walk without a head.

I was just starting to feel pretty smart when the hands flailed, reaching out for the head. The head itself was completely inert and expressionless, meaning the soul animating the body was further down. I hopped down off the horse and lopped off the arms and legs of the zombie. The torso continued twitching, but the dismembered limbs lay motionless.

It seemed the soul was contained in the torso, or at least it remained there when all the extremities were gone. My original plan of chopping off heads and plucking souls from unmoving bodies evaporated. It'd take forever to dismember this many zombies, so I'd have to take another approach.

I touched the soul catcher to the body, but nothing happened. I reached into the rotting corpse and pulled on the soul. Once it was completely free and clear of the body, the soul catcher took it. Booping zombies on the nose with the black ball wouldn't cut it. My work was cut out for me.

When facing superior enemy numbers, even if they're complete morons, the best policy is to isolate the stragglers and work your way in. I hopped on Mortis and urged him toward a lone zombie. I leaned down, yanked out the soul, and stuffed it into the catcher in one smooth movement.

I rode up a rise and looked down at the shambling horde. The narrow streets were packed tighter than a zombie sardine can. There was no way for me to thin the herd in such close quarters.

Screams echoed behind me. I turned and saw another horde making its way from the opposite direction. Living people were fleeing from the dead and right toward the other horde.

"Mama mia, that's a spicy meatball." I didn't know why I said that, but I knew if I didn't do something in a hurry, a lot more people would die.

7

I turned Mortis in a circle, looking for a solution to the zombie sardine problem. I zoomed in on the soul beacon map and finally located a possible answer. The people fleeing the zombies couldn't see me and I didn't want to kill them from fright, so I hopped off Mortis, ran into a diagonal side-street, and removed the hood.

I stepped out and shouted at them. "This way!" I motioned into the street. "Come!"

They might not understand English, but they were panicked enough to veer toward a voice of reason. They ran past me and down the street. One woman's eyes widened when she saw my skeletal hands, but she kept running.

I hopped back on Mortis, raised my cowl, and rode back to the converging zombie hordes. The gurgling shrieks and moans of the undead increased in volume when they saw me. They instinctually knew that I and I alone could free their souls.

Raising my scythe like a banner, I led the zombies toward a large open plaza, the pied piper of Hamelin trying to save the town from something far worse than rats. Some zombies were faster than others, pushing through the shambling ranks and racing toward me. I plucked their souls as they reached me, leaving their bodies in the streets.

There were living people dining outside restaurants or sitting on benches, apparently unaware of the crisis. The moment the shrieks and moans reached their ears, the people began rising slowly, concerned looks on their faces. When they saw the mass of rotting bodies entering the plaza, they panicked like a herd of sheep, funneling down streets on the other side of the plaza.

"It's the end!" a man cried out in Italian. "We are doomed!"

"Have you considered our lord and savior, the Flying Spaghetti Monster?" I shouted back.

His eyes flared even wider, and he screamed like a boy who'd just been kicked in the crotch for the first time. "Death has come for us!" Despite his portly build, he sprinted away like a track star.

Apparently, talking directly to a mortal revealed me. Or perhaps it was intent that did it and not merely talking. I'd have to be careful. I looked around and noticed Ithia was nowhere to be seen.

Once I reached the plaza, I rode Mortis in wide circles to loosen up the horde, then started taking the souls of those at the edge of the crowd, careful not to let any of the others touch me. The last thing I needed to do on the first day of the job was unleash a swarm of wraiths on the world. I lost track of time as I repeated the pattern over and over, circling the plaza more times than I cared to count.

At long last, the plaza was full of unmoving bodies. I took a moment to catch my breath. I wasn't as tired as I should be, but that was probably due to the supernatural powers granted by the death cloak. I glanced at the death beacon. More crimson dots were scattered along the streets, along with many more that were green, meaning the horde had killed other people recently.

I sighed. "This is going to take a while." I guided Mortis back down the street and we headed toward the next batch of souls.

We reached a newly dead body, a young woman whose throat had been torn out. I reached in her body and was surprised when my fingers felt silk rather than rough wool. Her soul came free, drifting limply in my grasp. The souls of the recently deceased were much different than the insane ones.

I hesitated before putting her in the soul catcher, a stray thought giving me pause. Would putting her inside with all the insane souls harm her? Or were they all compartmentalized somehow? I had no idea how the thing worked or how many souls it could hold. Ithia wasn't around to ask, and I doubted she knew.

Still holding gently onto the soul, I took out Garrick's manual and began reading more about the soul catcher. According to him, he'd never reached a limit on the number of souls it could hold. Souls that remained in Purgatory had told him the inside looked like a honeycomb, every soul kept in a separate cell. I could safely put this soul inside and it would be kept separate from the others. I held up the soul catcher and let it draw her soul inside.

The next question looming on my mind was, would the insane souls ever recover their sanity? Or were they forever doomed? It was an important question, but one for which I didn't have an answer. I also had far too much on my plate to even stop for a moment. This was going to take a while.

My phone rang. I looked at the caller ID and saw it was Hannah. I'd completely lost track of time because it was already three AM back in Atlanta. Surprisingly, my bony fingers worked on the touchscreen when I swiped the icon to answer.

"What's up?" I asked.

"Cain, are you okay?" Hannah sounded worried. "You usually check in if you're not coming home."

"I can't wait to tell you about my day, but it's going to have to wait." I sighed. "Long story short, I had to take over as Death for a while since Garrick is in a coma. The backlog of souls is massive and I've got to stop a zombie uprising."

"Wait, what?" Hannah's voice rose an octave. "Turn on your video!"

I activated the camera and Hannah appeared on my screen. Her eyes widened.

"Oh my god!" She motioned offscreen. "Shae, come look at Cain! He's Death!"

Shae appeared on screen and her mouth dropped open. "Whoa, Cain, what's going on?"

"Cain had to take over for Garrick." Hannah grinned. "That's so cool."

"It's not really," I grumbled. "I'm fighting zombies out here, not prancing around in a Halloween costume." I noticed a lone zombie shambling down the street toward me. "I've got to go."

"Wait, Cain!" Hannah's face filled the screen. "I heard Aura is back at Voltaire's."

I paused. "Our Aura?"

She nodded. "Aura Prime, not the one from Alpha."

The zombie lunged. Mortis dodged left and its rotting hand narrowly missed my leg. The phone was hindering my ability to grab the soul, meaning it was time to say goodbye. "Thanks for the info. I'll talk to you later."

"Good luck!" Hannah blew me a kiss.

"Yep." I ended the call, tucked away my phone, and reaped the mad soul of the zombie. I checked the death beacon and groaned at the number of dead still in the city. There was no time to feel sorry for myself, so I twitched the reins, and Mortis galloped toward the next soul to be reaped.

I lost all sense of time as I continued my task, cleaning up Italy and then moving onto the next soul and the next until I found myself in the Baltic region. By then, I was starting to feel the mental and physical strain of the job wearing on me. The cloak obviously gave me extra strength and stamina, but I was still just a mortal beneath the cowl.

I took a moment to read up on the death beacon. Tapping on one side caused a readout to display the number of dead in the world, and the number of those who'd die within the next twenty-four hours. There were still one thousand, three-hundred and ninety-two currently dead worldwide. It didn't show how many were of the insane variety Every few seconds, the number ticked up as someone else died. Some parts of the world were completely dark, presumably because there were no Christians there. I gave silent thanks that I didn't have to worry about them because the populations would make it impossible to keep up with.

Given the locations I had to visit, it seemed unlikely that people would be dropping like flies every few seconds if not for the pandemic and murderous rampaging zombies.

I urged Mortis to the next location. He pawed the ground and neighed, then looked back at me expectantly. He'd been galloping pell-mell to the next group of undead every time I'd been ready earlier. I wondered if he thought it was time for me to go home and rest.

"Are you tired?" I leaned back in the saddle. "Do you need rest?"

He shook his head and snorted.

"But you think I need rest?"

He bobbed his head.

"Not yet, but soon." I sighed. "Let's go." I checked the beacon and realized we were in South America. Judging from the lack of blips in Argentina and the lower half of the continent, I'd been working my way up from the bottom.

We reaped our way through Bolivia and headed to Brazil. The rural areas were significantly easier to deal with because there weren't roving hordes of zombies. Some of the smaller villages were completely empty. Signs scrawled in Portuguese warned of the walking dead. Others claimed the rapture had already happened and they were living in the end days.

Unfortunately, they weren't entirely wrong. If Fate's loom were destroyed, would that put us on a path to Armageddon? I didn't know enough about her job to even hazard a guess, but the two of us needed a good sit-down and talk as soon as I was finished with my task.

Despite my harsh training in the Oblivion Guard, I would have found a place to rest hours ago without the cloak sustaining me. I just hoped this thing could keep me going until I cleared the board of crimson blips. But when I reached Rio de Janeiro and saw the size of the undead horde gathered downtown, I felt the weariness in my bones.

I arrived just outside the massive Maracanã Stadium where they hosted soccer—excuse me—football. Either the locals had been storing the dead inside, or they'd herded the undead in there. Some cities had been unable to keep up with the bodies, resulting in overflowing morgues, so they'd resorted to piling corpses where they could. A football stadium seemed reasonable. Unfortunately, it was now teeming with zombies.

On the upside, there were only a few scattered crimson blips elsewhere the city, meaning the majority were contained here. On the downside, I was slumping from weariness in the saddle. Collecting insane souls was hard work and I couldn't afford to slip up, not even once.

I didn't know much about wraiths except they were typically the most pissed off kinds of ghosts. Add extreme PTSD to their insanity and just one of these wraiths could do as much damage to the psyche of living people as a horde of zombies could do to their bodies.

It was time to go home and rest.

Mortis innately understood what I wanted and raced forward. The city skyline thinned to cardboard cutouts, folding down around us like someone closing a pop-up book, and then the dark realm unfolded beneath us. Moments later, we were back in Purgatory.

"This isn't my home." I sighed. "I'm not sleeping in a stranger's house. Take me to Sanctuary."

Mortis snorted and stomped a foot, then turned and nipped at my feet in the stirrups.

"Who's a grumpy little horse?" I said.

He glared at me, dark mist billowing from his nostrils.

"What is that stuff coming out of your nose?" I asked.

Mortis snorted and shook his head, then turned around and galloped. The woodlands around Sanctuary unfolded before us moments later. It was already broad daylight in this part of the world. Mortis skidded to a stop at the gate. I was surprised that he hadn't been able to deliver us directly to the house.

"You can't just skip past the wards?"

He didn't offer a response.

I'd always hoped my heavy-duty wards protected against divine invasions, and this seemed to validate that hope. Caolan, the druid, with the help of a local elemental had ringed the entire place with silver and iron. I'd thrown in some fae magic to seal the deal. Whatever magical form of travel Mortis employed didn't seem capable of breaking through the wards.

I disabled the wards, led Mortis through, and closed the gate. We raced down the gravel road, through the graveyard, and up to the front doors of the church I'd converted into my home. I hopped off Mortis and patted his neck. "I don't have a stable."

He snorted in disdain, then wandered out into the nearby field where he lay down. His head tilted forward, and the glow in his eyes winked out.

"Sleep well and dream of large mares," I said. Then I disabled the wards on my doors and went inside. Hannah and Shae weren't home, presumably because they'd gone to school. Their special school didn't offer much for demigoddess training, but they'd found the lessons useful while posing as daughters of a witch.

I went to my room, disrobed, and crawled under the covers.

Without the cloak, I no longer felt the tug of the dead on my consciousness. That was quite a relief, because it would have nagged the hell out of me while trying to fall asleep. I gave myself a mental time to wake up. Much as I needed rest, the world needed to be rid of the walking dead even more.

I woke up precisely six hours later to dishes rattling in the kitchen and Hannah talking excitedly. Fred, my former octopus now turned Baby Cthulhu, chimed in with simple sentences every now and then. I really wanted to duck out without getting caught up in conversation, but soon realized they were talking about seeing Mortis in the front yard.

Despite being invisible to most people, Shae could see through just about any kind of glamour. As the daughter of Nyx, I doubted any form of death could hide from her.

I sighed and opened the bedroom door.

Hannah looked up from a pitcher of pancake batter and grinned. "Cain!" She dropped the whisk and ran over to me, gripping me in a tight hug while hopping excitedly.

Shae waved shyly from behind the counter. Fred waddled over, his mouth tentacles twitching.

I pried myself loose from Hannah and held up my hands. "Look, I don't have much time to waste—"

"Cain, shut up and eat breakfast." Hannah pointed to a pile of already made pancakes and a plate of bacon. "I know you're hungry."

My stomach grumbled in agreement.

"Hannah made breakfast for dinner for you," Shae said.

"I can see that." I made myself a plate and sat down at the table.

Fred climbed awkwardly into a chair and stood in it so he could look over the edge of the table. "You are Death?"

I nodded but was too busy stuffing my mouth to say anything. I swallowed. "Too much to talk about. Too many zombies to deal with."

"Zombies!" Shae gasped in delight. "I've always wanted to see a giant horde descending on a town while the villagers run screaming!"

"She's a huge Walking Dead fan." Hannah rolled her eyes. "Negan is her fave."

I grunted. "To each their own."

"I know you didn't ask, but school is going great." Hannah traced a sigil and a tiny ball of light hovered above her hand. "We're not much better with our demi powers, but at least we can do the basics."

I paused chewing a pancake. "You can do ordinary sigil magic?"

She grinned. "Yep. Pretty cool, right?"

It made sense. As a demigoddess, she already had more magical potential in her little finger than most wizards had in their entire bodies. "Maybe learning sigils will help you connect to your god powers."

"I hope so." Hannah sat down and chomped on a piece of bacon. "Shae is already so much better than me with her shadow magic and mega-true sight."

"I was forced to learn quickly. Esteri was extremely cruel when it came to teaching." Shae shivered. "She'd hurt me if I didn't perform well, and when that stopped working, she'd capture animals and threaten to kill them in front of me."

Hannah patted Shae's back. "I'm sorry my doppelganger is so evil."

Esteri was Hannah, but from Dimension Alpha. The Cain in Alpha had made a mistake resulting in horrific injuries to Hannah Alpha and that sent her down a different life path than my ward here in Prime.

Shae shrugged. "We all make our choices. Esteri is just a twat."

Hannah giggled. "Yes, she is."

Shae regarded me. "How did you become Death?"

"It's just at temp job." I munched another piece of bacon. "The original Thanatos decided he no longer wanted to be in the soul reaping business, so he turned it into a regular job for mortals. Garrick still holds the office. I'm just filling in."

"That's insane!" Hannah's eyes widened. "You put on a cloak, and it just turns you into Death?"

"More or less." I slapped some butter on my pancakes. "Now I'm stuck with the job since Garrick is in a coma. I really needed his help finding the original Thanatos so I can figure out how to free Layla and Athena from Soultaker. Now all that is up in the air, and I've got Zeus and Mars breathing down my neck since they need Athena to help them defend their part of the divine realm."

"Thanatos is Nyx's son." Shae leaned her elbows on the table. "I guess we're like half siblings or something."

"Wow, that's so cool." Hannah poured herself a glass of orange juice. "I wonder what Nyx is like."

"I wondered that myself, so I started reading about her." Shae leaned back in her chair. "She's a Titan. She had a lot of kids. Rumor has it even Zeus was afraid of her." She turned to me. "Maybe Nyx can help you find Thanatos."

"Maybe." I stuffed more pancakes in my mouth, hurrying so I could get back on the job and get the zombie uprising over and done with.

I knew only basic myths about the gods since the fae didn't want people to learn the truth. Most of the supernatural world still believed the gods were dead, slain by the fae. They'd probably be horrified to know the truth—that the fae had made a bargain with Shub-Nuggurath in order to gain dominion over Feary and Gaia. Now that I'd disrupted that plan, I wondered what came next.

I sipped orange juice and nodded. "Zeus was afraid of the Titans in general since they were the original Elder Gods. According to legend, the Titan, Prometheus, is actually the one who designed humans from clay."

"Yeah, but weren't all the Titans actually humans from the previous cycle of the universe?" Hannah quirked her lips. "It's not like they had to come up with humans from scratch. Prometheus just made us in their image."

I shrugged. "He went with what he knew best, I suppose."

Shae stabbed a pancake with her fork. "Then Prometheus pissed off Zeus by giving humans fire."

Hannah quirked her lips. "Zeus and company were just kids revolting against their parents."

"Yep." I finished my bacon and scooted back the chair. "I've got to go."

Hannah sighed. "Good luck, Cain."

I headed toward the door.

Hannah banged the table with a fist. "Look, I know you're repressing a lot of negative emotions right now, but that's no excuse to act so impersonal to us."

I stopped at the door and considered what she said. "I didn't realize I was being impersonal."

"You haven't kissed me on the top of my head in weeks, Cain!" She slumped. "You barely hug me back anymore."

"Cain angry," Fred said. "Very sad and angry for Layla."

I was more than angry—I was furious. But that was normal and easily controlled. My adoptive father, Erolith, would expect nothing less. I was filled with the cold certainty of duty, and that was all I needed. My duty right now required reaping a multitude of souls so

I'd be free to pursue finding Thanatos, among other things. It also opened other doors that hadn't been available to me before.

I nodded. "I'm sorry, but there's a lot on my mind."

Shae kissed Hannah's forehead and took her hand. "Cain still loves you."

Hannah leaned her head against Shae, tears trickling down her cheeks. "I know, but it's like ever since Mars killed Layla, the joy of life has just drained out of him."

It occurred to me that I hadn't even considered that. My love for Layla seemed like a distant memory now, as did my brotherly or fatherly feelings for Hannah. I tried to think back to the moment Mars drove Soultaker through Layla's chest and tried to feel what I'd felt at that moment. It was there buried inside—a distant emotion with no depth.

This draining of emotion and concern had been happening slowly but steadily since then. I still felt anger about her death. I still felt determined to bring her and Athena back to the land of the living. But I had no explanation for this strange turn in my emotions.

"I'm sorry, Hannah. Once this is over, things will be better." That statement was more hope than fact, because something else was going on with me and the only correlation I could draw was that ever since being relieved of the ghosts haunting me, I was steadily becoming the old emotionless Cain again.

And that wasn't good for anyone.

8

When I'd murdered a house full of women and children, innocent bystanders in the Fae-Human War, their ghosts haunted me as they might haunt a house. It wasn't possession, but it was like having dozens of extra voices whispering in my head. After discovering my origins as Ekhsis, a member of the original humans from a past universe, Garrick had told me I'd also been haunted by them after they'd been slaughtered by Torvin Rayne and the Oblivion Guard.

It seemed those ghosts had left me as well.

Without ghosts acting as an external conscience, I was slowly returning to old form, a machine torn down and rebuilt by Torvin and the Oblivion Guard. A machine built for one purpose— following orders without question, without emotion. I still felt anger and determination, but love and caring for others had been beaten out of me during training.

Thinking back on my feelings for Hannah and Layla were like trying to use a missing limb, a ghost arm that still tingled, but wasn't there.

While I'd had emotions driven from me during my training, my haunting had taught me how to feel, how to empathize, and how to be human. It was hard to believe that I couldn't simply hold onto what I'd learned and continue to evolve. I shook my head and went outside. There would be plenty of time later to analyze my feelings. For now, I had business to attend to.

Mortis stomped a foot when I stepped outside. He seemed just as eager to get going. I slid on the cloak and felt my flesh melt away once again. Once we were past the outer gates, Mortis galloped at full speed toward downtown Atlanta. He apparently didn't transition through the dark realm when the destination was relatively close.

I wondered if there was information in Garrick's manual about his strange form of travel. It probably wasn't necessary for me to know, but it could be useful.

There were very few crimson blips scattered around the city since most of the undead were concentrated in one spot. We soon reached a large penitentiary surrounded by tall brick walls. Judging from the dull roar on the other side, the inside was teeming with zombies. A black animal control truck drove past, rocking violently on its wheels as if a grizzly bear was trying to break out.

Lines of police in riot gear stood outside the wall and rows upon rows of animal control vehicles parked along the street. Crowds of people stood across the road from the perimeter waving signs and shouting at the police. The signs read:

We Want Answers!

Bill Gates is controlling the dead with 5G!

Let our loved ones go!

It seemed the conspiracy theorists were having a field day with the zombie apocalypse.

Mortis slowed to a trot, and I passed among the police without any of them noticing.

One officer shivered and looked around. "Did you feel that?"

Another frowned uncertainly. "That freezing cold air?"

"Felt like a ghost just walked through me." The first officer shuddered again. "This shit is getting to me. I never signed up to handle zombies."

"Me either." The second officer watched as people in animal

control uniforms walked toward the arriving truck, long dog catcher poles in hand.

It seemed someone had come up with a way to corral the zombies, at least temporarily.

"We should burn them," the second officer said. "If we burn the bodies to nothing, they can't move, right?"

The first shrugged. "I don't know. Guess people finally got the zombie apocalypse they've been wanting."

The outer gates opened as the truck drove inside. Mortis and I paced alongside it with the animal control workers. I assumed he hadn't taken us directly inside since that might put us in the middle of a zombie swarm. If they touched me, it would free countless wraiths, so it was best to play this cautiously.

The outer gate closed, and the inner gates swung open. The babble, shrieks, and screams rose to a dull roar. Heavy barbed fences that looked as if they'd been recently constructed blocked a small portion of the courtyard off from the inner gates. Hundreds of the undead threw themselves against the fence, arms clutching at the living now walking so close.

They suddenly stopped and the courtyard went deathly quiet as the undead felt my presence. Almost as one, they turned and began shambling toward me, some babbling incoherently, others screaming for salvation.

"What in the actual fuck?" One of the animal control workers stopped in place, a shocked look in her face. "Where are they going?" She looked straight through me as if trying to understand what invisible source was attracting the zombies.

The zombies were packed so tightly into the courtyard that there was no way I could get inside and liberate the souls one at a time. I needed space. I didn't like involving nubs in supernatural activities, but I also needed their help if I was going to get through this. So, I decided to take a risk.

I focused on the woman and her only. "They're coming for me."

Her eyes flared comically wide, and she dropped the animal control pole. Her mouth opened in a silent scream.

I lowered my cowl and revealed my face. "It's okay. I'm not here to hurt you."

"Holy Mary, Mother of God!" The woman backed away slowly. "Do you guys see this?"

Her coworkers looked around in confusion. "Abby, what in the hell are you talking about?"

This was going to be a lot messier than I wanted, but there were only ten nubs present, so it wouldn't be too out of hand. I focused on them and allowed myself to be seen.

Since my head was normal, the others didn't react quite as horrified as Abby, but most of them jumped when a man in a dark cloak on a skeletal horse appeared out of nowhere.

"Fucking shitballs!" A man dropped his pole, turned and smacked into the side of the animal control truck.

"Calm your tits!" I shouted. "I'm not here to hurt you, okay? I'm here to help."

Meanwhile, the zombies had pressed themselves up against the fence closest to me, screaming for release.

Abby recovered her wits first. "Who are you and how did you get in here? Is this some kind of sick joke?"

I slid off the horse. "I'm Death and I'm here to release the souls of the undead." I pointed to the zombies. "Their souls have gone insane from being trapped in dead bodies. If I don't carefully free them one at a time, they'll fly free as wraiths and harm a lot more people. If you could pull them out one at a time and let me take their souls, it'd make things much easier."

Abby gulped. Reached out a hand and touched mine. She recoiled. "This can't be happening."

I shrugged. "Like it or not, it's happening. Now, do you want me to fix the problem quickly, or should I go invisible again and try to fix it on my own?"

One of the others stepped forward. "I always dreamed magic was real. Now I've got zombies and the Grim Reaper all in one day. This is great!" She thrust out her pole. "I'm ready."

The truck continued rocking violently as its cargo tried to escape.

I nodded toward it. "Let's start with the ones inside."

She motioned toward a pair of control workers wearing heavily padded clothing used in encounters with rabid dogs and larger animals. "Taylor and Higgs, get one of the zombies out here."

The men were still staring in fear and confusion at me. The woman clapped her hands and they snapped out of it, walked to the back of the truck and unlocked the rear doors. They tossed out one body at a time and the others quickly snared the undead around the necks with the control poles.

I went to the nearest struggling zombie, reached in, and pulled out its soul. The corpse collapsed immediately. I held the soul to the soul catcher and sucked it inside.

"Holy shit, he did it!" Higgs clapped his gloved hands. "This shit is legit!"

I moved to the next and the next, freeing a dozen souls in less than two minutes. "Damn, this was a lot easier than Rome."

"Rome?" the woman asked.

"I've been all over the world, but I've still got thousands of souls to free." I grimaced at the thought of what waited in Brazil. "It's a fucking mess."

"How did this happen?" Abby asked.

"These souls weren't taken in time and they've gone insane since they were trapped in dead, rotting bodies." I looked toward the couple hundred undead behind the barbed wire. "Help me get those done so I can get this worldwide mess cleaned up."

Abby turned toward the woman in charge. "How do you want us to handle this, Belmarie?"

Belmarie pursed her lips and looked at the gate to the fenced-in area. "Maybe we can lure them out."

Taylor shook his head. "We don't have the manpower to hold back that many if they all make a run for the gate."

Higgs gave me a sideways look, as if afraid to look at me head on. "Uh, do they feel pain? I know they don't go down from bullets."

"They feel the constant existential pain and torment of being trapped in rotting bodies." I shrugged. "I don't think it's the same as physical pain, though."

Higgs made the sign of the cross on his chest. "God help these poor souls."

"Technically, that's my job." I sighed because there didn't seem to be a good way to handle this. On the other hand, this part of the courtyard was about as large as the fenced-in area. "Open the gate and I'll draw through a few at a time. Noose them with the control poles and then close the gate again when I lure the others back the other way."

Belmarie nodded. "That's as good an idea as any." She motioned to Taylor and Higgs. "Get ready to control the gate."

The pair stepped up to the gate.

"Open it," she said.

They did. The zombies were too fixated on me to realize they had a way out of their cage. I walked toward the open gate and the outliers in the mob turned and shambled toward us. Even then, most of them didn't seem to realize they could simply walk through the open gate and pressed up against the barbed wire next to it.

"Poor people." Belmarie wiped a tear from her eye and adjusted her surgical mask to keep it from getting wet. "Taylor, pull a few through."

He obliged, reaching inside and yanking through four undead. The others noosed them, and I freed their souls. We washed, rinsed, repeated for the next hour until there was nothing but a massive pile of motionless corpses.

Abby walked a distance away from the dead and fell to her knees, tears pouring down her cheeks. She raised her gaze heavenward and clasped her hands in prayer. Several others crowded around her, hands on her shoulders. Others watched me, a mix of hope and wonder on their faces.

Belmarie walked up to me and took my hand. "Thank you, Death. I take some small comfort knowing that you'll be there to help me when I pass from this body." She looked up. "Is Heaven as beautiful as they say?"

I shrugged. "I've never been there. It's a lot more likely everyone here will go to Hell anyway."

"How could you say that?" Her eyes flared. "Am I going to Hell?"

"I don't know." I realized that what I was saying might traumatize her, but there was no reason not to tell her the truth. "Hell is basically a place where you torture yourself for whatever you feel most guilty about. If you can overcome that, Lucifer says you can go on to Heaven."

"And you believe the King of Lies?"

"I've found that Lucifer is one of the most truthful people I've ever met. I'm not saying he's a wonderful person, but the rumors about him are untrue." I patted her shoulder. "Just try to confront whatever you feel the guiltiest about in life and try to get over it before you die. I think that'll increase your odds."

Belmarie looked ready to faint. "You're a terrible inspirational speaker."

"This isn't even my job. I'm just a temp." I donned my cowl and felt the flesh melt from my face. The others gasped. "Thanks for your help. I just might be able to avert the apocalypse."

There was some scattered clapping at this declaration, and then I hopped on Mortis, and we headed toward the next blip. We worked our way up through Tennessee, over to Alabama, working gradually northward. The infestations were much smaller than Atlanta and easier to handle.

Chicago was another story.

I cleaned up the scattered blips in rural Illinois and headed toward the Windy City where naturally, the largest concentration waited. The police had herded the undead into whatever large buildings they had—stadiums, warehouses, and even a mega-church, but most of them were at Soldier Field. While I'd slept, the worldwide death count had risen by another two thousand and about four hundred of them were located here, packed like cattle in a hundred yards of barricaded football field.

"Well, fuck." It looked like I'd have to request help from the locals again.

Chicago wasn't using animal control officers, but it had an army of cops, riot tanks, and other militarized weaponry guarding the perimeter against thousands of sign-waving protestors. The signs here were much the same as those in Atlanta and other cities I'd visited along the way.

Big Pharma is responsible!

The End is Nigh!

Where is Rick Grimes?

I couldn't blame the populace for wondering just what in the fuck was happening in the world. First a plague and now zombies. This was something that only happened on television in their boring little lives. Now that it had overflowed into the real world, they felt like sheep being led to slaughter.

They weren't wrong.

I guided Mortis past the outer line of police, over a concrete barricade, and into the stadium. The police had erected chain link fencing around the football field and reinforced it with concrete barricades. A small police squad patrolled this side of the barricade. I went past them and looked at the undead inside the fence.

According to the death beacon, there were three hundred ninety-eight dead inside. Now that I'd arrived, they were stampeding toward this end of the fence, pressing desperately against it. Cops fired shots, temporarily dropping a few zombies, but not doing much otherwise. This was going to be a horrific mess if I tried to handle this mob without help.

The police had no animal control gear, but their riot gear would protect them against bites. The zombie bites weren't contagious, but having your skin torn off by a ravenous zombie probably didn't feel great.

I steered Mortis back to the nearest patrol, lowered my hood, and revealed myself to them by willing it.

"Excuse me, but I need your help."

The first cop turned. His eyes flared, and he shouted in surprise. The others turned with him, weapons coming free of holsters. Gunfire exploded before I could say another word.

9

A hail of bullets flew toward me.

This is off to a great start, I thought.

I reflexively threw up a shield, uncertain if the death cloak would protect me from bullets. The shield sparked with every impact, cracking, but holding. An officer at the back waved his arms and shouted, "Cease fire! Cease fire!"

Most had already stopped only because they'd run out of bullets. Others fumbled to reload.

The same officer approached me. "Identify yourself! Get off the horse."

"I am Death." I slid off Mortis, hands upraised, but with a shield in front of me. "I'm here to free the souls of the undead."

Nervous laughter rose from their ranks.

"What the fuck, you moron?" One of them shouted. "We could've killed you!"

Another cop stared in disbelief. "How the fuck did we miss?"

I slid the cowl over my head and the flesh fell away. Their laughter turned to shouts of surprise. Some screamed, dropped their weapons, and ran. Some froze in fear, wet spots forming at the crotch of their pants. Seeing the Grim Reaper in person was enough to make grown men and women shit their pants. However, scaring them half to death wasn't a good idea. I needed their help, not their fear.

I lowered the hood to reveal my normal face again. "You just shot at me and didn't hit me a single time. I think that's proof enough that I am who I say I am."

The lead officer held up a hand to quiet the other police, then walked toward me, his gun aimed at my chest. "I want your identification."

I cast a shield around the man's gun hand and twisted it sideways. He cried out in pain and the gun fell from his grip. Using another shield, I yanked the gun through the air toward me. Reaching over my shoulder, I summoned the scythe and slashed the pistol in half just before it reached me. The pieces clattered to the asphalt at my feet.

Another cop ran away, leaving only a squad of four.

This wasn't going the way I'd hoped. I sighed. "Look, if you help me, I can get rid of your undead problem in a matter of hours. The only reason those corpses are walking is because the tortured souls of the dead can't escape and go to the afterlife. So, stop asking me for my ID, stop screaming, and just fucking help, okay?"

The officer pushed up to his knees, hindered by his large stomach. He looked up at me, eyes filling with realization. "How did you do that?"

"Magic." I banished the scythe, summoned it, then banished it again. "See? Magic!"

Another cop stiffened her shoulders and faced me. "You can get rid of the zombies?"

I nodded. "I can't handle them all at once. If a zombie touches me, it frees the insane soul. If I don't grab the soul before it escapes, it will become a wraith that will haunt and torment the living." I gave them a moment to digest that, then continued. "I need to free one zombie at a time in a controlled manner so that doesn't happen. Once I capture the soul the body is dead for good. Capiche?"

Another cop wiped tears from his eyes. "My wife is in the zombie pen. She died of the plague two weeks ago. Another buddy lost his kid in a car accident and he's walking around in there too. I'll do whatever you need if it brings them some peace."

The lead officer, Jergens, according to his name tag, climbed to his feet with a loud grunt. "I can't believe you're really Death."

I motioned toward the fence. "You see how they're all clamoring to touch me? It's because they know I can free them from their torment. Bring me one and I'll prove it."

Jergens brushed off his pants, then turned to the others. "We didn't exactly design this place to make it easy to pull zombies out one at a time."

A woman with short blonde hair jogged around the corner and stormed up to the four cops. "Jergens, what in the fuck is going on over here? Half your patrol ran past me like the devil was on their heels."

Jergens looked from me to her, apparently confused because she couldn't see me. "Uh, you don't see him?"

"Right there, Sergeant Murray!" Another cop pointed at me.

She looked straight at me, frowned, and then to the others. A sudden realization passed through her eyes, and she looked back in my direction. "Reveal yourself, whoever you are, or I'll call someone who knows how to deal with your kind."

That took me off guard. This woman had apparently dealt with the supernatural. I willed myself to become visible. She flinched but didn't shrink away. I waved. "Hi."

She breathed a sigh of relief. "If you are who I think you are, it's about damned time."

I raised an eyebrow. "Oh, is it?"

She turned to the others. "You're not to breathe a word of this to anyone, understand?"

Jergens spluttered. "B-but this proves what you been saying all along! Everyone calls you Crazy Murray!"

Her gaze turned stony. "I've learned over the years that proving myself right would only put others in danger. Besides, do you really think anyone else will believe you? Do you want to be called Crazy Jergens for the rest of your life?"

He looked down at the ground and scuffed his shoe like a naughty kid who'd just been caught. "No."

"Then let's help Death do what he needs to do before the world ends, okay?"

The other cops nodded.

Jergens sighed and shook his head. "Death said he's gotta touch them one at a time but the second we open that fence, those things are gonna swarm us."

I took out the soul catcher. "If a zombie even brushes against me, their soul will fly free. I've got to manually pull them out one at a time and stuff them into this thing because if they escape, they'll become wraiths."

Sergeant Murray frowned and looked around. She pointed to stacks of fencing not far away. "Jergens, are those the temporary barriers?

He followed her finger. "Yeah."

"Let's drag those over here and set up a cattle chute. That'll funnel the undead so only one at a time can get through." She turned to me. "Does that work?"

"Excellent idea." I slid off Mortis and headed toward the fencing she'd indicated. Upon closer inspection, I realized it was heavy gauge fencing with a wide base, designed to stand on its own and be hooked into a neighboring section of fence.

Everyone chose a section and began dragging them over to the nearest gate in the zombie pen. We hooked the sections to the chain link outside the gate, then angled the sections into a maze of narrow funnels. We reinforced the sections by stacking more fencing against the outsides to keep the zombies from breaking free by sheer force of numbers.

Then it was just a matter of opening the gate and letting the zombies fill the pen. Sergeant Murray jogged through the maze of temporary fencing without hesitation and opened the gate. The zombies pressing against it fell through, piling atop one another while others crawled over them in their haste to reach living flesh and me. Their moans and cries sent shudders of fear through some of the cops.

Completely unfazed, Murray jogged back through the chute and the other cops closed the makeshift gate behind her. Now it was all up to me. I waited for the zombies to finally make it to the end of the chute. It was so narrow that they had to turn sideways to squeeze through. This made it next to impossible for the zombies behind them to touch me.

When the first one reached the end, I yanked out its soul and vacuumed it with the soul catcher. The body went limp but couldn't fall due to the narrow confines of the cattle chute.

Jergens stared in awe. "Y-you did it! Holy shit, this guy's the real deal!"

The other cops whooped and cheered.

Murray rolled her eyes. "Jergens, get the body out of the way so he can do the next one."

He flinched. "Oh, yeah, sorry." He opened the temporary gate a slit. Lips curled in disgust, he pulled on the rotting corpse and dragged it across the pavement, leaving a trail of putrid bodily fluids.

The next zombie pushed into the vacated space, and I liberated its soul. The next cop dragged it off. We did the same to the next and the next.

Murray snorted. "It's like a zombie Pez dispenser."

I barely knew the woman, but I already liked her. She was fearless and driven and at least as bossy as Layla.

She raised an eyebrow. "You didn't think that was funny?"

"It was hilarious," I said in a deadpan voice. I freed another soul and let Jergens drag it out of the way.

Murray grinned and quickly repressed it. "You're not anything like I expected Death to be."

I grunted. "You're not anything like I expected a cop to be."

Jergens frowned. "What do you mean by that?"

I stared at him. "Don't make me put the hood back on."

He paled and shut his mouth.

It took a long time to clear out the pen, but Murray's occasional quips and observations made it far more tolerable than my earlier experiences. Everyone except for me was sweating and covered in bodily fluids by the time the last undead was freed of its soul. I checked the death beacon and noted with distaste that there was another large group of the undead further north near the shores of Lake Michigan.

"I still can't believe it." Jergens stared at the pile of completely dead bodies. "I don't even know what's real anymore."

"Well, the afterlife is real. If you're Christian, I hate to say it, but you're probably going to Hell." I shrugged. "So, just enjoy life and don't be a dick, okay?"

Jergens gulped. "Fuck me."

"I gotta get to church," another cop said. "I'm gonna bathe in holy water if that's what it takes."

A third cop seemed to be having an entirely different crisis. "Do we need to worry about vampires too?"

"And werewolves." I waggled a hand. "Just avoid Seattle and you'll probably be okay."

"Seattle?" Her eyes widened. "My sister lives there!"

"It's infested with vampires." I offered a shrug. "At least they don't sparkle."

"That's probably worse though, isn't it?" She shivered and made a sign of the cross. "Seattle is infested with vampires, and we're all going to Hell."

"That sums it up pretty well," I said.

"All these poor bastards whose souls you're freeing are going from this hell to another?" Jergens spat on the ground. "Why the fuck would God make us just to endure the shit storm we call life only to die and end up in a lake of eternal fire?"

"That answer is above my paygrade." I shook my head. "I'm sorry. All I know is that Hell is filled with people who can't overcome their guilt."

"Enough with the twenty questions." Murray turned to me. "A friend of mine really needs your help."

"I'm not here to help anyone but the dead, Sergeant."

"Call me Sharon or Murray." She walked over to Mortis and petted his nose. He whickered gently.

I blinked in surprise. "He's not even all that friendly to me. Are you a pale horse whisperer?"

"I've been touched by Death." Murray stroked his mane. "I probably should have died, but my friend saved me." She turned to me. "I'm not asking for a personal favor. My friend has been trapping the undead ever since they started roaming the streets and he's pretty pissed about it."

"He wouldn't happen to be keeping them here, would he?" I showed her the map on the death beacon.

"That's the place."

I sighed. "He's not exactly doing me a favor."

"Maybe not you, but he's certainly helping ordinary citizens." She patted the saddle. "Mind giving me a lift over there?"

I shrugged. "Since you and the horse get along so well, maybe you'd like to take over my Death duties."

Murray snorted. "Oh, no you don't. You got this."

I climbed into the saddle, then reached down. Murray gripped my wrist, put a foot in a stirrup and pulled herself up behind me. "Let's go horsey."

"Hey, wait!" Jergens held out a hand, but Mortis galloped away before he could get out another word.

Murray held on but didn't say a word as we flashed through the streets, weaving between traffic and dodging pedestrians without any of them being the wiser. Mortis leapt atop the L train rails and followed them into a tunnel. We ran through what looked like a solid wall and into a dimly lit tunnel.

It was impossible to see anything, so I pulled on the Death cowl and wasn't surprised when I was suddenly able to see everything in shadowy grayscale.

We took a sudden left turn and entered a well-lit tunnel blocked by rusting derelict train cars that looked more suitable to holding cattle than human passengers. The rails in this area were smaller and closer together and this section of tunnel looked as if it hadn't seen maintenance in fifty years.

"These are old, abandoned freight tunnels," Murray said. "Good place to store zombies."

The wails and shrieks of the undead echoed hauntingly through the corridor. Mortis slowed as we reached an area where a junction of several tunnels formed a wide space blocked off by small freight cars, lumber, and anything else that could be assembled into a barrier.

Shouting that was too coherent to belong to the undead emanated from somewhere ahead. Pinpoints of glowing light became visible in the darkness of an adjoining tunnel, growing closer until I realized they were eyes that belonged to unseen creatures. The gray night vision provided by the cowl wasn't enough to reveal them, but thankfully, they seemed unaware of my presence.

Gunfire, the clang of swords, and explosions of magic grew louder. There was a major conflict underway and that didn't bode well for this being a quick soul-collecting operation.

The sources of the glowing eyes entered the light. Some slithered with bodies resembling giant black eels, their upper bodies humanoid but with fishlike heads and grayish-green glossy skin. Others walked on hind legs, their bodies morphing into monstrously-headed angler fish complete with tentacle-like protrusions dangling from their foreheads and mouths full of jagged teeth.

Many wielded rusty metal weapons while others brandished what looked like whalebones or even ship anchors. Even without weapons, their long, clawed hands looked as if they could rend flesh to the bone in a matter of seconds.

Murray stiffened. "What in the fuck are those things?"

I knew what they were but had no idea why they were here. They were minions of Cthulhu.

They were the deep ones.

10

The deep ones were a bizarre mix of human and deep-sea creature anatomy. Some were outright human hybrids, fish people birthed from the unholy pairing of deep ones with villagers as outlined in Lovecraft's journals about Innsmouth, Massachusetts. This small army was comprised of hybrids and deep ones.

I tried and failed to formulate a reason why Cthulhu would have sent his minions here unless he also saw the zombies as a threat. Was it possible he was trying to quell the zombie uprising in his own way? Then again, Lovecraft's journals never specifically said Cthulhu controlled all the deep ones. Maybe these were just concerned citizens who'd roused their underwater brethren to help them stop the apocalypse.

I shuddered. "Reeks like the dumpster behind a Red Lobster."

Murray snorted. "Night of the living sushi."

"Good one."

She raised an eyebrow. "I can't tell if your skull is grinning or not."

"It's always grinning."

Mortis skirted between the monstrosities and raced around the bend until we found the source of the commotion. A pack of werewolves were battling a group of deep ones in one tunnel while a group of magic users clashed with fish people coming from another tunnel. Humans with automatic weapons guarded another of the tunnels.

It seemed my theory about the deep ones trying to stop the zombie uprising was wrong. Then again, if they showed up without warning and didn't explain their intentions to the defenders, this battle might be one huge mistake.

The defenders were about to be overwhelmed by the reinforcements coming behind us. Thankfully, I could easily take care of the problem. I guided Mortis a short way around the bend. I hopped off, drew the scythe, and stalked down the tunnel to make fish stew out of the oncoming creatures. The best part was they'd never even see me.

I whirled the scythe and swung it at the lead eel creature. My muscles seemed to freeze before the weapon even started its arc. I flexed, making sure something wasn't wrong with me, then tried another swing. Once again, I was unable to attack.

Mortis stomped a hoof and blasted mist from his nostrils.

"I think he's saying you can't do that," Murray said calmly as the deep ones slithered, crawled, and limped past her on the horse without ever seeing her.

"Are you kidding me?" I banished the scythe. "Why even carry the stupid thing?"

"You're Death." She shrugged. "You collect souls. Maybe killing is against the rules."

I hadn't even thought about that. Death was a deity, meaning he couldn't act against people unless they acted against him first. Then again, the rules might be completely different for this job. There was only one way to find out.

I spotted a lagging angler hybrid and willed to reveal myself to it. The creature hissed. Its forehead tentacle lashed out at me. I swung the scythe and blocked the attack. It should have cleaved right through the flesh but didn't so much as nick it. I spun, still swinging the unfamiliar weapon and brought it down on the neck of the deep one.

It slammed the creature to the ground, pinning it, but the blade didn't cut the skin.

"I think that proves it," Murray said. "You can defend yourself, but you can't kill anyone." She shook her head. "Do you even know what you're doing?"

"I'm new, okay?" I willed myself to be hidden again and the deep one climbed to its feet, fish eyes rotating wildly as it tried to find the being that had attacked it.

Renewed shouting erupted as the fresh wave of deep ones hit the defenders. Automatic gunfire erupted and wolves howled. Gouts of fire exploded from around the bend.

Murray drew a pistol. "We've got to help them." She fired a shot and struck an angler hybrid in one of its eyes. It went down like a sack of bricks, blood and goop exploding from the eye on the other side. A pair of its comrades stopped and stared straight at her.

Mortis snorted and stomped a hoof.

"Well, looks like I can't hide up here anymore." Murray hopped down and blew out the brains of the pair of deep ones. The rest of the creatures were already engaged with the werewolves and magic users. "Let's go!" She raced around the bend.

I considered my options and realized there was only one way I could fight. I didn't particularly want to fight deep ones, but they now stood between me and a small horde of zombies. Casting off the cloak, I draped it over Mortis.

Reaching back, I summoned my staff and was relieved when it appeared in my hand. I'd been fearful that taking on the vestments of Death had fundamentally changed me. Then again, I wouldn't know until I tried to kill one of those fishy bastards.

I hurried after Murray and caught up easily, thanks to the strength enhancement sigils tattooed on my legs. She'd already dropped another of the angler deep ones, but one of the slithering eels had turned on her and was approaching fast, despite the multiple bullet holes in its head and torso.

"I don't think this one has a brain!" Murray ejected a magazine and clicked another into place.

I ignited my brightblade and ghostwalked just in front of and to the side of the eel hybrid. I slashed across its throat. The scaly skin was tough, but the energy blade cut through it like cold butter thanks to its forward momentum. The creature flopped to the ground twitching madly like a beheaded snake.

Murray's eyes widened. "Who in the hell are you and where did you get a lightsaber?"

I put a finger to my lips. "It's a brightblade and definitely one hundred percent not a lightsaber. If you think deep ones are scary, wait until Mickey Mouse comes after you."

She chuckled. "You're weird. I like that."

I spun and raced after the other deep ones. A werewolf lunged at me as I came out of the dark. I ducked beneath its claws and cast a shield ahead of the nearest angler hybrid. The creature smacked into it with a wet sound. I cut it in half before it knew what happened.

The werewolf growled and ran back toward the others, apparently apologizing for the near friendly-fire incident.

A wizard brandishing a staff burned a pair of creatures with a fire spell, then drew a revolver and blasted another pair. The deep ones seemed unaware that I was behind them. I cut three of them down, then deactivated the brightblade and switched to longshot mode. Brandishing the staff like a rifle, I sheared the top of the head off an eel hybrid, then annihilated a pair of anglers. Switching back to brightblade, I lopped an eel creature into neat slices.

It was over within minutes. All that was left was blood and the headless flailing bodies of a couple of eel hybrids.

The wizard frowned at me for a long moment, then blinked and looked to my right. "Murray, what the hell are you doing down here?"

"Saving your ass again, apparently." She checked the ammo in her pistol magazine, then clicked it back into place. She motioned toward me. "This is Death, or at least some random dude who's doing Death's job."

The wizard frowned. "How in the hell does that work?" He peered at my glowing blade. "And where in the hell did you get a light—"

"Brightblade." I shook my head. "Don't bring the wrath of the mouse down upon us."

He grinned. "I like this guy already. Where'd you find him?"

"He found us." Murray looked at the bodies. "Can someone explain why fish monsters are attacking us?"

"It's a long story." The wizard shook his head. "I ran into them a few days ago when I was rounding up the zombies. Some of these things can talk, but man do they have a lisp."

"Hold up, they talked to you?" I'd fought deep ones on Gaia Alpha, but I didn't recall any of them talking.

"Yeah, but the talking ones looked more human than these things." He shook his head. "I don't know how familiar you are with Lovecraft, but—"

"Intimately."

He nodded. "Well, the man wasn't writing fiction. There was a town called Innsmouth just south of Plum Island, Massachusetts. Legend had it all the hybrids were wiped out, but it looks like they weren't. I don't know where these came from, but the one that talked told me to cease my actions against the undead. It was on orders to ensure the apocalypse happens so its master could rise."

I hissed air between my teeth. "It wants Cthulhu to awaken."

He nodded. "That's what I thought too. Truth is, I've very rarely had to deal with anything like this. It's usually mundane stuff like vampires and fae."

I narrowed my eyes. "You're Henry Quaid, aren't you?"

"Yep." He tilted his head. "Who are you and how do you know me?"

"I've heard of you." I scoffed. "Anyone who knows anything would definitely know you way before they'd know me." I whistled to summon Mortis and was pleasantly surprised when he trotted around the corner. "We need to clean up these zombies before another wave of deep ones comes, though." I looked at the makeshift barriers. "I need to get to them one at a time so I can safely capture and contain their souls. Otherwise, this city is going to have an even bigger problem on its hands."

He grimaced. "Wraiths?"

I nodded. "Wraiths."

"Yeah, let's do it." He leaned on his staff. "But we need to talk afterward."

I banished my staff and slipped on the Death cloak. I must have vanished when I did it because Quaid blinked and looked around. "Well, that's neat."

I willed myself visible to those present.

One of the people armed with a machine gun approached. "Someone mind explaining what's going on here?"

A werewolf morphed into a young nude woman. "I've never been more confused in my life. Who is this guy and why does he look like the Grim Reaper?"

I shrugged. "My mom fucked a skeleton."

Murray cackled.

I examined the pen holding the undead. If we cracked open one of the barricades, I could probably get to them one at a time. "Long story short, Death is just a job created by the original Thanatos a long time ago. The current Death was incapacitated by the other three horsemen of the apocalypse because he wouldn't end the world with them. Now I'm stuck cleaning up the mess created by his long absence, and I barely know what I'm doing."

Murray clapped my back. "You're doing just fine."

Quaid snorted. "Hell's bells. Sounds like we're working the same problem from different angles."

"Why are two completely different groups so intent on ending the world anyway?" Murray pressed her lips into a thin line. "Cthulhu is an outsider but the horsemen of the apocalypse are Christian deities."

I shifted one of the barriers just enough to allow one zombie out at a time. They were already pressing against it, desperate to touch me. "Can someone regulate the flow of zombies from the enclosure?"

Quaid grinned. "That's a statement I never planned on hearing this lifetime."

"Yeah, I can't believe I just said that either." I yanked the soul from the first zombie and let the soul catcher do its thing. "I've dealt with regular necromancer zombies before, but these things are something else."

"At first, I thought this was the work of a powerful necromancer." Quaid cracked open the barrier to let another zombie spill out so I could free the soul. "Then I realized these still had souls."

Werewolf howls echoed from a distant tunnel. The female werewolf sighed. "More deep ones incoming. We'll try to hold them off." She morphed into a large gray wolf and bounded away.

Murray checked her pistol. "I need more ammo or another weapon."

"Ask the mobsters," another woman said. "They brought enough firepower to light up the entire city."

Murray scowled. "I don't like being in bed with Brusca. This whole thing stinks to high heaven."

"It ain't perfect, but we're not stopping this invasion without help." Quaid nudged his boot against the body of a corpse I'd just liberated. "Be better if you helped us move the bodies."

Murray holstered her pistol and looked at the corpulent corpse. "Quaid, there's no way in hell I could move that thing by myself." She looked at the barrier. "I'll crack the fence, and you move the bodies."

He grimaced. "I shouldn't have worn my good duster today."

"That's the only one you have." She cracked open the barrier to let another zombie out and I freed it. To save time, I caught the body and flung it away. Deaths' cloak granted me supernatural strength. It wasn't enough to pick up cars, but it made moving rotten corpses a breeze.

We worked through the trapped horde until all souls were freed. The werewolves and mobsters returned just before we finished. Several mobsters were missing, and the werewolves were covered in blood. Some were limping and whining. A gray wolf morphed back into the woman from earlier. A long, gory slash ran down her leg, and blood trailed down her bare shoulder.

She leaned against a wall. "We can't keep this up much longer, Quaid."

"Hopefully you won't have to." Quaid wiped his filthy hands on the brick wall. "Looks like the temp worker here will have things cleaned up in no time."

"Maybe." I checked the death beacon and counted the remaining dead in the city. "I've still got South America to finish."

"What about China?" Murray said. "India?"

"Different religions, different death gods." I shuddered. "Otherwise, we'd be hip-deep in zombies."

"We need to sit down for a recap when you're caught up." Quaid examined unidentifiable fluids on his leather coat. "I'll see if I can find where the deep ones are coming from and why they're so keen on triggering the end days."

"That would be really helpful." I climbed onto Mortis. "I've still got to figure out what's wrong with Garrick once I'm caught up on souls. It's possible this was triggered by Loki and his trickster god crew."

Quaid's eyebrows rose. "What makes you think the trickster gods are behind this?"

"Are you aware of the dimensional split that happened a while back?"

He shook his head. "I don't usually deal with that kind of stuff."

"Me either, but Loki tried to alter an event and it split our dimension into three. The world's been going to hell in a handbasket ever since."

Quaid nodded solemnly. "That would explain a lot. It explains why the outsiders are so much stronger than usual."

"Yep." I nodded at him and Murray. "Been a pleasure. Let's never do this again."

Murray scoffed. "It never ends until you're dead."

"Oh, it doesn't even end then, unfortunately." I shrugged. "Afterlife and all that."

"Great!" She threw up her hands. "Life is pain, and death is torture. I've got nothing to look forward to."

"Become an atheist, maybe?" I shrugged.

Quaid snorted. "Solid plan."

I urged Mortis onward, and he galloped down the tunnel. The

place was a maze, but he knew where he was going. Before long, we reached the next closest zombie, and I went to work.

We zipped around town, cleaned up Chicago, and moved on to the rest of the state. Then we moved eastward, where the concentrations of crimson blips were depressingly high. Mortis shifted to the dark realm to get us to New York City and promptly skidded to a halt.

Three figures on horses blocked the path ahead.

War, Famine, and Pestilence had found us.

11

The first figure rode a red horse and carried a massive sword on his back. A thin woman rode the black horse next to his, and the third, a white horse, bore a stout woman with a bow and quivers of arrows across her back.

I was still rusty on the Christian mythos, but War was the red one. I wasn't sure about the other two, but they'd probably tell me if I asked nicely.

I waved. "Can any of you tell me how to get to Burger King from here?"

The woman on the white horse scowled. "Who are you and why do you wear the cloak of Death?"

"My name's Peter, and I always wanted to have superpowers." I shrugged. "How about you?"

"Lower your hood." War guided his horse closer. The others moved to flank me.

"Uh, can you get us past them?" I murmured to Mortis.

He stomped a foot and shook his head.

"Can they go anywhere we can?"

He bobbed his head.

They couldn't harm me while wearing the cloak, but it seemed they could delay me from doing my job. "Is this about my car's extended warranty again?"

The woman on the white horse scoffed. "He mocks us."

"I would mock us for failing to secure Death's vestments." The thin woman scowled. "Will this dread existence never end?"

The pain in her voice made me wince. "Maybe you should go drink a mangorita and relax."

"Lower your cowl." War's horse stopped inches from Mortis. "I will not ask again."

Revealing my identity wasn't much of an issue. If Mortis couldn't breach my wards, I doubted these deities could either. I doubted they'd even know who I was in the first place. But I also didn't like them thinking they could boss me around.

I crossed my arms. "Good. I'm tired of you asking."

He drew his sword and pointed it at my face. "Do it now!"

I ignored him and turned to the other two. "War is pretty obvious, but which of you is Famine, and which is Plague?"

"I prefer Pestilence," the woman on the white horse said. "Some call me Conquest."

"Conquest?" I looked from her to War. "Wouldn't that be in War's wheelhouse?"

She shrugged. "Conquest and plague are merely other forms of pestilence."

I turned to the thin woman. "Famine, I presume?"

"Yes." Her voice was thin and gravelly. "Whoever you are, you must bide your time and prepare to ride with us. The end days are upon the world."

"The end days are here because you put Garrick in a coma." I leaned back in the saddle. "Did Loki put you up to this?"

War lashed out with a leather boot that was meant to knock me off Mortis. I reflexively powered the sigils on my body and leapt to the ground. War pounced off his horse and rushed me, sword at the ready. I didn't know if he could hurt me and didn't feel like taking chances, so I summoned Death's weapon of choice.

Metal clanged as scythe met sword. Our feet slid backward,

sending puffs of black dust into the air. War's sword blurred. His attacks were quicker even than Torvin's, but my speed nearly matched his, allowing me to block blow after blow. Deaths' cloak came with its share of advantages, but Garrick wouldn't have stood a chance against this being without training.

I blocked another strike, then went on the offensive, driving War back. I considered ghostwalking behind him but didn't want to lay all my cards on the table just yet. He blocked my successive strikes but was back on his heels, unable to muster a counter. I didn't think I could kill him, but I could probably lay him out.

That was when I recognized the pattern of his retreat. It was a feint, intended to make the attacker overconfident so they'd over-commit and open themselves to an easy counter. I'd fought enough sword masters during my training to recognize even the most subtle patterns. Fortunately for me, this baiting technique carried risks. It required him to intentionally be off balance just enough to convince the attacker to overcommit.

The ground was chipped and rugged, but there weren't any real tripping hazards behind him, so I made one. I cast a shield just behind his right foot. It wouldn't have worked against a master retreating normally, but War's gambit betrayed him. His ankle hit the shield, throwing him off balance for real.

I swung the scythe low at his other foot and War threw himself backward. He flung his sword in the air, caught himself with a hand, and flipped sideways. I cast a shield to deflect the path of his sword, but it smashed through the small barrier without even slowing and landed perfectly in his hand.

War sheathed his sword, a savage grin on his face. "By God, you are skilled. Now I must really know who you are."

"This is the Death we've been seeking." Famine pressed hands to her gaunt cheeks. "It was said he was the Grim Reaper among men."

"A true killer." Pestilence nodded approvingly. "But will he ride with us?"

War looked at me questioningly. "Well, Death. Will you ride with us and put an end to the chaos on Earth?"

"I'm going to need a much better reason than that." I watched them carefully, looking for any sign of trickery.

"I can finally end my existential pain." Famine breathed deeply, as if warding off powerful emotions. "I have waited forever to finally end it all."

"I have witnessed human depravity on grand scales." Pestilence clenched her fists. "I have waited even longer than Famine to see the blessed day of reckoning."

"I have witnessed more wars than any of them combined," War said proudly. "I have grown tired of human conflict and have been promised endless wars on a galactic scale against outsiders. Does that not sound glorious?"

I frowned. "I'm no expert on the subject, but don't you need the Antichrist to help end the world?"

"Lucifer has done nothing to yield offspring." Famine hugged herself and shivered. "But we can ride without the Antichrist."

"Lucifer seems like the last person to father the Antichrist." I frowned. "Are you sure it's his responsibility?"

War shook his head. "It was never plainly stated where the Antichrist would come from. God is not forthcoming with his plans."

I'd already connected enough dots to put together a bigger picture. "This new plague is your doing, Pestilence. Famine is complementing it with worldwide food shortages. The multiple regional conflicts that have erupted due to food shortages are obviously the work of War. But you need Death to do his part and not collect the souls, so the world is overrun by the undead. And as the undead kill the living, they destroy the loom of Fate, forcing the Christian god to advance his plans for the apocalypse."

War nodded solemnly. "You have the reflexes of a warrior and the mind of tactician. But the Morrigan is removing the souls from those slain in battle and refuses to join our cause. We need you to bring a harvest of souls from the afterlife and implant them in the dead."

"What's the big deal with riding together, anyway?" I still hadn't figured out the significance of it. "It sounds like I could help the cause just by staying at home eating cheezy poofs."

Pestilence shook her head. "Don't you know anything about Judgement Day? We ride in order to slay all humans upon the Earth."

"Even the non-Christians?" I asked.

"Even those who are not of the same religion will fall." War smiled as if enjoying the thought. "Death may slay humans while riding with the horsemen."

"Uh, horsepersons," I said. "In case you hadn't noticed, two of you are women and I can't let you ignore that any longer."

Famine hissed. "We are the Horsemen."

I shrugged. "Once all the humans are slain, then what? We get to retreat to paradise with an eternal supply of mangoritas?"

"I will retreat to the divine realm and bask in the glory of wars among the gods and the outsiders." War reached down and touched his crotch. "It will be glorious."

"Did you just jizz in your pants?" I wrinkled my nose and turned to the others. "Are you like me, a human filling a role?"

"No." Famine stared at me with hollow eyes. "Unlike Thanatos, we never had the option to throw off our roles and live as we wished. We are trapped." She flinched and pressed a hand to her temple. "Stop it! Stop it!"

The others flinched in unison as if they were sharing in the pain, then blinked and stared at me while their horses neighed in agitation.

Apparently, I'd struck a nerve.

War regarded me. "You are the one we've been waiting for. Join us that we may bask in the glory of eternal war."

There couldn't have been a group of deities more ready to end the world if they'd been individually hand-picked. I could understand being sick and tired of doing the same thing for thousands of years, but why had it taken so long for it to come to this? Something didn't mesh.

"You were created for specific purposes and to follow the rules." I watched them carefully. "Why now, of all times, are you suddenly revolting?"

"It is simply time to end this." Famine touched her gaunt cheeks. "I felt as if my mind was finally awakened to who and what I am, and I want it to end."

"Precisely," Pestilence said. "It is time to move on."

I grunted. "That sounds very nihilistic for Christian deities."

"The peace of oblivion calls to me," Famine said.

"But that's totally against your religion." It felt as if these deities had been turned against their very natures. There was little doubt Loki was behind it, but I couldn't fathom how he could do such a mind-fuck on Christian deities.

"No, this is God's will." War twitched and put a hand to his temple. "Revelations are upon us."

"I'm gonna be upfront with you." I climbed onto Mortis's back and banished the scythe. "I know Loki is behind this, but I'm totally lost as to why you'd listen to him. By ending the human worlds, you're just giving the outsiders like Cthulhu enough power to wipe us out of existence. This glorious eternal war you're looking forward to will be over in the blink of an eye because without worshippers, the Elder Gods won't have the power to stop them."

War frowned. "Loki? What does a Norse god have to do with this?"

Famine shook her head. "I've never spoken to Loki about anything."

"Me either," Pestilence said.

Their responses threw me for a loop. "Then who told you to end the world?" I half expected a shadowy figure to appear and reveal himself with a well-prepared villain monologue. Unfortunately, that didn't happen.

War narrowed his eyes. "You don't sound willing to join us."

"Yeah, no." I shook my head emphatically. "The world can go to hell, but not if it's taking mangoritas along with it. If you guys are so ready to end the world, I think you need to take a step back and give a long hard look at your priorities. Maybe you should do what Thanatos did and leave your jobs. I'll bet if you asked God nicely, he'd be willing to make accommodations."

"No!" Famine wailed. "We must end it! Humans have no place in the new order."

Pestilence growled "It is time to purge the world."

I frowned. "That sounds like something an outsider would say."

Famine pressed her hands to her temples and screamed. "Not the truth!"

The others flinched in pain. I saw an opportunity to get the hell out of there and took it. I nudged Mortis and he galloped between the distracted deities. We unfolded on Gaia at the outskirts of New York City. I urged Mortis to go faster, then guided him behind a building where we took cover and watched. The other horsemen didn't appear. They may have been so distracted that they didn't know exactly where we'd gone.

"Can they follow us?" I asked Mortis.

He whickered but didn't nod or shake his head, probably because he didn't know. It made me wonder how War and the others had known where to wait for me in the dark realm.

Several minutes ticked past and still no sign of the other horsemen, so I decided it was safe to get back to work. But there were graver implications to worry about already. If they could wait for me in the dark realm and even block my path, what was to stop them from doing it all over again?

The only answer, it seemed, was to avoid the dark realm and take the long way from place to place. Unless there was an alternative, there was no way I'd ever stem the zombie tide.

12

Our next stop was at a nursing home.

The grounds outside were littered with body bags, some of which flopped about like fish on dry land while the occupants screamed and moaned. The orderlies tending to the dead were already scared shitless, some of them hiding behind cars, others recording the incident from a safe distance with their cell phones.

The moment I started unzipping body bags was the moment the remaining orderlies screamed at the tops of their lungs and ran for the hills. They might not be able to see me, but they could see the zippers moving by themselves. They probably assumed the zombies had figured out how to work them.

I chuckled at their expense.

Plucking the souls one by one was made easier by the body bags, but it still took the better part of an hour to clear the pile and then free the souls of those locked inside the building.

"Bloody hell, it's true!" A man with shoulder-length silver hair booted the body bags. "I was thinking we'd have to destroy another city block just to get them to stop." His British accent was snooty and educated.

"I'm not so sure we did stop them." Another man with shorter hair appeared around the corner of a building. "But we sure as hell made a mess."

A black dog stood near them, its eyes like burning coals. And it was looking straight at me.

"What is it, boy?" The British man looked up and around as if trying to spot something.

I suddenly realized who the men were. I knew of them more from reputation than anything else. I was certain he hadn't been kidding about destroying a city block. From what I heard, they considered destruction an art form.

I didn't have time to stay and chat, so I urged Mortis on to the next destination. There were still hundreds of souls left to free. We spent the rest of the day racing around New York City and its environs before I could finally declare it free of zombies.

The next group of undead was far enough away that Mortis would need to slip through the dark realm to get us there quickly. He was fast but spending an hour traveling to the next soul wasn't a good use of our time.

I plucked Garrick's Death manual from the cloak and found a section on traveling. The name for the dark realm was Limbo, the place in between the planes. According to Garrick's manual, he wasn't sure if Limbo was a Christian realm or if it existed outside the pantheons.

During travel, Mortis entered the folded version of Limbo, never entering full Limbo, which was vast and endless. Points in folded Limbo corresponded with exit points in Gaia and the divine realm. There were also paths to Feary and Oblivion, but he wrote that visits there were very rare.

War and the others had been able to wait on me in folded Limbo because only a small portion of it corresponded with the places I was travelling. All they'd had to do was wait and I'd eventually come across them. Garrick estimated that one mile in folded Limbo equaled a thousand in Gaia. Given the speed of travel, it seemed he was right.

Unfortunately, it meant I'd have to travel a thousand miles across Gaia to ensure I didn't bump into the horsemen the moment we entered folded Limbo again. Then again, maybe all I needed was a few hundred feet. We were over two hundred miles from our arrival location. Maybe that was enough buffer to keep away from the others.

I made up my mind. "Let's go." I nudged Mortis's ribs and he lunged forward. Nearby skyscrapers turned into cardboard cutouts and folded in on themselves, then a moment later, unfolded into the stark nothingness of folded Limbo. I spotted War and the others less than a hundred yards away, each of them facing a different way so they'd see me coming.

I didn't think a camouflage blind would hide me from them, so I didn't bother. Mortis was galloping parallel to their position which made sense, given our next destination was Vermont. Pestilence raised a finger and shouted. The other horsemen wheeled around and galloped after me. I was willing to bet that they'd follow me into the mortal realm this time.

I instantly regretted my decision. "Wish there was somewhere to hide in this place."

The distant mountains abruptly expanded, and the obsidian plain seemed to swell beneath Mortis's hooves. Mist rose from the ground, and whispers filled my ears. The sudden fog obscured the other horsemen from my vision, but there were other figures, wisps, and shadows haunting the corners of my eyes.

A man wearing clothes from the late eighteenth century stepped in our path. He looked up at me with fear and screamed. Anguished wails rose from around us. Silhouettes appeared in the fog, all of them drifting like wraiths toward the warm light of the living. They reminded me of the insane souls trapped in corpses on Gaia, but these seemed fundamentally different somehow.

They were trapped in Limbo, a place neither Heaven, Hell, nor Purgatory. They were outside the system that should have taken their soul and sent it to an appropriate afterlife. Despite my guise as Death, they sensed my life force and were desperately hungry for it.

Houses and other buildings rose like boxy shadows in the mists.

Street signs, stores, and other remnants from the land of the living appeared, alone and without context. There was no continuity, no completeness to the landscape. It was as if objects lost from reality made their way to this land of the lost.

I ducked under a tree branch that came from nowhere. "Maybe this is where my lost socks end up."

The fog cleared and an all-too-familiar structure rose from darkness. It was Sanctuary, but different. The structure was plain, raw, and foreboding. The gravel road leading to the church wound through a graveyard with only two tombstones.

A middle-aged man shouted at a young boy who was filling a large granite tub with buckets of water from the well that I'd covered over years ago. Distant chants echoed from the nearby forest. I wasn't surprised by much, but my mouth dropped open in shock at the sight.

"What in the hell is happening?"

Mortis slowed to a trot and stopped. Dark mist billowed from his nostrils, but that was all the reaction he offered. I opened the manual and flicked through the section on Limbo. There was only one paragraph that even hinted as to where I was. It said simply: *Do not, under any circumstances, enter Limbo entirely. The souls crave life and not even Death is immune to them.*

"Just great," I muttered.

Oddly enough, the boy and man didn't notice my arrival, nor did they seem drawn to me as the souls had. The chanting from the forest grew louder. Moments later a group of people emerged from the forest, their naked bodies covered in painted symbols. My eyes flared in recognition. Not at the people, but the symbols. They were R'lyehian.

The woman leading the procession looked full to bursting with child. Judging from the pain on her face, she was suffering contractions. The boy filling the stone tub sprinkled something from a bowl into the water. The man with him raised his hands as if surrendering, palms out toward the procession, and dropped to his knees.

A pair of women helped the pregnant woman into the stone tub.

She gritted her teeth and began shouting in a language so convoluted that not even Death's vestments could fully translate it into something coherent: "Nyar, the under is of what we surrender a void wholly not for our blood."

She spoke alien words, and that was about all I could make of it. But one of them stuck out—Nyar. And I knew what it meant. The water in the tub bubbled and a baby floated to the surface. The woman lifted the child overhead and began spewing more nonsense.

The other women helped her rise from the bath while she held onto the baby, the umbilical cord still trailing between her legs. She set the baby on a stone table and the man who'd greeted her, handed her a knife. She began chanting, eyes closed, the knife clasped in both hands.

I finally understood one word the rest of the crowd was chanting. "Nyarlathotep! Nyarlathotep! Nyarlathotep!"

I realized that she wasn't going to use the knife to cut the umbilical cord. She was going to sacrifice the baby. I leapt off Mortis and raced toward the crowd, shoving them roughly to the sides. None of them reacted to my presence in the slightest. In fact, most of them barely moved when I ran into them.

The knife flashed downward.

An explosion deafened me. The woman's head shattered in a shower of blood, brains, and bone. The knife dropped next to her headless corpse. Another explosion blew a gaping hole in the greeting man's chest. Behind him stood the boy, a pump-action shotgun in his hand. The chanting abruptly stopped as the cultists realized what was happening.

The boy stalked forward, blasting people left and right as they panicked and fled. He dropped the weapon after he'd emptied it and unslung another one from his back. Pump, aim, obliterate. One of the women who'd helped the pregnant woman into the tub had been hiding behind it. She shrieked and tried to run.

A final blast took her down.

The boy walked around calmly, kicking the bodies and checking for signs of life while the baby remained uncharacteristically quiet and calm, watching him with the blind eyes of a newborn.

The front door to the church vibrated as someone pounded on it from inside. The boy went to a bush and removed a box of shotgun shells from beneath it. He began calmly reloading the shotguns as if this was just another day and he hadn't just slaughtered a dozen people. He slung the second over his back, cocked the first one, and went to the door.

The boy traced a symbol and the door unlatched. A girl about his age, ten or eleven, stood on the other side. "Joaquim, what happened? We heard gunshots!"

"Are the other children still downstairs?" he said.

"Of course, they are. We're ready to drink the blood of the newborn to give glory to Lord Nyar." She looked past him and saw a bloodied body on the lawn. She screamed. "Joaquim, what—"

The shotgun barked and the girl flew inside and out of sight, arms and legs trailing. The boy went inside and closed the door behind him.

There was no question what I was witnessing. This boy had grown up to become the farmer who'd given me Sanctuary. This was the day he'd killed off his family and all the cult members.

These people were Ekhsis like me. But they were the ones who'd left Oblivion so they could worship another god—an Elder Thing by the name of Nyarlathotep. I went to the door and opened it. The girl, eyes wide with shock, lay motionless on the floor, guts spilling out, blood bubbling from her mouth. The shotgun barked and children's screams echoed up the stairwell leading down to the basement.

I ran downstairs not because I was eager to see the massacre of children, but because I wanted to see what the library had looked like before Joaquim burned all the books. But the stairwell didn't end where it should have. Instead, it kept going and going, spiraling down into eternity even though the screams sounded just as close as they had moments ago.

Frustrated, I turned around and went upstairs. I wasn't surprised to find the door right around the bend. Whatever strange vision this was, it didn't want me going downstairs. Was this a vision? A dream? How was I able to see something that had happened so long ago before I was even born?

I'd been so fixated on the stairs that I hadn't even paused to look at the inside of the church. It was nothing like my Sanctuary. Wooden pews encircled a wide stone pedestal. The metal statue atop it was monstrous, reaching all the way to the vaulted ceiling. The being it represented was only vaguely humanoid, with three legs, four arms, and several thick tentacles emerging from its torso. The head resembled a tentacle but with a gaping, roaring maw of sharp teeth. Small, spiny worms coiled around the feet.

I now knew what the old farmer had done. He'd purged the cult of Nyar completely from the world, even melting down the statues and burning all their writings. The graves in front of Sanctuary held adults and children, and in all my years living there, I'd never even known. There had been no reason to exhume bodies. No reason to ask details about his dead family. I'd found a safe place to hide from the fae and that was all that mattered at the time.

I walked through the blood of the slain girl without tracking footprints behind me. It seemed I was the ghost here—wherever here was. I went outside. The baby still lay on the stone altar, the umbilical cord stretching from it to its dead mother. It was a boy, I noted, and the only living human in the vicinity.

A pair of men emerged from the forest to the west, garden hoes and other farming implements slung over their shoulders. Their eyes flared when they saw the carnage. Neither of them seemed to see the baby from their position.

"Abigail!" The taller of the two ran to the corpse of a dead woman. "Our sister is dead!"

The other man fell to his knees, hands clasped. "Has Nyar come already to reap our sanity? Is this the end?"

"No, this bespeaks of other foul intent, brother!" The taller man scowled. "This is murder!" He stormed toward the house and flung open the front door. A shotgun blast took him full in the face, caving it in and spraying the porch with fine red mist.

The other man, still on his knees, tried to rise, but a load of buckshot caught him in the shoulder and spun him around. Lying on his back, crying in pain, he said, "Joaquim, why?"

The stony resolve on the boy's face wavered slightly. "I read the forbidden books, Jacob. I know the truth about what is to come. Nyar has corrupted your minds beyond repair and made you blind to the awful future that he and the others plan."

"But you are one of us, Joaquim! You have basked in Nyar's glory with us!"

The boy nodded. "Then I met a...man. A being who told me the conflict did not need to happen. That all creatures could coexist. He cleared my mind and gave me a task."

The wounded man, wincing and moaning in pain, managed to rise to his knees. "What heresy is this, Joaquim?" His eyes flashed with anger. "The Elder Gods would see Nyar and his kind dead! I will kill you myself!" He lunged forward and the shotgun boomed. Jacob fell like a rag doll, his face and neck torn to shreds.

The boy dropped the shotgun and looked straight at me. "I'm glad to see you again, Cain." He morphed slowly into the old farmer I'd met years ago. "I am glad you've found your destiny."

I flinched in surprise. "Old Joe, you can see me?"

"I sensed you because we are connected in life and death." He turned toward the baby. "Both of us were always part of the plan."

"What plan?" I ran toward him. "What did you read in the forbidden books? Who is the being you encountered?"

Joaquim looked away from the baby to me. "I'm sorry I had to kill your mother." He shivered and faded to shadow, taking Sanctuary and everything else with him.

13

I barely had time to think about what he'd just said because as the world faded, the shadowy ghosts of limbo appeared at the fringes, arms outstretched toward the lifeforce they so craved.

Mortis appeared at my side, pawing the ground, ready to go. I hopped on. "Get us the fuck out of this place."

We rode through the eternal night of Limbo, legions of lost souls clamoring to escape the cold nothingness. I couldn't stop thinking about Joaquim, or as I'd called him, Old Joe. How had he found me in Limbo? How had he created that vision? Was any of what I'd just seen a true accounting of that day?

If he truly was Joe, then his apology for killing my mother meant only one thing. I was the baby on that table, and he'd saved me from becoming a sacrifice.

I thought back to the conversation I'd had with Tythus, the dragon I'd met on Oblivion. An elder Ekhsis had told him the story of the Disciples of Nyar and it mirrored everything I'd seen almost exactly. My gut feeling said it was true, but one thing didn't make sense.

If I was that infant and Joe was that boy, then how had Joe been so old when I met him? I'd left the Oblivion Guard at age twenty-eight and gained my freedom by age twenty-nine. I'd found Sanctuary just after I turned thirty. If the boy in the vision was twelve, then Joe couldn't have been much older than forty. He'd looked at least sixty when I'd met him.

Then again, Joe had destroyed a library filled with the horrors of the Elder Things. There might have been enough dark magic and outsider artifacts to prematurely age him. It could have also been punishment from Nyar for what he'd done. Joe hadn't told me anything about the church except the number of graves, three hundred thirty-three, and that his family had owned it since the eighteenth century. Joe barely lived another year after I found Sanctuary and seemed happy to die, all things considered.

Maybe that was because he'd served a purpose and it was over. He thought death would bring him final peace and allow him the comfort of oblivion. Murdering that many people in cold blood couldn't sit well with anyone's soul. I knew that from experience. Maybe killing people who were about to sacrifice an infant and drink its blood didn't weigh that heavily on him, or maybe it haunted him for the rest of his days.

The only way I'd know for sure is if I tracked down his soul in the vast emptiness of Limbo. I was Death, after all. Maybe there was a way I could do it, especially if, as he claimed, we were connected.

The darkness and fog abruptly vanished. A giant moon hung low, framed by halos of white clouds that formed a tunnel all the way to the ground. Brilliant stars twinkled in the backdrop, though their light should have been overpowered by the moon. A sense of peace washed over me, and the cries of lost souls faded.

Mortis slowed to a walk, his pale eyes looking up at the moon. I also looked at the moon. It looked like Gaia's moon, but I was no moon-ologist so I couldn't be sure. The oasis was surrounded by the fog of Limbo, but it seemed like a different place altogether.

"Where are we?"

Mortis, of course, didn't answer, but he seemed content basking in the moonlight, so I let him have a moment. Sometime later, he neighed softly and jolted forward. The moon and the barrier of fog collapsed into two dimensions. He dashed through folded Limbo for several minutes and then another city skyline popped up around us. I checked the death beacon and saw we were in Baltimore, Maryland.

I was still shaken by the brief time in Limbo, but the weight of the world once again settled on my shoulders. There was still a metric shit ton of souls to reap and zombies to put down, so I put my head down and we rode, clearing hundreds of scattered zombies in the streets of a city that looked as if it had barely survived a war.

When it came time to leap through Limbo again, I braced myself for another meeting with the others. But as we passed into folded Limbo again, they seemed to be absent.

Mortis and I continued across the northeast, moving up into Canada, across, and back down. The souls were so spaced out in some areas, that we had to skip through Limbo for nearly every trip. Each time we did, I readied myself for a confrontation that never came. Even as I felt weariness sink deep into my bones, I refused to stop, refused to rest until I at least had North America cleared of the infestation.

And then we reached St. Louis.

I was concerned the legendary protector of the city might come flying after me on his foul-mouthed unicorn. I'd heard he was close friends with Death and might not take too kindly to the temporary employee occupying the position.

It seemed nearly every zombie in the city had been rounded up and incinerated in a quarry on the outskirts of town. The amount of carnage was absolutely savage and gave me a grim feeling. Especially since the quarry was now filled with walking skeletons.

It was a freakshow, pure and simple. The souls clinging to the skeletons were visible, at least to me, their forms distinctly humanoid, but without faces or other features. It looked as if someone had skinned a stuffed doll and left the stuffing in place.

The place was surrounded by emergency personnel and the news media. A devilishly good-looking man stood atop an expensive car, basking in the media spotlight while those closest to him watched uncertainly.

His voice boomed across the quarry. "As my acquaintance would say, we gave those zombies the D."

There was simply too much of a media presence for me to appear out of nowhere and ask for help, so I took a count of the undead, one hundred eighty-three, and examined the terrain so I could devise a plan of attack. It took far longer than I wanted to admit for a strategy to come to mind because my brain was addled by the lack of sleep.

"I should go home and sleep first, shouldn't I?"

Mortis stomped a foot but didn't nod or shake his head. If anything, he seemed impatient to get to work. The sides of the quarry were steep, but there were a few places that were just tall enough to suit my purpose. I guided Mortis to one of the lower ledges and the skeletons began migrating toward me.

It was quite a sight watching a veritable army of skeletons on the march and reminded me of classic fantasy movies from the old days of special effects. These skeletons weren't stop-motion animated, but their movements were still jerky and awkward, as if the souls animating them hadn't quite gotten the hang of it yet.

That worked just fine for me.

The ledge was just tall enough so the skeletons below could barely reach up and touch the lip. As they did, I reached down and yanked out their souls. The texture of the essence was rougher than any I'd felt before. I tried not to think about the implications of insane souls and whether they were scarred for eternity or might return to normal once they reached the afterlife. Or would every insane soul I freed end up in Limbo?

Bright lights focused on the crowd of the undead and I realized the media had noticed the rush of skeletons toward my location. As I reached down and freed them one by one, I had to move laterally to avoid building a pile of bones that the others could climb and reach my position. Thankfully, no one came down to investigate in person. I didn't want to see a walking skeleton chow down on living flesh. Then again, it might be interesting.

I worked my way back and forth until finally, the last of the skeletons were inanimate. Unfortunately, there were still souls in the pit that needed collecting. The bodies of those few had been blown to bits, leaving the souls no physical frame to move. Apparently, the souls were anchored in place and the best they could do was roll the bones back and forth.

I freed the last of them and stumbled back to Mortis. I needed to keep going, to keep working, but I simply couldn't. Not even Death's cloak could overcome the weariness I felt.

I was too tired to even go home. "I don't suppose you could transport us inside a nice hotel, could you?"

Mortis snorted and stomped a hoof. I climbed on his back. "I'm thinking a five-star."

He galloped up and out of the quarry before jumping into Limbo. When the world unfolded again, we were in a dim room. A man lay on a bed, a bag of blue and red pills next to him. He stared up at me with fright.

"It can't be true." He rubbed his eyes. "It must be the drugs."

I climbed down off Mortis and noticed a white blip on the death beacon right in front of me. "Are you committing suicide?"

"No. But I think these drugs are laced with something bad. Maybe fentanyl. I must be hallucinating right now."

I checked the death beacon. "You died about a second after I got here, so I don't know how you're still talking."

"I'm dead?" He shivered. "That's why I feel so cold, isn't it?"

I nodded. "Probably."

"Well, fuck. Either I'm hallucinating, or I'm actually talking to the Grim Reaper." His bluish lips trembled. "I was just expecting oblivion when I died."

"You're not a Christian?"

He scoffed. "I'm atheist."

I frowned. "I have no idea why I'm here, then. I thought I only collected the souls of believers."

He laughed hoarsely. "Even the divine don't know what they're doing."

I shrugged. "Well, maybe it's not too late. Maybe now that you've seen me you can believe and go to the afterlife."

Fear lit in his eyes. "I'll go to Hell, won't I?"

"I don't know. You might go to Limbo which in my experience, seems even worse. I'm kind of new to this so I don't know anything for certain. I will say that going to Heaven seems like a long shot."

He shook his head with difficulty. "No." His body began to stiffen. "Don't give me a cruel afterlife, please. Give me the mercy of nothingness."

"I don't think—" I stopped talking because the body had gone still, the eyes glazed in total death. I reached down and extracted his soul. The moment it came free, it began to drift apart like fine ash, fading into nothing before I could even bring out the soul catcher. A knot formed in my stomach because I knew without a doubt the man had gotten what he wished for—the sweet release of oblivion.

Mortis whickered gently and bumped my shoulder with his nose.

I looked up at him. "I guess mercy exists after all."

He bobbed his head.

The death beacon showed that we were in Singapore, of all places, and specifically in Marina Bay Sands hotel. I chuckled grimly. "Thanks for the five-star hotel, Mortis."

He snorted and then wandered through the doorway and into the den beyond where he lay down. I picked up the dead man and moved his body to the couch along with his pill bag, then stripped, showered, and went to sleep, completely unbothered by the death cooties infecting the bed.

POUNDING on the hotel door woke me with a start.

"Alex, open the door! You're two hours late!" More pounding and the man shouted again. "Open up!"

I rubbed the sleep out of my eyes and checked the time. It was nearly noon local time. I didn't even know what time I'd gone to sleep. All I knew for certain was that I hadn't gotten nearly enough rest. I'd overworked myself the day before and would likely do so again today. But the crimson wave of insane souls was steadily growing in South America and I couldn't afford to rest.

"How the hell does Santa Clause do it in one night?" I said to myself as I stretched. I snagged a bottled water from the fridge and gulped it.

"I'm getting security to open the door, Alex!" The man pounded again, then must have walked away.

I sniffed the Death cloak for body odor, but it seemed to magically remain clean. I wasn't even sure what the cleaning instructions would be for something like it. Dry clean only? I didn't have a change of clothes, and the dead man, Alex, was too short. I slipped on the cloak and went into the den. Mortis, still resting on the floor, looked up at me.

"Do you eat?" I said.

He bobbed his head.

"I'm going to get something from the lobby. I think they have free continental breakfast."

Mortis bobbed his head again, then closed his eyes.

I opened the door. A short man in a business suit looked up from his phone in surprise, looking right through me. "Alex?" He brushed past me and went inside, shivering violently when he touched me. "Oh my God! Alex!"

I turned and watched as the man tried to awaken his friend, or whatever the two were to each other.

"God damn it, Alex! I told you to quit!" The man rested his head on Alex's chest and sobbed. "Why did you hate life so much?"

"Friends, then," I said to myself, trying not to think about Layla. My emotions still felt distant but watching the atheist's soul dissolve in my hands had shaken me. Why that bothered me the most out of all the horrors I'd witnessed in the past two days, I had no idea. Maybe it was because I didn't know what was worse—eternal damnation, or oblivion.

Mortis watched the man grieve, black mist puffing from his

nostrils. I wondered if the horse was curious or annoyed about having his sleep interrupted again.

I pressed the call button on the elevator. The doors opened and the few people inside looked confused since they couldn't see me and assumed no one was boarding. They all wore surgical-style face-masks, probably to avoid spreading the plague. I stepped inside and stood in the middle since the other riders stood at the sides of the car, apparently to keep a safe distance from each other. The doors closed and the other riders began shivering.

"I feel like a ghost just walked past me," a woman said in her native tongue.

"Close enough," I muttered.

Another woman shivered violently. "Me too!"

The doors opened in the lobby and I followed the others to a dining room where breakfast was being served. It wasn't free, but it was a self-serve buffet, so I considered the best way to serve myself without creating a panic. Since I hadn't read the entire instruction manual, it was likely I'd missed some helpful tips and tricks to eating while in the Death cloak.

If willing myself to become visible worked, how about willing things I picked up to become invisible? I plucked a fork from the start of the line. A man gasped and flinched. I willed the fork to become invisible like me and the man blinked, looking around as if he had no idea what had just happened.

I touched a plate and willed it to also vanish. The man didn't notice when I picked it up and waved it under his nose. Satisfied that this would work, I made myself a nice large plate of bacon, pancakes, and other goodies, then sat at a table in the far back and scarfed it down. No one noticed.

The cloak didn't offer true invisibility, of course, but its high level of camouflage glamour seemed able to adapt and hide anything I touched, at least within reason. I didn't think I could touch a house or car and make it vanish. Then again, it was worth a try when I didn't have an apocalypse to avert.

I crunched a piece of bacon and sighed with contentment. I was exhausted and so ready to be done with this shit—but thank the gods for bacon.

"Please tell me you're almost done." Ithia sat down next to me, took a piece of bacon and bit into it. "I don't think the loom will last another day."

14

S omehow, I wasn't even surprised by her sudden appearance. "How in the hell did you find me?"

"The loom guides me if I search hard enough." She finished the slice of bacon and sighed. "Within a few hours it won't matter anymore. When the loom is destroyed, I don't know what will happen to us and the world."

I knew. It was all a part of War's plan. "The horsemen will ride with or without Death." I sighed and finished off my carton of chocolate milk.

Ithia shook her head. "How old are you? Twelve? What adult drinks chocolate milk for breakfast?"

I resisted the urge to burp loudly in response and set down the carton. "It's not a mangorita, but it'll do for now."

"A what?" Her fists clenched. "You and your chocolate milk are wasting time. Fate is about to be destroyed."

"Will you blow up if the loom breaks?" I looked her over. "That could be messy."

"Heartless bastard!" She yanked another piece of bacon from my plate. "Get to work."

I stood and headed for the door. Not because she told me to, but because she'd ruined a semi-enjoyable breakfast.

I picked up a piece of bacon, letting it remain visible to the others, and floated it around the room while making ghost noises that I also let the other patrons hear.

An American man, easily identifiable due to his cargo pants and New Balance sneakers, leapt up and pointed at the flying meat. "Jesus H. Christ, the bacon is haunted!"

Phones came out and people started recording while gabbing excitedly in their native tongues. They seemed more delighted and surprised than frightened despite the ghost sounds accompanying the bacon.

I sighed and ate the bacon, earning another collective gasp from the crowd, then left the nubs to wonder if the rest of the bacon was safe to eat.

Mortis waited in the hallway outside, a steady stream of people obliviously walking around his nightmarish form. I touched him and willed us to become visible for just a second.

People gasped and screamed in alarm, falling backwards over themselves to get away. The next instant they looked around in comical confusion as the source of their fright abruptly vanished.

"Did you see that?"

"I thought I saw something!"

"It was a skeleton man!"

"Skeleton? That was Death! The end days are truly here!"

I hopped on Mortis. "Well, that was fun. Let's go."

He whickered in what sounded suspiciously like a horse laugh, then bounded forward. Despite the rocky start to our relationship, it seemed he was starting to like me better.

We shifted to folded Limbo and raced across the dark landscape. Thankfully, there were no other horsemen present.

I was starting to understand a little better how the shift worked. What I saw when the world folded into two dimensions was basically like folding space, making the world look like a popup book as we passed through it and into another layer. Rather than fully commit-ting to Limbo, Mortis raced along the folded realm, covering relative distance much more quickly, and then passing through the layer and back to Gaia once again.

My limited human perception had no other way to translate what was really happening, so it took the available information and tried to make the best of it. I wondered if this was similar to the shadow walking that the gods used. I'd only seen the Greek gods use that method of travel, so it was possible other deities utilized other methods.

Lucifer, for example, had traveled through the divine realm on angel wings. Then again, maybe a fallen angel wasn't powerful enough to use shadow walking.

Gaia popped up and unfolded into three dimensions. I checked the map to find we were in Mexico. I would have girded my loins for what was to come but turning the Death cloak into an adult diaper would have just looked silly.

There were hundreds of zombies in the border towns, but they were scattered all over the place. It seemed people were locking up their own dead relatives however they could, and the government hadn't stepped in to help round them up. In many cases, the undead had been buried or shoved into caskets that were nailed shut.

We had to travel all over the place to free souls, but it took less time since I didn't have to figure out a crowd control plan. We moved south through Central America and finally reached Brazil at nightfall.

Now that I'd had experience dealing with zombies packed into stadiums, I hoped this would go a bit easier. Instead of police, I found a group of people in uniforms patrolling the area. The uniforms were single-piece spandex with a yellow top, blue bottom, and a green cape.

I rubbed my eyes and guided Mortis closer to one of the guards. Several of them had wizarding staffs. Those people that didn't were werewolves, as I was able to discern from the way they sniffed the air and cocked their ears. Even stranger, there were vampires mixed in with them. The group consisted of a bizarre mix of supers that usually didn't get along but now seemed to be part of a team.

"What in the actual hell is going on here?" I found a wizard and revealed myself to him.

He yelped and jumped back a foot. "Mother of God!" he said in Portuguese. "Who are you?" Sweat beaded on his forehead and he pressed a hand to his heart.

"Death." I waited for him to calm down.

"Death?" His eyes widened. "I thought you were just a myth."

"Most humans think wizards, vampires, and werewolves are a myth." I shook my head and looked around. "Yet, I see a whole group of you dressed in superhero costumes guarding a stadium full of zombies."

He produced a bottle of blue potion and downed it. "I'm sorry. I've seen enough strange things that I should expect anything by now."

"I was thinking the same thing myself." I frowned. "You even have capes."

"We are the Guardians, a group of supers dedicated to keeping the world safe." He straightened and managed to regain a modicum of dignity. "We have chapters all around the world, except in places where the Mage Guild Knights hold sway."

"Yeah, they don't like nubs knowing about supers." I shrugged. "Probably for the best that we don't go parading around in superhero costumes, especially such ugly ones."

"These are the colors of our nation's soccer team." The wizard huffed. "The people welcome us with open arms and appreciate our help."

"So, technically, you're just keeping Brazil safe."

"For now. Some day we will be world protectors."

I grunted. "What's your name?"

"Alejandro."

"Well, Alejandro, I'm here to help with the zombie problem." I nodded toward the stadium. "I just need some help getting the zombies to come out one at a time so I can free their souls." I told him an abbreviated version of the events leading to the disaster. "Can the Guardians assist me?"

"Proudly!" He tapped a finger to his ear. "Guardians, assemble!"

"I think the Avengers already use that phrase."

He was too busy talking to his fellow superheroes to hear me.

The others gathered and I revealed myself to them. A few of them ran away briefly, only to return after a solid chastising from Alejandro. Once they'd accepted my presence as a reality, they got to work. Despite their ridiculous uniforms, they were efficient and professional.

There were an ungodly number of zombies locked in the stadium and even the most streamlined process was going to take a while. The Guardians arranged temporary fencing into cattle chutes much like what we'd done in Chicago and started letting a few zombies into them at a time.

I walked back and forth along the multiple chutes, freeing souls and sucking them into the soul catcher. The spherical device had collected over two thousand souls by my estimation and I still didn't know what I was supposed to do with them. Thankfully, most of South America was clear since only a few people had died since my original sweep through the continent.

Howling arose in the distance and more howls answered back.

Alejandro ran over to me. "Another attack is coming."

I frowned. "Another one?" I thought back to Chicago. "Are they deep ones?"

"Deep ones?" He looked puzzled. "They're fish people if that's what you mean."

"They call themselves deep ones." I looked in the direction of the howls. "I take it you've been attacked by them before?"

He nodded. "They only attack at night, so we've been able to repel them with the help of our vampire brethren. But each time, they've returned in greater and greater numbers. We still don't understand why they attack us."

"They want to release the zombies, so they'll run free and kill people who aren't supposed to die right now. Enough untimely deaths will eventually break Fate's loom and start Armageddon."

Alejandro gasped. "My God, I knew things were bad when the

dead started walking, but I didn't realize it was leading to the end days. Do you prepare to ride with the other horsemen?"

I shook my head. "I'm trying to avoid it at all costs. So, if your people can keep the deep ones off my back, I'll free the rest of the undead. This is the last major hotspot in the world. Once we clear it, the deep ones should go home."

"Home?"

I nodded grimly. "Back to the ocean depths where their master, Cthulhu, lies sleeping."

Alejandro made the sign of the cross on his chest. "Almighty Father, protect us."

"Unfortunately, I'm all you've got." I grinned and was rewarded when he flinched away.

"Please don't do that. It's unnatural seeing a skull stretch like that."

"It stretched?" I touched my bone chin and felt it move when I smiled. Whoever designed the outfit obviously had a morbid sense of humor.

A pack of werewolves ran past, shifting into wolf form, green capes flowing behind them as they raced toward the incoming threat.

That was when I saw the actual threat. It wasn't just a handful of deep ones, but a small army of them.

"They're coming from the lake across the road," someone shouted.

Cthulhu's deepways led to nearly all bodies of water on the planet, small and large. I'd seen deep ones moving through them during my time on Gaia Alpha, so it was no surprise that they were using a nearby lake as their beachhead. I could choose to fight them, or I could take away the entire reason for their fighting and get rid of the zombies. The death beacon showed I still had nearly a hundred to go. It didn't sound like a lot, but when I was the only one dealing with them, a hundred was a lot.

Magic attacks lit the night sky, punctuated by howls and shrieking vampires. A pair of bridge trolls thudded past, looking absolutely ridiculous in their superhero outfits. I was impressed that the Guardians had managed to recruit trolls. It seemed they did things differently here in Brazil where the Mage Guild wasn't all-powerful.

I went for the nearest cattle chute of zombies and walked down the line of them, yanking out souls while avoiding the groping hands of the others so I didn't accidentally free a wraith. Several deep ones made it past the Guardians' blockade, but I remained invisible to them, plucking souls as fast as I could.

Those who made it to the cattle chutes began tearing apart the fences, releasing the zombies back into the wild. Naturally, the undead came straight for me, crying and begging for me to free their souls. The deep ones spoke with ungodly squeals, squeaks, and squawks that Death's aura had trouble translating. But I didn't have to speak their language to know that they were flabbergasted as to why the zombies were running in circles.

It was because I was running in circles while they chased me, taking one soul at a time. To anyone who could see me, it probably looked comical, the Grim Reaper running from the undead. It was definitely something I wasn't going to go home and brag about.

At long last, I sucked the last soul from the undead, leaving the deep ones with piles of inert bodies. It was difficult to read their fishy faces, but judging from the volume of their voices, they were terrified to return home and face their master. I had to wonder if that meant Cthulhu was awake, or if he spoke to them telepathically in dreams as he had with me.

Howls of triumph echoed in the night as the deep ones retreated to the lake, leaving a trail of dead and wounded behind them. The Guardians had lost fifteen of their own, a staggering loss given that I counted only about forty of them total.

I checked the death beacon and counted a few scattered crimson blips remaining. The light at the end of the tunnel was finally here. The zombie uprising was nearly over.

Alejandro staggered out of the dark, the side of his face bloody from a cut above his eyes. "We did it." He leaned heavily against a barrier. "We drove them off. You can complete your work."

"Hey, buddy, sit down." I guided him to the curb where he sat with a moan. "I freed all the souls, so they had nothing left to fight over."

"Thank God." He signed the cross over his chest. "His mercy

knows no bounds."

"Oh, it knows a lot of bounds." I shook my head. "You're on your own. The god you worship hasn't done a thing to help you."

His forehead creased. "How do you know this?"

I didn't want to bring up Lucifer because he'd just think he was lying. "I live in Purgatory, and the big guy hasn't shown his face for eons now."

Alejandro shook his head. "He is omniscient. There is nothing he cannot do. He doesn't have to be present to help us."

I shrugged. "Sure, you keep on believing that. I've met Greek gods in the flesh, and they're not good people. Maybe it's a good thing the Christian god takes a hands-off approach." I climbed onto Mortis. "Might want to get that cut looked at before it gets infected and your god does nothing to save you from an infection."

"Why would you blaspheme God so?" Alejandro wiped blood from his eye. "And mock our beliefs?"

I sighed. "Sorry. I just think it's bullshit." I bowed. "Thanks for coming to my TED talk." Then I urged Mortis forward and we galloped toward the next undead.

Within an hour, the death beacon was clear of crimson blips and only a few newly forming white ones remained.

Mortis and I crisscrossed the globe once more and the world was finally free from apocalypse-inducing zombies. I was beyond happy to be done with this so I could concentrate on the next major issues— fixing Garrick and finding the original Thanatos.

I must have been sitting still too long because Fate stepped out of the shadows. I looked down at her. "Is there a problem?"

Ithia shook her head wearily. "The loom is safe for now, but you cannot rest a moment. There are new kinks forming in the threads due to the interference from the other horsemen. They must be stopped."

"They'll just have to wait." I sighed. "A person has to sleep."

Ithia massaged her temples as if warding off a headache. "Yes, of course, but bear in mind that the fate of the world is in your hands, and your hands alone."

15

"Fate of the world?" I scoffed. "Isn't that your job?" I bumped Mortis with my heels, and he took off for our next destination—a place I hadn't visited for far too long since the owner had gone AWOL.

Aura had taken off from Voltaire's and gone to be with her lover, the druid apprentice, Grace. I'd skipped over to Gaia in the Alpha dimension since the Aura there made mangoritas just as well as her counterpart here, but if Hannah was right and our Aura was back in town, I wanted to stop in and celebrate with the best mangorita in the known universe.

I deserved it.

Mortis delivered me to the edge of the fae safezone minutes later.

"You can't arrive inside a safezone either?" It should have come as no surprise to me.

He ignored the question. I wondered if he might be hiding some of his capabilities since he knew I wasn't a permanent replacement for Garrick. It was smart keeping some of his master's secrets just in case he ever had to act against me. Not that I knew of a reason I'd ever want to go up against Death.

Then again, you never knew what the next day might bring.

When I dismounted, Mortis stomped his hoof and bumped his nose against my arm. It took a second to realize that he wanted me to hold up my wrist with the death beacon. Once I did, he stomped a hoof and gave me a long, hard look. I hadn't the foggiest idea what he wanted, so I consulted the manual and read the section on the device.

A few paragraphs in, I found what I was supposed to do. Several faint green dots were already blinking in various places around the world, representing those souls that would need reaping within the next few hours. By running my finger along the edge of the maps, the green dots stopped blinking and put the deaths in a holding pattern. I didn't even want to know how that worked because the magnitude of stopping death seemed way too large for one being to control.

I skipped the section with the explanation and tucked the manual back in the cloak. It occurred to me that I was wearing the same normal clothes beneath the cloak that I'd been wearing since yesterday—or had it been two days ago? I'd completely lost track of time in my mad dash to free the zombies.

Stepping across the line marking the fae safezone, I took some satisfaction in noting that it didn't dispel my appearance as it did most illusions. The magic powering the cloak was strong enough to resist it.

Taking out the manual once more, I read up on the Death cloak and discovered it had more versatility than I'd realized. I removed the hood and willed myself to look normal to everyone else. Then I headed toward the stairs leading into Voltaire's. A vampire and a wizard converged on the stairs at the same time as me.

A wizard, a vampire and the Grim Reaper enter a bar, I thought to myself. It sounded like the start of a joke, but probably not a good one.

They looked at me, eyes flaring when they recognized me—not as Death, but as normal old Cain. They stopped, motioning me to go ahead of them. I knocked on the speakeasy door, gave the code, and Durrug let me inside.

He frowned. "You look like Death, Cain."

I raised an eyebrow. "How did you know?"

"You look pale. Tired. Not good."

That was when I realized he meant it figuratively. "Oh, yeah. Saving the world again."

Durrug nodded matter-of-factly and showed me a romance novel he was reading. "Tell the me in Alpha that this book good. Lots of sex."

On the cover, a reptilian cecrops wrapped her tail lasciviously around a pair of troll males. That told me all I needed to know. "Three Shades of Green." I nodded. "Got it. You really like cecrops novels, don't you?"

He nodded. "My wife cecrops. They are most beautiful of all races."

"They are exceptional," I agreed. Cecrops, griffins, and other sentient beings had once been allowed as slaves on Feary. I'd freed many of them, forming a beast army with the sole purpose of creating enough leverage against the fae that they would free me from the Oblivion Guard. In the end, the fae outlawed all slavery and released me from their service.

I'd done it for myself, but the fringe benefits of being known as the Liberator by certain groups had been very useful. Durrug appreciated me because his wife had once been a slave.

Durrug grunted and turned to the vampire and wizard, letting them inside. Then he sat back down and resumed reading.

I went straight to the bar and felt deep relief when I saw Aura behind the counter. Her stand-in, Shalia, had been the absolute worst when it came to making drinks, driving me to jump dimensions just to find another Aura.

Aura looked up and gasped. She lithely leapt over the bar, rushed over, and hugged me, much to the amusement of the other patrons, judging from the oohs and aahs rising up around us.

"Cain, I'm so happy to see you." Aura kissed my cheek and released me. "I can't believe you did it."

"Did what?" I walked toward the bar.

She punched my shoulder. "Overturned my curse, jackass."

"Oh, that." I feigned a yawn. "Nothing to it."

Her gaze turned sad. "How are you dealing with Layla's death?"

"I'm not." I sat down. "Not yet, anyway. I will be soon, now that I can finally take a break."

"A break from what?" She ducked under the bar door and began mixing a mangorita without asking. "I didn't even realize my curse was gone until Hannah called me."

"Hannah called you?" I raised an eyebrow. "I tried calling you before our little adventure and never got through."

"My phone was usually off. She got lucky and reached me when I turned it on." Aura paused making the drink, took a shuddering breath and released it. "I thought the curse was about to hit me so I did everything I could to not think about it. My birthday came and went, and nothing happened. At first, Grace thought maybe Caolan's protections around her home were protecting me, but he said that wasn't the case."

"What made you come back?" I said. "Not that I'm complaining."

"I missed it." She sighed, eyes dreamy. "Living with Grace was like finally finding my true center. But she has so many duties as an apprentice and Caolan was about to take her on another training adventure, so I decided it was a good time to come home and pick up my life where I left off."

I nodded. "Think you'll ever have kids?"

Aura laughed as she set down my drink. "Gods, I have no idea. I never thought it would be an option or even a choice!" Her gaze went distant. "I don't think I ever wanted kids. The responsibility is staggering, and I'm too selfish with my time."

I snorted. "Hey, I've got a couple of kids if you want to adopt them."

Aura reached out and touched my hand. "Cain, you're a better father figure than I ever could have imagined."

"Not by choice." I inspected the little umbrella and the pirate sword speared through pineapple, grape, and a slice of orange. "This is fucking perfection."

She looked amused. "Aura Alpha didn't make them perfectly?"

"The drink was perfect, but she didn't put enough fruit on the plastic pirate sword."

Aura gasped. "The blasphemy!"

I nodded. "I know." I took another long sip. "Gods almighty, I needed this."

Aura leaned her elbows on the bar. "Cain, what have you been doing? You look like death warmed over."

"I am Death." I leaned back in the stool. "Literally. For the time being at least."

She blinked rapidly. "I'm sorry, but what does that even mean?"

"How much did Hannah tell you about what we did to remove the curse?"

"Not much." Aura straightened. "Something about a forest and Medusa and lots of tentacles. The main gist of her call was to say that you saved my ass even though I didn't deserve it."

I chuckled. "That kid knows how to nurse a grudge."

"Can't blame her, really." Aura sighed. "So, what's the full story?"

I sipped on the mangorita. "As usual, it started right here. I met a gorgon who wanted to lift Medusa's curse from her bloodline." I told her an abbreviated version of events with all the high points and then reached the point where Layla and Athena met their ends. "That was when I found out Death is just a job. A guy named Garrick holds the office now and he has no idea how the magic of Soultaker works. For us to extract Athena's and Layla's souls, we need to find the original Thanatos and hope he can tell us how to do it."

"That doesn't explain how you became Death," Aura said.

"Famine, Pestilence, and War want Death to ride with them." I let that sink in a moment. "They want the end days to start. Garrick wasn't down with that, so they cursed him into a coma. Without Death to free souls of the dead in the Christian world, the trapped souls began to go insane, causing the dead to rise. With dead people killing the living, it threw destiny for a loop, causing Fate's loom to nearly break. If the loom broke, then it would've started the end days. I finally reaped the last of the insane souls today and avoided the apocalypse for the time being. Unfortunately, Pestilence, War, and Famine are trying to trigger the apocalypse on their own."

"Good job." Aura patted my hand. "The mangorita is on me."

I scoffed. "Such reward. Wow."

She grinned. "You've earned it." Her gaze narrowed. "What now?"

"Now I'll use the powers of Death to search the underworld and find Thanatos while simultaneously looking for a way to revive Garrick and avoid the other three horsemen so they don't drag me into their apocalypse scheme."

Aura laughed. "I would say I don't know how you get yourself into these messes, but I'd be lying."

"You're responsible for most of them." I raised my glass to her. "Just be glad you know how to mix drinks."

Her gaze went distant. "What are we going to do about Gaia Beta? Did the Aura there really destroy the world?"

I pressed my lips together. "I have no idea." The one thing I'd left out of the story was that I hadn't destroyed the apocalypse weapons from the original armory of Hephaestus on Oblivion Beta. Aura Beta had hidden an entire cache of them in a mysterious interdimensional warehouse that was only accessible using a ring that was also from the armory. The smart thing would have been to take them to the armory on our Oblivion and melt them to slag in the forge I'd relit using a fire of creation. But now that a god had murdered Layla and threatened me and mine, I'd decided that keeping the weapons was a good insurance policy.

The only surviving weapons from the armories on Oblivion Prime and Alpha were the Soultakers from each dimension. Destroying the swords would unleash the armies of the dead trapped within them. I'd placed them in the warehouse where Aura Beta had put her other weapons for the time being.

The weapons were akin to a nuclear deterrent, ones I could use to hold the gods at bay if they ever decided to threaten me or those close to me. I just hoped the decision didn't come back to bite me in the ass.

My thoughts went back to Dimension Beta. "I should probably

visit Beta and find out how bad it is. Aura Beta made it sound like there's not much left." I looked into my Aura's eyes and sensed none of the madness that had been in her Beta counterpart. "She's batshit insane."

"That could have been me, Cain." Aura shuddered. "My time with the Enders pushed me closer and closer to the edge. If I'd gotten my hands on the weapons from the lost armory first, then I might have ended Prime."

"Maybe." I shrugged. "Guess we'll never know."

"I'm just glad all the weapons are destroyed."

I nodded. "With your curse gone, you really don't have a reason to want to kill the gods anyway, right?"

"Yes, but I'm sure the Enders are still looking for ways to kill them." She looked at my almost empty glass. "I'll make you another."

I looked around, half-expecting to see Layla stroll inside with a group of her party friends, and then abruptly remembered that she was dead, her soul trapped inside Soultaker. Responsibility for reviving her and Athena weighed heavily on me, but I'd earned this break. Hadn't I?

I heard my name bouncing around the room as it typically did whenever I arrived at the bar. I turned and saw Glinda, the witch who'd interviewed me for an article, sitting with a group of other witches. She smiled and raised a glass toward me. I nodded back and turned around. She was attractive but getting involved with witches was bad news. The things they could do with bodily fluids simply boggled the mind.

Aura handed me a fresh drink.

I finished off my first one. "Can I get this to go?"

She frowned. "To go?"

I nodded. "I have work to do."

Aura raised an eyebrow. "I saw you ogling those witches. Maybe you should have a few drinks and get laid."

"Bad idea."

She pressed her lips together. "Cain, you look tired as hell and your face is gaunt. I seriously think you need to drink and relax."

"I agree, but I can't stop thinking about my responsibilities."

Aura took my hand and squeezed. "Then take the drink and go. I know how futile it is trying to talk you out of doing something once you've made up your mind."

"That's a strength, not a weakness."

She laughed softly. "Because you're usually right when you follow your gut. That Oblivion Guard training is still paying off."

I took the pirate sword from my first drink and put it in the new drink next to the new pirate sword since I hadn't had time to eat the fruit off it. "Thanks." I slid my hand from her grasp and stood.

Her brow furrowed. "Cain, could you get help from the Garrick in Dimension Alpha or Beta?"

The major gods supposedly existed across all dimensions simultaneously, but since Thanatos had handed off death duties to a mortal, that likely meant that Garrick had doppelgangers in dimensions Alpha and Beta.

"I wish I'd thought of that during the zombie crisis because an extra Death could've gone a long way." My needs now, however, were much different. "Right now, I just need the powers of Death to search for the original Thanatos. I'm an expert tracker with a particular set of skills. Garrick, on the other hand, is just a normal guy when he's not wearing the Death cloak. I don't think his doppelgangers from other dimensions will be much help at tracking down Thanatos."

She pursed her lips. "I guess you're right. If anyone can find a lost god, it's you."

"I hope." I took a sip from my to-go mangorita. "So long and thanks for all the fruit." I turned and headed toward the door.

"Is that a souvenir glass?" someone whispered as I passed by their table. "I want a souvenir glass."

I nodded at Durrug on the way out, walked up the stairs and into the parking lot. I kept walking until I was out of the fae safezone. There wasn't anyone around, so I reached behind my back and summoned my oblivion staff. My hand wrapped around the hilt as it appeared out of whatever pocket dimension it resided in.

The hilt bore a gray band that wasn't normally there. Any self-respecting member of the Oblivion Guard would sneer in disdain if they had any idea what it was. It was a magical life hack I'd discovered, useful for hiding small things and required nothing more than duct tape. That's right—the tape people use for repairing everything from car windows to structural beams in houses.

In this case, it was merely holding something I didn't want to leave laying around, or chance losing if, for some reason, my pants were ripped off while it was in my pocket. I unwrapped the duct tape and plucked a small, silver ring from the adhesive side.

I'd learned long ago that some very small objects could be adhered to the hilt of the staff and they'd go with it when I banished it to its pocket dimension. If the ring had been a fraction thicker or larger in circumference, it would've remained behind when I tried to banish the staff. One day when I had nothing better to do, I'd investigate where, exactly, my staff went when I banished it. For now, I'd be content to use this simple life hack to keep apocalyptic weapons out of the hands of others.

Because they could literally lead to the end of the world.

16

I slipped on the ring and my vision split, showing me different places as if viewing them through multiple eyes. The parking lot was in one frame, the next frame was dark, the next was the inside of a warehouse. There were many more places: a desert, a frigid wasteland, and so forth, but I hadn't taken the time to investigate them.

To put it simply, the ring allowed me to travel between the various frames. Every time I put it on, though, my head ached, the pain worsening gradually until I removed the ring. I willed myself through the frame and into the warehouse. The center frame shifted from the parking lot to the warehouse. I removed the ring. My view returned to normal, but the headache lingered for a few seconds.

If there was a way to keep my vision from splitting into multiple frames, I hadn't figured it out yet. Aura must have known how but she was supposedly strung up on the same rock where Prometheus had been bound, unable to die and tortured every day by an eagle that ate her liver. Zeus had instructed Hermes to tie her up next to Prometheus. According to legend, Prometheus had been rescued by Hercules, but Zeus made it sound as if the Titan were still being endlessly tortured.

Mortis could presumably take me to her so I could ask about the ring, but I didn't want her to know I had taken it. I'd punched her senseless before slipping it off her finger, so she probably thought one of the gods had taken it.

I went to a nearby sword rack and took the Soultaker marked with duct tape since it was the one used to slay Athena and Layla. Duct tape really could be used for just about anything. I strapped the special sheath around my waist and considered where to conduct my risky experiment. Oblivion seemed like the best place to go.

I briefly considered summoning Mortis to pick me up from the warehouse so I could explore the area outside of Aura's vault. A keypad guarded the exit and I wanted to find out if this place was on Gaia, or possibly in another dimension altogether. My smartphone didn't have a signal here, so I couldn't use its GPS. I'd brought a dedicated GPS as well, but it couldn't find a satellite signal. That meant this vault was likely on Oblivion or Feary, but just as likely, it might be somewhere extremely remote on Gaia.

The vault door was mithril and not even Soultaker could cut through it. Even the rock walls were nigh impervious to a sword that could cut through nearly anything. It seemed no amount of explosives or magic would allow me to bypass the lock, so I'd simply have to find the right code if I wanted to see what was on the other side.

I put on the ring and stepped from the frame with the vault back to the frame with the parking lot outside Voltaire's. Once there, I taped the ring back to my staff and banished it. Then I mentally requested Mortis and waited. It took him a few minutes to show and when he did, his eyes were glowing with something that might have been anger.

Mortis stomped his hoof and blew plumes of black mist from his nostrils.

I shrugged. "Yeah, I know I should be resting, but this is something I need to do."

He snorted and shook his head vehemently. Just when I'd thought we were starting to get along, it seemed like he decided he didn't like me after all.

I gripped his reins and pulled his head closer to mine. "Look, I know you're pissed about Garrick. I know working with me isn't exactly at the top of your favorite things to do, and I know you think we should both be resting. But I can't sleep until I know if this works."

He blasted mist into my face. It wasn't wet and it didn't smell, but it was frigid, like a blast of subzero air. Then he sighed as if resigned to his fate and the glow faded from his eyes. He probably didn't have a choice as long as I wore Death's vestments, but it would've been nice for him to show a little enthusiasm.

I mounted the saddle and imagined where I wanted to go. "We need to go to Oblivion."

He lunged forward, blurring to top speed and shifting into two-dimensional Limbo. Though we were moving forward, the ground beneath us started rotating sideways. We passed through a shimmering barrier and suddenly, the dunes of the Kameni desert popped up around us. Mortis stopped atop a crimson dune in the middle of nowhere.

We were somewhere north of the original Olympus in the heat-blasted wastelands of Oblivion, though it wasn't nearly so hot as before. Ever since our epic battle against Torvin, the weather patterns on Oblivion Prime had changed, becoming much cooler. I wasn't one to look a gift-horse in the mouth, so I allowed myself to enjoy not sweating my balls off the instant we arrived.

With that moment over, I slid off Mortis and drew Soultaker. I'd never actually used the sword to summon the army of souls it contained. I had no idea if I could release them, and even less idea as to how to control them or put them back in the sword. Everything might go horribly wrong in the next few seconds or it might go completely right.

Experience had taught me that the former was much more likely than the latter. But it was worth a try.

My premise was simple: Unleash the army, find Layla, and see if I could capture her soul with the soul catcher. Then I could take her newly freed soul and possibly put it back into her body. I hadn't exactly figured out that part, but it seemed doable.

Aside from a sand scorpion pit at the bottom of the dune, there was no other sign of life. Typically, a sand scorpion would have sensed the vibrations from the top of the dune and come for me already. Since I was wearing the death cloak it probably couldn't sense me. It was in for a rude awakening once I upchucked an army of the dead in its front yard.

I pointed Soultaker away from me and willed it to release the army. Nothing happened, so I pointed it at the sky and tried again. Still nothing. I held it over my head and shouted, "There can be only one!" That didn't do the trick, so I imagined souls exploding from the tip of the sword. "Release the army!"

Apparently, there was more to releasing the army of the dead than just willing it to happen. I had no instruction manual and no clue as to what to do. But there was another reason I'd chosen Oblivion as the perfect site for my test. Unless they'd somehow traveled to another realm, Noctua and Korborus still roamed the wastelands of this world.

Korborus, aka Mecha-Cerberus, had guarded the entrance to the lost armory. Noctua, a clockwork owl, had been inside. She was a repository for vast sums of knowledge. Her stand had enabled her to look out among the various realms and dimensions, giving her a livestream into more places than I could imagine.

After destroying the armory, she and Korborus had taken off for adventures of their own, but she'd given me an owl whistle that allowed me to contact her from anywhere. I'd also rescued her counterpart, the Noctua from Dimension Alpha, but that Noctua had been severely damaged and lost most of her memory. I'd thought she'd repaired herself, but the last time I brought her to Oblivion, she malfunctioned and hadn't recovered since.

I pulled the whistle from my utility belt and blew into it. A moment later, a voice emanated from it.

"Cain, is that you?"

"Hey Noctua. I need your help."

She hooted—a sound I'd never heard her make before. "I am quite excited to hear from you. Korborus and I have traveled far and wide across Oblivion and have experienced fascinating adventures. I have been eager to tell someone our story, but most beings we encounter here only wish to kill or enslave us."

I snorted. "That's Oblivion for you. I suppose Korborus dissuades most of them?"

"In some cases, yes, but there are creatures not even he can overcome." She paused. "Perhaps we can meet soon?"

"I'm in the Kameni desert," I said. "How far away are you?"

"Oh, we are halfway around the world." Noctua hooted softly. "If you have time, perhaps—"

"I don't really have time for stories right now. What I need is information."

"I am happy to help," she said.

"How do I release the souls from Soultaker?"

There was a long pause before she answered. "I am not certain I should give you that information."

My eyebrows rose. "You've never been shy about giving information to anyone who asks."

"Yes, but I have learned the hard way that giving away information is unwise." She made a clicking sound. "Especially when some beings will use that information against you."

I nodded. "That's a valuable life lesson you've learned, and I agree with it. But, there are mitigating circumstances surrounding my request."

"I am admittedly curious as to why you want to use Soultaker," she said. "Do you plan to use the army to take over the world?"

"Long story short, someone killed Athena with Soultaker, so her soul is trapped inside the sword. I am temporarily acting as Death and want to release Athena's soul from Soultaker so I can try to free it and return it to her body before the Greek gods decide to kill me."

Noctua clicked and hooted. "My goodness, Cain. Your adventure story already sounds far better than mine. I am relieved to hear you don't plan to use Soultaker maliciously."

"So, you'll help me?"

"I will." She paused. "One moment while I access the information." A solid two minutes passed before she spoke again. "Apologies, but the information is extremely old, and it took some time to find it. Lift the sword above your head, and say, by the power of Grayskull."

I blinked. "You're kidding me, right?"

"Oh, wait, Cain. That is actually for another sword." She hooted sharply. "Press the tip of the sword to the ground and shout, arise chaos!"

Noctua didn't often speak emphatically, so I took her exclamation to mean I needed to do it as well. I pressed the tip of the sword to the sand and shouted. "Arise chaos!"

And holy fuck did it ever.

Jagged black lightning ruptured the earth all around me, leaving lines of darkly glowing energy. The ground shook and rumbled. Shadowy figures rose from the lightning and not all of them were humanoid. Some had multiple legs and monstrous heads. Others resembled the giant creatures I'd seen the gods battling in the divine realm.

The humanoids nearest me looked as if they were flesh and blood bound by pure dark energy. They faced straight ahead, eyes fierce and hungry for blood, teeth bared, and fists clenched. Their chests heaved with breath, though I doubted they needed air. They had no weapons or armor that I could see which made me all the more curious about how they'd perform in battle.

The ground continued to quake as the black lightning spread in an oval pattern bisected by a thick jagged line. It took a moment for me to realize it was the Greek letter, theta, also a symbol for death. The rumbling stopped and it seemed my army was fully summoned up and down the dunes all around me.

A giant sand scorpion abruptly burst from its sand pit and grabbed the nearest solider, taking it beneath the sand in a heartbeat. Barely a second later, the same soldier was shot back up from the sand trap, his body bloody and torn, as if chewed up and spit out. He staggered to his feet and hobbled back into formation. The scorpion scurried out of the sand trap and vanished over the dunes.

I approached the nearest soldier to my right, a soldier of

unknown nationality with dark skin and thick, black hair. His torso and loins were wrapped in white cloth, and like the others, he had no weapon.

Not far away, giant humanoids towered over the army, the tallest nearly three stories high, with giant mouths and lips pulled back over flat teeth. Nothing covered their bodies, leaving massive private parts free to dangle. The non-human beings also had no clothing. The shock value of a naked giant charging the enemy frontlines was probably enough to make most commanders call it a day and order a retreat.

Tentatively, I reached out and touched the soldier. The skin was cold and tingling with the dark energy. I stepped in front of him, but his gaze seemed to look right through me. "Who are you?" I asked. His eyes widened and locked onto me. Animalistic grunts and growls rumbled in his chest. Apparently, he didn't speak any language I was familiar with or one that the cloak could translate.

I looked around and realized it'd take me a while to locate Athena or Layla in this mass of bodies.

Noctua's voice emanated from the owl whistle. "Cain, did you summon the army?"

"Yeah, and it's big." I turned and looked at the soldiers lined up in a giant theta pattern. "Can I call specific people to come to me?"

"Unfortunately, I don't have much information about how to command the army," she said. "Mars slew many beings with Soul-taker, but he only used the army once and was apparently displeased with something."

"What, specifically was that?"

"Something to do with strategy, but that is all I can recall about his conversation with Hades since they blocked me out of the conversation." Noctua hooted softly. "There is a command to summon only specific souls. Mars pleasured himself by summoning a handful of souls and making them fight."

I grimaced. "Pleasured himself?"

"Not in a masturbatory sense," Noctua said. "He enjoyed the raw, animalistic fights, but quickly grew tired of the spectacle."

I stepped away from the row of undead making up the line across the theta symbol and looked up and down to see if I saw Layla. "How do I summon specific ones?"

"You identify the ones you want, give them a name, and then say the same phrase, but substitute their name for chaos."

"Any name will do?" I said.

"Yes."

I pursed my lips. "What if I already know their name?"

"I believe that will work, but I think you must look at them first, or at least visualize them."

I knew every curve and angle of Layla's body, so I imagined them, and named her. "Layla." Athena was easy to remember, having watched the goddess battle giant outsiders in the divine realm. I did the same for her. "How do I get rid of the army?"

"Put the sword to the ground and say, "Chaos undone!"

I did as instructed. With hardly a whisper, the army dissolved into black vapors and was sucked into the ground, leaving a massive theta symbol burned into the desert sands. Taking a deep breath and hoping for the best, I said, "Arise Layla!"

Black lightning crackled and a single spirit rose from the ground. Eyes glowing with dark power, fists clenched, and teeth bared, Layla stood before me.

17

I flinched and tears stung my eyes. It felt as if I hadn't seen her in years, even though it had only been weeks. I reached out and touched her face. Like the other soldier, her skin was cold and tingling with dark magic. I pulled her toward me, and she came, unresisting. I wanted to kiss her on the lips, but they were peeled back in animalistic rage, so I would've only kissed her teeth.

"Layla?" I snapped my fingers. "Look at me."

Her wild gaze locked onto mine. She looked ready to murder someone in an instant if only I gave the command, but there was no recognition in her eyes.

"Layla, can you hear me? Can you talk?"

She opened her mouth and a horrific shriek tore from her throat.

I backed up a step. "What's your name?"

Layla screamed again, eyes boiling with dark clouds of energy.

I spoke into the owl whistle. "Noctua, what in the fuck is wrong with Layla? She just screams when I tell her to talk."

"I believe the souls are stripped of all rational thoughts and are in a constant frenzied state," Noctua said. "They were supposed to be a relentless army, not unlike berserkers. The souls are placed into conjured bodies that can be injured, killed, and reborn every day."

"Fuck me." I took out the soul catcher. "If I use Death's soul collector to get her soul, will she return to normal once I put her back in her body?"

"You would first need to kill her and free the soul from the temporary body." Noctua paused. "Even then, I'm not sure it would work. Death's soul catcher is used to reap the souls of dead Christians so they may be released into Purgatory and judged before going on to their destinations. Souls in the grasp of Soultaker may not be affected by Death's abilities."

"Can I put her soul back into her body by summoning it from the sword and commanding it back in?"

"I do not have all the information pertaining to Death's abilities, but in most cases, he can only control Christian souls. There are times where souls that belong to no particular religion must also be collected, but they are rotated among the various death entities from other religions."

"Like atheists?" I said.

"Precisely. There are no atheist deities despite Pastafarian attempts to create the Flying Spaghetti Monster."

I frowned. "That's an atheist thing? I thought it was just a joke."

"I think it can be both," Noctua said. "Even if Layla were Christian, I do not think her soul is free to take. The sword is her prison. Destroying it will only release her in her current form. Without a sword to control her or the others, the army will run rampant."

"How do I free her soul then?" I looked away from Layla's crazed face. "Is her real consciousness trapped somewhere in the back of her mind, unable to break free?"

"The Greek Thanatos helped Hephaestus enchant the sword with his magic. He might know the answer, but he vanished centuries ago and not even I was able to discover where he went." Noctua hooted sadly. "I'm afraid I have no answers for you, Cain. But..." she trailed off.

"But what?"

"I hesitate to say it, but perhaps Nyx can help you."

"The goddess of night?" I frowned. "How is she supposed to help me?"

"She is imprisoned in Tartarus, though it is rumored that she is allowed to leave in human form during the winter solstice on Gaia and enjoy a night of freedom before returning." Noctua made a clicking sound. "Unfortunately, the winter solstice is several months away, and even then, I do not know where on Gaia she would be at the time."

I wasn't waiting around for months, but if Nyx could help me, then I had to see her at any cost. "Tartarus is in Hades, right?"

"It is an abyss in Hades," Noctua said. "It is where horrible creatures and the vilest of humans are sent. I would not recommend going there even if you have the powers of Death."

"I don't have a choice if I want to rescue Athena and Layla from Soultaker."

Noctua went silent for a moment. "Death's vestments should give you free reign of several underworlds and afterlives regardless of religion, but it will not offer complete protection, especially not in Tartarus since it is a place used to imprison beings as mighty as the Titans."

"Is there a map of the place? A way I can locate Nyx quickly?"

"None that I know of. Perhaps you should consult with other gods before venturing there. Hades would be a good start."

I nodded. "That's good advice. Thanks, Noctua."

"Cain, you are a good friend to do this."

I scoffed. "I'm a horrible friend. I'm only doing this because I have to."

"I do not believe that is true."

"Before I go, I have to ask about a ring from the armory."

"There are many of them, Cain." Noctua clicked her beak. "Describe it, please."

"Thin and silver. When I wear it, I see into several places at once."

"Ah, the ring of Panoptes, also called Allseer." Noctua hooted softly. "It was originally designed to allow the wearer to see everything all at once—something not even the gods can do. Hephaestus was inspired by Argus Panoptes, a giant with one hundred eyes on his body. He thought an all-seeing ring would be useful. Unfortunately, it never worked very well, and gave the wearer terrible headaches. Hephaestus tried reworking the enchantment several times, but eventually gave up."

I examined the ring. "When I wear it, I see multiple places, including a warehouse. I can travel to the warehouse and presumably to the other places I see."

"Instant travel to the places the wearer of the ring saw was part of the functionality, but extended use caused psychotic side effects." Noctua clicked her beak. "I would advise to only use it in short bursts."

"You're saying I'd have to wear it for a long time to cause psychosis?" I grimaced. "It's like the One Ring?"

"Yes. Allowing your mind to rest in between uses should avoid such complications." She paused. "Such mental damage is unlikely to heal even if you have godlike powers."

I suddenly understood why Aura Beta had gone so far off the deep end. She'd probably used the ring for too long at once and slowly driven herself mad. "The Aura from Beta set this ring to a warehouse where she stored some apocalypse weapons. The place is locked, and I can't figure out where it is."

"Is it filled with old computers and a mithril door?" Noctua said.

I blinked. "Yeah, that's the place. How do you know about it?"

"There is a group of beings dedicated to finding dangerous arti-facts and storing them secure, magic-proof vaults." Noctua hooted gently. "There are other groups dedicated to finding and destroying these vaults, freeing the dangerous artifacts back into the world. It seems Aura Beta is utilizing one of these hidden vaults. Not even I could tell you where this one might be located."

I began to form an idea as to where this vault might be. "Can Panoptes see across dimensions?"

"Yes, provided the user attunes it to a place while they are there."

"Then it stands to reason this vault might be on Gaia Beta." It also stood to reason that Aura had killed everyone in the facility to secure her trove. The same vaults on Prime and Alpha were hopefully still functional.

"I think this is enough information for now. Thanks, Noctua."

"My pleasure, Cain. Please be careful."

I scoffed. "I'll try." I put the whistle back in my utility belt, then took Layla's hand. It was cold, but I didn't care. I looked deep into her eyes. Somewhere beyond the berserker insanity, I sensed the real Layla pacing back and forth in a mental prison. At least, that's what I hoped for. "Layla, I swear I'll free you even if it means finally letting you die."

A single tear pooled in the corner of her eye and that was when I knew my Layla was still inside.

I gripped her hand tighter. "I fucking promise."

There were no more tears from her, no other signs that her inner spark could hear me. I sighed, pressed the sword tip to the ground, and said, "Chaos undone."

Nothing happened, so I rolled my eyes and shouted, "Chaos undone!"

She puffed away in black vapors.

I sheathed Soultaker and grimly considered my next steps. Mortis stood on a distant dune, apparently content to watch the proceedings from a distance. I'd been so preoccupied I hadn't even noticed he'd left my side. He returned in a heartbeat, regarding me suspiciously. "I need to visit Hades."

He stomped a hoof and shook his head.

"I know you don't want me to, but I have to."

Mortis snorted and bowed his head, apparently resigned to having an insane person in control of him. He seemed different—agitated. I thought he was warming up to me, but now there was a wild look to his glowing eyes. When I'd left him to go to Aura Beta's vault, he'd apparently had time to reconsider our relationship.

I was just reaching for his reins when movement caught the corner of my eye. A red meteor slammed into the dune across from me, sending a cloud of dust into the air. A strong wind carried it away, revealing a thickly muscled man in a superhero pose in the center. He drew a giant red sword and blurred toward me.

I dove sideways at the last instant, supernaturally fast, thanks to Death's cloak. But I couldn't move fast enough when the red blur changed direction and rammed into me with bone-jarring impact.

I flew off the dune, tumbling head over heels in midair. I reflexively activated my tattooed sigils and flung a shield spell behind me. Twisting like a cat, I flung out a foot and landed on the shield, a good twenty feet above the ground, then bounded forward toward the slope of the dune where the god who'd just hit me stood.

Blood trickled down his face from multiple cuts, one of them above the eye. His broom helmet was missing, and his giant red sword was coated in green fluid. Mars looked furious and ready to take it out on me. "Where is Athena, mortal? Why have you not yet freed her soul?"

Before I had a chance to open my mouth, he blurred toward me. I instinctively reached for my brightblade and instead found the scythe in my hand. Mars' sword was already halfway toward my neck. His blade clanged against the haft of the scythe. The handle was made of bone, but it withstood the brutal impact.

The blow rattled my bones. My feet slid backward in the sand, but I managed to remain standing. I'd barely absorbed the impact of the first blow when Mars swung his sword again. If not for the supernatural aid of the Death cloak, I probably wouldn't have even seen the next blow coming.

Somehow, I had time to duck. Pivoting on my foot, I swung the scythe at Mars's ankles. He leapt over the blade, twisted in mid-air, and swung his sword down at my head. I rolled toward him, thrusting the haft of the scythe straight up and caught him in the chin.

Roaring in fury, Mars lashed out with a foot and connected with my chest. I tumbled backward, rolling at least three times before managing to stop myself. I checked myself for broken bones and was surprised to find none, but my ribs ached, and my kidneys felt like ping-pong balls after a championship round.

Apparently, Death's cloak had protected me from being crushed but only just barely. Mars rubbed his chin and glared at me but didn't attack me again.

"When asking a question, it's usually best to wait for an answer." I stopped a few feet away, grimly aware that there was no safe distance to stand from a god who could apparently find me anywhere and move faster than a vampire on cocaine.

Mars sneered. "My patience wears thin, mortal."

"I know you're the god of war, but try asking politely next time, or I'll do more than bloody your chin." Cold anger welled inside me, and I distantly realized this was the old Cain talking. The assassin who'd just killed a high fae rival for the Winter Court and thought nothing could touch him. By channeling my old Cain, I was antagonizing a being who could probably kill me despite the protective Death cloak. It wasn't the soundest strategic decision I'd ever made. On the other hand, I also had access to an armory of godlike weapons.

Maybe I can take him.

Mars's eye blazed. "Do you challenge me to a duel?"

I banished the scythe and drew Soultaker. "I'll send you to meet Athena if you'd like."

He regarded the sword. "What do you mean to do with that? Prick me?"

I reached into my utility pack and withdrew a silvery-gray length of rope. I spun it once, and it coiled in midair, hovering like a venomous snake. "I mean to defend myself and send you into the next life if need be."

Mars backed up a step when he recognized the rope. It was, of course, no ordinary rope, but a mortal coil taken from the armory and used by Aura Beta to kill Athena. If he touched it, he'd be mortal and I could strike him down—temporarily, at least. His body might heal the moment it was no longer touching the mortal coil, but Soultaker would claim his soul just as it had Athena's.

He sneered. "You're quite brave when you have those weapons, mortal."

I sneered back. "You're quite brave when you have divine powers, god."

Mars burst into laughter and sheathed his sword. "You have quite the spirit for a speck. Frail as you are, I can respect that."

It was a double backhanded compliment, but I took the opportunity to deescalate and find out what the pompous bastard wanted. The tip of the mortal coil twisted, following him like a wary snake. "I assume things are not going well in the divine realm."

He took a handful of crimson sand and wiped down his red blade, removing the blue fluid from it. "Athena is a mighty warrior. She had my back, and I hers. Now I am alone except for that fool Hermes. We were stretched thin already, and now the situation worsens."

"Are the Norse gods and other pantheons helping?"

He nodded. "Of course. Odin and his Valkyries have secured much of Yggdrasil, while Thor and his companions fight Níðhöggr at the roots. The great serpent has been particularly agitated as of late, no doubt due to Loki's machinations."

I didn't know much about the great serpent, but it was way above my paygrade if it took gods to fend it off. "As you can tell, I'm wearing the vestments of Death. Garrick was waylaid by the other three horsemen because they want to bring about the end days. I've been busy ending a zombie uprising and have only just found time to find out how to free Athena."

Mars pursed his lips and sheathed his sword. "It would seem the gods of chaos are working hard to bring about the end days, for what reasons I know not. They would unleash the Elder Things in our worlds and bring about end of humankind, leaving the universe in the hands of abominations."

In other words, the gods were growing desperate. Maybe it was time to test just how desperate. "Perhaps it's time to free the Titans and other Elder Gods that are imprisoned in Tartarus."

Laughter boomed across the hills. "Oh, little speck, that would be even worse. But your limited mind simply cannot comprehend what that would mean."

I resisted the urge to claim his soul with Soultaker since the world apparently needed him. "I tried to directly remove Athena's soul from the sword by using the powers of Death. Unfortunately, the souls within the sword are insane and demented and the soul catcher doesn't work with them."

Mars scoffed. "I could have told you that."

"But you didn't. Your vast, ancient mind did not conceive that my tiny, limited mind would need information that might help me achieve a goal."

The sarcasm seemed to escape him. "It is quite difficult, but even I do not have all the answers. We are simply too busy to hold your hand, little one."

I nearly let the mortal coil lash out at him. *Resist! You need this insufferable bastard.* "I need to find Thanatos, son of Nyx since he helped craft the sword. Do you know where he is? Is there a quick way to find him?"

"I heard he grew so weary of life that he ended himself and went onto oblivion." Mars shrugged. "He was always a grim one."

"Probably because he's the son of the goddess of night." I sighed. "I hope you're wrong, because he might be the only person who knows the trick to freeing souls."

Mars didn't seem concerned. "Then you will have to discover the trick yourself."

"Where is Hephaestus? At the very least, he might have some idea what to do."

"He does not." Mars knelt and looked at the theta symbol carved from glassy, black sand when I'd used Soultaker. "I questioned him thoroughly, and he only said that he gave Thanatos the finished weapon so he could enchant it."

"He didn't watch Thanatos?" I gritted my teeth. "How in the hell am I supposed to unravel the enchantment of a fucking god if no one has the slightest clue about the magic he used?"

Mars shrugged. "I have wasted enough time here. Perhaps the death gods of other pantheons can aid your quest." He raised his sword above his head and leapt into the sky, becoming a red streak that vanished into the clouds.

This day was getting worse by the moment.

18

I didn't know much about the death gods of other pantheons. I had no idea where to start or how much time it would take to track them down. The Morrigan seemed like the best person to start with since I knew where to find her but given that she was working with the Greek gods to supply them with souls for the dead, I had a feeling they'd already asked her about freeing Athena.

Even if she didn't know how to free the souls, she could probably point me in the direction of other gods of death. It wasn't a lot to go on, but it was worth a try. I sheathed Soultaker and put the mortal coil back in my utility belt. My ribs were still aching from the short scuffle with Mars. Had he not already been exhausted from battle in the divine realm, the outcome wouldn't have been nearly so favorable for me.

Mortis watched from a neighboring dune. If I didn't know any better, I'd have thought he looked amused. It was apparent that he was resigned to helping me, but his loyalty was with Garrick. I had enough problems trying to free souls from Soultaker. Trying to awaken Garrick and stop the other horsemen from starting the apocalypse was simply too much to deal with.

I was also exhausted. Skipping out on mangoritas and getting some shuteye would've been the wise move, but I'd become a lazy creature of habit over the past few years. My life of bounty hunting had been easy compared to my time in the Oblivion Guard. Any humans, supernatural or otherwise, hadn't been much of a threat to me even if they knew my habits.

But dealing directly with the Greek gods was something I hadn't prepared for. I wasn't even sure I could prepare for a showdown with a full-fledged god. I needed to be at the top of my game to even stand a chance at surviving what might lay ahead. I blew out a sigh and waved Mortis over. I wanted to sleep in my own bed.

It was daytime when we arrived back at Sanctuary. The girls had gone to school and Fred was nowhere to be seen when I walked inside the church. I walked over to his pool in the corner of the room and peered into the dark water. I splashed the water to alert him, but he didn't surface. After his metamorphosis from octopus to spawn of Cthulhu, he'd started sleeping almost as many hours as he was awake.

I wondered if his fate was to eventually enter an eternal slumber like his dear old dad. Gods knew I felt like slumbering for a month after everything I'd been through over the past few days.

I showered and dropped into bed.

VOICES from the den woke me sometime later. I sat up and winced at the deep ache in my ribs. I pulled up my shirt and winced again. My ribs were black and blue. If I hadn't been protected by the Death cloak, I probably wouldn't have survived that first blow from Mars.

I understood his anger, but what if that pompous moron had killed me? What good would all his impotent rage have done him then? Trying to make sense of something so senseless only made my head hurt. The gods did as the gods willed, and it certainly wouldn't have been the first time Mars acted impulsively and killed someone.

Shae's and Hannah's voices rose into an argument, and it wasn't about which movie to watch as usual. I threw on some street clothes and opened the door. They flinched in unison, eyes wide.

"Cain?" Hannah ran over and hugged me. "You've been gone for days! I was really worried."

"Me too." Shae watched from afar as usual. She wasn't one who liked to be touched no matter how much she might like someone.

I mussed Hannah's dark hair and freed myself. "What were you two arguing about?"

Shae's lips pressed into a thin line, and she looked away.

Hannah huffed. "Boys."

I blinked and looked back and forth between them. "I thought you two were an item."

Shae sighed. "We are, but—"

"We are or we aren't, Shae!" Hannah wiped a tear from her eye. "Shae has a thing for a boy at school."

I had no idea how to respond, so I just stared blankly.

Hannah looked at me expectantly. "Well, that's wrong, right? If we're dating, then she shouldn't be looking at other people like that."

"It's normal human behavior," Shae shot back. "Just because I love you doesn't mean I can't find other people attractive too!"

I was tempted to call Mortis so I could escape to the divine realm because I was the worst person to ask about relationship advice.

Shae continued pressing. "Look at Cain. He bangs whoever he wants even though Layla is his girlfriend." Her eyes flared and she grimaced. "Oh, shit, I'm sorry, Cain. It just kind of slipped out."

I went into the kitchen and heated up the stovetop to make breakfast even though it was late in the day. "I think you two should just do what feels right."

"But what if what feels right for one person really hurts the other?" Hannah's tears flowed freely now. "Shae is the first person I've felt like this for. I don't even know how she can trust boys."

"Not every boy is bad." Shae threw up her hands. "We've both been through bad shit, Hannah. I've been abused by men and women. Just because I find a boy attractive doesn't mean I don't love you anymore."

"But it means you might leave me." Hannah's voice broke and she crumpled to the couch. "I don't want to lose you."

Shae's lips trembled. "You won't, Hannah. I swear."

"That's not a promise you can keep." I cracked an egg into my mixing bowl and whisked it. "You two are demigods, so you'll probably have a thousand lovers in your lifetime, and that's putting it conservatively."

Their mouths dropped open in dismay and they turned on me.

"Are you serious, Cain?" Hannah shook her head in disbelief. "Do you know how horrible I feel right now, and then you decide to tell me it's meaningless?"

"Yeah!" Shae wrapped an arm around Hannah and kissed her cheek. "That was cruel!"

I shrugged. "Facts of life. Maybe I'm wrong, but I'm probably not."

"You're wrong!" they said in unison.

I added some cinnamon to the pancake batter and threw in some pecans. "Sure, whatever you say."

Shae kissed Hannah on the lips. "I promise I won't look at boys like that again. I love you."

Hannah shuddered in relief. "I love you too!"

The well-worn tactic of ending an argument by giving the aggrieved parties a common enemy had worked once again. Even better, it saved me from having to hand out terrible relationship advice.

I poured batter into the pan. "You two want breakfast for dinner?"

They snapped out of their moment.

Hannah frowned. "We were going to meet some friends for dinner, but I feel like I haven't seen you in forever."

"I've got to eat quickly and go anyway." I checked the death beacon and grimaced at the number of imminent deaths that were accumulating. They were on hold, but the price of that seemed to be that the number kept piling up.

"Are you sure?" Shae's nostrils flared. "It smells really good."

I sighed. "It's me you're asking. Just let me know if you want some or not because I only made enough for me."

Hannah nodded. "Yes, I do." She patted Shae's hand. "We can still meet the others, but I want some time with Cain."

Shae smiled. "It's been a while since our last family breakfast."

Water splashed and Fred stumbled out of his pool. "Brekkie?"

"Yes, brekkie!" Hannah clapped her hands.

I shook my head and started mixing more batter. Not two minutes ago they'd told me I was cruel and now they wanted family breakfast. *Family.* That word still made me cringe. I wasn't Dom Toretto, for gods' sakes. These attachments I'd formed had taken root and they were spreading deeper. It was dangerous, but oddly enjoyable at times.

Hannah and Shae helped me cook while Fred pulled himself clumsily onto a barstool and watched, his tentacles twitching in anticipation.

I tossed him a sausage which he snatched from the air with a mouth tentacle. "Were you sleeping earlier?"

Fred gulped it down. "Yes. Sleep."

Something in his eyes told me that wasn't the complete truth. "You weren't playing with yourself, were you?"

"Ew!" Hannah giggled. "I can't believe you just asked him that!"

Shae coughed as if choking. "Gods, Cain, why would you ask him that?"

I shrugged. "I splashed the water when I got home but he didn't answer. That usually wakes him up."

Fred shook his head, tentacles twitching. "No play myself."

Shae and Hannah broke into fresh giggles.

"Brings a whole new meaning to tentacle porn," Hannah said between bouts of laughter.

I grunted and continued cooking. Once breakfast was served, I ate quickly. The next phase of my plan was to locate the Morrigan and use her to meet other death gods. But first, I had to catch up on soul reaping.

"Tell us what you've been up to, Cain." Shae leaned her elbows on the table. "A lot of people at school were worried about the zombies."

"They're taken care of," I said. "But I put death on hold so I could get some sleep, so today will be busy."

Hannah's eyes widened. "You can stop death?"

"It's more of a pause, really." I shook my head. "I can't actually stop it from happening."

"Not even if you keep it paused forever?" Shae said.

I grimaced. "I don't even understand how it works, so pausing death might be torture for those in pain or dying from terminal illnesses. I just need to get Garrick back up and running so I don't have to do this anymore. It's only been a week or so and I'm already sick of it."

"I can't blame you." Shae munched sympathetically on a piece of bacon. "It sounds like a horribly stressful job with no rewards."

"Basically, yeah." I finished my pancakes and transferred my coffee into a to-go mug. "I've got to go, but I'll try to check in more often."

Hannah hugged me. "Be careful, Cain. And let us know if we can help."

I kissed the top of her head. "If I need anything destroyed, I'll let you know."

She laughed. "I can grow stuff too, remember."

I thought back to the monstrous carnivorous plants she'd grown while angry. Even her creations were destructive. I went to my closet and picked out the Death cloak, then went outside and found Mortis resting among the gravestones. Something vibrated softly from within the cloak. I reached into the inside pocket and pulled out the soul catcher.

It hadn't vibrated before, so I assumed it was an indicator of some kind. I hadn't emptied it yet and that seemed like the most logical reason for this behavior. I climbed onto Mortis and guided him toward the gates. Once we were outside of the protective ring surrounding Sanctuary, I had him take me to wherever it was I needed to go to empty the soul catcher.

He took me through Limbo and past Garrick's house in Purgatory. We journeyed down a path through a forest and stopped at the edge of a wide river. There was a large dock and moored to it was a small boat. A withered old man with papery-thin skin sat on the dock, a fishing pole in his hand.

I recognized the man immediately because I'd met him before. He was Charon, the ferryman.

The end of the pole bent, and he gasped in delight, reeling in the catch. I watched, curious to see what kind of fish lived in the river. He gave a final yank and a ghostly looking catfish wiggled on the end. Charon watched it for a long moment, then wrestled it off the hook and tossed it back into the river. He put aside his pole and stood, turning to face me.

"What in Hades' name have you been doing, Garrick? I've had nothing to do for a week except fish."

"Looks like you enjoy it," I said.

"I love it!" He picked up a mug from the dock and drank the contents. "But I'm not too fond of hearing that the dead are rising on Earth."

I lowered the hood to reveal myself. "I'm not Garrick."

He hissed. "You're the young fool who gave my coin to a dragon."

"Sorry." I shrugged.

Charon's brow pinched. "Where is Garrick? What in Hades' name is happening on Earth?"

"How is it you didn't just go to Garrick's house when he straight-up vanished for a week?"

He frowned. "Yuki won't let me near the place." He belched loudly and took another gulp from his mug. "She doesn't like me for some reason."

I showed him the soul catcher. "Garrick is in a magical coma thanks to the other three horsemen. I was drafted to clean up the mess on Gaia. Now I'm here to do whatever needs to be done with the souls."

Charon shrugged. "Well, get on with it, then."

I shook my head. "What do I do?"

"Just dip it in the Styx and then release it in the air. It'll do the rest."

I looked at the river. "That's the River Styx?"

He nodded.

"Can I become invulnerable by dipping myself in the water?"

Charon looked at me like I was crazy. "That only worked if you did it in the Styx on Earth, but after the Achilles fiasco, the gods removed the magic from it."

"Oh." It would have come in handy against Mars, but I didn't bring that up. "Do you ferry all the souls to their final destinations?"

He waggled a hand. "I used to work exclusively for the Greek gods, but there aren't many going to Hades these days. Most of them are going straight to Hell, so there's not much to be done except waiting on their personal demons to fetch them."

"Ah." I walked to the river's edge and paused. "Some of these souls were driven insane when Garrick wasn't around to collect them."

Charon nodded. "Not the first time we've had the dead rise. The soul catcher usually cleans them up, so maybe it's a good thing they've been incubating in there for a while."

"So, we're not about to have thousands of insane souls flood the dock?"

"They should be recovered by now." His eyes flared. "Gods almighty, things really got out of hand this time, didn't they?"

"They did, indeed." I knelt and dipped the soul catcher in the water. Ghostly shadows scattered in the frigid water, leaving it clear enough to see the bottom. I yanked my hand back up and watched as the inky darkness closed in again. "What are those things?"

"The drowned." Charon poured ale from his cup into the river and the darkness scattered. "The souls of those who leapt into the river rather than face Hell."

I blinked in surprise. "That's a choice?"

"If you can do it before the demon collects you." He shrugged. "I can't say it's a better option than Hell, though."

I looked at the vastness of the dark waters and shook my head. "My gods, there must be hundreds of thousands of souls in the water."

"And the gods only know what else." Charon wheezed in laughter. "Let's just say that not even Death wants to swim in these waters."

"And you?"

He spat into the water. "Oh, they've tried pulling me in, but it's impossible to wrest me from my boat."

The soul catcher started vibrating strongly in my hand, so I tossed it into the air. It began to spin. A flood of gray erupted all around it, spewing countless souls onto the river shore. Though the souls had been little more than gray humanoid shapes when I'd reaped them, they were far more defined here, ghostly versions of their former selves, complete with faces, clothing, and other mortal accoutrements.

And they were all screaming madly, faces carved with insanity.

I backed up, uncertain if I'd just unleashed nearly three thousand wraiths in Purgatory. If I had, things were about to get nasty.

19

The soul catcher continued ejecting souls, lining them up neatly along the shore and out into the fields beyond.

After initial screams of fear, most of the ghosts calmed down, quieting my concerns they might be wraiths.

"What? Where am I?" A ghostly man nearby spun in a circle, face gripped with fear.

"The pain is gone!" A woman fell to her knees. "Almighty Father, thank you for your deliverance! I knew my faith would cure me!"

Dark pools coalesced on the ground. A creature with skin as black as pitch leapt from the darkness and gripped the woman. "Mary Sue, it's so good to meet you!" The demon licked her cheek with a forked tongue.

The woman screamed. "God help me!"

"Oh, Mary Sue Riggins, you put on a good show, didn't you?" The demon cackled madly, dancing in a circle around her, its grotesquely large private parts bouncing between its legs. "But your hatred and judgmental behaviors have made you unworthy of the kingdom!" It wrapped its arms around her. "Welcome home, Mary Sue."

With a final scream, she vanished into the dark pool, and it closed behind her and the demon.

A man shouted in fear as a red arm reached from the ground and jerked him down into Hell. Other demons leapt from the ground, from flaming holes, raw earth, and pits of lava. The demons were all shapes, shades, and sizes. Most were humanoid. Naked succubus wrapped themselves erotically around men and women alike, taunting them with lurid talk and gestures before taking them away. None of the other souls seemed aware of the chaos erupting around them, as if each demon were putting on a show seen only by its intended target.

"What a reaping." A female with red skin and great black bat wings stood next to me. She moaned in pleasure. "We wondered why we hadn't seen a new soul in over an Earth week."

I stumbled back, trying to figure out how she'd sneaked up next to me. "Who in the Hell are you?"

She laughed and traced a black claw down my cloak. "You're not Garrick."

"You just noticed?"

She bit her lower lip. "It is simply unexpected to see someone that is not Garrick. Who are you and what happened to him?"

"Tell me your name and maybe I'll tell you."

"I am Deva, an archdemon of my lord, Satan." She walked behind me, tracing her claws along the cloak as if that was supposed to be sensual. "Do you not feel my presence, stranger?"

I shrugged. "Um, sure?" There was certainly a power to her presence, a radiating sexuality trying to pry its way into my mind. I was trained to resist mind-altering magic, but the cloak probably helped me too.

"Not even Garrick could completely withstand my presence." She completed her walk around and stood in front of me, face sure and calm despite the constant screams of souls being dragged into Hell behind her.

Another group of souls had formed on the other side of the soul catcher, many of them young children with only one or two adults among them. Charon was herding them onto his boat.

"Who are they?" I asked.

Deva shivered and moaned in pleasure. "They are going to Heaven, my dear." She closed her eyes and sighed. "How I envy them."

"Because you're trapped in Hell?"

Deva released another sigh and turned back to me. "It would be nice to have a change from the eternal screaming, the burning, the torture. Don't get me wrong, I dearly love it, but I would enjoy a vacation. I cannot even go to Earth like Ashatha did because Lucifer would be furious."

"I can talk with him if you'd like. Even demons need a holiday every now and then."

Her eyes widened. "Would you?" She gripped my hands, sending sexual tingles straight into my groin. "I would be forever grateful!"

I yanked my hands back as my body responded to her touch. "Okay, I felt that."

She laughed. "I am the archdemon of lust, my dear. It would be a problem if you felt nothing at all."

I tried to think about baseball, but it didn't help. "That was intense."

Deva moaned and licked her lips, revealing pearly white fangs. "And torturous, I hope."

I nodded. "Yeah, it's definitely torturous. Like the worst blue balls I've ever had."

"Excellent. I was worried I'd lost my touch when you didn't respond right away."

I reached into the cloak and adjusted myself. "Nope, you've still got it."

Deva frowned. "You are different from Garrick. Very few humans can resist my presence even when protected by supernatural vestments such as your cloak."

"I'm just a super ordinary guy." I cleared my throat uneasily. "Do you come here for every reaping?"

She shook her head. "Not unless there are some particularly nasty souls to collect. I like watching their faces when they realize where they're going."

The soul catcher stopped disgorging souls and flew toward me. I caught it and tucked it into the cloak. Scores of souls were being dragged into Hell, but there were plenty more to go. "Do you have enough demons to take them all at once?"

"We do, but they all have day jobs as well, so scheduling was a real bitch." Deva reached up to her forehead and stroked one of her small black horns. "There are thousands of underlings, but not all of them are suited to this particular task. We take pride in doing this right and personalizing every experience."

I watched as a man in a business suit fell to his knees before a demon taunting him about his charitable giving.

"You gave millions of dollars so people would think you're such a wonderful humanitarian, George!" The demon cackled maniacally. "But you were only doing it to make yourself feel good, not because you wanted to help!"

Deva stroked her horn a little harder. "I love watching this kind get their due. The politicians are even better, but there don't seem to be many in this batch."

"You have a lot of politicians in Hell?"

She laughed. "All politicians go to Hell."

"Even Gandhi?"

"You wouldn't believe how many people ask that question." Deva sighed. "He wasn't even a Christian."

"Ah." I grunted. "I don't know much about Christianity or other Gaian religions, so this is a learning experience."

She smiled. "Gaian is such a Greek way of putting things."

"I grew up on Feary, and that's what they call it." I shrugged. "Calling it Earth sounds weird to me."

Charon's boat left the shore with a group of wide-eyed children and two adults on board. They seemed oblivious to the cries of those destined for Hell but were interacting among themselves. One of the children laughed and pointed across the river. I peered in that direction and saw people gathered on the distant shore.

"Mommy!" A boy cried out. "It's my mommy and daddy!"

"It's not really them." Deva's smile faded. "But it's easier for young souls to adjust if they think their parents are with them. Unfortunately, most of their parents are bound for my domain."

I grimaced. "Do they remain kids forever?"

"I don't know." Her gaze lingered on the boat. "Perhaps keeping youthful ignorance and bliss is the greatest gift of all."

Her comment struck a chord deep in my chest. I'd never had a chance to be an innocent child, especially not if that vision in Limbo had been accurate. I'd been born in blood, orphaned twice, and raised to be a killer. I tried to remember a time I'd been ignorant or blissful as a child and couldn't. Erolith had started my training young. Fun had been a luxury I wasn't afforded.

"You seem troubled, Death."

I blinked out of my reverie. "My name is Cain."

"I love that name." Deva touched my shoulder briefly. "What troubles you?"

"Everything about this." I scoffed. "But who am I to say that this is fucked up?"

"On that we can agree." The last of the damned souls vanished into the ground and a demon with a face that was half chiseled masculine perfection and half feminine beauty climbed from one of the black pools in the ground.

"My queen, the souls have been secured." The demon's voice was masculine one moment and feminine the next. Both sides sounded exhausted. "May I retire to my chamber for now?"

Deva nodded. "You did an excellent job reallocating resources, Helfin. Enjoy your rest."

"Thank you, my queen." They bowed and leapt into the hole they'd crawled out of. It closed behind them.

"You're a queen?" I said.

She nodded. "I am an archdemon, after all." Deva brushed my hand, sending another torturous wave of lust right to my groin. With a devilish grin, she dropped into the ground and vanished.

"Bitch!" I walked in circles as if that might help me not pitch a tent in the Death cloak. I walked to the river and dipped my hand into the frigid waters. Shadows scattered beneath the surface. The chill and thrill almost instantly banished my body's carnal desires.

I peered across the river where Charon's boat had already finished ferrying the souls to Heaven and was making its way back. The boat bumped against the dock moments later and remained in place despite having no mooring lines.

Charon pursed his withered lips. "I wasn't sure how the demons would handle it, but they did a good job."

"I suppose they did." I stared out at the black waters. "I didn't realize Heaven was across the River Styx."

He shrugged. "This is the divine realm. There are no set physical locations. As the ferryman, I just like having it set up this way."

"Oh." It made sense, but sometimes it was just better to accept things and move on, especially when the death beacon was lighting up like a menorah. "Can I cross the river and take a look in Heaven?"

Charon snorted. "Not even I can enter the gates of Heaven."

I grunted. "Figures that it's a gated community."

"There's a path on the other shore. Not far from there are the gates, guarded by angels and Saint Peter." He shrugged. "You'd think they'd let in visitors, especially those who have served for so long, but they're very picky."

"Too picky, if you ask me."

"No one cares." Charon shook his head. "Especially not them."

I patted down the cloak as if looking for car keys. "Well, I've got souls to reap and a conundrum to solve. If you think of anyone who can remove the curse from Garrick, let me know."

"If Yuki lets me into the house, I'll visit him and offer my prognosis." He bared crooked teeth. "But I don't think she will."

I turned around and nearly ran into Mortis who stood right behind me. I climbed onto his back and checked the death beacon. "Let's go."

Our first stop was no surprise—a hospital where a woman in a coma lay in a bed surrounded by family. Two teary-eyed boys sat in chairs, one of them much younger than the other. A girl slept on a cot next to the mother's bed, and an exhausted looking man, presumably the husband, stood next to the bed holding her hand.

"I don't understand," the husband said to a nurse. "Her body is healing, but she's not waking up."

"We don't understand it either." The nurse shook her head sadly. "It's a miracle she made it here alive after the car wreck. We just don't know if or when she'll come out of her coma."

I looked at Mortis. "If I keep the timer paused, could she recover and go on living?"

He snorted and stomped a hoof.

The youngest boy's eyes widened, and he looked straight at me. "Are you here for Mommy?"

His brother frowned. "Who are you talking to?"

"The skeleton man." The little boy's eyes filled with tears. "Please don't take Mommy. Please!"

I put a finger to my lips. "The others can't see me."

"Please don't!" He ran to me, gripping the cloak and falling to his knees. "Don't take Mommy."

The father wiped his eyes and went to the boy. "David, she'll be okay." He picked him up and took him to the bedside. "The nurse thinks she'll be fine."

"But the skeleton man is here to take her!" David buried his face in his father's shoulder. "I just know it!"

"Fuck me." I blew out a breath and walked over to the woman. I reached my hand toward her body, but the soul refused to come free.

Mortis stomped his hoof again.

"The horsey is so angry!" David bawled.

I realized I hadn't unpaused the death beacon, so I slid my finger along the edge and the steady green blip on the map began blinking. Everyone in the room seemed to freeze in place.

The woman gasped and opened her eyes. "Where have I been?" Her eyes widened when she saw me. "No. Please, no."

I looked at the tears frozen in place on David's little face. "I'm sorry, but I don't have a choice."

She looked at her family and tears trickled down her cheeks. "Tell

Mark it wasn't his fault. I was angry for no reason. If I hadn't left the house—" She began sobbing. "I wasn't paying attention to the road. Please, just give me another chance!"

"I don't have that kind of power." I reached in and took her soul, and the soul catcher did the rest. The world resumed around me. The vitals console beeped loudly, and the heartbeat monitor flatlined.

"No!" David screamed and pointed at me. "He took her! He took Mommy!"

"Debra!" The father's hoarse cry of pain echoed in the hallways. "Debra!"

I climbed on Mortis. "Get me the fuck out of here now!"

He galloped down the corridor and away from the screams. I didn't draw another breath until we were in Limbo. Before I blew it out, we were in a forest. A half-eaten body lay at the bottom of a hill. Despite his throat being torn out by a wild animal, the man twitched and stared at me with wide eyes. I took his soul, ended his torture, and the body went limp.

The next trip took us to a small, dingy house in the middle of nowhere. Mortis stopped outside, so I climbed off and went into the front door. The house reeked of spoiled food. Rats scattered from a garbage can piled high with refuse. I followed the sound of a television droning in another room.

A morbidly obese man was slumped over in an easy chair, a half-eaten steak on a plate in front of him. The body twitched. I reached in through the man's back and pulled out his soul. The edges were slightly frayed and rough, as if it had already started going mad.

The house was packed with newspapers, old mail, and garbage. I wondered if anyone would discover the body for a very long time. Probably not before the rats ate it. I left the house and mounted Mortis.

"Next."

The next stop took us to a cube-shaped mansion in southern California. It was an ugly gray block on a cliff overlooking the ocean, but apparently, someone rich called it home.

"All the money in the world and zero taste." I hopped to the ground, leaving Mortis in the driveway next to the five-car garage. The beacon led me inside the garage where several exotic supercars were parked next to an old, blue minivan.

The blinking dot seemed to be right in front of a Lamborghini, but there was no one there. I checked inside the cars and saw nothing. The minivan was completely empty, lacking anything except for two seats in the front. The interior was coated in black rubber. There were leather straps stained with what looked like dried blood.

A mop and container of bleach sat on a nearby bench. There was no question in my mind that I'd just entered a murderer's house.

20

"Blood, bleach, and a mop." I grimaced. "That doesn't look suspicious at all."

I checked the death beacon again, this time rotating the image, and realized the blip was about a hundred feet below me. A narrow passage in the wall led to a network of chambers. I walked to the wall and felt a tugging sensation, as if a sixth sense were telling me something.

Letting it guide me, I found a small indentation in the wall and touched it. A seam appeared in the wall, opening into an elevator. I stepped inside and pressed one of the two unmarked buttons. The door hissed shut and the car dropped. It slowed and stopped a moment later. The doors opened into a well-lit tunnel.

I followed the tunnel to a cave that looked as if it had been partially finished with concrete and support beams. I walked past a tunnel leading to the right, continuing toward the blip on the map.

A satisfied sigh drew my attention up from the beacon and to a series of clear cubes, each one holding an occupant. A naked man lay next to a teenaged girl in one of the cubes, idly stroking her breasts as he fondled his privates.

Young women in various states of undress were in the other cages, many of them with dull, drugged gazes. One of them lay on the cot in her cage, sobbing uncontrollably.

Judging from the deep bruises on the neck of the teenager next to the man, she'd been strangled to death. She was young—so young. I thought of Shae and Hanna and my fists clenched. I entered the open door of the cube cell.

The man flinched, looked up and around, then reached into a pile of clothes on the floor and pulled out a pair of glasses. He put them on, gaze wandering until it settled on me. "Ah, Death, here you are again."

I froze. "You can see me?"

He frowned. "I thought we settled that months ago." He shook his head. "It took you much longer than usual to come this time. Were you on holiday?"

"What kind of sick fuck are you?"

He stood and looked me up and down. "Something is different about you. The last few times you've been no fun at all, just taking the soul and leaving without so much as a word."

I couldn't believe what I was hearing. Garrick actually let this sicko murder people? "Not on my fucking watch you degenerate piece of shit."

He laughed. "I feel like we're repeating our first encounter again, Death."

I bared my teeth. "You've got the wrong person this time."

"Oh, do—" His eyes widened, and he froze in place.

"What are you doing?" Ithia stepped from the shadows right next to me and snapped her fingers in front of my face. "Cain, look at me!"

I tore my eyes off the psychopath and looked at her, fury burning through my veins. "What do you want?"

"To stop you from further damaging the loom, you idiot." She huffed. "Our offices and responsibilities are tied very tightly together, Cain. Why do you think the loom nearly broke during the zombie outbreak? What do you think will happen if you kill this man?"

"What will happen if I don't?" I looked down at the lifeless body of the girl and couldn't stop seeing Hannah's face even though the two looked nothing alike. "This man—this monster needs to die."

"He will meet his fate, but Death will not be the one to do it." She gripped my cloak. "You have a job, Cain, and right now it's more important than ever that you don't get off track!"

My body trembled with rage and disgust.

Ithia sighed and wiped away a tear. "Bad things have to happen, Cain. I'm sorry, but they just do."

I took deep breaths and walked outside the transparent cube cage. "I don't know why I'm suddenly emotional. Just hours ago, I felt nothing, and now I'm so furious I can barely stand it."

She looked at my bony hand. "Did you meet Deva?"

I flinched. "Yes, why?"

"She's the arch demon of lust, but her touch will incite emotions that are hard to control." Ithia squeezed her eyes shut as if calming herself. "It takes time to recover."

"So, this isn't me?" I felt somewhat relieved. "I thought I was losing it."

"You are losing it." She scoffed. "But you're not wrong to want Alistair dead."

"Alistair?" I looked from her to the frozen man. "You know this dirt bag?"

"He is obsessed with death in general and Death incarnate." Ithia took my bony hand and squeezed it. "Alistair is a powerful necromancer. Years ago, he found a way to watch when souls passed from the body. Those glasses of his are one of his tools. He also has spells stolen from the fae that allow him to detect nearby deities."

"Why didn't Garrick tell someone mortal where to find this sicko?"

"Because that would be breaking fate!" Ithia shook her head. "Neither of us can act on our feelings and snip threads that are not supposed to end."

"Maybe they're supposed to end by our hand." I stared at the dead girl. "Maybe they should end by our hand."

"I thought that way when I first took office as Fate." Ithia released my hand. "I discovered that my best friend was going to die, so I intervened." She shivered violently. "I cut the thread of a man who was going to go into her office building and shoot people because he thought he was unfairly fired. Sheana would have been struck in the stomach and died a painful death. I prevented it."

I grunted. "I sense the moral of the story coming."

"Her thread and the threads of the others grew longer, indicating normal lifespans." Ithia swallowed hard, as if forcing a lump of regrets back down her throat. "Later that day, two of the people who would have died of gunshot wounds, perished when their elevator plummeted twenty stories. A man who should not have died until thirty years later died with them."

"Freak accidents happen," I said.

"A woman who should have died that day was driving home on the interstate when the straps on a logging truck broke. Massive logs fell onto the interstate, crushing cars and causing a horrific pileup. One of the logs speared into her car and decapitated her."

"That's some Final Destination shit right there." I frowned. "Are you making this up?"

"I wish!" She threw up her hands. "Sheana tripped on the sidewalk outside her building and hit her head on a bench at a bus stop. The blow broke her neck."

"Are you saying the loom is self-correcting?"

Ithia nodded. "The zombie uprising nearly broke it, but so long as it has time, it will recover and reset the pattern. Destiny can be restored."

I pushed back the anger and desire to murder Alistair and left it boiling beneath the surface. "He's going to kill all these girls. This prison is the last place they'll ever see."

"He converts some of them into his followers. Not all of them will die."

"Doesn't make me feel any better."

Ithia sighed. "I know. But you must do your job and move on. Please, trust me in this. Alistair is what I call a nexus. Ending him prematurely will affect an entire web, not just one thread. The ripple effect of such a nexus event would be devastating."

I went into the cube cage and stood over Alistair, thinking about how easily I could take off the Death cloak and cut him to ribbons with my brightblade. If I did that and caused a nexus event, a lot more people would die. Fate itself might be shattered. As a former assassin, I didn't generally have a problem with killing. But I'd never cared for indiscriminate murder and seeing Hannah reflected in these young faces made me sick to my stomach.

I knelt next to the dead girl and put a hand to her forehead. In a low whisper, I said, "I will avenge you."

"I heard that," Ithia said.

With time frozen in this area, I couldn't take her soul. I looked over my shoulder at her. "Can we get on with this?"

She nodded.

"—I?" Alistair finished his earlier sentence flinched in confusion and spun around when he realized I was behind him.

I gently slid out the girl's soul and let the soul catcher take it.

Alistair rubbed his hands together. "Now the true joy begins."

I shoved past him, eager to leave before I killed him in one violent reflex.

Ithia was gone, apparently satisfied that I'd control myself.

"You never stick around to see the fun!" Alistair hurried in front of me. "The ceremony doesn't take long."

I stopped. "Ceremony?"

"Yes. I reanimate her and bring out the others." He rubbed his hands together and shivered. "You of all people would love it."

"Love what?"

Alistair grinned broadly and strode toward a door in the cave wall. I followed him, a morbid sense of curiosity drawing me along for the ride. He threw open the door and revealed a sprawling room with red carpet and a giant round bed piled with dozens of people. He snapped his fingers and the people lurched to life, rising in jerky motions.

They were teenagers, mostly female, but with a few males scattered among them. They were dressed in garish costumes. Their bluish skin and glassy eyes told me these people were dead, their bodies reanimated.

Alistair motioned to a woman, and she lurched forward, body jerking grotesquely. "My preservation methods are almost flawless. Their souls might be gone, but their bodies will live forever." He traced a finger down her neck. "They can satisfy any desire."

Rage boiled over. My vision filled with red. The scythe was in my hand and at his neck in an instant, but try as I might, I couldn't kill him with it. I regained my wits and remembered that Death's vestments wouldn't allow it.

Alistair laughed and pushed away the blade. "Haven't we been through this before? You tried this the first time we met, and it didn't work any better then than now." He shook his head. "Are you the same Death I met all that time ago? Has something befallen my dear friend?"

I spun around and stormed out. "Mortis, get your ass down here right now!"

"You really must be someone new." Alistair hurried after me. "You know the horse can't come down here with my protections in place."

I entered the elevator. He tried to follow, but I shoved him back as the doors closed. The elevator shot up and deposited me back in the garage. I continued outside and found Mortis waiting on me. "How is it I can go down there, but you can't? Is there some kind of selective magic in place?"

Mortis bobbed his head. "Fuck!" I prowled back and forth in the driveway, trying to calm the rage I felt. Mortis snorted gently and nudged me with his nose. I met his glowing eyes. "This job sucks. I don't know how Garrick does it!"

Mortis whickered softly and bobbed his head. He flinched suddenly as if someone cracked a whip and backed away, shaking his head.

I wondered if I'd be so furious if Deva hadn't touched me, or if I'd be just as infuriated. I guided Mortis to the street and checked out the next blip. It wasn't far. "Let's go."

His tail flicked with annoyance, and his eyes glowed angrily, but he calmed down and let me onto the saddle.

The next five visits were quick and simple by comparison, but all I could think about was Alistair and how much I wanted to kill him. My phone buzzed in the pocket of my street clothes. I pulled it out and saw it was Hannah. "What's up?"

"I hate her!" Hannah sobbed. "I can't believe she'd do that to me!" She started talking a hundred miles a minute, blubbering so much I could barely understand her.

"Slow down. What happened?"

"We went to dinner with our friends." Hannah sniffled. "Shae went to the bathroom but she was gone a long time. Then I went out back and found her kissing Gabe!"

I groaned. "You didn't kill anyone, did you?"

"No!" Hannah sobbed and sniffled uncontrollably. "C-c-can you come get me?"

I checked the death beacon and counted another dozen souls to collect. Most of them had been on hold for hours before I'd resumed collection. I hated to let them suffer, but hearing Hannah's voice, all I could think about were the girls imprisoned by Alistair.

"Where are you?"

"I'm in that yellow strip mall with the sushi restaurant."

"I'll be there in a minute." I hung up and patted Mortis on the neck. "Can you take me to her?" I envisioned the place in my head, and he took off without so much as a derisive snort. The mall unfolded around us, and I saw Hannah sitting at the base of a street-lamp, crying beneath its dull glow.

I took off the Death cloak and folded it across Mortis's saddle, then walked over to her. Hannah jumped up when she saw me, ran over, and gave me a bone-crushing hug.

"I-I hate them, Cain!" Sobs shook her body. "I can't believe she'd do that after her promise at breakfast dinner!"

I kissed the top of her head. "I'm sorry, Hannah. I don't know why she'd do that either."

She looked up at me, eyes dark pools of sadness. "Take me some-where. Anywhere but here. I don't want to see her ever again!"

I wanted to point out that it'd be really difficult since Shae lived in the same house, but I simply nodded. I'd discovered that was some-times the best thing to do when dealing with other people's feelings. What they felt right then was the most important thing in the world even if it meant nothing in the long run. I thought of Alistair again. Emotion overwhelmed me. I hugged her tighter. "I love you, Hannah." Maybe I was still suffering from Deva's touch, but I didn't care.

Her sobbing grew louder and stronger. "I l-love you t-too, Cain!"

"Let's go on a horsey ride." I pried her arms loose and led her to Mortis. "Mortis, can she come with us, please?"

He gently nudged her shoulder with his nose.

"You're so pretty." Hannah smiled through her tears and rubbed the top of his nose. "Thank you."

He whickered and turned sideways for us to mount. I put on the cloak, allowing myself to remain visible to Hannah. I climbed on first and pulled her up after me. She leaned her head on my back.

"Thanks, Cain."

"Yep." I looked at the death beacon and sighed. "I guess it's take your daughter to work day."

She laughed. "But you're my bro."

I shook my head. "Nah, I'm pretty sure I've morphed into a dad by now."

"But without the lame dad jokes."

I raised an eyebrow. "The what?"

Mortis stomped a hoof, obviously ready to go.

I nudged his ribs with my feet. "Giddy up!"

He took off and we arrived in eastern Europe outside a hospital. I hopped off Mortis and approached a line of gurneys with equipment rigged to them. It looked like the hospital was unable to keep up with the number of people being admitted due to the plague, so they were improvising. I reaped the soul of a woman who hadn't survived. Just as I turned to leave, another dot appeared, blinking white to green as a man in a neighboring bed passed away. I took his soul, then went back to Mortis.

"Did you take their souls?" Hannah said, eyes wide.

I nodded. "Not much to it."

"That was so fast." She stared at the gurneys. "Over in the blink of an eye."

"Maybe I should take you home. This is pretty morbid work."

Hannah shook her head emphatically. "No. I want to see."

"Okay." I climbed onto Mortis, careful not to kick Hannah when I swung my leg over the saddle.

I fetched several more souls across Europe and then we crossed the Atlantic to the eastern coast of the United States. We stopped in the corridor of a hospital, a common theme this night, thanks to the plague.

"Can I watch you up close?" Hannah said.

"People will see you if you get off Mortis."

Mortis bumped my hand and nodded toward Hannah.

She smiled. "I think he wants you to hold my hand, and that'll make me invisible."

"You got all that from him nudging my hand?"

She nodded.

Mortis snorted.

I shot him a look. "He doesn't like me, but he sure likes you."

Mortis bobbed his head.

Hannah's smile brightened. "I can't blame him. You're an ass sometimes."

"Mhm." I slid off Mortis, took Hannah's hand, and willed her to be invisible to any nearby humans. The beacon led us into a nearby room.

My breath caught in my throat when I saw the person on the bed.

21

Hannah gasped. "Oh no."

The tiny figure on the bed was no one we knew personally, but that didn't matter. She couldn't be any older than four or five, all her hair gone, her little body punctured and bruised from IV tubes and needles.

The death beacon indicated the end was almost here.

Hannah touched the little girl's arm.

Her eyes opened and she looked up at us. "Hi."

"Your pain is about to end." Hannah gently stroked her forehead. "We're going to take you somewhere much better."

"Heaven?" she said weakly.

Hannah nodded and wiped away tears. "Heaven."

I cleared my throat to drive away the lump forming there. "How long have you been in the hospital?"

"A long time." The girl smiled. "But I met Miss Jenny and Mrs. Abby and Doctor Walls, and they bring me snacks sometimes and they even brought me puppies to pet one day." Her smile brightened. "And Wonder Woman visited me too!"

Hannah looked at a picture on the wall with the actress who

played Wonder Woman posing with the girl. "Oh, wow, you really got to meet her!"

The girl nodded. "She promised to save all the other kids in the world for me even though she can't help with cancer."

Hannah's lips trembled and more tears spilled out. "I'm so sorry you didn't get a better life."

The light on the death beacon blinked green and the girl's smile faded. Her little body went limp and the alarms on the monitors blared. I reached in and gently pulled her soul free. It was pure and white, softly glowing.

Hannah gasped and shuddered. "Let's take her to Heaven, Cain." She looked up at me imploringly. "Can we do it now?"

I cleared my throat again as the soul catcher took the soul. "Yeah."

Nurses rushed into the room, blindly brushing past us as we left.

Hannah hugged Mortis for a long moment. "I can't imagine the pain of seeing so much death. You're a good, good horse."

Mortis nudged her hair gently, then spared me a glare as if to say I didn't appreciate him enough.

I blew out a sigh. "Let's go."

We rode into Purgatory and found Charon sitting on the dock drinking from his mug. He rose unsteadily to his feet. "Back already?"

I nodded. "I cleared most of the backlog."

"Good." He took another swig. "Let's get to it."

I dipped the soul catcher in the water, then let it do its thing. Twenty-seven souls emerged. The murdered teenaged girl appeared, looking frightened and confused.

"Where am I?"

The cries of other ghosts echoed her sentiment, many of them in different languages, but she didn't see anyone else. Before I could answer, the demons appeared.

"Your mother tried to warn you, Rebecca." A demon with yellow skin and an overly sexualized body danced around her. "You told your daddy to go fuck himself when he said you shouldn't go to wild parties. But you never listen, do you? Now look what's happened to you."

"I didn't know!" She screamed. "I didn't know!"

He cackled with laughter, flouncing around her. "Youth is wasted on the young and wisdom is wasted on the old." He laughed again. "Perhaps you'll learn a lesson over the next eternity."

"Please, no!" Her screams trailed off as he dragged her into the hole, straight down to Hell.

I'd known what to expect, but that didn't make it any easier to accept. "Fuck."

Hannah watched in horror as the other souls were dragged to Hell. "All of them deserve Hell? What kind of sick god would allow that?"

Charon, meanwhile, had taken the little girl by the hand and led her onto his boat. "You're going to love Heaven. Did you know that's where all the puppies and kitties go when they die?"

"Puppies and kitties in heaven?" The girl's eyes widened in delight. "What about bears and tigers?"

"Plenty of them too." He sat her down. "And you can ride them all you want."

"Yay!" she giggled and clapped her hands. "What about Mommy and Daddy?"

"They're still alive, but they get to visit you."

"Oh, I can't wait!" she said. "It feels so good not to be sick anymore."

Hannah looked back and forth from the screaming souls to the happy little girl, her face torn with mixed emotions. "This is bullshit, Cain. If the only way to be innocent enough to make it into heaven is to be a kid, then the system is broken!"

"Do you hear that Father?" Wings rustled and Lucifer landed next to me, grinning widely. "Your system is rubbish!"

I frowned. "I thought you didn't like coming to the divine realm."

"I don't, but I wanted to see how things were going." He patted Hannah's shoulder. "I'm glad to see you're educating the girl on the horrors of the Almighty's everlasting love."

"I thought Jesus was all people needed." Hannah watched in distraught horror at the lone soul being ferried across to Heaven.

"The bible thumpers told me as long as you accept Jesus, you're forgiven and saved."

"Yes, except most people don't really accept him." Lucifer shook his head sadly. "They just pay lip service to it. Also, it doesn't help that the people who rewrote the Bible repeatedly across the centuries, managed to leave out some important bits."

"Important bits?" Hannah's eyes widened. "Like what?"

"Let's just say that kings, priests, and politicians managed to create a book that grants them control over the population without actually providing worshippers the information that could save them." He chuckled. "You see, you have to genuinely live life like Christ. Be loving, forgiving, and non-judgmental, or at least try your level best to do it. Love your neighbor as yourself, and all that."

She spun on him. "Is that really all there is to it?"

Lucifer laughed. "All there is to it? Goodness, young lady, living like that in an age of social media makes it harder than ever!"

I thought it over. "So, the important part that was left out is that you have to genuinely live by his example?"

"Exactly. Simply paying lip service to being saved isn't enough. The interpretations make it sound like once you're saved, you're always saved, but it's not that simple. It's a constant struggle to make the world a better place." Lucifer shrugged. "Father has never seen fit to correct mankind on their mistake, so most Christians get baptized and think they're Heaven bound."

I pursed my lips. "Can people ever earn their way out of Hell?"

"It's possible, but rarely happens." Lucifer watched Charon's boat reach the other side. "People in Hell are much like those on Earth—simply too caught up in their own guilt and issues to even think about redeeming themselves."

Hannah shivered. "The system is broken. Someone needs to fix it."

"Are you volunteering?" Lucifer grinned and turned to me. "I'm glad to see you stopped the zombie uprising, but have you made any progress on saving your friend and Athena from Soultaker?"

I shook my head. "I had to catch up on soul reaping, but now I'm going to find the Morrigan and ask her a few questions. Maybe she or another god of death can lead me to Thanatos."

"That would be a good start." He turned away from the river. "Well, please come see me if I can be of any service. Things are boring without you around."

I nodded. "Thanks."

Lucifer's wings flared and he shot into the sky.

"Lucifer?" Deva appeared from a fiery hole, looking around wildly. "I felt his presence!"

Hannah grimaced. "Just missed him."

She glanced at Hannah, then to me. "Did I?"

"Just barely." I shrugged. "Sorry."

She blew out a breath. "Curses! He hasn't visited the riverside in years."

"I forgot to put in a good word about your vacation time," I said. "I'll try to remember next time."

"You're absolutely gorgeous, by the way." Hannah fluttered her eyelashes, totally fan-girling over the arch demon of lust. "Wow, can I touch your wings?"

I groaned. "Her powers are affecting you, Hannah."

Deva frowned. "No, I'm not using my aura right now."

I returned the frown. "You're not?"

Hannah huffed. "God, Cain, she's got perfect fingernail claws and that black hair cascading down her red skin is just to die for."

"Well, thank you, darling." Deva bared her fangs in a smile. "There's something quite powerful about you as well, but I can't put my finger on it."

"She's a demigod," I said. "Very powerful. Very dangerous."

"Ooh, I love danger." Deva approached her.

I held up a hand. "And she's a teenager, so you're way too old, okay?"

"Age is just a number." Deva stepped closer.

"No, it isn't. Back off."

Hannah giggled. "You're so cute when you're protective."

I took her hand. "Let's go. Now."

Hannah groaned. "But—"

"No buts. I am not letting the arch demoness of lust get near you."
I tossed her up on Mortis and climbed on.

Deva watched me with a wicked smile. "It's no wonder Lucifer
came here. You are two of the most interesting beings I've met in
eons."

"And we bid you farewell." I turned Mortis. "Let's go home."

We galloped into Limbo and emerged in the forest outside the
perimeter of Sanctuary's protections.

Hannah stiffened. "I really don't want to go home yet. I don't want
to see Shae."

I sighed. "Look, this won't be the last time someone lets you down.
You need to deal with it head on."

"She betrayed me!"

"Maybe, maybe not. Do I need to ship her back to Alpha to stay
with the Cain there?" I gave her a steely look. "Because I've got too
much going on to deal with this kind of drama."

Hannah slumped against me. "I'm sorry, Cain. I've never really
liked anyone enough to date them. Most of my tween and teen life
was pretty shitty until I met you."

"You battled Torvin Rayne with godlike weapons on the shores of
Oblivion." I patted her hand. "I think you can handle a little romantic
trauma."

"I don't know." She groaned. "This feels worse than anything ever."

"Well, don't let it control you." I stopped Mortis outside the church
and slid off after Hannah. "Confront it and deal with it."

"That's a very Cain way of dealing with things."

"It gets better results than ignoring it." I patted Mortis on the neck
to see if he'd give me a friendly nose nudge, but he flinched and
trotted off into the darkness. "Fuck you too, then."

"Wow, confronting Mortis sure is paying dividends." Hannah
giggled. "He probably doesn't like that you haven't done anything to
help Garrick."

I threw up my hands. "When have I had time to deal with that?"

"He thinks you've stolen the job from Garrick." Hannah nodded emphatically. "You're a homewrecker. Mortis thinks he'll never get his friend back and he's sad."

"I don't want this job, as I've made abundantly clear." I really needed to get going so I could find the Morrigan, but I was starving.

Hannah's gaze settled on her clockwork car where it was parked at a crooked angle to the side of the garage. "Shae is home."

"Good." I marched up to the front door, disabled the wards, and went inside to make a sandwich.

Shae jumped up from the couch when I came in and immediately looked disappointed. "Is Hannah with you?"

I continued to the counter and took a loaf of my homemade bread from the breadbox. "Maybe."

"Yes." Hannah stood in the doorway, dark eyes locked on Shae. "I saw you kissing Gabe."

"First of all, he kissed me." Shae held up her hands imploringly. "He lured me away from the others and said he wanted to talk to me and then just started kissing me!"

"He was grabbing your ass too!" Hannah shot back.

"Right before I picked him up and threw him in the dumpster." Shae huffed. "But you didn't stick around for that part, did you?"

Hannah bit her lower lip and looked down. "No. I just saw you kissing and ran away."

"If you'd confronted her right away, you would've seen her throw the kid in the dumpster," I said.

Hannah and Shae turned to me. "Shut up, Cain!"

I went back to making my sandwich.

"I'm not gonna lie," Shae said. "I liked kissing him, but I like kissing you more. I like the way your hands feel on my body."

I harrumphed. "Gods be damned, can you talk about this where I don't have to listen?" I picked up the cutting board with the tomato and other ingredients on it and took it into my room where I closed the door and activated the silencing sigils, muting their discussion.

The last thing I wanted to hear was my two wards talking about their sex and love lives. I hated the protective instincts it triggered in me when I wasn't even related to them. They were eighteen—grown ass adults that didn't need me making decisions for them.

I finished making my sandwich and bit into it. The taste of my garden-grown tomatoes was enough to elicit a groan of pleasure. It was a slice of Heaven in this god-forsaken hell I was currently trapped in. There were too many moving pieces, too many unanswered questions between me and a solution to reviving Garrick or releasing souls from Soultaker.

"Just need to think this through." Except I didn't know where to begin. Was tracking down other gods of death the best next step, or should I confront the other horsemen and force them to release Garrick from their curse? There was simply too much I didn't know. But there might be someone who did. I just had to go talk to him.

I finished my sandwich and opened the bedroom door. Hannah and Shae jumped back from the door, fists raised as if knocking.

"God, Cain, are you deaf?" Hannah threw up her hands.

"I put a silencing spell on the door." I walked past them and started cleaning my dishes in the sink.

"We're sorry we started getting personal in front of you." Hannah stood across the island counter from me. "We know you don't like that."

I began drying my plate. "It's none of my business. You're both adults and can do what you want."

"But you hate it when people get personal in front of you." Hannah looked amused. "And we're sorry."

Shae nodded. "We'll try to get down and kinky where you can't see or hear us."

I glared at her. "Someone's about to get banished to another dimension."

Her eyes widened. "I was just joking."

I finished drying the dishes and grunted. "So was I. Mostly."

Hannah laughed, but Shae just looked at me uncertainly.

I picked up the cloak from the couch and headed toward the door.

"Where are you going?" Hannah said.

"Feary. I've got some questions that need answers." It was a long-shot and if it didn't pay off, I was on my own.

22

Mortis took me to Feary, delivering me to Imperial University in a matter of minutes. His method of instant travel was one I'd certainly miss once I was done with the job.

Thanks to the cloak, not even pixies seemed to see me. They could usually look through any kind of glamour, meaning the cloak was using some very powerful magic, indeed.

I entered the history building and walked down a winding hall. A familiar voice emanated from ahead, leading me to the room where Raghat the orc was teaching a class. I took a seat in the back and took out the Death manual while I waited for him to finish. It was time to fully educate myself on my duties and abilities, not to mention discover answers to a few troubling questions.

For example, if the wards around Sanctuary and Alistair's mansion prevented Mortis from fast traveling inside of them, was there a way to prevent Death from reaching a body? Could someone like Alistair physically block me from reaching bodies and create a massive zombie uprising?

I found the answer in the first section. The Death cloak, it seemed, allowed Death to draw nearby souls to him if the corpse couldn't otherwise be reached. I studied the section, thinking it might offer a solution to reaping souls from zombie mobs without ever having to get close to them.

I'd just reached the halfway point of the manual when the class broke into applause as Raghat finished acting out his latest history lesson. The orc had a flair for the dramatic and he could tell a story like no one else. He was far different from any orc I'd met, which was probably why he was the only orc allowed at the university.

I waited for the crowd to thin out and headed down the aisle of the stadium-seating room where he stood at the podium. A pair of female elves had cornered him and were making eyes at him.

"We'd love some private lessons, professor," one said. "You're amazing!"

No one noticed me still shrouded in the cloak.

Raghat cleared his throat. "You're both simply too kind, but I will be busy writing, I'm afraid."

"You don't need any fun time?" The second elf winked at him. "You're a legend, having survived the Dead Forest and driven off a scourge!"

He bared his tusks in a grin. "That's quite a compliment, but I was merely there to record history. Had not the Oblivion Guard swooped in and saved the day, all of Feary might have been doomed."

"That can't be the total truth." The first elf pursed her lips. "Perhaps you can tell us what really happened while we share the comfort of your bed."

"That would be inappropriate, I'm afraid." He packed his books into a satchel. "Now, if you'll excuse me, I must go."

The elves looked at each other and nodded, as if mentally communicating something, then drew swords.

"You will tell us what happened, or things will get unpleasant." The first bared her teeth. "We know the fae are covering up something and the people deserve to know the truth."

Raghat groaned. "You conspiracy theorists need to leave me alone. I didn't cover up anything!"

They stepped forward, swords pointed at his chest.

Raghat could handle himself, but I was in a hurry. I willed myself visible to the three of them.

The elves cried out in surprise as the Grim Reaper appeared, massive scythe at the ready.

"What ghoul is this?" one cried out. "The fae have sent an assassin!"

"Run or die!" I growled. "Flee, you wretched things!"

The elves dropped their swords and sprinted out of the classroom.

Raghat stared at me, mouth hanging open in astonishment. "I did not know Death made visits to Feary. Are there Christians here?"

I lowered the cowl and smirked. "Not that I know of, but I've seen stranger things."

He gasped in pleasure. "Cain, my friend! How did you—" he looked me up and down. "Create such a convincing illusion?"

"It's no illusion." I willed the cloak to resemble street clothes. "I'm temporarily reaping souls since the current Death is bewitched by a curse."

"My goodness." Raghat sat on a stool. "I take it this is not a social visit?"

"It is not." I pulled up another stool. "Did you publish a fae approved accounting of our adventures in the Shalthaes Woodlands?"

Raghat sighed sadly. "Erolith assigned a minder to me during my writing. They demanded a full and true account of our experiences. Then they edited and altered it substantially, making the Oblivion Guard and the high fae the heroes of the story."

"They left me out, I suppose?"

He shook his head. "Raze, the high fae who led the cult of Shub-Nuggurath is never mentioned. They tried to make you the villain, but I convinced them to place you in a minor role. You were blamed for attacking and burning Ecrin to the ground."

"That's not exactly minor." I scoffed. "The drow murdered those people at the command of the fae."

"Precisely. But it was much better than them making you the cult leader. The propaganda pieces they publish about you are terrible.

Did you know the account of the Beast War makes you the villain and claims you were murdering and enslaving griffins and other sentient beasts to wage war?"

"I haven't read it, but I don't doubt it. The fae leadership wants me to be seen as a villain, not a savior." I blew out a breath. "I need to have a talk with the high fae one day. It's enough that they call me a traitor and send their minions to kill me every time I visit Feary. But claiming I burned a village to the ground is just too much."

"It's pure madness." Raghat blew out a breath. "I should have left you out of it altogether, but I had no idea they'd go through such lengths to brand you as the arch villain of the story."

"Well, enough about me." I leaned back on the stool. "I've got some major problems and I hope you have useful information."

"Ask away." Raghat looked at the door at the far back of the room. "We should have some privacy here."

"I don't care who hears this." I summarized the adventures of the past few days for context, then told him what I needed. "I need to find the original Thanatos, but I have no idea where to start looking. I was considering asking other gods of death if they could help."

"That would be a waste of time," Raghat said. "Though most of my evidence is anecdotal and based on myth, the fae allowed me access to their secret library when I wrote about our time in the Shalthaes Woodlands. I discovered that there is almost no cross-communication between pantheons, and especially not between the gods of death. The few exemptions would be between the Greek and Norse gods. I suggest you find Loki's daughter, Hel, and speak with her first."

"The Norse goddess of death?"

He nodded. "Your timing is quite fortunate. I was given a book only recently that detailed a romance between Hel and Thanatos. He supposedly went to Helheim to be with her. Even if he's no longer there, she might know where to find him."

I narrowed my eyes. "Who gave you this book?"

"One of my students." Raghat dug into his satchel and produced a leatherbound tome. "She wanted me to do a lecture on Thanatos because he was such a tragic figure."

Receiving a book about Thanatos right now seemed almost too fortuitous. Ever since meeting Raghat, I'd come to rely on him for hard-to-find historical information. If someone wanted to indirectly provide me with information, giving it to Raghat was a clever way to do it. I wondered if another god was trying to help me without making themselves known, or if I was overthinking this.

I was grateful for the information, but I was also wary and suspicious without knowing the source. However, since I had no other leads to follow, I couldn't afford to ignore valuable information, no matter the source.

I opened the book. The pages were yellowed and ancient, but slick to the touch—probably from a preservation enchantment. The text was written in an ancient dialect of Faeicht used by high fae scholars. It was definitely not a book an average student would simply have on them or find in a library, much less hand over to their history professor.

Someone was helping me. Someone who knew I relied on Raghat for information. Who that someone was, however, was a mystery. Solving said mystery could wait until a later time. For now, I had a date with Hel.

"Thank you, Raghat." I handed him the book. "This information is invaluable."

Raghat nodded solemnly. "I'm glad to help. Layla was—is—a great warrior and a good friend of yours."

"Yeah." I blew out a breath. "I don't suppose you know anything about overturning the curse on Garrick, do you?"

"Can you better describe how he was cursed?"

I nodded. "Garrick still maintained an apartment on Gaia. His companion, Yuki, told me that he would slip away to play video games, watch TV—just do normal human stuff. The three horsemen wanted Garrick to ride with them and start Armageddon, but he refused. So, they waylaid him in the apartment and put a combo curse on him. A shaman and an angel looked at him and neither knew how to unbind the curse. They said only the ones who placed it could remove it."

Raghat tapped a fingernail against a tusk as he thought. "There are some universal cures to most curses, such as unicorn hearts, but the cost of such a magnificent, endangered creature is too high. The only way to remove most curses is through death."

I scoffed. "That's the kind of solution that doesn't help anyone."

"Ah, but in this case it might." He grinned tuskily. "As Death, can you not return a soul to a healthy body?"

I frowned and gave it some thought. "One of the Greek gods told me they couldn't convince Garrick to move souls into their soldiers in the divine realm, so the Morrigan was doing it. But those bodies are probably new ones created by the gods. I don't know if I can put a soul back into its original body even if it was restored to life."

"If you killed Garrick's body in some way that was repairable, perhaps you could hold onto his soul and return it to the body." Raghat tilted his head and gazed at the wall for a moment. "It would likely require divine help. Perhaps Hera or the Morrigan could advise you."

"Killing Garrick to save him is an awful idea, but it's the best I've heard so far." I blew out a breath. "There's no way I'll convince the other horsemen to remove the curse willingly, so unless I can somehow overpower them and force them to do it, there's nothing else I can do."

"It seems best to avoid them at all costs." Raghat shuddered. "If they're successful in bringing about the end days, what would the apocalypse mean for those of us in Feary?"

"Probably nothing." I shrugged. "It would mean death on a massive scale in Gaia though."

"Would that also affect non-Christians?"

"Almost certainly," I said. "I don't think War, Famine, and Pestilence are limited as much by religion as Death is."

"I suggest you speak with Hera or the Morrigan next." Raghat took out a quill and jotted notes in a book. "Would it be okay if I document this, Cain? I think others would enjoy reading about your trials and tribulations as Death."

"Sure." I raised an eyebrow. "As long as you're not asking to ride along with me."

"Rest assured I'm not." He grinned. "I simply ask that you give me a detailed accounting so I might accurately depict the story. Whether you desire it or not, you are an important historic figure."

"Not by choice."

"Certainly not, but you are out of necessity." He continued writing. "If only the fae weren't so determined to make you the villain."

I stood and patted him on his broad shoulder. "I'm afraid that's how it will be so long as the fae rule."

"Then they should not rule." He scowled. "I strongly oppose their censorship and heavy-handed dealings."

I shook my head. "Stop." I looked around for pixies, but the fae had multiple ways to spy. "You're on their list now. I wouldn't doubt it if they're listening to our conversation right now."

Raghat flinched. "The thought never occurred to me."

"Well, it should." I blew out a breath. "The faes' minions just forced you to rewrite history. They know your words are more dangerous than most, due to your popularity. You need to be careful."

Raghat nodded solemnly. "Perhaps. But I am beginning to believe that perhaps the path I'm meant to follow is not that of a history teacher. Perhaps my words can lay bare the sins of the fae and hold them to account."

"Raghat, if you do that, you're signing your own death warrant." I slapped a hand on the table. "The Oblivion Guard isn't simply a defensive, reactionary force. The fae use them to silence dissenters as well."

"You know this from experience, I suppose?"

I nodded. "I followed orders without question. I was brainwashed like the rest of them."

"Until the Hollow Hills incident."

I raised an eyebrow. "Very few outside the Guard even know that name."

"It was the name of the farm where the humans hid their children and spouses so the fae couldn't get to them." Raghat sighed. "The human-fae war was already quite brutal, but when most of the human safehouses were hit in the span of a night, it turned the war into a bloodbath of the innocent."

"I was literally haunted by the ghosts of the Hollow Hills." I dropped back onto the stool. "After saving Hannah, the ghosts were ready to go onto the afterlife, so Death took them. Lately, I feel as if I've been returning to old form, and I'm not sure that's a good thing."

"Worry not, friend. You were indelibly changed, I think." He smiled. "You're no longer a brainwashed minion of the Oblivion Guard."

"It's not so much that but my range of emotions seems to have withered lately." I shrugged. "Maybe I'm just realizing that I'm not a family man."

"I believe you're too overwhelmed with emotions," Raghat said. "Mars murdered Layla. Aura from Beta murdered Athena before your very eyes. It was a terrible betrayal even though she wasn't either of the Auras you know."

I almost disagreed on principle but sat back and gave it some thought. I'd gone from emotionless murder puppet to a haunted free man that had developed connections over the years. One of those had been with Aura. When one of her alternate dimension doppel-gangers had betrayed me, it felt as if she'd just driven a dagger into my chest.

As usual, I'd pushed that aside, rationalizing that Aura Beta was damaged goods from another dimension. A poor soul that had followed her dreams of killing gods and ended up an insane train wreck thanks to constant use of the ring, Panoptes.

My Aura was not that Aura. But if she'd followed her original path, then she would have become that terrible person. That poten-tial had seeded mistrust in me whether I wanted to admit it or not. Yes, my Aura had betrayed me once already, but that was nothing compared to the destruction of an entire world.

"Cain, here is something else to consider." Raghat looked around the room as if expecting an incursion from the Oblivion Guard at any moment. "Death is not a major deity, correct? In fact, Garrick is but a mortal man fulfilling a job. Is it possible Garrick is still awake and well in dimension Alpha?"

"I just had this conversation with Aura."

"You did?"

I nodded. "I wish I'd had an extra Garrick to help me during the zombie uprising, but the road ahead involves tracking down Thanatos. The Garrick here had no idea how to find Thanatos, so I don't think his doppelgangers would either."

"Ah, yes. Quite right." Raghat clicked his tongue. "And here I thought I had a wonderful idea."

The hairs on the back of my neck rose. I turned toward the source and saw nothing. Pulling the cowl over my head, willed it to let me see what I sensed. Five cloaked figures shrouded in glamour were fanning out to positions around the room, effectively surrounding us.

"Fuck." I growled. "The Oblivion Guard is here."

Raghat's bushy eyebrows rose. "Well, it seems my time has come to an end."

23

Another figure entered the room, but he was clearly visible.

"It's your father, Cain."

Erolith cast his gaze about the room, a look of calm confusion etched into his brow. He waved a hand in the air before him, tracing sigils so quickly, his fingers were a blur. He looked past me, then did a double-take. "Cain, is that you?"

I put a hand on Raghat's shoulder. "Maybe you're not dead just yet."

My adoptive father peered toward me. "I'm impressed by whatever glamour you're using. I cannot hear you, and your body seems to be two-dimensional."

I willed him to see me. His eyes flashed with something like surprise, but it was so brief as to be hardly noticeable to anyone who didn't know his stoic nature. Keeping the hood over my head to preserve the mystery, I said, "Why are you here, Erolith?"

"Cain, I know that's you," he replied. "I heard Raghat's half of the conversation."

I glanced around at the still hidden guardians fanned around the room. "Is there a reason you have five guardians surrounding us?"

Erolith pursed his lips. "You can see them." It wasn't a question.

I reached back and summoned the scythe. "I'd appreciate it if they left the room before I'm forced to reap their souls."

Some of the shrouded guardians gave uneasy glances at their companions, but their training had put them through far more frightening situations than fighting the Grim Reaper.

I drew Soultaker to reinforce the point. "Or, I can simply add them to the army of the dead in my magical sword."

Now some of them looked concerned. It was one thing to die and yet another to have your soul drafted into an army of the undead. They might not know about Soultaker specifically, but on Feary, it was best to take any magical threat seriously.

Erolith's fingers flicked in minute gestures that only trained guardians would notice. The hidden figures faded into sight and quickly marched up the aisles and out the door. I banished the scythe and sheathed Soultaker. My father walked down the stairs of the auditorium, approaching in a slow but sure manner as if to telegraph that he meant no harm. "I have excused the others for now, but I'm afraid your orc friend has spoken treason against the high fae and must be arrested."

"Treason?" I scoffed. "What about the elves who tried to coerce him into telling the truth about the events of the Shub-Nuggurath incident?"

"They were arrested once they left." He nodded curtly at Raghat. "It is unsurprising that you have become a flame to insurrectionists."

I lowered the cowl and let my flesh face return.

Erolith watched with interest. "Your part of the conversation was muted, but I gathered from what Raghat said you are now employed as a death deity of some sort."

"I am Death." I bowed grandly. "The Christian version, anyway."

"An interesting choice of human religions." He continued watching me in his typical unnerving way. "Perhaps if you shared more information with me, I would be willing to overlook Raghat's grave crimes."

"You're only here because he said my name." I returned his gaze. "The treason is just trumped-up bullshit to use as leverage."

"It is leverage, yes, but he did commit a crime."

Raghat scoffed. "I have talked about such things with others and never had a visit from you."

"He doesn't care what you say, Raghat." I shook my head. "Erolith isn't like Torvin who would send out kill squads at the slightest mention of treason. Erolith likes to identify the roots, the trunk, and the branches before uprooting the tree."

"An apt characterization of my methods, Cain." Erolith bobbed a nod. "But that does not mean I will not take Raghat into custody should I not receive a full accounting of your situation."

I gave the offer some thought. Erolith didn't make idle threats, but he also didn't make threats simply to gain information either. Not unless that information was valuable. Then again, this was a strange situation, so he might just want fresh gossip.

Doubtful.

I folded my arms over my chest. "Tell me why this information is so valuable to you. You wouldn't have come barging in here if something Raghat said hadn't alarmed you."

"Perceptive." Erolith nodded approvingly. "Naturally, I am aware of the situation on Gaia and have been monitoring it closely. The queens want the mortals—the nubs, as you call them—to remain unaware of the supernatural world. The dead rising and walking the streets is unacceptable for obvious reasons. Due to the complexity of the various pantheons, I was unable to discern the root cause of the zombies. I am not surprised to find out you're involved."

Raghat snorted in amusement. "Cain seems to find a way to be at the epicenter of most apocalyptic events."

"Let me assure you that my involvement is neither voluntary nor desired." I sat back on the stool. "After being forced to take on this job, I have since stopped the zombie uprising, but haven't fixed the root cause."

"I would hear the entire story." Erolith located another stool and pulled it up to the table.

I sighed long and loud because I felt like I'd told the story a million times already. "Garrick is the fulltime Grim Reaper, but War, Famine, and Pestilence put a hex on him so he's in a coma. Garrick was going to help me find the original Thanatos so I could figure out how to retrieve Athena's and Layla's souls from Soultaker. But with him in a coma there was no one reaping Christian souls. The bodies were reanimating as the souls went insane. I was forced to temporarily take up the mantle of Death since no one else could. Since then, I've culled the zombie uprising, gotten into a cat and mouse game with the other three horsemen, and managed to help Hannah deal with some personal issues. But I'm no closer to finding Thanatos or a way to free souls from Soultaker and I don't know how to free Garrick from the curse."

Erolith pursed his lips. "I knew you were destined for great things, Cain. Serving as a deity is quite an accomplishment."

I flinched at the unexpected compliment. Erolith had paid me perhaps two other compliments in my entire life, making them easy to remember. "I'd say it's more of an inconvenience than anything else."

"I met Thanatos long ago when Christianity was but a novelty among the humans." Erolith's gaze went distant. "He was the brooding sort, which was natural, given his lineage comes from gods of night and darkness. He had a fondness for Christians, primarily because he approved of the new direction Yahweh decided to take with his new forgiveness policy. He befriended Jesus and became the new god of death for Christians even though the number of believers in the Greek gods was still quite high at the time."

"That was excellent timing on his part." Raghat looked up from writing. "Is it okay if I document this?"

Erolith nodded. "It's already documented in the secret fae library which you have access to."

"How exciting!" Raghat continued writing.

I tried not to get my hopes up. "I assume you don't know where Thanatos is presently?"

"I'm afraid not." Erolith seemed to nod to himself. "As Christianity spread and the number of living people multiplied, he became quite disenchanted with his role. Some say he asked for a final death from gods of another pantheon and received it. Others say he found happiness with the Norse gods."

Raghat spoke without looking up from writing. "Perhaps in Helheim?"

"Perhaps." Erolith leaned forward. "Cain, it is imperative that Athena be restored to life. Though the queens are loath to admit that they need the gods, I will tell you that our forces in the divine realm are spread very thin already. Losing a goddess of war has amplified that issue greatly."

I barked a laugh. "So, the high fae need their favorite punching bag to help them?" I scoffed. "Now I know the real reason you came here when you heard my name."

He raised an eyebrow. "Well, you are impossible to find on Gaia unless you're at Voltaire's."

"By design." I grunted thoughtfully. "The sooner I find Thanatos, the faster we can free Athena, provided Thanatos knows how to undo Soultaker's magic."

"I will ask around and do what I can to help," Erolith said.

A thought occurred to me. "Did you indirectly give Raghat a book about Thanatos and Hel?"

His other eyebrow rose. "No."

He couldn't lie, but he could misdirect. Since helping me aligned with the interests of the high fae, there was no reason for him to be indirect. Someone else must have made sure the book fell into Raghat's hands. I switched back to the subject at hand. "Do the fae have forces fighting in the divine realm?"

"Yes." Erolith paused as if that was all he would offer on the subject, but then he continued. "There are armies of goblins, orcs, ogres, and so forth who are raised and trained in the divine realm. The Morrigan crafted special spells to keep their bodies and souls intact no matter how badly they are slaughtered. The bodies regenerate over time, allowing the same beings to enter battle where they die time and time again, resurrect, and return to fight again."

I grimaced. "What a hellish existence."

He nodded. "Unfortunately, some outsiders have forged weapons which destroy souls, meaning the fighters will no longer resurrect. Only the rarity of those weapons has helped us maintain numbers."

"I have two Soultakers. Why not use them to fight?" I almost slipped up and told him I had three of them, but I didn't want anyone knowing about my access to Dimension Beta's apocalypse weapons.

"It has been discussed, but Mars told us that many of the outsider souls that are trapped in Soultaker will not follow the commands of the sword's wielder and will eventually turn on whoever holds it. Any being who is killed by the undead soldiers from Soultaker will also have their soul join the undead army."

That was something I hadn't even considered. "The wielder would just be building an army of outsider souls that could turn on you."

"Precisely."

Raghat chuckled. "You might say it's a double-edged sword."

"In all senses of the word," Erolith said. "It is a weapon that should never have been crafted."

"Amen to that." I stood. "It's been fun chit-chatting, but I need to get back to work. Souls to reap, a long-lost death god to find—you know, the usual."

Erolith rose. "Check in with me in a few days and I will let you know if I've uncovered any new information."

"I will, thanks." I patted Raghat on the shoulder. "Thanks for your help."

"A pleasure as always, Cain!" His eyes widened. "Oh, and if you do visit the Norse gods, be sure to see if Andhrímnir will give you a taste of Sæhrímnir."

I stared at him in confusion. "Who and what are you talking about?"

"Sæhrímnir is a boar that's killed and eaten every night, according to Norse mythology." Raghat rubbed his hands together. "If true, it's literally bacon of the gods. I'm quite curious to know if it's the best bacon in existence."

"Oh, really?" I didn't even have to think about my response. "I'll definitely find this Andhrímnir and ask for a taste of the good stuff then."

"Yes, please do!" Raghat rubbed his hands together again. "And bring me back a piece, please."

"I'll do what I can." I nodded at Erolith, then hopped onto Mortis who'd been standing in the corner unseen by the others all this time. "Hi-ho Silver and away!"

Mortis gave me a dirty look and stood still.

"Oh, you need somewhere to go." I gave it some thought. "Helheim?"

Mortis leapt forward, traversing folded Limbo. Wood clopped beneath his hooves and vertigo pulled on my insides. We were galloping full speed down the branch of a massive tree. A great city glittered in its highest branches. Mortis leapt from the branch, carrying us down into the dense canopy of what could only be Yggdrasil—the tree of life.

I was perfectly safe in the saddle and trained to weather even the roughest rides, but our mad dash down a realms-spanning tree was the closest I'd come to feeling anxiety since the first time I'd seen R'lyeh in Cthulhu's dreams. Mortis leapt again and we entered freefall, nothing but stars and the void to one side and the enormous twisting trunk of Yggdrasil to the other.

The ground below rushed to meet us. Mortis shifted and his hooves sparked against the tree trunk, slowing us at the last minute for a smooth landing. Without pause, he dove beneath the ground, racing along a massive tunnel that followed an equally massive root. Chunks of the root were missing, torn out as if gnawed on by a giant rodent.

We dodged down another tunnel, traveling ever downward along the root and emerged in a sea of stars trapped in a mesh of giant roots. A giant serpent slithered along the roots next to us, its body thick around as a jumbo jet. It was gnawing on the roots with sharp teeth, barely making a dent despite its enormous size. Mortis ran right past its chomping teeth, black mist billowing from his nostrils. He glanced back at me as if hoping this close call frightened me.

I tried to raise an eyebrow but failed due to the lack of flesh on my face thanks to the cowl. "What in the hell has gotten into you?"

Mortis leapt into the void and we streaked like a pale comet into the mists below. Hooves sparked on gray rock, jolting me so hard my bones literally rattled. He skidded to a stop at the bank of a mist covered river. A narrow footbridge of glass spanned across the water, seemingly with no support but a single gleaming strand of something resembling spider web. It bobbed unsteadily, crackling louder than even the darkly churning river, sounding as if it might shatter at any minute. The river didn't so much roar as it screamed and wailed like lost souls.

I waited for Mortis to continue across the bridge, but he stood still, nostrils flaring as if waiting. I didn't know enough about Norse mythology to even hazard a guess about what was coming next, but if it was anything like the Greek mythos, I couldn't just merrily prance my way across the bridge.

I tried patting his neck but he flinched and nipped at my fingers. "Did I piss you off?"

Mortis stomped a hoof and shook his head, agitated. It was as if he'd suddenly gone from tolerating me to outright despising me.

Though the water shrieked, wind howled, and the glass bridge crackled, the mists and fogs remained unmoving, and an ominous silence hung over the shores. "Is Helheim over the bridge?"

Mortis snorted and stomped a hoof. Echoes scattered into the emptiness around us, louder than even the glass bridge.

Pale blue orbs danced in the mists, a pair of blue fire spirits trying to lure unwary travelers to their doom. But this wasn't Feary, and these weren't fire spirits. A great black wolf stalked from the fog, nostrils flaring. It looked down at us, apparently able to see through the magic that normally hid us. It was either that, or Mortis had made us visible of his own accord.

A skeletal woman glared down at us from her perch on the great wolf's neck, thin skin barely hanging from ill-concealed bones. She spoke in what I assumed was Old Norse, an incomprehensible mash of consonants slurred together, but perfectly translated by the cloak. "Pay the blood toll or Garm will feast on your soul, little thing."

The giant wolf bared its teeth and prepared to pounce.

24

I held up a skeletal hand. "Wait, I'm here on business!" I cleared my throat. "Death business."

Mortis snorted.

"What is it with underworlds and giant dogs?" I muttered.

The woman slid down the wolf's leg and lithely rolled onto the ground, a giant battleaxe appearing in her hand as if summoned from nothing. "There is no business but death here, little thing. I will extract the blood from you myself if I must."

I hopped off Mortis, reached over my back, and summoned the scythe. "I am Death, whoever you are, lady." It occurred to me that maybe I was already talking to the person I'd come to see. "Are you Hel?"

She bared her teeth. "How dare you compare me to our lady death? I am Modgud, sworn protector of Helheim. None may step upon Gjallarbrú to cross the Gjöll without paying the blood toll." Her eyes were little more than white meat orbs hovering in dark eye sockets, but they glanced at the glass bridge as she spoke.

"You're a poet and didn't know it." I waved a hand toward the glass structure. "The bridge is Gjallarbrú and the river is the Gjöll? And because of you, I have to pay a toll?"

"A poet?" She frowned. "I am no weakling artist, little thing. I am a warrior."

I returned a grim smile. "You certainly don't have a sense of humor." What concerned me the most about this encounter was her skeletal frame. The lack of muscles beneath the paper-thin skin made it difficult for me to read if she was tensing for an attack or merely biding her time.

Apparently, she was doing the former. Saying nothing, she took a step forward, battleaxe flashing.

"Well, that answers that." I moved the scythe to parry her first blow and was caught off guard when the axe abruptly shifted to her other hand and swung from another angle. Thanks to my newfound supernatural strength as Death, I was able to shift my position at the last second and metal clanged against the haft of the scythe.

Modgud continued her forward momentum, sliding and guiding the axe toward my legs. I leapt above the blow, used her head as a steppingstone, and rolled to the side, cloak billowing behind me in the wind. Massive jaws snapped as I traveled too close to the wolf, forcing me to fall to the ground and roll again.

I didn't know if either of them could kill me through the cloak, but I wasn't about to take the chance. I'd been eaten by a sea serpent on Oblivion in the recent past and didn't feel like adding "Being chomped by a giant underworld wolf" to my resume.

And then something latched onto my foot.

The world turned upside down as Garm lifted me off the ground with his teeth. The world flipped as he tossed me into the air like a doggy treat and opened his jaws wide to receive the blessing of my body. Reacting while in mid-air was hard but doing it while flipping was even harder. Using the scythe as a counterbalance, I whirled it and corrected my spin. Unfortunately, that did nothing to counteract gravity and I plunged toward the dark pit of teeth.

It seemed my resume was about to get another interesting bullet point whether I wanted it or not.

I'd never owned a dog or any other pet except for Fred. I had, however, encountered Korborus, the clockwork version of Cerberus on Oblivion, and had once become acquainted with a pack of Oblivion death hounds by giving them scraps of sand scorpion meat, at first to keep them from devouring me in my sleep, and then to become a member of the pack.

That was a story for another time, preferably when I wasn't falling toward certain doom. Suffice it to say I'd come away with a basic understanding of canine behavior that might help me, provided I timed my next action perfectly. Someone might wonder what could possibly save me from this certain fate. The answer?

Dogs don't usually chew their food.

Toss them a treat, and most dogs will chomp on it before trying to swallow it whole. It was the chomping part that I thought might save me. While the Death cloak might keep me alive, I would spend hours traveling through Garm's digestive system only to be shat out some inconvenient length of time later. I simply didn't have the time to waste, or Gaia would suffer another zombie uprising while I wormed my way through a giant wolf's intestines.

So, what was my marvelous plan?

Simple. I passed between the giant teeth and at the last instant, rotated my weapon. Garm chomped. The roof of his mouth and his lower jaw pinned the scythe between them like a giant toothpick. For an instant, I dangled above the dark gullet. Then I drew Soultaker and stabbed the giant son of a bitch in the tongue.

Garm howled and shook his head. I went flying once again, but this time much lower to the ground. I slammed the scythe handle to the ground, using it to halt my flight and catapult me in a controlled manner to the ground. My huge goth boots scraped against stone and Soultaker dug a glowing trench in the rock, doing little to slow me since it cut through just about anything like butter.

I finally ground to a halt and watched Garm rub his face against the ground, a wounded animal unable to salve its pain.

Modgud stared with unnaturally wide eyes at Soultaker. "You bring that soul-thieving sword to our domain?" She gripped the battleaxe with both hands. "You will never steal the souls of Helheim while I still draw breath."

"Do you draw breath?" I asked. "Because I can't tell if you're alive or dead, to be honest."

Mortis snorted.

I turned to him. "Laugh it up, fuzzball. It'll be your fault if Gaia ends up in another zombie apocalypse."

His head twitched and he pawed the ground. It was bizarre behavior considering how duty-bound he'd been only a day or so ago.

"I'm going to tell Garrick he needs a pale horse that cares about his job." I turned back to Modgud. "I'm not here to steal souls. I'm here to talk to Hel so she can help me find Thanatos so we can release the souls trapped in the sword. Now, be a good, uh, skeleton woman and tell me how to talk to her."

She regarded me warily for a solid thirty seconds before shaking her head and marching forward. "Loki's minions shall not pass."

"I'm not with Loki!"

"That is what Loki's minions would say!"

I gripped the scythe tightly enough make my knuckles crack. "Then bring Hel to me. I'll wait here."

"I cannot simply summon the goddess of the underworld at the whim of a pretender!"

I grasped for every shred of knowledge I had about the Norse gods. "But isn't Loki Hel's father? Why would he send someone with a Greek-made weapon to steal souls from his own daughter?"

Modgud paused, staring at me for another long moment. While her fighting skills were unquestionable, she obviously wasn't much of a thinker. The battleaxe lowered just a hair, then another hair, and finally she dropped her arms altogether. "You make sense, little one."

I didn't want to damage the fragile peace with something else for her to think about, so I banished the scythe and sheathed Soultaker. "May I please pass and ask Hel if she knows where I might find Thanatos?"

Garm crept up beside her, whining as blood trickled from the prick in his tongue. Modgud petted the giant beast with one hand as she considered the request. After another awkwardly long pause, she nodded. "If you are lying, Hel will end you."

I wanted to ask her how she knew what Soultaker was and how she thought I could steal souls from the underworld with it, but I really didn't feel like waiting another minute for an answer. "Thank you."

Modgud grunted and turned to tend to her giant wolf friend.

Mortis was already walking toward the bridge without me, so I hurried to catch up. "Hey, are you going to let me ride?"

He glanced over his shoulder at me and snorted as if that were the dumbest question I'd ever asked. Then he gingerly stepped onto the glass bridge. Cracks radiated from beneath his hoof. He took another step and the spiderweb of cracks spread further.

"What the fuck?" I tried to grip his reins and pull him back, but he continued onward. I stepped onto the glass after him, putting my feet where the glass wasn't cracked, but it was so narrow, that there was almost no way to avoid the fissures.

The glass fractured even more, grinding and creaking as if it might shatter at any instant. The wind howled harder, and the screams of the river grew louder, a cacophony of air, water, and earth that was enough to give even me anxiety.

"Can this bridge even break?" I shouted above the din.

Mortis might have responded with a snort, but it was impossible to hear him.

We continued our crossing for a small eternity, during which time dozens of questions crossed my mind. Why hadn't Mortis taken us directly to Helheim? Was he blocked from it like he was from Sanctuary? Could neither of us typically cross into the afterlife since it wasn't in the job description?

The fact that Mortis had chosen this route rather than taken us directly into Helheim indicated that despite his vast abilities as the pale horse of Death, there were barriers both earthly and divine that he couldn't simply cross at will. Even Death, it seemed, had some limitations.

The crossing seemed to stretch into eternity, given our languid pace. We eventually reached the other side, a rocky path carved into an icy canyon. Mortis stopped and waited for me to climb on as the wind pelted us with sleet and ice. Even with the cloak protecting me, I still felt a slight chill penetrating it.

We forged onward along the winding path as it led us up the side of a mountain, across an icy wasteland, and eventually into a cave. Torches along the tunnel walls lit the way, taking us into a valley surrounded by rocky cliffs. A village sprawled along the shores of a mist-covered lake. A snow-capped mountain rose in the distance and thick forest surrounded the town.

Muddy streets wound between buildings of heavy tarred timbers and steeply pitched roofs. It was like entering the old world, a place where Vikings still roamed. I'd expected something much less like a village and more like a pit of darkness and doom. Instead, it was as if an ancient civilization had simply picked up roots and moved into the afterlife.

People in rustic garb tended herds of goats and sheep. A few oxen roamed the fields, and chickens abounded. An old woman stopped gabbing with a neighbor at the local well, watching me curiously, but apparently not overly concerned about a skeleton riding a flesh-tattered horse.

Then again, she was dead already and that was probably why she could see me.

Blacksmith hammers chimed against metal, and a tanner hung several hides on ropes to let them dry. It was business as usual in the Viking village of the dead.

The village didn't seem large enough to contain all the Viking dead throughout history, but it also wasn't the only afterlife for the Norse. Valhalla was Viking heaven, a place reserved for those who died bravely in battle. Helheim was where everyone else ended up. It was possible Valhalla held a lot more souls than this place.

Smoke billowed from the chimney of a large town hall in the center of the village. Judging from the number of people waiting to enter, it was the place to be. Mortis took me there without guidance and stopped outside. Curious eyes watched as I dismounted and clomped up the wooden steps in my overly goth boots. The bleats of frightened goats emanated from within, presumably as they were being led to slaughter for a town feast.

No one tried to stop me as I squeezed past those waiting in line and entered the hall. Fires blazed in great hearths along the walls. Some iron spits held well-cooked goats. A group of men roughly shoved a spit up another goat's ass and out through its mouth then hefted it onto the supports over a mound of wood.

A great table and throne atop a raised platform sat at the far end of the dining hall, but it was currently unoccupied. Then I noticed a dark-haired woman slashing the throat of a black goat. As it struggled in its death throes, she dipped a finger in its blood and traced runes on the foreheads of its butchers.

When she straightened from the ritual, she stood at least a head taller than the tallest people present. She was attractive, at least from what little I could see of her face from this angle. Then she stiffened as if feeling me watching her and slowly turned to face me.

One side of her face was beautiful with fair, youthful skin and a piercing blue eye. The other side was a bare skull etched with an interlacing pattern and a cloudy white eye. She was tall, broad of shoulder, and seemed every bit the definition I'd have expected of a Viking woman aside from the exposed skull part.

She marched toward me, cloak billowing to reveal the body beneath it. As with her face, one side was youthful and muscular while the other side was skeletal. Yet, as with her face, the symmetry was somehow perfect and beautiful. Hel looked like the perfect embodiment of death, both beautiful and terrifying at the same time.

Her flesh side was tattooed in a similar pattern as her skeletal side, but in black ink whereas the bone was tattooed in crimson. The pattern held no meaning for me, but I doubted a goddess would decorate herself in such as way if there was no symbolism behind it.

Hel pushed through the crowd, ignoring everyone and everything except for me. I found myself rooted in place, entranced by the visage of a goddess whose domain I had trespassed upon. The mantle of Death might protect me from a lot, but if my brief battle with Mars had been any indication, the gods could probably still kill me, especially when I was in the seat of their power.

The bustling hall became deathly quiet as Hel stopped before me, looking down at me from her height advantage. "Who dares enter the land of the dead without my permission?" Her voice was youthful but haunting.

I tried to speak but found it hard to utter a sound. Her presence was much like the other gods—overpowering and overwhelming no matter how I prepared myself for it. Here in her domain, it weighed on me even more heavily. Clearing my head, I found my words and used them.

"I'm looking for Thanatos. It's a matter of great urgency."

She flinched, eyes flaring dangerously. "Then you have made a grave mistake, mortal. For none who enter my domain may leave."

25

Entering Helheim was apparently like checking into Hotel California. Once you went in, you could never leave. Then again, maybe Hel was just being dramatic.

"You'd think your doorkeepers could have told me that before letting me come in." It took all my training to gird my mind against her presence, but I slowly adjusted the best I could, wondering if the cloak was protecting me against the worst of it. I slid on the ring, Panoptes. My vision split, showing me the places where the ring led.

I tried to reach inside the warehouse, but intense cold raced down my arm and blocked me from shifting through. It seemed not even this ring could get me out of this place.

Hel's eyes narrowed, even the one on the bare skull side. "You are not cowed by my aura as most are."

"Probably because I'm currently employed as Death."

She scowled and the overpowering feeling suddenly abated as if she'd turned off a switch. "The mantle does not protect you, this I know from experience. Your mind is stronger than most mortals."

I had nothing to say to that, so I went back to my largest concern. "Why did you say I can't leave Hel?"

"Not even I can grant you leave from this place." She motioned in the direction of the river. "Once you have stepped foot on land after crossing the bridge, it will not allow you to turn back. Should you try to do so, it will shatter unexpectedly and cast you into Gjöll where your soul will be shredded and bound to the river, screaming for all eternity in a state suspended between death and oblivion."

I nodded matter-of-factly while trying not to show my alarm. "That does sound bad. Are you sure the Death cloak won't protect me?"

"It may for some time, but you will be swept along the river, unable to escape its icy grasp." Hel shook her head slowly. "This place is an eternal prison."

"Can you leave?"

"Yes, but I cannot take anyone with me, and my travels are limited to specific places. If I leave, my time is limited. If I do not return within a few days, I will die." Hel shook her head again. "It is a curse my own father put on me to keep me out of his affairs, and there is only one way to break it." She stared at the distant mountain. "It is also the only way out of this world."

That piqued my interest. "So, there's a way out for both of us?"

"For anyone brave enough to attempt it." Hel pursed her flesh lips and her skull side mimicked it. "One must fight their way through the monsters of the badlands and reach the lake where they can raise a challenge. A Valkyrie will fly down to face you in holmgang—a duel. Whether you win or are slain, you will have earned passage to Valhalla."

"Uh, how is that supposed to help me?" I threw up my hands. "Exchanging one afterlife for another doesn't work for me. If I don't return to the mortal realm to resume collecting souls, then Gaia will be overwhelmed by another zombie uprising and start the apocalypse."

Hel grunted. "That does sound like a grave problem. But not even I have the power to free you from Hel."

"You mean Helheim?"

"That is not the proper name," she replied coldly.

"Well, it helps me separate the place from the person." I shrugged. "No offense."

"You will use the proper names for me and my kingdom." Hel changed the subject as if there was nothing else to say about the matter. "What brings you here in search of Thanatos?"

I drew Soultaker. "The souls trapped in this sword must be freed."

She flinched, eyes widening. "Why have you brought this wretched creation into my domain?" Hel scowled. "I told Thanatos that he tried too hard to impress his brethren. I told him that no matter what he did, they would never accept him into the upper echelons, the inner circle of Olympians."

I frowned. "So, he helped Hephaestus make the sword just to impress Mars?"

"He did it to impress Athena!" She hissed breath between her teeth. "Then Hephaestus instead presented Soultaker to Mars as a gift solely from him. Naturally, the gift was rejected, and the misshapen god had no better success impressing his brethren than Thanatos would have had impressing Athena."

I couldn't help but crack a grin. "Wow, that's really ironic, and not the Alanis Morrissette kind, either."

Hel blinked. "Is she the goddess of irony?"

"No, I mean she was god in a movie once, but—then again, maybe she was the god of irony for writing a song about irony without any irony in it." I waved away the tangent. "The real irony is that Athena was slain by Soultaker and her soul is trapped inside. I need Thanatos to help me figure out how to free her soul. If he does that, she's sure to notice him and promptly toss him in the friendzone."

Hel's eyes brightened and she burst into laughter, much to the surprise of the men and women patiently waiting to slaughter their goats for the feast. She continued laughing until tears of mirth streamed down her cheeks. When her laughter subsided, she wiped her flesh and bone cheeks, head shaking. "You must tell me how this joyous slaying of Athena happened. If Thanatos were here, I would dearly love to see his reaction when I told him his dear, sweet Athena the bitch was nothing but a wraith in his sword."

"Jealous much?" I sighed and leaned against a table. "You might find this hilarious, but if I'm trapped here for eternity, then the world is going to Hell in a handbasket."

Her forehead creased on both sides as if the bone were also malleable flesh. "Why would the world travel here in a handbasket?"

"H-e-double hockey sticks Hell. The Christian Hell." I shook my head. "And that's just a saying."

"Ah." She nodded. "I have not traveled into the mortal realm in some time and have become woefully ignorant of current idioms."

"Hell in a handbasket has been around a while." Though it was probably just a heartbeat relative to the span of her existence. "Getting back to the subject, do you know where Thanatos is? Rumor has it he came here to be with you. Since no one can leave Hel except for you, it stands to reason he's still here."

"Alas, though our time was lustily well spent, he pined for Athena." Hel sighed. "Knowing he would never have her, he opted for the screaming oblivion of the Gjöll."

"You've got to be fucking kidding me!" I gritted my teeth. "He jumped in the river?"

"He thought it would destroy his consciousness entirely, allowing him the sweet sleep of oblivion." Hel's gaze grew somber. "I assured him it would not bring him the peace he sought. So, he left for the badlands, intent on facing a Valkyrie that he might reach Valhalla and ask for the respite of true death."

"Can I get back to the mortal realm from Valhalla?" I asked.

She shook her head. "Valhalla is likewise blocked from the mortal realm. Only Odin and his kin can freely travel between it and Asgard. There is a barrier that obliterates anyone else who tries to leave."

I frowned. "But travel between Valhalla and Hel is obviously permitted."

"Only if you face the challenge of the Valkyrie."

I considered that again. "Can I fly over the Gjöll?" I asked.

She frowned. "Do you have wings?"

"No, but theoretically, could I fly over the river?"

Hel shrugged. "I have never considered such a thing. I do not think the Gjöll would prevent someone from flying over it."

"Good."

She raised an eyebrow. "What is good about that? As you said a moment ago, you have no wings."

"Then I'll figure out how to get some." I already had one idea, but the challenge would be surviving to earn those wings. "Are you certain that the living are barred from leaving Hel?"

"Deadly certain." She shook her head. "I have seen some few try over the centuries and all ended up in the Gjöll."

I blew out a breath. "Well, I need to get going then." I checked the death beacon and counted several souls waiting to be reaped on Gaia. I traced a finger along the side and put them on hold to prevent them from going zombie. "Which way to the badlands?"

She put a hand on the cowl. "I would see your face, brave soul."

I'd grown so used to the new outfit that I'd forgotten to lower the hood. I pulled it back and shivered at the still strange feeling of flesh growing back over my skull. "My name is Cain."

She touched my cheek with her bone hand, sending not so unpleasant chills down my flesh. "It has been too long since I've encountered a living being worthy of tarrying with. Perhaps you should stay for the feast before starting a difficult journey."

I was feeling a mite hungry, but now was not the time to risk my body or sanity by sleeping with a powerful goddess who'd nearly overpowered me with her aura only moments ago. The old part of me was sorely tempted and not easily convinced that it would be a terrible idea and I found myself considering the offer for much longer than I should have.

Clamping down on the lust, I forced myself to shake my head. "I'm sorry, but I really have to go."

Her lip trembled. "Do you find me hideous?"

I also didn't want to sadden or anger the being who could slay me or keep me here against my will. I reached out and stroked her skull cheek. "No. You are a unique and beautiful being. But I cannot tarry, or the world will suffer." I leaned closer and kissed her, gently. Visions of snow and ice, of a great river being carved from a dead rock floating in space passed through my head. A giant of a man with a patch over one eye dragged a great spear across the land, a scowl on his face.

"That abomination must live here for eternity!" the giant man boomed. That was no man, but the god Odin.

Loki floated in the void nearby, face downcast, a baby cradled in his arms. "Why do you punish me for love? For fathering children?"

Odin clenched his teeth. "Do not feign sadness, trickster!"

The vision abruptly vanished, and I found myself still kissing Hel. I flinched back with a gasp. "What the fuck was that?"

She stroked my cheek. "You also had visions? Most of my lovers do."

"I saw the creation of this place."

"Thanatos often saw visions during our lovemaking. Especially of animals which he loved so." Hel sighed. "Memories are powerful things."

"You can say that again."

She nodded. "Memories are powerful things."

"Uh..." I offered a smile. "Yep."

"Did the repetition help?"

I nodded. "It was perfect."

Hel smiled. "And to think I meant to kill you when you first turned me down. But you are quite charming."

I felt myself balancing on a razor's edge between life and death. "Does that mean it's okay for me to go to the badlands now?"

"Yes, of course, love." She abruptly kissed me again.

Another wave of visions raced through my head. Ice, snow, wind, Modgud and Garm herding souls across the glass bridge. Of ice giants storming the Gjöll, only to meet a final end in its brutal, screaming waters.

I stumbled back. "Did ice giants attack Helheim?"

Hel blinked. "That was eons ago. Loki sought to destroy this prison, so Odin relented and allowed me to move freely into and out of Hel, but with the price of mortality and death should I linger too long."

"Odin sounds like a real twat."

She tilted her head. "That strange term does not translate well into Old Norse, yet perfectly conveys that he is the ass of a donkey."

Violent images still danced in my head from her last kiss, and I knew without a doubt that my mortal frame couldn't handle the vast power of this goddess. "I must ask your leave, beautiful Hel, but I thank you for the taste of your sweet lips and your hospitality."

Hel grinned, the skull part also curving up like the lips on her flesh side. She motioned toward the people lifting a spitted goat from the fires. "Make this hero a feast and guide him to the badlands. He must be well fed and strong for the battle that awaits."

The people hurried to comply with her command.

I bowed again. "Thank you, Hel." Those were words I'd have never in a million years imagined saying.

She left me to continue blessing the other slaughtered goats while a group of men and women worked feverishly to prepare me a to-go order of goat. They packed it in a leather satchel and gave me a leather skin reeking of mead.

The group spoke among themselves, obviously arguing about who would escort me until a brawny woman finally rolled her eyes and shoved through the men. "I will take you, godsfriend."

I nodded. "Thank you."

She slung the food satchel over one shoulder and grabbed a large haunch of goat then headed out of the dining hall. Mortis stood outside munching on the black grass growing around the hall. He saw me and snorted.

"We're going on an adventure!" I flashed a fake grin. "All because no one told me that we can't leave this place."

Mortis flinched, lips peeling back from his teeth as if he wanted to convey some emotion. Then it was as if a door slammed shut on his emotions and he stared dully at me.

"Please tell me you didn't know that and decided to make this our forever home." I scowled. "We might be permanently fucked."

"This is a good place to live," the woman said. "We eat and drink the days away. The only bad part is dying of sickness or old age every few years rather than being allowed to die honorably in battle."

"Why not go through the badlands and take the challenge to get into Valhalla?"

Her eyes flared. "The creatures of the badlands will devour you and shit out your soul at the edge of the valley." She pointed toward the distant tree line. "Dying of sickness and old age is bad enough but being returned as a pile of shit is a terrible dishonor even among us."

"Are you reincarnated after dying like that?"

She nodded. "But you are conscious of being a pile of dung. Once the dung has dried, the other villagers can burn it and the soul will be reborn as a child, barely old enough to walk. The memories of your past lives remain no matter how many times you die and are reborn."

I grunted. "It's not the worst punishment imaginable, but it does sound like it'd get old after a few eons."

"It is enormously tiresome." She sighed and looked skyward. "Oh, to bask in the glory of Valhalla."

It seemed impolite to ride Mortis while the woman walked, so I continued on foot. "What is your name?"

"Astrid, godsfriend."

"I like that name."

"It means divine beauty." She burst into laughter. "And I am anything but!"

I hesitated to pay her an untrue compliment. I found her Viking proportions attractive in their own way. "You are a very strong woman and that is beauty enough."

Astrid beamed. "You are too kind, godsfriend." She navigated the rutted path into the forest. "I was a warrior, a leader. I should have died in battle and instead caught the sick and died." Her smile faded. "I should have dragged myself into battle, but I waited too long, hoping for a recovery that never came, so I was too weak to even crawl beneath my enemy's sword."

"I'm sorry the rules of the afterlife suck." I sighed. "In fact, most rules governing afterlives are just dumb."

She spun on me. "The rules are the rules, godsfriend. I did not honor the gods with my life and so I have no right to join the warriors in Valhalla."

I faced her down. "Wrong. You didn't honor the gods with your death. You might have lived your life honorably until the day the sickness took you, but instead you were sent to Helheim for something out of your control. The gods should have healed you and given you a chance to die in battle instead of such an ignominious death."

Astrid's eyes flared. "By Odin's beard, you are right." She looked up fearfully, as if lightning might strike her. "I toiled my entire life, fighting for my people, building a village, a community, and then to be struck down as if Loki himself poisoned me."

"It's not right and just." I shook my head. "There are cowards who will never stand up and fight. They belong here, not you."

She sagged. "But I am not warrior enough to reach the holmgang. I will be devoured and shat out at the village's edge for all to see and that memory will fill me with regret for eternity."

I stopped walking. "What do you know of the beasts between here and the battlefield?"

Astrid stared ahead with dread. "I have heard they are the spawn of Garm and other animals. Giant boars, wolves, and even serpents birthed by Loki himself. They were banished here by Odin that they would not destroy Midgard." She shivered. "I cannot imagine even a god defeating them and reaching the battlefield."

26

I considered her statement and had zero doubt it was accurate. I turned to Mortis. "Can you outrun the beasts in the badlands?"

Mortis stomped a hoof.

"Not even a supernatural steed can outrun the monsters," Astrid said. "You will be relentlessly hunted across the terrain. The only blessing is that the badlands only stretch for a day's ride."

"And you know this how?"

"Hel told the last challenger how far it was when he asked her." Astrid shook his head. "We found the mound of shit days later and burned it. When he was reborn, he was not the same. Now he lives alone in the forest somewhere, too ashamed to show his face."

It seemed that even with Mortis it would be extremely difficult to make it across the badlands without help. A plan began to form in the back of my mind. I shuffled it to the front to give more processing power to the thought and realized it might be my only chance.

"Fuck," I muttered.

"Yes, godsfriend. Gladly." She began tugging off her leather shirt. "Sometimes a vigorous fuck will grant even more bravery. You are also a fair sight if I might say so."

I held up a hand. "No, wait, that's not what I meant."

Astrid paused a disappointed look on her face. "Oh, you were cursing." She sighed. "The men here are wretched at pleasing anyone but themselves."

"I'm sorry." I switched subjects quickly. "Astrid, how many people live in Helheim?"

She slipped her leather shirt back on. "Thousands? I cannot say for sure."

That seemed like plenty. "Any idea how many creatures inhabit the badlands?"

"Not many, but they are deadly, each and every one."

I rubbed my hands together. "Astrid, how would you like to earn a way into Valhalla?"

Her eyes widened. "I told you, I dare not make the attempt."

I turned back toward the village and started walking. "I think I have an idea that can benefit everyone."

Astrid hurried after me. "What idea? What are you talking about?"

I held onto the idea until we returned to the great hall in the center of the village. More and more people had come to the feast, ringing the building with hundreds, maybe even a thousand people. Most were filing inside. Judging from the size of the building, I had no doubt it could hold them all.

"Why are we going back?" Astrid said. "The entrance to the badlands was just ahead."

"You'll see." I squeezed through the crowd outside and made my way into the hall. People occupied dozens of tables, each one with a cooked goat sitting in the center. Hel sat at the head table upon a throne of skulls. Her gaze locked onto me immediately. I continued up to the platform and bowed. "Hel, may I address the crowd when everyone is seated?"

"Join me, Cain." She patted a chair next to her. I would know why you have returned."

Mortis snorted. I turned to see he'd followed me all the way.

Hel smiled. "Your pale steed may also join us."

Mortis walked up the stairs to the platform and stood at the edge, gazing regally down at the revelers.

Hel turned to me after I sat down. "Why have you returned? Did you reconsider my earlier offer?"

I'd been a bit concerned that she would ask me that and had prepared a response. "My goddess, unfortunately my mortal form could not handle such a divine experience no matter how much I desire it. Even your kisses are enough to threaten my sanity."

She shivered with delight. "Your words are sweet as honey, Cain. I have not been regaled with such high compliments since my dear Thanatos left."

"What I would like to do is propose a path for your subjects that they might earn a warrior's death and that you might earn your rightful place."

Hel looked at me expectantly. "Explain."

I did and found her unexpectedly supportive. "This is a grand venture, Cain. I have not felt such excitement in a very long time." She shivered again. "So much death, blood, and glory in the name of Hel!"

"Uh, yeah, exactly." By now, most of the hall was filled. Despite the food and drink before them, the revelers seemed to be waiting on something. Judging from the way they were looking this way, it seemed that something was the blessing of Hel.

She rose, a goblet of mead in hand and raised it. "Welcome denizens of Hel." Her voice boomed across the room, reaching even the far corners. "I would normally give you a few short words and leave you to enjoy the meal as we have done countless times before. But today we have been blessed with a rare opportunity." She turned to me. "Tell them of the glory that awaits, Cain."

I stood, cleared my throat, and used an amplification spell so everyone could hear me. "How many of you wished to die in battle when you were alive?"

In almost unanimous precision, fists raised from men and women as they roared and cheered.

I held up a hand to quiet them and the room went silent. "Is it true that Hel is filled with the souls of the valiant dead? Of those who deserved a chance at glory only to have it stolen from their grasps?" I clenched a fist. "What a travesty crafty Loki has committed upon each and every one of you. He struck you down with sickness, old age, and never once gave you a war to fight in." I raised a goblet. "To the valiant dead!"

Roars of approval filled the room.

I silenced them once again. "Well, valiant dead, today you will have your chance at redemption. Today, I am gathering an army that will march across the badlands and to the challenge arena so that we can all earn our place in Valhalla!"

The cheers were much more muted this time as people looked uncertainly at each other. A few groups here and there rose to their feet, cheering loudly and banging their fists on the table as they chanted, "Re-demp-tion! Re-demp-tion!"

I joined the chant for a time until more joined and I was able to gauge how many were definitely not into this idea. I put up a hand to silent the crowd again. "Tonight we feast, for tomorrow we go to war. The beasts of the badlands will have no chance against our might and soon all worthy warriors will journey out of Hel and into the golden lands of Valhalla!"

Hel rose beside me. "Now eat and make merry, for tomorrow there will be blood and battle for the glory of Hel!"

"To the glory of Hel!" the enthusiastic revelers roared back. "To the glory of Hel!"

I wasn't sure if they meant glory for Helheim or the goddess, but it didn't much matter. I raised my goblet and joined the chant. This was going to take longer than expected, but we were off to a promising start.

It was my first Viking feast and as the hours slipped past, I didn't know how I'd lived all my life without enjoying something so violently festive as this. Many roasted goats were consumed. Much mead was drunk. Many fights were cheered, and many songs were sung while men and women danced upon the tables.

Hel gripped my hand and pulled me up onto the head table with her and we danced and laughed the night away. I knew I was way drunker than I'd ever been when I started dancing for fun. Hel's aura probably didn't help matters any. I'd learned dancing to become a better fighter, and certainly not for enjoyment. Before I knew it, the goddess swept me away and we ended up in her bed.

"You are mine, Cain," she murmured in my ear as her hand ran down my body. "I promise not to damage you too badly."

Abandoning all sense, I took off the death cloak and welcomed the madness and pleasure that was Hel, goddess of the Norse underworld. Her kisses planted visions of creation, of battle and torture in my head. When she mounted me, I saw the Norse universe, Yggdrasil and its realms rotating in a sea of stars.

Its gravity sucked me in, and I orbited the great tree, a helpless meteor caught in its inescapable wake. Distantly, I heard Hel moaning and crying out. Then I fell into the dark vastness, tumbling down a black hole and into infinity.

A nebula appeared before me, hues of green and violet gasses. Cacophonic music drifted across the void, piercing my ears with an unholy melody. I spun and discovered the black hole was the gaping maw of a gelatinous creature so large, I could barely comprehend its enormity. Creatures the size of planets circled around the massive being. Pipe-like orifices along their undulating bodies were the source of the incomprehensible and chaotic melody.

Another creature drifted across space toward me. It was human sized, but with three legs, long arms, and clawed hands. Its head was shaped like a worm with a sharp-toothed maw. If there were eyes, I couldn't see them.

I reached for my staff, but it didn't appear.

"Madness consumes you, Cain. Hel's appetite has brought you to me as planned." The creature flinched as its maw stretched into a horrendous grin. "Nyarlathotep welcomes you to Azathoth's domain." It spoke with a bizarre accent and with emphasis on unexpected syllables, as if speaking in my language was completely alien to it.

"Long have I wished to see my lost disciple." It flinched again, its worm head wiggling grotesquely.

"Disciple?" I struggled to stop spinning and to gather my thoughts, but it was futile. Hel's moans echoed through the void and I knew without a doubt that I'd completely lost my mind.

Nyarlathotep hissed in laughter. "Embrace madness, Cain. It is the way of existence. All else is futile yearning." He flinched so quickly it was like watching a movie skipping frames.

Steeling myself, I clenched my teeth and concentrated on breaking this mind trap. Madness and despair wrenched my thoughts from me time and time again as I fought to hold onto a shred of sanity. Nyarlathotep continued laughing.

A brief instance of sanity showed me what I was doing wrong. Fighting was only making it worse. I did indeed have to do what Nyarlathotep said. I had to fall into the madness and embrace it, but to do so without accepting it. This was a different kind of madness than what I'd faced before.

I took a deep breath and concentrated on Hel's moans. I found them beneath the chaotic music of the creatures entertaining Azathoth and let them fill my mind.

My grip on sanity grew stronger.

"What do you want, Nyarlathotep?"

His laughter ceased. "You are a strong one, disciple. Though you were stolen away from me, you will return to your world and continue your good work. Do not fear the Elder Things, Cain and do not believe everything the Elder Gods say. We are two halves of a whole." He reached out with his crooked hands and gripped my arm. "We cry out for unity. Nurture the gift and all will be made whole. The universe will exist in the utter madness of complete harmony." His worm head flinched twice.

I struggled to focus on Hel's heavy breathing, on her soft gasps of delight. "What...are...you talking about?"

"I am talking about the end of this universe and the start of the next." He traced a claw down my face. "Nurture the seed, Cain. Embrace the apocalypse."

"You planned this?" I forced my mind to be at peace with the surging madness. "How?"

"Tangling fate's threads always brings me what I need." He hissed softly. "And my agents do the rest."

I felt sensation from my physical body again, felt Hel's soft half and the hardness of the skeletal half pressing against me. Felt her lips on mine. Something surged from deep within me, an eruption like none I'd felt before. The music began to fade. Nyarlathotep and Azathoth faded from view.

And then I lurched back to my mortal coil, exploding with sweet relief while Hel cried out in pleasure.

"Gods be damned," I shouted. "Gods be damned!"

Hel laughed and pressed her skeletal hand to my cheek. "Cain, you have survived me." She rolled off and lay next to me in the great bed. "I am pleased with your resilience."

Gasping, I lurched to my feet, staggered to a stone column and braced myself on it. My legs were trembling and a fine layer of sweat covered my body. "Holy fuck." I dropped to my knees and huddled against the stone column, shivering with the fever of madness, pleasure, and too much drink.

Hel propped her head on an elbow and watched me with amusement. "Oh, I have missed having a real lover. The souls here are simply too weak to survive my attentions, and the men have no skill."

Still shivering, I manage to speak. "I-I'm too fucking fragile for this shit, Hel!"

She laughed and patted the bed. "Come to bed, my sweet. I will let you rest, for in the morn, we rise for battle."

I didn't feel real fear very often, but this was absolutely one of those times. I couldn't survive another round with Hel. If I slept in the same bed, I had no doubt she'd use me again and I might lose the rest of my sanity in the process. I also didn't want another encounter with Nyarlathotep. Everything he'd said to me tangled in my mind and I needed to make sense of it all. Had he somehow been responsible for luring me here because he knew Hel would take advantage and drive me mad? I didn't see how that was possible.

I held up a hand. "No offense, Hel, but I'm going to sleep some-where else."

She laughed. "Very well, my sweet."

I gathered my clothes into a bundle and hurriedly left the room, marched down stone stairs, and out a door. I emerged in the great hall, completely naked in my walk of shame. Thankfully, nearly everyone else was in such bad shape, that they barely even noticed my bare ass and dangling bits.

It also helped that others were having sex with abandon on tables, the floor, and anywhere else they could while other revelers completely ignored them. I put on my clothes and noticed Mortis watching me judgmentally from across the room.

I sighed and shook my head. "How in the hell did I end up in this mess again?" The path I'd taken seemed incomprehensible. From trying to help Dusa and Aura to getting fucked by the Norse goddess of death seemed like an impossibly long and convoluted journey.

Had Nyar manipulated me into ending up here?

I continued making my way through the hall. It looked likely that I'd have to find a place to sleep on the floor, but then a familiar face found me.

Astrid gripped my hand. "Cain, did you truly bed Hel?"

I shivered uncontrollably. "No, she bedded me."

"Oh, you must be quite durable to survive that. Many have entered and few except you and Thanatos have emerged unscathed."

Another shiver ran through me. "I'm definitely not unscathed."

She laughed. "Where are you going?"

"To find a place to sleep. I'm completely drunk and half insane."

"Then you can come with me." She took my hand, and I didn't have the willpower or the strength to resist. I was just done. She took me outside, down the dirt road, and into a sturdy wooden home where she tucked me into bed like a child.

Astrid sat at the edge of the bed, smoothing back my hair, and singing an old Norse song about a village preparing for war. I drifted into an uneasy sleep, images of Azathoth and Nyarlathotep haunting my dreams. What had he meant by continuing to nurture the seed?

What halves cried out for unity? Who were his agents? How had he possibly engineered my coming to Hel?

By saying I should continue nurturing the seed, it meant I was already doing it whether I knew it or not. Without even knowing or understanding it, I was fulfilling a task for a creature that was hell-bent on destroying the universe and recreating it in perfect madness.

27

I jerked awake alone in bed, heavy animal furs weighing down on my chest.

My body ached all the way down to the bones, and my head was pounding. That wasn't the only thing that was pounding. Metal clanged with the steady beat of blacksmith hammers. Astrid was gone, but a bowl of cold porridge waited on the table for me. Despite having eaten nearly half a goat the night before, I was famished. I forced down the tasteless muck and drank water straight from a stone pitcher.

My street clothes and the Death cloak hung on a wooden chair. The cloak was clean as usual, but my street clothes had gotten covered in mud at some point I couldn't remember the night before. I didn't relish putting them on, so I went commando beneath the robes, and willed them to resemble jeans and a t-shirt. The cloak obliged and I stepped outdoors in all black, my oversized goth boots clomping in the mud.

A cold rain drizzled steadily, and a heavy mist hung over the forest. The Vikings bustled about the streets in their heavy furs and leather armor as if the weather were perfectly fine. Men, women, and children were dressed for war, most of them carrying heavy wooden shields and a variety of iron weapons ranging from axes, swords, bows, and the occasional two-handed battleaxe.

A horn trumpeted from the center of the village and people began heading toward the great hall, faces lit with excitement. Astrid appeared at my side, a grin splitting her face.

"Whether we survive or are shat out by a beast, this will be a great day for all." She slapped my back. "I don't know why we have never thought of this before!"

I flexed my sore back. "Is everyone fighting?"

She scoffed. "Hardly. We have discovered the true cowards among us this day, for they have taken refuge in the forest to the southeast. Old Finni joked that the weaklings are ready to risk jumping in the Gjöll if it means they don't have to pick up a sword."

I shook my head. "Why wouldn't they fight? Being crapped out and forced to reincarnate as a baby isn't the end of the world, and this is the best chance any of them will ever have at reaching Valhalla."

"They are as frightened in death as they were in life, Cain, and undeserving of reward." Astrid mussed my hair. "You are a cute little man, especially when you look confused."

I stared at her for a long moment. "Don't talk to me like a child even if you are bigger than me."

She laughed and offered a curt bow. "Pardon me, oh great assassin, oh wielder of Death."

I groaned. "You remind me of Layla."

Her eyebrows rose. "Who?"

"Doesn't matter." I nodded toward the crowds headed toward the village center. "Let's get this party started."

Astrid snorted. "You are very good at starting parties, but not so good at finishing them."

"I don't normally allow myself to lose control." I pinched the bridge of my nose in the vain hope it would stave off the headache, but it didn't help. I hoped the Death cloak would lend some supernatural healing before battle.

She patted my back. "It is good to lose control sometimes, Cain. Living life is not always about perfect order, but about sometimes letting chaos add excitement."

"Sounds like something Loki would say."

Astrid scowled. "Though I love our lady Hel, I do not like her father. Please don't compare me to that scoundrel."

I grunted and kept walking.

Mortis emerged from a branching street and joined us on our way. His gazed judged me.

I scowled. "I fucked up, okay?"

He snorted and whickered.

"Your horse doesn't seem to like you much," Astrid said.

"He's not my horse." I blew out a breath. "He's a coworker."

She frowned. "A what?"

"An associate."

"Those words to not translate well to Old Norse." Astrid pursed her lips. "A partner, perhaps?"

"Sure. Either way, Mortis is his own horse and doesn't belong to anyone. He's friends with Garrick, the guy who's usually working as Death, but he and I haven't gotten along since I took this miserable job." Despite my words, I had a hard time understanding why Mortis seemed happy to watch me fail. It just wasn't in keeping with his attitude when all this started. He hadn't been pleased, but he'd done everything he could to support the mission.

Astrid squeezed my shoulder. "Well, in any case, I cannot thank you enough for this glorious opportunity to redeem ourselves."

A throne of skulls sat upon a newly erected wooden tower in the square before the great hall. It didn't seem like something the people could have thrown up overnight, so I suspected it was Hel's doing, especially since she was currently seated on said throne.

A man blew a giant ram's horn and the murmuring of the crowd ceased. Hel rose to her feet and gestured at the throng. "All great warriors have heeded my call. Today, we will fight our way to the proving grounds and earn our places in Valhalla. Only the cowards shall remain behind while the rest of us claim victory!" She raised a great sword, its handle made from human skulls, and the blade from black metal. "Even I will journey with you that I might escape this place."

The crowd roared with approval.

I watched her then turned to Astrid. "What happens to Hel if Hel goes to Valhalla?"

"I don't know." Astrid shrugged. "Only she can say for sure."

"Who will rule Hel in her absence?"

"The cowards can have it for all I care." She spat on the muddy road. "I just pray that Odin grants me the skill to make it to Valhalla."

I'd been worried about our chances even with an army, but having Hel fighting alongside us made this a cinch. She was a goddess. The beasts of the badlands wouldn't stand a chance against her.

A shiny black mare trotted out of the great hall and up to the platform. She locked eyes with Mortis and neighed. He nickered back and stomped a hoof.

I raised an eyebrow. "You old devil. Did you get down and dirty with Hel's mare last night?"

He snorted.

Astrid laughed.

Hel leapt from the tower and landed neatly on the mare's back. She pulled back on the reins and the mare reared up, neighing loudly, black mist billowing from its mouth and nostrils.

I turned to Mortis. "What is it with death horses and black mist?"

He stared at me silently as the crowd began to form ranks and march behind Hel and her mare.

I climbed onto his back and looked down at Astrid. "May the gods grant us favor."

She raised her great battleaxe. "For Hel and the glory of our Lady Hel!"

The chant rose in a thousand voices. "For Hel!"

I nudged Mortis and we weaved our way past the long lines and caught up with Hel. She regarded me with a wicked smile. "You look tired, Cain. Did you sleep well?"

I scoffed. "After you used me like yesterday's newspaper? Hardly."

Her grin widened.

I leaned back in the saddle. "So, you plan to break your curse so you can go to Valhalla?"

"Precisely. This is my best chance to do it."

I grunted. "And you'll just leave Hel behind?"

She scoffed. "Hardly. This is my realm. But it will be glorious to finally find my place in Asgard and to prove my worth to Father and the others."

"I get it." I looked ahead. "Well, this should be easy with you and that fancy sword of yours."

Hel looked straight ahead and said nothing.

"Do we even have to fight?" I leaned forward. "If these beasts are spawn of Garm, couldn't you command them?"

She shook her head. "They are guardians against all who enter the badlands, even me."

"And you've never considered doing this before?"

Again, she said nothing, and that was when I knew there was something she wasn't telling me.

"Why are you so close-lipped all of a sudden? What aren't you telling me?"

Hel sighed heavily. "I cannot lift a hand against the creatures of the badlands. Odin protected them against me, so if I were to attempt the badlands on my own, they could ravage me, and I wouldn't be able to defend myself."

"Fucking hell, Hel." I glanced back at the army behind us. "You could have mentioned that during your speech. These people are expecting to see you fighting alongside them. When they see you're not, they'll lose all that piss and vinegar you just pumped them full of."

"They will rush into battle and become engulfed in the fog of war, hardly looking to see what I or anyone else is doing." Hel shrugged. "We have the numbers to make this work with or without me."

I didn't like the sound of that. "You might not be able to fight the creatures, but what's stopping you from riding to the proving grounds by yourself and skipping the beasts?"

"Not even my mare can outrun the beasts of the badlands." She bared her teeth. "But our combined might will crush them."

"I hope so." I began to wonder if I'd be able to fight while wearing the Death cloak. Fighting naked wouldn't be pretty, but if it came down to it, I'd do what I had to. Though I'd been unable to fight the deep ones a few days ago, I had been able to fight Mars, Garm, and Modgud. The only difference I could think of was that I'd tried to strike down deep ones while hidden by the cloak. I'd been the one to attack first and that had blunted my ability to kill them. Maybe if the enemy attacked me first it gave me the green-light to fight back.

I had a feeling I'd be getting attacked a lot in the upcoming battle.

We entered the forest and followed the path to the mouth of a canyon. The ground was littered with bones, battered shields, and rusty weapons.

Hel held up a fist and the march stopped. "The first challenge is upon us."

I frowned and looked at the boneyard. "Do we have to get through without stepping on bones?"

She turned to face the army and her voice boomed across the forest. "There is something I did not tell you, my brave warriors. I am not allowed to fight the beasts. That honor is for mortals only. For that reason, I can only watch you fight."

"Then we will make you proud," a warrior cried out from the front ranks. He raised his sword. "For the glory of Hel, may she reign forever!"

"For the glory of Hel!" The cheer raced along the ranks.

Without warning, the lead ranks charged toward the bones. The moment they stepped out of the forest, the bones sprang to life, snapping together until a small squad of skeleton warriors barred entrance into the canyon, most of them armed with the old weapons that had been scattered on the ground.

If only one person had been trying to enter the canyon, the dozen or so skeleton warriors would have been a challenge. The army rushing them now could simply crush them underfoot. Surprisingly, the skeletons seemed to realize that. Bones clattering, they turned tail and ran into the canyon, a Viking army roaring after them.

I glanced over at Hel. "Well, that was an unexpected start."

She sighed. "I'm afraid it will get worse. Much worse."

Astrid ran past grinning at me and shouting a battle cry. She'd probably go hoarse before reaching her first enemy.

Once the army was past, Hel and I guided our horses into the canyon.

"Thveri is quite fond of Mortis," Hel said casually as we trotted after the army. "And I am quite fond of you, Cain."

"Can we not do this right now?" I was about to say something else, but the cries of the army had suddenly gone deathly quiet. "Shit. Something's happened." I urged Mortis faster and we reached the end of the canyon moments later. A valley spread out before it. It looked as if it had been carved from the ground with a broken shovel and sprinkled with boulders, rocks, and splintered trees.

The footing was uneven. Fissures, chasms, and cracks in the hard soil would impede even the surest-footed supernatural horse. Mortis neighed in apprehension. He might not be able to die but racing across this broken terrain was a sure way to break a leg.

The skeletons had stopped running and now stood before a line of monstrous creatures. Elephant-sized wolves, two great serpents that could swallow a man whole, a pair of horse-sized rams, and even a big hairy beaver. I counted thirteen enormous beasts. A pair of ravens circled overhead, cawing loudly.

Hel gasped. "Huginn and Muninn!"

"Huh?"

"Odin's ravens." She scowled. "The Allfather knows of our plan, but it is of no matter. Let him enjoy the show!"

Our army had spilled out into wide ranks, the villagers staring in awe at the monsters they'd have to battle. It seemed all the war cries in the world couldn't buff their courage enough. I couldn't imagine how an army, much less one person could possibly fight through such odds especially with only melee weapons and wooden shields.

It didn't matter. I'd raised this army with only one goal in mind, and that was to keep the creatures diverted while I raced past them and all the way to the distant finish line at the far end of the valley. It didn't look like more than a mile or two from this position. Mortis would have to be careful crossing the rugged terrain, but we could probably bypass the beasts.

"What is on your mind, Cain?" Hel watched me uncertainly. "Do you doubt our chances?"

I shook my head. "No, I don't. Unfortunately, I can't stay to fight."

She flinched. "What do you mean?"

"I mean that I'm going to lead them into battle and then leave them behind." I reached over and touched her hand. "Hel, I have to get back to Gaia or souls will be trapped in dead bodies. I can put the reaping on hold for a while, but sooner or later, the dead will rise, and Armageddon will destroy the world."

She yanked her hand from mine. "Then go, Cain. Abandon the valiant dead you have led into this hopeless battle and return to your little world."

I blinked a few times. "Uh, Gaia is Earth. You know, the mortal realm and all that? Do you really want the apocalypse?"

"I care not what happens to it if you run like a coward from this battle!" Hel wiped tears from her eyes. "I had thought you better than this!"

"I had no idea I'd be trapped in Hel when I came here!" I threw up my hands. "Look, I offered everyone a chance at reaching Valhalla. This is their chance, and they can do it without me!"

Beasts roared and charged, trampling over the skeletons on their side without a second thought. Scattered cries rose from the Viking ranks and they gathered into formations that would do nothing to stop the charge of the giant beasts.

"Fuck my life," I growled. I nudged Mortis and we galloped toward the front lines. The moment the beasts hit the Vikings, that would be my perfect chance to escape.

Regardless of what Hel said, it wasn't because I was a coward, but because I had responsibilities, gods damn it! I had a responsibility to humanity. Fighting and dying in Hel sure as hell wasn't going to solve that.

This was my chance to get out of this miserable underworld and I was going to take it.

28

I saw Astrid on the front line bracing herself for the brutal impact of a massive wolf. The beast would run right over them without even slowing down. I spotted Vikings with long pikes scattered among the throng. "What are those idiots thinking?" I turned Mortis parallel to the ranks and shouted out at the warriors. "Pikes to the front! Pikes to the front now!"

The pikemen rushed forward without hesitation until most of the front line bristled with the long weapons.

I raced around to the front of the formation. "Plant your pikes!"

The nearest fighters looked at me in confusion. I leapt down from Mortis, grabbed a pike and planted the haft into the ground, then angled it out. I showed the pike wielder how to brace it, then shouted down the row. "Plant your gods damned pikes!"

The others followed by example. I glanced at the rushing beast army and saw we had only a few seconds before they reached us. "Swords form up behind pikes! Slash the tendons!" I kept shouting the commands as I raced down the front line. Just as I reached the end, the wave hit the Vikings.

Giant animals roared as they impaled themselves upon the pikes. The wolves howled as swords and axes swung against the backs of their legs, severing tendons. Vikings drove axes down on the toes of the beasts, crippling them. But the animals weren't finished. Jaws flashed out and tore men, women, and children to shreds.

The beaver spun, knocking scores of Vikings aside with its broad tail. The rams lowered their heads and butted attackers so hard, shattering bones splintered through their skin. Thankfully, the initial damage was already done, and many of the beasts were hobbled by the damage to their legs and paws. It didn't matter how big you were if you couldn't walk. The beaver, having been a slow runner hadn't impaled itself, and it sat low enough to the ground to keep swords away from its feet.

I had no idea what the fuck a big hairy beaver was doing here, but it was giving the Vikings a hell of time. Another squad of Vikings ducked as the goats spun, kicking and butting anyone who came close. A few fighters made it beneath the horns and rammed swords up into the giant dangling balls of a ram.

The bleat and screams of pain were enough to make my eyes water. "I feel you, buddy. I feel you."

The wolves went down beneath a swarm of hacking and stabbing Vikings. The rams were nearly done for as their giant balls took a beating. But the fucking beaver was just too much for anyone to handle. The pounding it was taking only seemed to make it fight back harder. I turned Mortis toward the beast, and we galloped at full speed. Timing the beaver's spin, I guided Mortis up the broad tail and onto the beaver's back. I drew the scythe and leapt off Mortis, swinging down with all my might. The massive blade cleaved through the tail, neatly severing it.

The beaver made a horrible squealing sound and thrashed wildly as blood rained down. Vikings rushed in with pikes, ramming them into the monstrous creature's neck and jaw. At long last, it fell into a quivering heap on the ground.

The battlefield was littered with the carcasses of giant beasts and countless Viking bodies. Less than half of our original numbers were left—staggering losses to be sure but considering the weaponry and the size of the creatures, it was to be expected. The giant serpents seemed to have killed the most people since they had simply slithered between the pikes and bitten scores of fighters with their venomous fangs.

Aside from a few remaining skirmishes, the battle was over in less than an hour. All that lay between us and the proving grounds was a few miles of dangerous terrain.

Hel galloped toward fallen warriors and leapt off her horse. She knelt and pressed a hand to the forehead of a boy. "Old Sven fought his way here across countless lives only to fall again."

I joined her. "The poor guy has been reincarnated and crapped out a few times already?"

"At least a hundred times. He never gave up trying to reach the proving grounds, but now he is dead again."

I frowned. "Is he, though? I mean, if he didn't get eaten and crapped out then he's still a soul, right?"

"He is dead until we burn the body." Hel sighed and rose. "Then he will reincarnate as a baby again."

"How long does it take? And does someone have to give birth to him?"

She shook her head. "The baby rises from the ashes the morning after."

"What if you leave him to rot?"

She grimaced. "Then he would remain truly dead."

A voice weakly called out my name. I turned and saw movement in a pile of bodies. I raced over and rolled bloodied bodies away, revealing Astrid. Her skin was jaundiced. Blackened veins stood out in her neck. A giant puncture wound in her leg told me all I needed to know. She'd been bitten by a serpent.

"No!" I dragged her out of the pile. "Mortis, come! Hold on, Astrid. We'll get you to the proving ground so you can die like a warrior, okay?"

"Too late." She touched my face. "Thank you." A shiver stole her words, then she managed to speak again. "Y-you gave this old Viking faith again, Cain."

I stroked her hair. "Gods be damned, Astrid, no one deserves Valhalla more than you."

Bloody foam boiled from her mouth. She smiled and died in my arms.

My fists clenched. I shouldn't care about this woman I barely knew, but in the short time I'd known her, she'd proven that she and everyone who'd died on this field deserved a chance at Valhalla.

Hel stood by my side, a hand on my shoulder. "You did not abandon us, Cain. You fought bravely, and these warriors died good deaths."

"Did they, though?" I pushed Astrid's body off my lap and stood. "They didn't die where it counted!"

I paced back and forth talking to myself. "What the fuck are you doing, Cain? You should be long gone by now."

"Then let us gather the remaining army and go to the proving grounds." Hel took my arm. "We've made it, Cain."

A black meteor streaked across the sky, trailing dark smoke. It veered downward and smashed to earth a hundred yards away. A tall, thin figure rose from the smoldering crater, a crown of black horns on his head. The trickster god himself had arrived.

Loki approached us, a smirk on his face. "Cain, old friend, we meet again."

"Old friend?" I scoffed. "Buy me dinner sometime and we'll talk."

Hel froze. "Father? What are you doing here?"

"Checking in on my lovely daughter." His smirk turned into a wicked grin. "I'm afraid you must turn back, dear. There is no place for you in Asgard or Valhalla."

She gasped. "How can you say that?"

"In fact," Loki said in a booming voice, "there is no place for any of you in Valhalla. Turn back now, or you will all be killed and left here to rot. You will never reincarnate and will remain corpses for eternity."

I stepped forward, scythe in hand. "Will you kill them? Will a god raise his hand against mortals?"

Loki laughed. "What a cute toy you have there, Cain. It's a shame you cannot return to Gaia. It's a shame Midgard will soon be overrun with the walking dead and the three horsemen shall ride."

A retort died on my lips as puzzle pieces clicked together in my head. The Norse realms were the seat of power for Loki. Had the trickster lured me here with rumors of Thanatos so he could trap me?

He laughed again. "I see you have realized the trap long after it has sprung, little man. Yes, Thanatos was my daughter's lover for some time, but that was so long ago. All I had to do was plant seeds of rumors and let you follow them to Hel. My agents even supplied your orc friend with information that would convince you to come here."

I bared my teeth. "You conniving jackass."

Loki smirked. "I knew that once you crossed Gjallarbrú there would be no turning back. You would be trapped in Hel forever."

"But you didn't expect this, did you?" I managed a smirk of my own. "Your appearance has only confirmed that this is the way out of Hel, and you can't stop me."

"There is no path from Valhalla that will take you out of Hel, Cain. Whether you're here or there, you are trapped."

He was bluffing. Maybe there was no way out of Valhalla, but that wasn't why I was doing this. My plan, as usual, circumvented the rules. "If that's true, then let us pass."

"I will do nothing to stop you." Loki ran his gaze over the survivors. "But there is yet another gauntlet you must face, and I guarantee you will not survive it. Turn back now, or rot here forever."

The Vikings looked at each other and then at Hel, uncertainty plain on their faces. Hel looked ashen even by her standards. She backed slowly away. "Please father, I just ask—"

"Ask no more and return to your dirt pit, you little fool!" Loki thundered. "You have freedom enough without being granted entrance to Asgard!"

"But why can I not go there, Father?" Hel sounded like a pleading child. "Am I not a goddess? Am I not worthy?"

Loki thrust his finger back toward the canyons. "Go now. I will not repeat myself."

I knew then that the proving grounds had to be the way out or

Loki wouldn't be so Hel-bent on stopping us. I also realized how I could make sure everyone made it out, provided I could survive whatever secret weapon Loki threatened to unleash.

I mounted Mortis and turned him back toward the canyon.

"I see the little man has come to his sense." Loki giggled. "Enjoy your stay in Hel, Cain. Perhaps my daughter can make use of your frail body."

I hadn't turned Mortis to face the canyon, but to face the remnants of our broken army. "Hear me now, Vikings. Today you have fought, bled, and died as true warriors despite not having reached the proving grounds." I turned and thrust a finger at Loki. "And now the god of cowards, the underbelly of Asgard, the treacherous trickster, has made a special trip all the way down to Hel so he can threaten you with final death should you not turn back now."

"Cain, what are you doing?" Hel said softly.

"What is worse, brave warriors—to die and live eternity in a coward's paradise, or to die and slumber peacefully forever, having fought your best and striven for that golden paradise you were denied?" I raised a fist. "Because this cowardly god denies you now!"

The Vikings roared in approval. "Down with Loki!"

"We are not cowards!" I roared. "We are mother fucking Vikings!"

They began chanting. "Mother fucking Vikings! Mother fucking Vikings!"

Loki's smug smirk soured. "Very well. Face your final deaths, then." He swung down a fist and holes tore open in the sky, each one birthing meteors that trailed oily black smoke. They impacted the ground, spraying water as if giant water balloons had just exploded. I tasted salt on my lips and soon realized why.

A small army of deep ones appeared out of the craters. Snakelike creatures with arms and catfish heads slithered toward us. Bizarre centaur-like crustaceans with lobster bodies and human torsos skittered at us. There were smaller ones, fish-shaped bipeds bristling with spiky ridges along their backs and jaws full of sharp teeth. The most monstrous were the hulking angler-fish hybrids, their massive jaws filled with jagged teeth, and a single tentacle bobbing like fishing lures from their foreheads.

Clamshells popped open, revealing one-eyed blobs inside swarming with tentacles. The tentacles lashed out, dragging the clams across the ground and toward us.

The chanting stopped as Viking cried out in fear at these new monsters. I raised my fist. "Form ranks! Pikes to the front!"

There was a brief hesitation, then everyone scrambled to comply. We had maybe five hundred warriors left against an army of creatures that numbered nearly the same.

"So, you've completely thrown in your lot with the Elder Things, Loki?" I scowled. "Do the halves cry out for unity?"

He flinched. "Where did you hear that, little man?"

"Nyarlathotep told me." I readied my scythe. "He's playing you like a fool, Loki. The Elder Things will destroy the universe and remake it in their image. There will be no human gods left once they're done!"

"No, you're wrong." His smirk returned. "Did you know I once turned into a mare so I might bear the eight-legged stallion Sleipnir? Did you know I bore the serpent Jörmungandr?" He laughed maniacally. "I am the father of monsters, Cain. The Elder Things are my family, and I will rule them all."

"You're a fucking moron if you think that's true!" I shook the scythe at him. "Nyarlathotep told me who the new ruler will be, but I guess you'll never find out if your minions kill us. Call off the dogs and we can talk."

Loki paused as if considering it, then abruptly shook his head. "No, I won't fall for your ruse, little man." A cone of light formed around him. "When you die—and mark my words, you will not survive this day—I will turn your bones into a scarecrow so that all denizens of Hel will remember this glorious day." The earth cracked beneath him and then he shot into the air, a meteor escaping orbit, and vanished into the sky.

Once again, I considered running for the proving grounds, but something else held me back this time. It wasn't fear or pride. It was something else entirely.

It was my hatred for Loki.

There was one reason, and one reason only I was going to help these people and that was to beat that underhanded asshole at his own game. I leapt off Mortis and swung the scythe back and forth, judging the balance of the weapon. So long as the beasts attacked me first, I could kill them with the scythe.

The deep ones were eerily silent as they rushed toward us. There were no roars of battle, no cries, only clacking claws, ribbiting toad heads, and faint gurgling and slurping.

Pikes lowered, the Viking frontlines met the charge. Toad hybrids croaked in agony as their soft bellies were punctured. The pikes glanced off the hardened shells of crustaceans and strong claws cleaved through weapons and bodies alike.

I flanked from the side, swinging the scythe wide and hard. It slashed through bodies, spreading guts and gore across the ground. The crustacean shells were harder to penetrate. I considered using Soultaker, but I didn't want to claim any of these monsters' souls. A lobster centaur—lobstertaur—the size of Clydesdale charged me, claws snapping. The scythe parried the blows, but the shell was so hard, the blade glanced off it.

With a sudden thrust of its claws, I stumbled back, and the creature drove the pincers down to finish me off.

29

Hel's skull and bones broadsword parried the claws at the last instant. I rolled out of the way and Lobstersaurus Rex skittered after me while Hel dealt with another threat.

"How in the hell can Loki bring an army of living creatures here?" I said. "This is the land of the dead!"

"He has always been able to do things long thought impossible," Hel said as she thrust her great skull broadsword into a bipedal toad.

"I thought you couldn't fight with us."

"Not against the badlands creatures, but these monsters are something else entirely." With a mighty roar, she split a charging lobstertaur from crown to sternum. Shrieking, the creature fell in neat halves, displaying a small fortune in lobster tail meat.

"I wonder if that's edible."

Hel made a face. "Is it wrong that I wondered the same thing just now?"

I grimaced. "Let's not find out, okay?"

An angler fish hybrid barged between us. Hel began fighting it, her sword clanging against its rusty iron trident while I continued fighting Lobstersaurus Rex, the biggest lobstertaur on the battlefield.

The scythe was doing nothing, so I reached over my back and

summoned my staff. My palm wrapped around its hilt. It was as comforting as finding an old friend in a foreign land. "Gods, I've missed you." The brightblade hummed to life and I thrust it into Lobstersaurus Rex's human torso, piercing the shell with ease.

Flesh smoked and the monster shrieked and hissed as its innards were boiled. "I guess lobsters really do scream when you cook them alive."

Its claws snapped in my face, so I yanked the blade from its torso and swung up, cleaving the giant claws. A low-crawling crab creature with tentacles sprouting from the top of its shell rammed into my feet, upending me. Swinging out with the scythe in my other hand, I rammed the haft onto the ground and used it to vault backwards, away from the grasping tentacles.

I spun, swinging the brightblade across the crab's tentacles, cleaving them and cauterizing the flesh all at once. I reversed my grip on the hilt and drove the blade straight down into the crab's back. The creature hissed, spasmed, and died. Lobstersaurus Rex toppled sideways as it succumbed to its internal injuries.

I turned to the next challenge.

Hel was surrounded by anglerfish hybrids. Their forehead tentacles lashed out at her, slashing the flesh side of her face and drawing blood. She cut through tentacles but couldn't keep up with the onslaught. It looked like a scene from a video found on the last page of Pornhub and I wasn't down with it.

Layla might be, though, I thought. Thinking of her reminded me of why I was in this mess in the first place. I had to bring her back to life if only to bitch about all the shit that I had to go through just to get her back.

I ran toward the gang of anglerfish hybrids and drove the brightblade through the back of the first one with one hand while cleaving the head off another with the scythe. I leapt through the gap in the deep ones and put my back to Hel's, then held the brightblade and scythe at angles to cover a wider area.

A tentacle lashed toward me, but it never reached my face as the brightblade cleaved it cleanly. The hybrids lunged. I dropped to a knee and plunged the brightblade into the chest of one and shoved the other one back with the scythe. If not for the supernatural strength of the Death cloak, they would have easily overpowered me.

Rising from my knees, I shoved forward, pushing the anglerfish hybrid back on its heels. As it stumbled off balance, I drove the brightblade into its stomach and carved a ragged L into its flesh. Sizzling and screeching, the creature died. I spun and saw Hel slash another creature diagonally down its torso. It slid into pieces, guts spilling out.

Consumed by the flow of battle, I lost track of time. The fight could have raged on for minutes or hours, but I kept ducking, slashing, stabbing, and cleaving until at long last, Hel, a few Vikings, and I remained standing among a pile of bodies. The odor of rotting fish and seafood was enough to make my gorge rise.

"Gods be damned." I waded through the gore and found a clean spot of grass where I collapsed. "Smells like the bathrooms in a Captain D's."

The remaining Vikings dragged the wounded and dying from the field and over to Hel where she gave some of them last rites.

Less than two hundred out of our original numbers remained. If Loki sent down another army of deep ones, we were done for. A small dark cloud appeared overhead, and I began cursing Loki's name. "What do we have to fight next?"

Hel followed my gaze and flinched. "What is that?"

The strangely undulating cloud settled onto the battlefield and began creeping over the piles of deep ones' bodies. I staggered to my feet and went closer until the strange thing came into focus. It was a tiny octopus with dozens of eyes along its head. Dark vapors rose from its body.

I backed away, uncertain if this tiny thing might be as deadly as the rabbit in the Holy Grail. "I-is this another monster we have to fight?"

"I am the darkness," the octopus whispered in a strange language. "Tremble before the mighty Zushakon."

I readied my scythe. "Do your worst."

The octopus paused, its eyes blinking in seemingly random intervals even as its tentacles spread across another deep one. Greenish vapors seeped from the deep one and into a mouth on Zushakon underside. "Welcome home, deep one."

Hel gasped and knelt next to it. "You're a death god like us!"

"I am the darkness," Zushakon said. "I welcome the dead to the eternal depths."

"You're adorable." Hel cooed and reached over to pet the tiny god.

Zushakon slapped away her hand with a tentacle. "I am small but fierce. Do not test me, goddess." Then it continued claiming souls of its dead.

I looked at the corpses of the giant beasts we'd fought earlier. "Do they have souls? Are they actually dead or will they come back to life?"

"They are dead, and I can only assume they have souls." Hel shook her head. "But I do not know who collects them."

I followed Zushakon as it continued its duties. "Are you in on the plan to help Loki? Do you want the Elder Things to rule creation?"

The octopus paused, turning its eyes on me. "My only concerns are our dead. My reach spans from the outer worlds to the human realms. I go where I must and collect those who worship Cthulhu and others. The deep ones have part human souls, but I treat them as our own. We are all parts of the same cycle, life, death, creation, destruction. There is no us, no you, only the universe." Seemingly satisfied with its answer, it continued across the corpses, harvesting souls.

I sat down and watched it work. The Vikings looked with confusion at the bodies, apparently unable to see Zushakon. It seemed Hel and I were the only ones who could see the creature since we were death deities.

Loki must have thought there was no way we could survive the army of deep ones because he didn't return with reinforcements, or even pop in to make sure we were dead. Perhaps he was simply too busy with other schemes that he had no time to check in on us. Whatever the reason, I wasn't going to complain, but it was imperative that we get up and hurry to the proving grounds before we had to face a round three.

There was just one major problem with reaching the proving grounds. I was fucking exhausted. The rest of the Vikings could die at the hands of a Valkyrie no problem since they'd go to Valhalla no matter what. But for my plan of escape to work, I needed to remain very much alive.

I pushed to my feet. "We need to go before Loki makes another appearance."

Groaning with weariness, the other Vikings also rose and formed ragged ranks. Many of them looked at their dead comrades, tears in their eyes.

A woman covered in war paint jabbed her sword into the ground. "We can't just leave them to rot. They must be burned."

"And then what?" A man said. "We leave babies here to wander the badlands?"

"I've been reincarnated twice," the woman said. "We keep our old memories so even babies can walk back to the village."

I grimaced at the thought.

Hel shook her head. "The babes might die of starvation on the trek back and unless their bodies are burned again, they will not revive."

"What kind of fucking afterlife is this?" I said. "You might as well be back on Gaia if you can die here."

"This is the Viking underworld." Hel offered a wan smile. "What would you expect but hardship and toil? Odin thought that the worst afterlife a Viking could face would be that of an ordinary life. The denizens of Hel live without battle. They age and die and are reborn to do it all again. It is the place for cowards and weaklings, or so he thought."

"Those who came with us today earned a warrior's death." I pounded a fist against my leg. "Every Viking in this field, fallen or living has become a hero. There are no cowards on this field!"

A ragged cheer rose from the ranks.

I did the math and it just didn't work. We had miles of rugged terrain to cross before reaching the proving grounds and I wasn't sure if we could pull off what I was thinking. I turned to Mortis and Thveri who were nuzzling at the edge of the carnage. Apparently, this was what death horses considered a romantic spot.

I glanced at the fallen monsters we'd fought earlier and chose the big hairy beaver. It had exactly what we needed if we were going to make this work. "Come with me and we will help the fallen."

The Vikings followed me without question. With all of us shoving against the fat beaver, we managed to roll it onto its back, tongue lolling gruesomely beneath its giant buck teeth. I climbed onto it and ran a slash down from the throat to the asshole. Vikings gathered on the sides and began tugging at the skin, working with swords and axes to free it from the muscles beneath.

Before long, we had it laid out to the sides, leaving the now-naked beaver sprawled on it. It took even more effort to roll the large creature over so we could cut the skin free from its back, and then another concerted shoving session to roll the hairless beaver off the pelt entirely. There was no time to properly tan the hide, so the village tanner had everyone scrub the raw pelt with rocks to grind away the remaining flesh.

Once done, I examined the giant hide and nodded in satisfaction. It was nasty, but it would get the job done. The Vikings spread out across the field and began hauling bodies to the pelt, lying them out along it and piling them higher and higher. Some bodies had fallen into fissures or crevices and had to be hauled out. Thankfully, none of the holes went very deep.

Hel and I hitched Mortis and Thveri to the pelt with chains that some Vikings had used as weapons. Then we urged the horses forward. The supernatural equines had no problem hauling the load, but the uneven terrain caused corpses to roll down the mound and spill out onto the ground. So long as the pace was slow, the Vikings were able to pick up the fallen bodies and toss them back on.

"It's not perfect, but it will do."

"What is the plan, exactly?" Hel said.

I blew out a breath. "It won't be pretty, but I think it'll work."

"What won't be pretty?"

I told her and she laughed gleefully. "Oh, this will be wonderful."

I grimaced. "You're twisted, you know that?"

Hel looked confused. "Naturally. That which is twisted is beautiful."

I looked at her lovely half-flesh, half-skull face, and nodded. "In your case, yes."

Surprisingly, Mortis didn't seem the least bit put out about pulling cargo duty. If anything, he seemed proud of being a beast of burden to a mound of Viking corpses. It took us hours to cross the distance at the slow, steady pace required by the insane load of bodies, but at long last, we crossed the length of the valley and reached a crystal blue lake surrounded by cliffs. A black sand beach and forests surrounded the lake, but I saw no sign of anything resembling proving grounds.

Hel sighed. "This is a perfect place for a Viking funeral."

"We don't have a boat," I said.

"We don't need one." She turned to the Vikings. "Gather as much firewood as possible. We will make a pyre the likes of which not even the gods have seen!"

Exhausted though they were, the Vikings raised a cheer and got to work combing the forests for dead wood that would burn easily while others began chopping saplings.

Bright light shone down on the lake and a single Valkyrie on a flying horse descended from the heavens. The horse swooped low over the water, raising a rooster tail of water behind it. It landed on the beach and the Valkyrie leapt off, sword in hand.

If things worked out, that flying horse was my ticket back over the river and out of Hel.

"Who comes to challenge—" She broke off in confusion at the massive pile of dead bodies and Hel standing nearby.

The Valkyrie wore her hair shaved around the sides with a braided topknot running down her back. I'd only met one Valkyrie and it just so happened that she was that one. I strode forward. "We meet again, Kara."

She scowled. "Little man!"

I sighed. "Why do Norse people call me that? I'm over six feet tall!"

Kara strode forward and towered over me by a full head. "Cain Sthyldor, the little man. What are you doing in our afterlife?"

"That's a long story, but I'm working as the Grim Reaper right now and—"

She clapped her hands right in front of my nose. "Enough! You are here and that means I can kill you for the insults at Voltaire's. Thor was most displeased with me and demoted me to lesser duties. That is why I am in this forsaken pit!"

Hel stepped forward. "You will fight me first, Valkyrie. I will defeat you and earn the right to see Asgard and Valhalla."

Kara stared uncertainly at Hel for a moment. "I do not know how to respond to that, Lady Hel. You are the progeny of Loki, but you are also a god, and thus royalty."

"You can respond by fighting me."

Kara shook her head. "I cannot fight a goddess."

"What are the rules of combat?" I said. "We are weary from our travels and need rest before we can engage in honorable combat."

She glared at me. "You are allowed one night of rest and must face me by the time the sun rises to its peak tomorrow."

I grunted. "High noon?"

She nodded and sneered. "You will need all that time to prepare for your death, little man." Her sneer turned triumphant. "Because you have no chance at victory."

30

K ara and I had gotten off to a rough start during our first meeting. Our second meeting didn't seem to be going any better, so I decided to bluff. "You're assuming you'll win." I shrugged. "Don't be so sure."

Hel stepped forward. "You must fight me too. I will not be denied."

Kara knelt. "I yield to you, Lady Hel. There cannot be a fight between us."

A mote of starlight drifted from the sky and landed on Hel's head. There was a flash of light and she shivered with pleasure. "What does this mean?"

"It means you are worthy for you have defeated me." Kara rose to her feet. "I will not risk Thor's wrath by fighting one of his kin."

"Isn't Odin the one you should be worried about?" I asked.

She shrugged. "Odin has left many day-to-day functions to Thor."

Again, she turned to the corpses. "What is the meaning of this?"

I shrugged. "You'll just have to find out. Now, go away so you don't spoil the surprise."

She scoffed and glared at me, then reluctantly leapt on her winged horse and soared off into the heavens.

Hel laughed and spun in a circle. "I am finally worthy!"

"You've always been worthy," I said. "But now you have an official invite."

"And I will use it to bring Asgard to its knees!" She hugged me. "Now, let us finish this quest that you might get on with yours, brave man."

I was a bit disturbed by the first part of her statement, but at this point, I wasn't even going to ask. I went into the forest and used Soultaker to easily cleave down trees and chop them into logs. Green wood wouldn't normally burn well, but my brightblade had a way of making anything catch fire.

By the time night fell and a giant moon lit the lake, we had created a massive funeral pyre stretching for a hundred yards down the black sands. Bodies lined the top, most piled two high. I'd placed Astrid's body by itself at one end. Hel stood among the bodies atop the pyre and gave a speech.

"Your goddess has won her way to Asgard and beyond, my beloved warriors. You will tomorrow earn your place in Valhalla whether you win or lose your bout with the Valkyrie. Tonight, we will assure the honorable dead that they did not die in vain to reach this place. Let us honor them with a pyre worthy of the gods and praise all who made this possible." Hel raised her skull sword and uttered a word. Fire rained down from the sky all up and down the pyre, igniting it as easily as if it were dry kindling.

"Well, that saves me some work," I muttered. "Why in the Hel didn't she rain fire on the damned deep ones, though?"

Hel leapt down from the pyre as the blaze reached a hundred feet into the air and approached me. "I did not rain down fire because it would have killed our own people. Plus, it was more fun to fight without magic."

I grunted. "Not quite as much fun for the Vikings getting bitten in half by angler fish hybrids."

"The answer, Cain, is that I wanted to get bloody. I wanted to hack the monsters limb from limb. I had to watch like a helpless child during the battle of the beasts, but at long last, after so many eons, I was finally able to get my hands dirty!" She shivered and moaned with pleasure. "Soon Asgard will know how wonderful it feels."

I grimaced. "All Hel is about to break loose?"

She kissed me roughly, biting my lip hard enough to draw blood. "Oh, yes, my dear."

I backed away slowly. "Please, I really need my sleep tonight. I've got to fight a Valkyrie tomorrow!"

She nipped my lip again. "The battle worked me up and I must have relief." She gripped my hair and pulled. "I promise to be gentle."

I groaned. "You're not capable of that!"

"I insist, Cain."

Seeing there was no way out of this, I sighed and nodded. "But I'm keeping on the cloak so I hope you can deal with a literal boner."

Hel laughed. "Why do you think I loved Thanatos so dearly?"

It was no wonder Thanatos eventually fled Hel. She could seem so relatable at times and absolutely monstrous the next. Then again, she was the goddess of the Viking underworld.

Hel threw me to the ground right next to the pyre and had her way with me for gods only knew how long. The Death cloak gave me much needed stamina and strength to withstand the madness and her strength, so thankfully I had no more insane visions of Nyarlathotep or Azathoth. What I did have were some of the most intense and torturous orgasms ever.

When Hel was done, she waded into the water, singing a haunting melody. Farther down the beach, I saw Mortis and Thveri frolicking at the edge of the lake.

Despite the aid of the Death cloak, I was exhausted. I found my way to the end of the pyre where Astrid's body was nearly reduced to ash. I curled up in the sand, Hel's haunting song reaching me across the water, and fell asleep.

The laughter and delighted shrieks of children woke me early in the morning. Groaning, but thankfully not aching as I had the previous morning, I pushed to my feet and saw Vikings pulling naked toddlers from the ashes of the pyre. Other newly reincarnated Viking kids ran in circles while fierce warriors chased them down, big grins on their faces. It was such a surreal sight that I found myself staring in disbelief.

A little blonde girl with bright blue eyes walked up next to me, a smile on her face. She touched my hand and said, "Cain."

I immediately knew it was Astrid. I leaned down and took her tiny hand in mine. "Welcome back, warrior."

She giggled.

The beach was alive with jubilant kids and equally excited adults. Today was the day they'd finally earn a place in Valhalla.

Kara appeared on her flying horse right when the sun hit its high point and landed on the beach in front of the toddler army. Eyes wide with dismay, she dismounted and stared at the rows of babbling kids. "What is the meaning of this?"

"These brave Vikings died to reach the proving grounds," Hel said. "They will face the challenge and earn their way to Valhalla."

"You wish for me to slaughter children?" Kara bared her teeth. "There is nothing honorable about slaying babes who cannot even lift a sword!" She stalked over to a little boy who was struggling to lift a sword off the ground. "I will not do such a monstrous deed."

"They're reincarnated warriors, Kara." I stepped in front of the toddler army. "They knew what they were getting into and they're ready to fight you with bare fists if need be."

She paced back and forth muttering to herself, occasionally casting haunted looks our way. "You are monsters!"

I gave her a moment, then finally interrupted. "Look, you've got to kill them so they can go to Valhalla. Just leaving them here would be even crueler. They're Vikings, for gods' sakes."

Kara bared her teeth and growled at me. "I will kill you for this Cain."

I held up my hands. "You're duty bound to kill these toddlers and send them on their way to Valhalla, Kara. There is no way around it."

"Very well." She drew her gleaming sword and walked up to the first boy. Grinning with excitement, he charged her and started pounding his fists on her armored thigh. Looking down at him with disgust, Kara booted him away and swung her sword. The blade stopped a hair away from decapitating the boy. Sweat trickled down Kara's horrified face.

"Do it!" Hel shouted. "Send him to his reward, Valkyrie!"

Kara shook her head. "Not like this!" She knelt, tears of rage trickling down her cheeks. "I yield to this brave warrior."

A beam of rainbow light surrounded the boy. Laughing with glee, he shot into the sky and vanished in a pinpoint of light.

"Me next!" A girl shouted. "Me!"

All the kids started shouting to fight Kara next and the Valkyrie looked as if she wanted to be swallowed by the ground. She took several deep breaths, then calmed herself.

"Children, raise your hand if you challenge me!"

All the kids raised their hands. All except Astrid who still stood with me. I knelt next to her. "Astrid, go claim your reward."

Tears pooled in her eyes. She kissed my cheek. "Thank you, Cain."

I mussed her hair. "Enjoy Valhalla. You've earned it."

Raising her hand, she ran across the sand and joined the other kids.

Kara looked across the nearly thousand strong mob of children and nodded sagely. "You have all earned your way to Valhalla." She knelt. "I yield to the brave warriors."

Cones of rainbow light snatched the children in groups, taking them up into the sky. Before long, all that was left were the grownups.

Kara squared her shoulders and cast a grim look at the nearest man. "Do you challenge me?"

He drew a sword. "Yes, Valkyrie."

"Then fight."

He charged and went down without a head before he even got close to her. The rainbow light picked up his body and took him to Valhalla.

Kara faced the other few hundred adults. "Come at me challengers!"

They charged in groups or alone, but the end results were the same—they died without so much as landing a blow on the Valkyrie.

Within an hour, Hel and I were the only remaining people from the army.

It was my turn to face the supernatural Viking warrior. I might have been a top assassin in the Oblivion Guard and highly trained in multiple ways to kill people, but I knew my limitations. Even with the Death cloak, it would be an uphill battle to win against Kara.

If worse came to worst, I could use the mortal coil to even the odds. Thankfully, I still had it in my utility belt. I also had Soultaker but killing a Valkyrie with that would probably not go over so well.

Besides, my plan involved no fighting. Judging from the eager look on Kara's face, I had a feeling she wouldn't be willing to go along with it.

I held up a finger. "Before we fight, I would like to offer a proposition."

"Fight me, coward." Kara stepped closer, muscles bulging beneath her silver armor.

"Before we fight, you should know that I'm working as Death. If I die here, then the dead on Gaia will rise, and an apocalypse will destroy the world." I took a step back. "Do you really want to be responsible for that?"

She paused a moment. "I would gladly trade the world just to kill you for the way you insulted me the day we first met."

"Did I really insult you, though?" I waggled a hand. "I just wanted to be left alone so I could enjoy my mangorita."

"Mangoritas are an abomination!" She glared at me. "I tried one and found it sickly sweet and disgusting."

"They're not for everyone." I took another step back as she continued stalking closer. "Look, just fly me across the river on your horse and we can go our separate ways. There's no need for further bloodshed. Besides, I'm not a Norse worshiper, so I can't go to Valhalla."

"I don't care." A maniacal grin crossed her face. "I will kill you."

I turned to Hel. "Can you help me out here?"

Hel shook her head. "I have no control over Valkyrie, Cain, but I'm sure you'll do well."

"Well, fuck." I summoned the scythe and whirled it. "I just hope Odin or Thor aren't pissed when I kill this Valkyrie."

Kara laughed. "Oh, there is no danger of you winning this fight." She lunged, blurring toward me, metal wings springing from her back.

I parried a strike, twisted, and missed a blow to her ankles. The haft of her sword hit me in the stomach, knocking me back several feet. I rolled backward, narrowly avoiding a decapitating blow from her razor-sharp wings. Springing back to my feet, I caught several more blows against the haft of the scythe, but it was impossible to catch a breath as she delivered devastating strike after strike with the sword and wings. If not for the Death cloak, I would've been over-powered in seconds.

The scythe just wasn't cutting it, literally and figuratively. I needed to switch to a weapon I was intimately familiar with. I reached back and focused on summoning my oblivion staff. The cool, reassuring grip met my hand, and I banished the scythe back to whence it came. The scythe was a superbly crafted weapon and extremely light, but there was nothing like having my old friend with me for this duel.

The brightblade hummed to life just in time to meet Kara's sword. Energy crackled against her blade as she pressed it toward me. She bared her teeth in a grin. "I had heard the Oblivion Guard were fierce warriors. So far, I am not impressed."

"You're not that good yourself." I jumped back, hoping it would throw her off balance, but she anticipated the move and thrust the blade at my midriff. I arched my back but the tip grazed my abdomen. Had it not been for the cloak, I probably would've lost my intestines.

Kara pressed the attack, moving almost too quickly for even my Death reflexes to keep up with. Twice she nearly gutted me, and then tried to sever my arm all the while grinning like a maniac. She was enjoying this far too much for my comfort. Somehow, I had to even the odds. I slipped the mortal coil from my utility belt and let it wrap around my wrist. It only worked on bare skin contact, and that would be a major challenge with her armor.

If Kara had been wearing video game armor, it would've been a cinch to find bare flesh. Most female warriors in video games or movies wore armor that enhanced their breasts and legs, showing enough skin to leave almost nothing to the imagination. In real life, however, Valkyrie armor covered her nearly from head to toe. Only her neck and hands weren't protected.

The coil poised to strike. Kara backed away, staring suspiciously at it. "What do you mean to do with that? Snare me by my neck?"

"Nothing so dramatic." I faked a confident smirk. "Think of it as a surprise."

She slashed at it immediately, apparently hoping to catch me off guard. The coil dodged the strike on its own and struck at her hand, wrapping around the hand and the hilt. Kara gasped and staggered back. "What witchery is this?"

I lunged forward. Her sword swung up clumsily and I smashed it from her grip. I spun and donkey kicked her in the stomach. Kara flew back and rolled across the black sand beach. I dashed after her as she scrabbled backwards to avoid the brightblade. But without her supernatural strength and speed, I was on her in an instant, my blade hovering over her throat.

"Yield, Valkyrie. By doing so, you will agree to fly me over the Gjöll."

"Never!" Her eyes blazed with hatred and anger. "I would sooner die than yield to a scoundrel!"

"Hey, I'm not a scoundrel." I kept the blade just over her throat. "Look, I don't know why you hate me so much, but there's no need to die. Just fly me to the other side with your horse and you'll never have to see me again."

"I refuse." She rose to her knees, head raised proudly and baring her neck. "Kill me and be done with it. You will have nowhere to go and be trapped here for eternity."

"I'll just kill you and take your horse."

Kara laughed bitterly. "Vjormir will never let you ride her. She will depart for Asgard the moment you kill me. You will never escape Hel."

31

Kara wasn't going to help me even under pain of death. Her hands were behind her back, and it was obvious she was trying to unwind the mortal coil from her hand. Even without supernatural strength, removing the coil wasn't too difficult. Once it came free, we'd be back to fighting again. On the other hand, killing her would serve no purpose. My best bet was to ask Hel to go to Asgard and find another Valkyrie or maybe even a spare flying horse. I turned around and noticed that Hel was nowhere to be seen.

"What the fuck?"

Kara laughed again. "Hel has used you for her own purposes and has left you to die. How does that make you feel?"

I blew out a breath. "It makes me feel horrible, okay? Is that what you want to hear?" I banished the brightblade and stepped back as she struggled with the mortal coil. I held out a hand and recalled it. The length of gray rope snapped back to me and I stuffed it in my utility belt. "You got me, Kara. I'll be trapped here, and Gaia will suffer without the Grim Reaper harvesting souls of the dead. The remaining three horsemen will ride, and that'll be that."

She leapt lithely to her feet and recovered her sword. "Yes, it will." Roaring a battle cry, she charged me.

A column of lightning struck the ground not far from us, splitting the air with a sonic boom. A tall, heavily muscled figure emerged from the smoke, a scowl on his face.

Kara's progress died mid charge as she saw Thor. She dropped to a knee. "My lord why are you here?"

"Why is Valhalla being flooded with an army of children?" he roared. "Why is the goddess of the underworld flaunting herself at the palace in Asgard?" He stormed over to Kara, glowering. "You were put in charge of the proving grounds, Kara. What have you done to unleash this fresh Hel upon the rest of us?"

Kara trembled slightly and looked to me. "It is his fault."

Thor turned, eyes narrowed. "This is but one of the skeleton warriors that guard the badlands. How is it responsible?"

"It is Cain disguised as the Grim Reaper, my lord!"

Thor flinched. "What is the Grim Reaper doing in our underworld?"

I lowered the hood and bowed. "Apologies, Thor, but I am on a quest to save the mortal realm and became trapped in Hel."

He stared at me for a long moment. "You are the one who would not relinquish Soultaker to us."

"For good reason." I had an even worse feeling about this situation. Thor could take Soultaker from me and leave me here to rot. I had no way to return it to the warehouse by using the ring. The only good thing was that it was sheathed beneath the cloak, so he didn't know it was here. I decided to appeal to his sense of godly duty. "The sword currently contains the soul of Athena. I am searching for a way to free her soul, so I came here in search of Thanatos. Though he'd been here long ago, it turned out that Loki used old rumors to lure me to Hel, so I'd be trapped."

"Loki is a crafty one," Thor said.

I nodded. "Hel told me the only way out was through the proving grounds or perhaps by flying over the Gjöll. I'd hoped to convince a Valkyrie to fly me back over."

His eyes narrowed. Then he stormed forward and gripped the front of the cloak. "Did you raise an army of babes so you could reach the proving grounds?" His lips peeled back from his teeth. "Are you the one who showed Hel how to reach Asgard?"

It seemed my explanation was about to get me killed, but I decided to go all in rather than back off. I stiffened my spine. "I used the goddess of Hel and the denizens of the underworld just so I could get the Hel out of here."

Thor blinked. Thunder rumbled and lightning struck the ashes of the pyre. Then he burst into laughter and pushed me not very gently away. "Oh, Cain. I heard of your exploits in Feary and how you liberated the enslaved beasts simply so you could free yourself from the fae. And now you've done it again." He pursed his lips and nodded. "You are a true strategist—something sorely lacking among our ranks these days. I am amazed a mortal magician has such talent."

I almost scoffed at the term magician but shrugged instead. "My current strategy is to release Athena from Soultaker so she can once again aid the Greek pantheon defending the divine realm."

He patted me on the back hard enough to send me stumbling forward. "Then we shall aid you!"

Before I could ask how, he gripped the front of the cloak and raised Mjolnir. A column of lightning big enough to turn an elephant to ash coursed over us. We shot skyward in a funnel of rainbow light. My stomach should have shot out of my asshole at such incredible speeds, but aside from the stars streaking past on one side and the massive trunk of Yggdrasil on the other, it felt as if we were hardly moving.

We burst through cloud cover and the rainbow funnel turned sideways, flattening into a rainbow road. The road ended at the edge of the clouds not far from us. A city of silver and gold sparkled ahead.

I grunted. "You ever thought about racing go-karts on the Bifrost? Maybe add some twists and loops for fun?"

Thor frowned. "You are not the first to mention this to us. I took my best warriors to Midgard once and tried these go-karts you speak of. They are small but offered much entertainment. Perhaps other Asgardians would appreciate such leisure activities."

"Oh, I think they would."

He nodded sagely. "In these troubled times, it would be good to have diversions for the Valkyries. The battle to protect our realm has been more intense than ever recently." Thor looked me up and down. "That is why we needed Soultaker. The army of the dead would turn the tide."

"Actually, I have bad news about that." I looked around. "Uh, where's Mortis—Death's horse?"

Thor frowned. "We left your prized steed in Hel?"

I nodded.

"I saw no other creatures around." His eyebrows rose. "Hel, however, came into Asgard with two horses."

"Are you fucking kidding me?" I gritted my teeth. "Mortis left me in Hel!"

"There is no greater betrayal than a man's horse leaving him." Thor patted my shoulder. "You would do better to find another one whose loyalty is unquestionable."

"Technically, he's not my horse. He belongs to the office of Death."

Thor frowned. "Ah, yes. When you spoke of Thanatos earlier, I remember hearing that he had abandoned his post and given it to mortals. Shortly after that, there were rumors of his love affair with Hel."

I grunted. "I didn't realize rumors from Hel reached Asgard."

"With Odin's ravens constantly spying on everyone, we hear all the rumors in Asgard."

I thought of the ravens watching the battle in the badlands. "Then Odin knows about everything that happened in Hel already."

"No doubt." Thor pursed his lips. "I just now remembered a time when Thanatos came to Asgard after leaving Hel. He sought out Freya for advice since she is a goddess who also deals in death."

"What sort of advice?"

"She said he was asking about the horses of the Valkyrie and other supernatural creatures of Asgard. I think he wanted to know if they died." He scoffed. "At the time I would have said no, but as the battles in this realm grow fiercer, we have lost Valkyrie and their steeds."

I tried to imagine what creatures could kill someone as skilled as Kara. "Are they replaceable?"

"Hardly." Thor waved a hand and switched subjects. "Tell me this bad news about Soultaker, Cain."

"The souls in the sword are like berserkers—extremely hard to control, and just as likely to attack your own troops as the enemy. Anyone killed by the undead army will also be claimed by Soultaker, but the outsider souls do not always follow the commands of the wielder."

"Meaning they could turn on you?" Thor said.

I nodded. "You would be creating an army of undead outsiders that would eventually rebel."

He glanced at the waist of the cloak. "I assume that is Soultaker hidden beneath your clothing?"

Fuck, I thought. Apparently, it wasn't as well hidden as I'd hoped. "How did you know?"

"I am an ancient, experienced warrior, Cain. I could tell by your stance that you did not want me to see a large weapon hidden beneath your cloak." He motioned toward the city and the rainbow road began to move like a massive conveyer belt. "I believe we can negotiate about the sword, but first, we must free Athena." He shook his head in amazement. "If even she can be killed by the sword, then it is a grave danger to all the gods."

I considered telling him that killing Athena required making her mortal first. Not even cutting the head off an immortal god would steal the soul since their body could probably recover from even such a grave wound. Then again, I wasn't about to test that theory. So, I kept quiet about how Athena had died and simply nodded in agreement. "Soultaker is an abomination of a weapon that should be destroyed. Unfortunately, I can't do that without freeing the souls first, or the undead army will be unleashed upon the world."

"That is troubling, indeed. It is imperative we keep the weapon from Loki at all costs."

"And yet, Loki seems to travel freely anywhere," I said. "He came into Hel and attacked us with deep ones."

"My brother released eldritch horrors in the home of his daughter?" Thor growled. "My brother has always been cunning and devious, always looking to sow chaos. But his new obsession with the Elder Things seems beyond even him."

"He claims the Elder Things and Elder Gods must be unified and made whole." I shook my head. "He seems to think he's one of them."

"He has dabbled in Cthonian matters over the centuries, but his current obsession is on a whole new level." Thor hung Mjolnir on his belt and looked ahead. "It is rumored he even shifted into an outsider so he could birth children with them."

I grunted. "That dude is more fluid than water."

"Indeed." Thor blew out a breath. "We will fetch your steed in Asgard, and then send you back to Midgard so you can continue your quest. I would render you further aid, but I am due back on the frontlines. Before that, I must think of a suitable punishment for Kara's utter failure as a guardian of the proving grounds."

"She didn't really fail," I said. "Once someone reaches the proving grounds, they earn a trip to Valhalla whether they live or die."

"Do you know what chaos she unleashed on Valhalla?" Thor shuddered. "Babies as far as the eye can see, running, laughing, and shrieking with such pleasure in the middle of the great feast halls with some of our greatest heroes watching in utter confusion!"

I snort-laughed, tried to repress it, then burst into laughter. "Holy shit, can I see that? Because it sounds kind of awesome."

Thor growled in disapproval.

"Will they grow into adults eventually?" I said.

"Naturally. When people die in battles in Valhalla, they reincarnate as they do in Hel."

"Good. Those toddlers running amuck will have some good stories to tell about how they battled the beasts of the badlands, defeated an army of deep ones, and earned their way into the hall of heroes with other Vikings." I thought of Astrid and grinned. "They deserve it, Thor. Kara bears no fault for following the rules."

He regarded me for a long moment. "Perhaps you are right."

I nodded. "She was bound by the rules and she followed them."

"I have been disgruntled with her performance since her encounter with you in Voltaire's." He sighed. "Perhaps she should aid you in your quest to earn redemption."

My mouth dropped open. "Please, no. I've got enough problems already without having a Valkyrie questioning every decision I make. It sounds like the worst buddy cop movie never made."

Thor burst into laughter. "How entertaining that punishment would be." He grew serious again. "Let us get you on your way, Cain. There is much to be done."

"I know a certain druid who seems to think you're a real dick. But you're not that bad."

"I have done many great and terrible things, Cain." Thor's gaze seemed lost in the distance. "But I gained many worshippers thanks to mortal movies that make me out to be some kind of superhero." A smile crossed his face. "I rather like that image. More importantly, it made me reflect on my past. Somewhere along the way, we gods lost our path and purpose. We are here to protect our creations, not abuse and destroy them. With great responsibility comes great power."

I blinked. "Uh, I think you have that reversed."

He shook his head. "No. Those who accept their responsibility are powerful people indeed."

I had to admit it made sense. "Well, Uncle Ben had it half right, I guess."

The Bifrost took us up a rise at the edge of the city, giving us a magnificent view of the layout. Asgard didn't even remotely resemble what I'd seen in the movies. A mountainous fortress of silver and gold columns dominated the center. Tall walls divided the city into twelve sections, and in each one stood smaller palaces, some with domed roofs and Romanesque features, while others had the high-pitched roofs and rough dimensions of the buildings I'd seen in Hel.

Nearly everything had a golden or silver sheen to it, as if glossed over with precious metals just to certify the buildings were built for the gods. I took a moment to soak in the view and appreciate the fact that I was entering a place most mortals could only dream of. I wasn't sure if it was an honor or punishment for all the shit I'd gotten myself into recently.

A winged chariot waited at the end of the Bifrost. I followed Thor onboard, and he snapped the reins attached to the front. The two-wheeled chariot accelerated and soared into the air, taking us toward the fortress. It was further away than I'd thought, a testament to the sheer scale of the place.

"Is that Odin's palace?" I said.

"It is the seat of power, yes." Thor nodded and waved at people in the streets below. "It is mostly empty space though."

I looked over the side at the citizenry. "Who are these people? Gods?"

He chuckled. "No, they are families of the Valkyrie and other great heroes who were granted immortality and allowed to live here."

I frowned. "I'm no expert on Norse mythology, but I thought Valkyrie only remained immortal as long as they were virgins."

Thor scoffed. "Yes, an old and foolish rule that I overturned when Father gave me responsibility for the daily business of Asgard."

"What does Odin do with his spare time?"

"He has no spare time." He shook his head. "Father leads the war effort against the outsiders in Mistgard." He pointed vaguely to the side. "It is a middle area between our realms and the outsiders. We are dangerously close to losing our foothold, Cain. If that happens, the nine realms will fall, and the other parts of the divine realm will collapse like a house of cards."

32

Hearing Thor echo Zeus's warning about losing ground in the divine realm made me realize that disaster was far more imminent than I wanted to think.

"Your part of the battle is in Mistgard?" I asked.

"Precisely. All our battles are in places between our parts of the divine realm and those of the outsiders." He directed the chariot down to a courtyard in front of the fortress. It rolled to a stop before doors large enough to be on an aircraft hangar. We disembarked and he pushed on the doors. They swung open easily into a space between the outer and inner walls. Another large door swung open at Thor's touch, and we stepped inside the fortress proper.

Octagon stone tiles nearly fifty feet across covered a floor that stretched on for hundreds of yards in all directions. Runes were engraved in the tiles, most of which I didn't recognize. The ceiling rose high overhead, the peak a distant point. Crystals on the walls and ceiling glowed bright as day. Despite the vast space, there was no darkness or shadow except right beneath me.

The floor in the center of the structure rose to form stairs leading up to a massive gray bench.

"That's huge." I frowned. "That's Odin's throne?"

Thor waggled a hand. "Ymir, the first Norse, was a giant. His children, the frost giants, constructed it with the aid of Buri, the first Norse god. Later, Odin and Buri's other children were forced to help build the fortress. They eventually revolted, killing Ymir and taking over Asgard. Little has changed about this place since then, but it is the crown of Yggdrasil and a place of great power."

"I thought Odin was the first god."

"No, Buri was the first, but he died in the revolt." Thor stopped on a tile and looked down at the runes. They glowed to life. I was blinded for an instant, and then we stood inside a room adorned with all the trappings of a normal palace. A giant portrait of Odin graced the wall above a throne, and the vast ceiling looked as if Michelangelo had spent a dozen lifetimes filling it with murals.

The room was crowded with people. Among them stood Hel, a wicked grin on her lips as she regaled a crowd with the tale of our escape from Hel. Mortis stood to the side with Thveri, nuzzling her neck like a puppy in love. They were puffing out enough black mist to alarm the EPA.

A delicious odor tickled my nose. The source was a table on the far side of the room, every inch of it covered in roasted meats, vegetables, and fruits. A massive man with a huge carving knife was slicing meat and setting it on silver plates.

"What is this place?" I asked Thor.

"This is the place Father calls home." He waved a hand around the room. "These are descendants of the Valkyrie and other heroes I mentioned earlier."

"Shouldn't they be fighting with the other gods?"

"Many are," Thor said. "We rotate our troops frequently to keep them refreshed, or they grow battle weary, and their performance suffers."

I shifted to the side so I could get a better look at the man carving the meats on the table. "Is that Andhrímnir?"

Thor nodded. "He is our master chef."

I looked past the chef and at a massive roasted pig. "And that's Sæhrímnir?"

"I'm impressed by your knowledge. Few people know anything of our chef and the pig he roasts daily for us for our feasts."

"Can I try some bacon?" My mouth began watering. "I'm just curious to see if it's godlike."

Thor patted my shoulder. "Help yourself."

I locked eyes with Mortis. He didn't look happy or surprised to see me. "I'm going to have a word with my horse, eat some bacon, and then get back on mission."

Thor seemed distracted by Hel then nodded as if suddenly realizing I'd been talking to him. "Yes, well I must decide how to deal with our new problems."

"Loki didn't want Hel reaching Asgard, so I don't think she's in on his plans."

"Loki fears his daughter for good reason." Thor pursed his lips. "We Æsir fear her for good reason. There is no telling what chaos she might wreak upon our order. That is why Odin sent her away to govern Hel."

"Æsir?" I asked.

He nodded. "That would be Odin, Frigg, Höðr, Baldr, Týr, and me. Loki, Hel, and others are of the Vanir. We have been at war nearly as often as we have been unified. I had thought the outsiders would unify us, but Loki has chosen another path."

"Perhaps Hel can be convinced to join your side."

Thor grunted. "At best, she will agree to stay out of the way. Then I will have to worry constantly about her trying to usurp the throne while we are away."

I gave it some thought. "Does she believe in honor?"

"It is at the core of all our beliefs, but some interpret honor in their own way." He growled. "For Loki, it is as fluid to him as his shape and form. He once turned into a mare, mated, and gave birth to Sleipnir."

I nodded. "That level of fluidity would be a dream to some humans."

Thor grunted. "Yes, it is quite a gift."

"Well, let me have a word with Hel, and then I'll get on my way."

"Very well, Cain Sthyldor. May you succeed in your quest and prevent the end days."

"No pressure." I gave him a slight bow, but he gripped my forearm and shook it hard enough to nearly dislocate my shoulder even with the protection of the cloak.

He grinned at my discomfort. "Odin keep you safe."

"Thanks," I wheezed through the pain. I reclaimed my arm and strolled over to the table of food.

Andhrímnir looked down at me as he sharpened his carving knife. Without asking, he carved several thick slices of bacon from the pig and put them on a plate.

It smelled so good I almost cried. "How did you know what I wanted?"

He tapped his temple. "I just know."

I took a bite of bacon. The flavor melted perfectly into my mouth, flooding me with such strong sensations that I froze in place, unable to move or speak for a handful of seconds. "Holy shit. You've ruined all other bacon for me."

He simply nodded, turned, and began serving someone else.

I polished off a piece of bacon, then rolled the rest into a cloth napkin so I could save it for later. Then I got back on mission and walked over to Hel just as she finished telling the grand story about how we raised an army and were preparing to set out for the badlands.

I touched her sleeve. "A moment, please?"

She smiled. "Cain, you made it!"

"No thanks to you." I massaged my shoulder. "I need to ask you what your intentions are with regards to Asgard."

She smirked and pulled me aside. "I shall become the next King, I think. This place is far too orderly and clean for my tastes. Where are the sacrificial goats and fountains of blood?"

I sighed. "I was afraid of that. Odin and the others are having a hell of a time fighting off the outsiders. You're a great warrior and I think they could really use your help on the frontlines."

Hel's lips peeled back in distaste. "Odin banished me to the underworld. Why would I help him?"

"Did you ever ask yourself why Odin did that?"

She paused. "Because I am the daughter of Loki? Because he doesn't like me?"

I shook my head. "It's because he fears you, Hel."

Her eyes flashed with uncertainty. "The father of the gods fears me?"

"Yes, because you are a daughter of Loki, an agent of chaos. And yet, you ran Hel with precision and honor. You raised an army and fought your way to Asgard. Odin knew you were worthy of ruling a kingdom, but he is king here and won't relinquish the throne."

Hel pursed her lips. "But I do not wish to rule the Underworld. I think Asgard is more to my liking."

"There will be no more Asgard, Midgard, or Hel if the outsiders break through the defenses." I shook my head. "Loki, as you saw, is intent on helping them. Only you can help the others stand against him and the Elder Things. Once you show Odin your worth on the battlefield, he will have no choice but to accept you and acknowledge that you belong with the Æsir."

She gasped. "That is brilliant, Cain! Once I am proclaimed Æsir, I can command any of the other realms. There are many that would be more fun than this orderly place."

I was surprised I'd convinced her so quickly. Gods and goddesses were usually so egotistical and sure of themselves that using logic on them rarely worked, or so I'd learned in my encounters with them. Perhaps Hel was a different kind of goddess. Perhaps she'd been so mistreated and looked down upon that she had a slight edge of insecurity that made her easier to convince. I wasn't about to complain.

"With you defending the nine realms, the outsiders won't stand a chance." I nodded toward Thor. "Perhaps you should talk with him next." I almost called Thor her uncle but considering how Loki had birthed children ranging from an eight-legged horse, to frost giants and serpents, I wasn't sure these beings even used such familiarities.

Hel pursed her lips and stroked the cheek on the skull side of her face. "I do not relish being on friendly terms with Thor or his ilk, but I will do what I must to earn a place among the Æsir. Then I can ascend to whatever position I desire." She kissed me on the lips and murmured, "It has been a pleasure."

I couldn't even call the sex with her a pleasure. It had been torturous and maddening. Intoxicating and terrorizing. I wanted more but I also wanted to run away screaming. Being used and abused by such a powerful being was humbling. In theory, I'd always known that messing with powerful beings like high fae or gods was tempting fate. My dalliance with Hel only proved that. I would never be a master of my own fate so long as the gods and high fae existed.

As an Ekhsis, a descendant of the first humans made by Cha and Ord, I supposedly had the capacity to become a god. Considering that it had taken many of the Ekhsis centuries to even come close to ascension, it seemed unlikely that I'd be turning in my humanity card anytime soon. But maybe it was time I started taking my legacy seriously. Maybe it was time I started down the path of godhood so my fate couldn't be determined by these egomaniacal beings.

I watched Thor's expression with amusement as Hel began talking to him. He looked parts horrified and relieved as she presumably talked with him about joining the war effort. Gods, I hoped I'd done the right thing by pointing her in that direction. Hel wasn't just a double-edged sword—she was a multi-edged glaive, capable of spinning dangerously in any direction. I hoped Thor was up to the task of dealing with her.

Figuring I'd unleashed enough chaos in Asgard, I interrupted Mortis's party with Thveri, much to his disgust. He nearly stomped my foot and blew mist in my face as I stepped close to him.

I gripped his reins and yanked his head sideways close to mine. "Thanks for leaving me behind, asshole. Do you even care if I find a way to revive Garrick, or do you want the apocalypse to happen?"

He bared his teeth in a frightful horsey grin. For the first time, I began to question Mortis's loyalty. His anger and resentment at me because I'd temporarily replaced Garrick had been understandable at first, but this was bordering on dereliction of duty. It had manifested itself in the time leading up to our journey into Hel and had grown even stronger since. It got me to thinking, and I didn't like where those thoughts were leading me.

I led him to a clear part of the throne room and mounted him. "Let's go to Gaia."

Mortis cast one more look at Thveri, nickered, and then leapt forward. We shot out of the throne room and left the great palace behind. We sped across pastureland and reached the Bifrost. Mortis took us to the end and leapt off, galloping up a giant branch of Yggdrasil and into a void. We reached two-dimensional Limbo and nearly smacked into the dastardly trio of War, Famine, and Pestilence. It was almost as if they'd been waiting on me because a metal net met my face an instant later.

Mortis bucked and threw me from the saddle. I hit the ground, tangled in the net. I tried to reach for my brightblade, but my arms could barely move despite my supernatural Death strength. Naturally, Oblivion Guard training involved avoiding capture and escaping from snares and traps. Our trainers had thrown us into a pit on Oblivion with only one way out—through a maze of tunnels infested by cave spiders.

Cave spiders were intelligent creatures who lived on a steady diet of mole people and sand scorpions. They even had a language and left messages for each other with webs. Basically, if you put Charlotte from Charlotte's web on a steady diet of steroids, grew her to the size of a horse, and taught her to eat Wilbur instead of saving him with clever messages in her web, you'd have an Oblivion cave spider.

The three horsemen might have caught me in a metal net, but their snare tactics were no match for a determined cave spider. It made me wonder if they even knew how to use a net or had even bothered practicing beforehand.

It might seem counterintuitive, but the first thing to do when caught in a web, net, or snare was to stop struggling. Don't wiggle, squirm, or fight or you'll only dig yourself in deeper, just like quicksand. I paused and assessed the situation even as the others leapt from their horses and marched toward me while Mortis watched with satisfaction.

I found the edges of the net. Since I hadn't struggled, rolled, or panicked, they edges hadn't wrapped around me and become entangled with each other. I tossed off the net like a blanket and leapt to my feet. I summoned the scythe and assumed a defensive stance as the others fanned out around me.

Dozens of plans circulated through my mind as I considered the major threats. War, by default, was the biggest. I wasn't sure if Pestilence and Famine even knew how to fight. But another problem presented itself. Even if I fought free, how would I escape from folded Limbo without Mortis? He'd intentionally bucked me off and wasn't even trying to help.

My earlier thoughts about him resurfaced and it led me to a conclusion. Hatred at my taking Garrick's job couldn't possibly be enough to make Mortis do this. He had a duty to perform above all else, and by preventing me from doing my job, he was going against his very nature. I was no expert on him or the others, but deities who served specific purposes were in general not very flexible on their duties.

In short, they were hardwired to stay within the narrow confines of their job descriptions. Mortis was created for the sole purpose of taking Death to the souls he needed to reap. Famine, Pestilence, and War were created to sow misery around the world, providing enough conflict and hardships to keep the humans from growing too comfortable and stagnating. They were not created to initiate the apocalypse, but to perform their duties only when called upon to do them.

So why in the fresh fuck were these beings taking the initiative to act outside their parameters? I suspected the answer was connected to all the other puzzle pieces I'd experienced during my fun times as the Grim Reaper.

"Cain, you will ride with us." War drew his sword. "You will ride, and the humans will perish."

Pestilence bared her teeth. "Peace upon the Earth, bad will toward men."

"And starvation upon all!" Famine added.

Switching the scythe to my other hand, I summoned my staff and began backing away in a controlled manner, keeping distance between me and my would-be captors. I flipped up the true sight scope and looked through it, focusing on War's forehead. There was no minute speck of light, no binding on his head that told me he was bound like Garrick. In fact, there seemed to be nothing wrong with him at all. He had the brightly glowing aura of a deity, and a sword that hummed with magic all its own.

I switched to Mortis and saw nothing wrong with him either. It seemed I'd been completely wrong and these people just flat-out hated my guts.

"What the fuck is wrong with you?" I continued moving backward. "You've got jobs to do, and that doesn't include spontaneously ending the world! You weren't created to do whatever the hell you please!"

Pestilence blinked several times, as if confused by my logic. "It has been ordered and thus must it be."

"Ordered?" It was my turn to blink. "You mean the Christian god told you to start Armageddon?"

Pestilence flinched slightly, almost unnoticeably to anyone not trained to look for minute tells when facing opponents. It reminded me of mannerisms I'd seen a lot of recently, mainly when dealing with Mortis.

She flinched again. War and Famine mirrored her and it became obvious that something wasn't right. Not only that, but the flinch reminded me of someone I'd recently met.

Oh, shit.

I was in even deeper shit than I'd realized.

33

I switched the scope to thermal and looked at War once more. His body glowed with heat, but there was a small sliver of coolness in his head, something so small I might have missed it if not for being so focused on minutia. I examined the others and the horses and discovered every single one of them had the same sliver inside. I focused back on War and kept backing away while zooming in on the sliver.

"War, you are defying your god given duty. This is not your job!"

He slowed his pace and looked uncertain. "Not my—" The sliver wriggled in his head, and he flinched again. "The end will come. You will ride with us!"

I considered all my options and narrowed them down to zero. Because, frankly, I had no options. Without Mortis, I couldn't escape. I was convinced Mortis had only been infected recently because he'd willingly helped until a short time ago. But if he'd been infected for days, then why had he continued helping me?

Loki might have lured me to Hel, but I realized in retrospect that Mortis had been the one to make me cross the bridge and become trapped. He'd then become obsessed with Thveri. The mind worm, it seemed, was using external stimuli to tighten its grip on Mortis and override his innate sense of duty.

Then Mortis had taken me out of Asgard and delivered me straight into the hands of the other horsemen. That meant all the worms were connected and able to share information.

As for where the worms had come from, I already knew that part. During my fever dream meetup with Nyarlathotep, he'd flinched several times in the exact same way War and the others had. It wasn't because Nyar was infected, but because he was the one controlling the mind worms.

That led to other, even more uncomfortable questions: Was Loki infected? Could other gods be under Nyar's influence?

There was still one exception from all this—why hadn't Garrick been infected? There had to be a reason Nyar couldn't infect and control him. I suspected the answer would be very important to my future wellbeing. The question for now was, how could I get rid of these things? Was there even a way to get rid of them without destroying the mind of the host?

If I'd learned anything from Star Trek and the Wrath of Khan in particular, it was that mind-controlling worms weren't to be trifled with. Captain Terrell had, after all, vaporized himself with a phaser rather than endure the pain of trying to resist the thing in his head.

Mortis, however, had to have been resisting the worm for days, but its control was progressively getting stronger and stronger. Somehow, I had to reach him and get him to take me out of folded Limbo, because there was no escape from this place no matter how far I ran.

"Mortis!" I circled sideways and activated my brightblade so I could keep War at bay. "You're infected. There's a worm in your head that's making you do things you wouldn't normally do."

War and the others flinched.

Mortis flinched with them and snorted mist from his nostrils.

"Listen to me, Mortis! Nyarlathotep put worms in your heads. You've got to resist long enough to get me out of Limbo so I can figure out how to fix you."

Once again, Mortis and the others flinched. War lunged at me, feinting with his sword, then swiped sideways to drive me towards the others. Pestilence and Famine had recovered the metal net and were making no attempt to hide the fact that they were flanking me.

"Gods damn it, Mortis! Help me so I can help Garrick!"

Their heads jerked in unison again.

I ran a hand down my face, completely at a loss for what to do next. War leapt sideways and dealt a flurry of strikes that I barely countered with my brightblade. Famine and Pestilence ran at me from the side. I threw up ankle-high shields and they tripped over them, falling into the net. Using a shield spell telekinetically, I gripped the sides of the net and wrapped it tightly around them. The pair struggled and entangled themselves even more.

But even if I defeated War and kept the others trapped in the net, I still couldn't leave Limbo. I touched my face again and realized a crucial mistake. There was a way that might get Mortis to respond to my commands even though the hold of the mind worm was stronger now.

I raised my hood and let the countenance of the Grim Reaper cover my face. "Mortis, I command you to do your duties!"

Everyone flinched. All except for Mortis. Black mist puffed from his nostrils, and he strode forward as if fighting an ocean tide to reach me. He reared up, a neigh of defiance echoing in the emptiness around us. War lunged, his sword aiming for my chest once he realized what was happening.

The impulsive move threw him off balance and he paid dearly for it. I swung the scythe up, catching him on the chin with the flat of the blade and drove my brightblade down on his arm at the same time. Flesh sizzled and he cried out in pain, dropping the sword. His eyes widened as if having a moment of clarity.

"Death, help us!" he cried out before being seized with convulsions and falling to the ground.

With him disabled and the others trapped in the net, I saw a chance I couldn't afford to miss. I took the mortal coil from my pack and whipped it toward the net holding Pestilence and Famine. It snared the net. Gripping the mortal coil with my gloved hand, I leapt onto Mortis. "Take us to Seattle!" I envisioned the exact place.

Mortis lunged forward. Even with supernatural strength, my arm felt as if it might pop from the socket as I dragged the load behind us across the plains of folded Limbo. We emerged moments later, and Fitz's house popped up before us, unfolding into three dimensions. I hopped off Mortis, dragging the snared deities behind me and knocked on the front door.

There was a muffled exclamation from the other side and the door swung open. "Is that still you, Cain, or are you the other Death?" Fitz looked ready to run at a moment's notice.

I slid down the cowl and nodded. "Can you see the net?"

He leaned sideways and looked around me. "Dear heavens, what's trapped in that thing, Cain? What eldritch horrors have you brought to me now?"

"Pestilence and Famine." I motioned him inside. "Are you gonna ask me in?"

"Are you kidding me, man?" He shook his head. "This is far out of my league!"

"Nyarlathotep put mind worms in their heads and is controlling them. I need you to figure out how to extract them."

Fitz's eyes grew even wider. "You're crazier than a necromancer at Sunday service, Cain! How am I supposed to survive trying to play doctor to two mind-controlled gods?"

"I'll make them mortal so you can deal with them." I sighed. "Trust me, okay? If we don't do this, they'll start the end days at the bidding of an Elder Thing."

He backed up a step. "You're telling me that the Crawling Chaos has infected deities from the Christian pantheon and has been using them to initiate the end days?"

"Crawling Chaos?" I gave him a look. "How did you know Nyarlathotep's nickname?"

"Because you keep scaring the shit out of me with this madness,

Cain." He blew out a breath and stepped out of the door. "I knew it would be best if I learned all I could, so I read the copies of Love-craft's journals you gave me." He walked around the side of the house and opened the side gate. "I don't want you dragging Pestilence and Famine across my clean floors."

I snorted. "That's the least of your worries."

"Release us!" Famine rasped. "I will starve everyone you ever loved!"

Pestilence growled. "I will see them driven from their lands!"

"You two must be real fun at parties." I booted them through the net. "Now shut up."

Fitz opened the door to his cellar and headed down the stone steps. I dragged the captives down the steps, enjoying their angered cries as they bounced off each one.

I glanced back at them. "Pestilence, do you know what's best in life?"

"Killing you!" she screeched.

I shook my head. "Wow, I'm disappointed you don't know the answer. I thought one of your names was Conquest."

"Of course, I know." She hissed like a venomous snake. "To crush your enemies, see them driven before you, and hear the lamentations of their women."

I pumped a fist. "Yes!"

Fitz looked puzzled. "Isn't that from *Conan the Barbarian*?"

Once downstairs in the root cellar, I found a support beam. I untangled the net and quickly wrapped the mortal coil around the prisoners' necks as soon as I could reach them. Famine and Pestilence gasped, and tried vainly tearing away the gray rope, but their sudden encounter with human frailty seemed to frighten them into submis-sion. I shoved them roughly against the thick column of wood and used normal rope to secure them to it. With the mortal coil tied around their necks, they were too weak to break free.

They struggled anyway. Famine wailed piteously. "What have you done to me?"

"I'm trying to help you." I blew out a breath. "Those things in their heads are also affecting my horse. If we're going to help Garrick, we need to cure these two and War." I thought back to that moment when I'd injured War. "I think pain temporarily frees them from the mind worm. I burned War with my brightblade, and he regained brief control over himself."

Fitz hissed a breath between his teeth. "As usual, you have provided me with something that is likely out of my power to fix." He sighed. "But I will do my best."

"Fitz, you are without question, the ablest and most knowledge-able mortal when it comes to stuff like this. You're the only person out of hundreds of healers who correctly diagnosed that I'd been cursed by Cthulhu." I gave him an expectant look. "I'm counting on you to save the world."

He stared at me in horror. "You are the worst, Cain. The worst!" He threw up his hands. "First you nearly get me killed by vampires, and now you've got me solving Christian problems. If Christians knew what I was, they'd burn me at the stake."

I grinned. "Nah, they'd probably love to find out voodoo is real."

"You might be right." Fitz sighed and turned to shelves filled with jars and various containers, some of which contained live spec-imens. "I will do my best and call you the moment I know anything."

I nodded. "Thanks. Now I've got to hope Mortis can hold his shit together long enough to help me find Thanatos or it's game over for Athena and Layla."

"Where have you gone looking for Thanatos?"

"I just got back from Hel—Helheim, that is."

He frowned. "Isn't that the Norse underworld?"

I nodded. "Thanatos was there centuries ago and had a rabid love affair with Hel. But he left and she has no idea where he went. She said he was morbidly depressed and possibly suicidal."

"Can gods even commit suicide?" Fitz said.

I shrugged. "I mean, the original Death could probably kill himself if he wanted to."

"Would he not then simply go on living in the afterlife?"

I shrugged again. "No idea. There are ways to oblivion, or so I've heard."

Fitz pursed his lips. "I would say that unless he has a way to consign himself to oblivion, Thanatos would choose to keep existing as he always has since death would merely be a gateway to continued afterlife."

I considered it. "That's sound logic. But even if he's alive, I have no idea where to start looking. Before I ended up stuck in Hel, I thought about trying to find Nyx."

"Ah." Fitz plucked a jar of green liquid from a shelf. "Do you think Thanatos returned to his mother and resides in Tartarus?"

I was tired of shrugging, so I waggled a hand instead. "Living in his mom's basement seems even more depressing, so I doubt it. On the other hand, if that's the place where the Titans are imprisoned, I don't want to risk going there and finding out I'm stuck in yet another underworld. Getting out of Hel was trial enough for me."

"Well, there are other death gods that may have crossed paths with him." He tapped a finger on his chin. "The problem is if he hasn't been doing the job of death for centuries, then it's doubtful anyone encountered him recently."

I thought back to what Thor had said about Thanatos asking Freya for advice and wondered if he could put me in touch with the goddess. The odds that she knew what he'd gone on to do since then were slim, but it was worth a try. "Why do you think Thanatos would ask Freya if the flying horses of the Valkyrie could die?"

"Morbid curiosity?" Fitz said.

Something else about Thanatos came back to mind. "Hel said Thanatos loved animals. Maybe it has something to do with that."

"It's likely he was just making conversation, but in a death god sort of way." Fitz set down the bottle of green liquid and unscrewed the lid. He carefully measured two drops and put them into a pestle. Then he put it on the shelf and walked down the shelf to a basket of dry leaves.

"I even ran into the Cthonian death god, Zushakon, in the badlands of Hel." I shook my head. "He's a tiny octopus."

"Fascinating!" Fitz dropped two leaves in the pestle and added white powder. Using the mortar he began mixing them.

"Yeah, it was crazy."

Fitz stopped grinding the ingredients and gave me a pointed look. "Cain, can you go away and let me work?"

I realized that for whatever reason, I'd been trying to engage Fitz in small talk—something I usually avoided at all costs. It made me wonder if Nyar had put a worm in my head because this wasn't like me. "Yeah, I'll let you get to it." I headed upstairs and went back around the house, hoping Mortis hadn't run off and left me again.

I found the horse pacing in circles, shaking his head in agitation. He seemed to be fighting the influence of the thing in his head but wasn't having much luck. Keeping the cowl up so he didn't see my Cain face, I patted his neck. "You're strong. You can beat this."

The problem was, I had no idea what to do next. Going to Tartarus seemed extremely risky. I also had plenty of deaths queued up on the death beacon, but how much longer could I do that with Mortis's free will eroding by the moment thanks to the mind worm?

It felt like I'd reached a dead end, a no-win scenario, and that explained why I'd tried to make conversation with Fitz. It was because I had no idea what to do next. I decided that the best thing to do at this point was reap some souls and then go ask a Greek god about my odds of visiting Tartarus.

I mounted Mortis and he calmed down somewhat. "Let's go collect some souls, okay?" I slid a finger along the death beacon and the paused blips began blinking again.

Mortis released an agitated neigh, stomping back and forth while shaking his head. He was fighting the influence of Nyar but how much longer would he be able to keep it up? I just hoped we could travel through Limbo without running into War.

He lunged forward and the world folded around us, replaced by Limbo an instant later. We popped out at a location a few hundred miles from Seattle and I got to work, reaping the soul of a man who'd been on his deathbed for two days, thanks to the pause. The next was a woman who should've had her soul taken right after a terrible car accident and was now comatose in a hospital bed.

I worked through the list over the next few hours, then delivered the souls to Purgatory. Every single one of them went straight to Hell. As I stood there watching the demons collect them, I realized that I had nothing else on the agenda except for soul collecting. This was now my life and there was nothing I could do about it.

34

The other three horsemen needed to be dewormed, freeing them from Nyar's grasp. Then and only then would they release Garrick from their curse. I was no closer to finding Thanatos, nor did I have a solid lead where to search next.

Charon sat on the dock, a fishing pole in one hand and a beer in the other. Having seen the ghastly catfish creature he'd caught the last time, I had no idea why he fished in the Styx. I strode down the dock and sat on one of the mooring posts. "What do you know about Tartarus?"

He stared out at the water and took another sip of beer. After several seconds, he huffed and looked at me. "I don't like my fishing time being interrupted with stupid questions."

I looked out at the dark waters. "Why don't you go to a real river and fish?"

Charon scowled. "Because I like it here among the dead."

"Isn't this where you are ninety-nine percent of the time?"

He nodded. "Yep."

I resisted the urge to yank the fishing pole from his hand. "Have you ever had a mangorita?"

His scowl morphed to a frown. "Are you inviting me out for drinks?"

"Hell no—" I stopped myself. "Yes. Yes I am."

His eyes brightened and he dropped the fishing pole. "Let's go then!"

I hopped on Mortis. Charon climbed into his boat. "I'll drive myself. Where are we going?"

"Voltaire's." I paused. "I can't tell you how to get there from here."

He tossed me a coin. "Just hold that out when you get there, and I'll find it."

I nudged Mortis and we took off, skipping through Limbo and arriving just outside the fae safezone of Voltaire's. I dismounted and looked Mortis in the eye. He whuffed and twitched with agitation. I didn't know what else I could do for him, so I held out the coin. Mist drifted across the parking lot and Charon's boat drifted across the asphalt like water. He parked it in a slot and got out, rubbing his withered hands.

"I haven't had a boys' night out in a long time, Cain." He grinned. "Are there a lot of pretty ladies here?"

I winced. "Uh, sure, plenty." Not that his withered old ass had a chance with any of them. I led Mortis over to the stairs leading down into Voltaire's and left him there, hopeful he'd still be in place when I came back.

I willed myself to be visible to everyone inside and knocked on the door. Durrug took one look and let us inside without even waiting for the password. He nodded respectfully. "Looking good, Cain."

I still had the cowl over my head, so I wasn't sure if that was a sincere compliment or sarcasm. Then again, he was an ogre, so I probably did look fearfully good. "Thanks." I led Charon to the bar, feeling all eyes upon us. Most people gaped in astonishment or open-mouthed fear.

Aura waited at the bar, an amused smirk on her face. "Gods almighty, Cain. You know how to make an entrance."

I sat down and Charon took the seat next to me. "Two mangoritas, please."

Her gaze traveled between the two of us as if trying to divine just what in the hell was going on. "Two mangoritas coming right up." She skipped away and got to work.

Charon looked around the room and grimaced. "I don't see anything but dogs in here."

I followed his gaze and found plenty of attractive women. "Are you sure about that?"

He grunted. "It's okay. It's rare to find beautiful women anywhere I go."

"You never go anywhere."

He grunted again. "Exactly."

Aura set two frosty mangoritas before us. "So, Cain, what's going on?"

I took a sip and the glass clinked against my skull. "Nothing good." I lowered the cowl so I could drink with my face on. "I'm stuck."

"Oh, this is good!" Charon gulped on the mangorita without even using the curly straw. He made a horrible face, one that was only enhanced by his withered, papery skin. "Ow, my head!"

"Brain freeze." Aura tutted. "Don't drink it so fast."

"But it's so good!" He gulped more and grimaced in pain again. "Ow!"

I shook my head. "Press your tongue against the roof of your mouth."

Judging from the strange look on his wrinkled old face, Charon seemed to be doing just that. He nodded. "That helped." Then he gulped the rest of the drink and slammed the glass to the counter. "Another one, bar wench!"

Aura raised an eyebrow, then sauntered away and began concocting another.

"So, Tartarus." Charon snorted. "Are you thinking about visiting? Because I can show you a way in but getting back out is tricky."

"How so?"

"It's a prison." He scoffed. "They make it easy to get into, but almost impossible to escape."

I nodded. "Do you know a way out?"

"Yes, but I'm not sure you'd survive." His eyes narrowed. "If you're going there just to talk to Nyx, I wouldn't waste your time. Thanatos had a rocky relationship with his mother. I don't think he'd stop by for a visit."

Aura delivered another mangorita then hurried away to help another customer.

Charon traced a finger down the condensation on the glass. "This is better than ale by far."

"Agreed." I took another sip of mine and resigned myself to the fact that this wonderful evening with Charon was going to be an unpleasant waste of time.

"Nyx wouldn't let Thanatos keep pets and that caused a lot of problems." Charon chuckled. "Thanatos rescued a baby chimera whose mother had been killed by Hercules. When he brought it with him to visit Nyx, she kicked him out of the Night Mansion!"

I couldn't imagine what kind of special care a chimera took, especially considering it was more likely to eat its owner unless they were a god. "Why was she so dead set against pets?"

"Thanatos, being who he was, was fascinated with death. Naturally, he loved the deadliest animals in existence." Charon took another sip of his drink. "After Hercules killed the Lernaean Hydra, Thanatos brought home all the eggs from the creature's nest. Before long, the Night Mansion was infested with the things. Nyx killed them all and kicked Thanatos out. Their relationship was never the same after that."

I was trying to imagine the kinds of godlike shenanigans that led to a house infested with hydras. "That's quite a story."

He chuckled. "Thanatos was furious because he couldn't even ensure the hydras' souls were taken care of."

I took another long sip of my drink and abruptly stopped. "Do hydras and chimeras have souls?"

Charon nodded. "That's how they end up in the afterlife."

"There are hydras in the afterlife?"

"Yeah, they're in Hades keeping life interesting for the souls down there." He sighed with satisfaction. "There's a whole gauntlet of monsters that Hades lets brave souls attempt to navigate. It keeps the dead warriors entertained and lets the monsters enjoy mauling those who try to fight them. Everyone's happy—or at least as happy as the dead can be."

"You're telling me that someone delivers animal souls to the afterlife."

"I assume so, but animal souls don't come through Purgatory as far as I know." He examined the pineapple impaled on the plastic pirate sword in his drink. "I never gave it much thought."

I was giving it all the thought in the world right then. Piecing together the few things I learned about Thanatos, I suddenly had a very good idea what he'd been doing all this time. After leaving Hel, it seemed highly likely that Thanatos had followed his dreams. What better way to pass the time for a death god who loved animals than by becoming the being who guided their souls to Heaven, or wherever they needed to go?

Charon bit into the pineapple and gasped. "This thing tastes better than ghost fish!"

I raised an eyebrow. "You've never tried a girly drink?"

"Not like this!" He gulped another mouthful of mangorita and wiped his face with the back of his hand. "If only the women were better looking here!"

I took out my smartphone and started searching for animal death gods. After trying several search combinations, I came up empty. There was only one lead. I wasn't sure it would go anywhere, but I had no choice except to try.

"What do you know about Artemis?"

Charon polished off his drink and clinked the glass against the bar. "Bar wench, I need another!"

Aura shot him an irritated look from the far end of the counter and strode toward us. "If you call me a bar wench one more time, I'll ban you."

"Ban me?" Charon scoffed. "I haven't done anything wrong."

Aura scowled. "Listen here, you withered old bag of bones, you'll refer to me with respect, or your next drink will give you the worst case of diarrhea you've ever had."

Charon smiled. "You might be ugly, but you have spirit!"

Aura's face went red, and it was clear that the fae safezone was the only thing keeping her from knocking out Charon's teeth—not that he had many to begin with.

I took her hand. "Aura, this is the ferryman of the river Styx. He doesn't get out much."

She took deep breaths and calmed down. "I'd poison his drink if it didn't violate the safezone."

"I don't think it would even faze him, to be honest." I shrugged. "I mean, look at him."

Charon's attention had moved elsewhere, namely to a ghastly looking old hag who stood at the entrance to the bar.

"Gods be damned." Aura huffed. "I told that nasty crone that her coven isn't welcome here until they start taking baths!"

I raised an eyebrow. "Who is that?"

"Agatha and her wood witches." Aura shuddered. "They don't bathe or use potions to keep themselves looking young like most witches because they're about being all natural."

"Agatha is her name?" Charon rose from his seat and fidgeted nervously. "She is beautiful!"

Aura's mouth dropped open. "You've got to be fucking kidding me."

I saw a way out of the worst boys' night ever and nodded encouragingly. "Do you want me to introduce you to her?"

Charon nodded. "Yes, please! I haven't seen such beauty since Medusa's soul tried to stone gaze me."

Aura grimaced. "Please take lover boy over there, Cain. I've had enough of his wonderful manners."

I took Charon's bony arm and guided him to the door where Durrug was barring Agatha from entering.

"We are all natural!" she protested. "I use scented oils instead of deodorant."

"Aura say no." Durrug's nostrils flared. "My nose also say no. Go take bath and come back."

Agatha huffed and turned to face three others who looked just as old and haggard as she did. Their hair was patchy and stringy, and their skin was so saggy and wrinkled they looked as if they were nearing their two-hundredth birthdays.

I guided Charon past Durrug and immediately regretted getting within range of the witches. Their body odor made me want to fall to my knees and empty my stomach. I pushed Charon forward and took a step back. "This is my friend Charon, the ferryman of Hades, and he really loves your natural look."

Agatha looked him up and down. "This is *the* ferryman of the Styx?"

"The one and only, ladies." Charon grinned lasciviously, causing my stomach to spasm again. "You are the first beauties I've seen all night."

"You're quite handsome yourself." Agatha giggled nervously. "Would you like to taste my witch's brew?"

"I would love to." Charon turned to me. "Cain, this has been a great boys' night out. Thank you!"

"My pleasure." I gagged on the words as the witches' scent hit me once again. It was so strong I could taste it. I quickly backed through the door and headed for the bar, praying lover boy took Agatha far, far away from here.

Aura was grinning like an idiot. "You've got to tell me how you ended up agreeing to a boys' night with the ferryman. I didn't even think you were capable such a thing."

"It was out of necessity." I took a sip of mangorita to wash away the taste of Agatha's odor. "I wanted to ply him for information about Tartarus, so I could locate Thanatos."

She smirked. "How'd that go?"

"Nowhere." I held up a finger. "But I think I know what Thanatos is up to these days."

"And that is?"

"He's making sure all dogs go to heaven."

Aura frowned. "Huh?"

"Thanatos is apparently a huge animal lover." I blew out a breath. "I think he found a way to become the grim reaper for animals."

"That's actually wonderful." She paused. "Or maybe it's horrible to see dead animals all the time."

"I can tell you from experience that dealing with this much death really wears you down." I shook my head. "I don't know how Garrick does it. Reaping souls of dead animals sounds even more depressing."

"But you used to be an assassin."

"Yeah, but that's different," I said.

"Different how?"

"Do you know how many dead babies and kids whose souls I've had to take?" I shook my head. "And that's not even including the zombie kids I had to reap during the undead uprising."

"Ew, Cain!" Aura made a face. "That's awful!"

I waved off the conversation. "If Thanatos is collecting animal souls, I might be able to use that to reach him."

"Please tell me you're not planning to kill a puppy just to get Thanatos to come to you."

I pretended to give it some thought. "That might work."

Aura's eyes flared. "Cain, don't you dare!"

As evil as such a thing would be, Aura was onto something. While I wouldn't kill a puppy, what if I went to an animal shelter and waited while they euthanized an animal? On the other hand, what if Thanatos had nothing to do with domesticated animals and only dealt with deadly supernatural creatures?

I ran several more searches for animal death gods and came back empty. One search result stood out consistently and I came to the conclusion that checking it out would be better than watching a kill shelter euthanize dogs.

Aura gave me a long hard look. "What did you find, Cain?"

I finished off my drink and stood. "I've got a lead. Hopefully, it'll pan out."

She pursed her lips. "Do you need help? I could use a break from the bar."

I shook my head. "No, it's much better that you don't go."

Her eyebrows rose. "Why is that?"

"Because I need to go see a god, and after what Aura Beta did to Athena, they might just tie you up to Prometheus's rock right next to her."

Aura's eyes flared with anger. "My variant might be crazy, but eternal torture is wrong. You need to free her, Cain."

I blinked. "Variant?"

"Yeah, she's a variation of me, so a variant." Aura scowled. "Free her, Cain. Put her in a prison or something, but get her off Prometheus's rock, okay?"

I sighed. "One step at a time, okay? I've got to free Layla's and Athena's souls from Soultaker and then remove the mind-worms an Elder Thing put into the heads of Pestilence, Famine, and War. Saving your lunatic doppelganger from torture is something I'll have to consider long and hard."

She held up her hands. "I get it. You've got a lot on your plate."

I barked a laugh. "My plate is the size of a banquet table and it's groaning under the weight." I dropped payment on the bar and left. Mortis, thankfully, was still waiting near the top of the stairs. He neighed and reared back when I reached for the reins, and I quickly remembered that I'd taken off the cowl. I covered my face again and turned back to him. He calmed once again, but flinched every few seconds, as if Nyar was tugging the worm in his mind like puppet strings.

I climbed on his back and envisioned who I needed to see. "I need to find—" Mortis leapt forward before I could finish talking. We raced through Limbo. Thick underbrush and towering trees sprang up around us. Mortis skidded to a stop just feet away from a giant white stag. A woman with long braids and dark skin sat on the back of the stag, an arrow nocked and aimed.

35

Thankfully, the arrow was aimed at something other than me.

She glanced at me out of the corner of her eye, then released the arrow. It sang through the forest and thudded into a tree trunk. Green ichor spurted and the tree collapsed in a very untreelike manner. Tentacles flailed and the camouflage hiding the beast faded to reveal pale skin. The arrow jutted from the squid-like head of a creature with long, spidery legs and countless tentacles around the mouth.

It was huge and unlike anything I'd seen before, but if I had to guess, it was Cthonian in origin. My suspicion was confirmed when seconds later, the little black octopus death god showed up to take its soul as it softly whispered, "I am the darkness." It vanished before I could talk to it.

Artemis, goddess of the hunt, looked down at me expectantly. "You are out of place here, Death." She slid from the back of the stag as they both shrank to human size. Her spotted green dress blended perfectly with the foliage as it swished around her legs. "Why have you sought me out?"

I dismounted Mortis and walked toward her. "I'm looking for

Thanatos. I have dire need of his help."

Her eyebrows rose. "And why would I know anything of him?"

"I'm sure you've heard of Athena's fate."

Her head tilted slightly. "I have been hunting and Hermes has not delivered a message to me for some time."

I waited for her to follow up with more information, but that was all she had to say. "Hunting Cthonians?"

"Any minions of the Elder Things who slip past the wall." Artemis looked at the dead thing on the ground. "Some come from the Norse lands, others from the Egyptians, and countless others whose defenses are not as sound as ours."

"What good is it if a few slip past the wall?"

"There are places where they could trigger Cthonian wormholes and invade us from our flank." She knelt and put a hand to the ground. "Our section of the divine realm is especially ideal for that due to the power of Mount Olympus."

I returned to my original inquiry. "You haven't heard of Athena's death because you've been in the wilderness."

Her eyes flared. "Athena is dead?" Artemis blurred to me and gripped my shoulders. "What mighty creature took her down?"

I hesitated to tell her it was an elf with a grudge, but figured it was best to just get it out there. "Centuries ago, she cursed the bloodline of an elf. One of the elf's descendants carried out an elaborate plot and assassinated Athena as revenge. Her soul is now trapped in Soultaker and only Thanatos might know how to free the soul."

Artemis released me and backed up a step, smirking one moment and frowning the next. "I always told her that mortals are far more dangerous than we believe. Her wrath was bound to spring back upon her like a sling that breaks mid-swing, or a bowstring snapping and slicing open your finger."

None of which, I was sure, could affect a god, but I didn't point that out. "I have concluded from various sources of information that Thanatos gave up reaping human souls and found a way to become the god of death for animals, particularly the deadliest ones. You are the goddess of animals and the hunt and also Greek like him, so it seemed likely—"

She held up a hand. "As I was saying, mortals are cleverer and more dangerous than we believe. You have discovered Thanatos's shameful secret—one that he would never want his mother to discover." Artemis scowled. "Nyx always thought animals were beneath him. Poor Thanatos withered from unhappiness until I caught him playing with the creatures of my secret preserve."

This was going in an unexpected direction, but I kept quiet and listened.

"Many of our ancient creatures were going extinct, especially on Feary where the fae did nothing to keep them safe. I made a secret preserve in the divine realm for chimeras, hydras, and other magnificent animals that would otherwise be gone forever." Artemis's gaze grew distant. "I found Thanatos grieving over a baby chimera that died in the litter. He looked up at me and asked who would tend to its soul. I had no answer because there was no god assigned that duty. We had never considered what to do with animals, and I discovered that their souls were simply fading into oblivion."

Artemis shuddered. "In our hubris, we had omitted a plan to care for creatures because they were not human. I convinced Zeus and the others that all animals in our creation were worthy of the afterlife. He and the others granted me the ability to find a new god with the power to reap the souls of dead animals. I secretly chose Thanatos." Her eyes filled with tears. "I have never seen someone so happy. Besides creation, it was the best moment of my existence. I saved animal souls and aided a gentle god who wanted to be happy but also did not wish to disappoint his mother."

"That's a very heartwarming story. I'm glad you helped achieve his true purpose." The sincerity in my voice surprised me. It wasn't often that a god did something so selfless. "I need Thanatos to help me with Soultaker since he supplied the magic that steals souls. Do you know how I can reach him?"

"I do." She took my hand and pulled me toward her stag. "Come."

I didn't have much choice except to follow. She picked me up and popped me onto the back of the stag like I was a little kid, then leapt onto its back. The stag took off in great bounds. The forest blurred around us.

"Mortis, follow us!" I shouted before we were out of range. I lost sight of him before I could tell if he was listening.

The forest blurred around us. The stag bounded down a raging river and leapt off the cliff at the end. We plummeted alongside the roaring waterfall toward a great frothing pool of water at the bottom. A hydra sprang from the depths, fangs flashing as it snapped at us.

I gripped Artemis around the waist and waited for impact. The stag landed softly on the shore, somehow missing the hydra entirely. It turned and faced the pool calmly even as the hydra's heads swooped toward us.

Artemis leapt off the stag, growing larger as she strode toward the striking monster in the water. Its fangs struck her arm. She laughed and gripped one of the monster's heads, stroking it. "Oh, you are feisty today."

The snapping heads calmed, and the hydra hissed softly.

She kissed its snout and released it. "Thanatos has been very keen on checking the progress of the unicorns lately. There was quite a scare that their queen might be sacrificed to save a mortal." She clenched her teeth. "If that had happened, I would have killed the mortal myself."

I gulped. "Queen Shraya?"

Artemis frowned and nodded. "How do you know her name?"

I didn't want to answer that question. "So, uh, what kind of progress are the unicorns making?"

Her eyes brightened. "They are expecting foals very soon. Thanatos never leaves them unless he must reap a soul."

I simply nodded, not wanting to get back on the subject of Shraya. "Does he reap the souls of all animals?"

"He has many minions who help him with all the creatures of the world. They themselves were once mere animals."

I frowned. "So, he uses other animals as reapers?"

"Precisely." She smiled. "There are many now."

Artemis shrank back to my size and took my hand, forcefully leading me through the forest for a hundred yards or so until we emerged in a glade. Golden and silver hides sparkled as unicorns pranced in the sunlight. The sight was so enchanting, I nearly tripped as Artemis continued pulling me after her.

A unicorn with a golden mane, immaculately white hair, and an onyx horn stood at the edge of the glade, her belly swollen. She was the only one with such coloring, as the others had ivory, silver, or golden horns, and none were quite as large as her. There was no doubt that she was Queen Shraya even if I'd never met her before.

Artemis took us to her. "My lovely, I have brought someone here who seeks Thanatos. Has he visited today?"

"Visited?" Shraya nickered. "He is frolicking with the colts."

I flinched in surprise at hearing her speak out loud. The last time we'd met she'd had to use a virgin to talk in my head.

"Cain, it is a pleasure to see you again." Shraya bent her foreleg and bowed ever so slightly. "I thought you had died from your curse when you did not eat my heart."

Artemis's eyes blazed. "Cain?" She spun on me. "Are you not the mortal known as Garrick?"

I blew out a sigh, lowered the cowl, and braced myself for a fight I couldn't win. "I am Cain Sthyldor."

Artemis glared at me for a long moment. "This is the mortal who nearly ate your heart?"

"Yes, Artemis, but he spared me even though I had promised it to him."

The goddess grew slightly larger, and her voice echoed with godly power. "Why did you spare her, mortal?"

"Because the unicorns would have gone extinct. And also because she is the most beautiful creature I have ever seen." I looked Artemis dead in the eyes. "Even more so than you and the other goddesses."

Artemis glared at me for a moment, bow drawn, arrow nocked. "You are lucky I am not vain like the others, Cain." She slung the bow over her back and shrank back to normal size. "Shraya is the last of the first unicorns, and my crowning joy as a goddess. You were wise, Cain Sthyldor, and you have good taste."

I nodded uncertainly. "Thanks?"

"Ah, here they come." Shraya bobbed her head at three young unicorns, one of them bearing a pale but beautiful young man with long flowing hair as dark as night.

Artemis laughed. "Thanatos, a word please once you've had your fun."

His eyes lit on Artemis and brightened. "My lovely friend, you've come to see the birth of miracles?"

"I am here to see you."

Thanatos sprang from the back of a colt and landed before her. He hugged Artemis and kissed her cheeks. Uncertainty flickered in his eyes when he saw me. "Who is this bearing my mantle? What foul tidings do you bring on this joyful day?"

This guy was probably a lot of fun at parties. "No foul tidings, Thanatos. I have a question regarding this." I slowly drew Soultaker so Artemis wouldn't think I was about to attack.

"Foul tidings, indeed." Thanatos grimaced. "A thoughtful gift spurned by Mars, though I crafted the magic lovingly for Athena." He huffed and crossed his arms. "He did not like the way the souls behaved. I tried to explain that sentient souls must be made mindless if you desire absolute obedience." He shivered. "Why did you bring this rejected gift to me except to spoil my mood?"

I didn't need to be an expert at reading people to tell that this guy was super sensitive and prone to moodiness. Approaching this the wrong way would send this guy into a downward spiral and depression, making him useless to me. Asking him to remove the magic he created would be hurtful and insulting, so I needed to come at this from another angle.

Thankfully, I knew just the thing to say. "Thanatos, I'm here on a mission of mercy. Athena was slain with this blade and her soul is trapped inside. You are the only being who can tell me how to free the soul of a goddess from the bondage of your powerful magic."

His eyes brightened. "Athena is trapped?" He laughed. "Oh, that conniving, loathsome bitch is one of those who turned me away from Olympus many a time. She scorned me as the dark, unwanted offspring of the night."

Artemis scowled. "Athena has spread many evil rumors about me, saying I am not chaste, and that I am a whore. I would as soon leave her in the blade."

Thanatos rubbed his hands gleefully. "That would be a perfect torture, would it not?" He waved me away dismissively. "Athena will receive no relief from me. Let her writhe in mindless torment forever."

And just like that, it was over.

36

My clever idea had completely backfired. I should have known that Thanatos, a god spurned by the Olympians, would have a grudge against most of them. Artemis was probably the only one he got along with due to his love of dangerous animals. Thanatos turned toward Shraya, already acting as if I didn't exist. Artemis didn't look inclined to help either.

There had to be a way to turn this around—one that didn't involve bringing Zeus's wrath down on Thanatos if he refused to help. I considered threatening to tell Nyx about his duty collecting animal souls, but the odds were I wouldn't leave here alive if Artemis had anything to say about it.

The answer to the dilemma struck me an instant later. I posed a question to Thanatos. "The souls in the sword are mindless?"

"Yes," he said without turning around.

"Then Athena does not even know she's being tortured—at least not consciously." I sighed. "That's too bad."

Thanatos stopped dead in his tracks and slowly turned toward Artemis, a look of dismay spreading across his face. "The mortal is right. The magic suppresses sentience so the souls can be controlled. So long as they're in the sword, torture is meaningless."

"Here's a question," I said. "Even though their sentience is suppressed, their memories work fine, right? If they're released from the sword, will they remember the torture they were subjected to?"

His gaze went distant as he considered it. "Yes, they would remember the horrors of the soul trap."

Artemis raised an eyebrow. "What horrors are there? Are they not simply trapped in the sword until summoned?"

"They are trapped in a plane where they fight and murder each other only to come back to life the next day and start all over again." Thanatos looked wistful. "I thought it would be more useful if the souls constantly trained for battle, so they'd be useful when summoned for war. The souls must take on a physical form when released from the sword, and that physical form can die."

I blinked. "You're telling me that the army released from the sword is killable?"

He nodded. "But their physical forms can be recreated again the next day."

"The recyclable army." I scowled. "And they practice by murdering each other endlessly in the soul trap."

Thanatos smiled brightly. "Brilliant, yes?"

I forced a smile of my own. "It's pure genius." It sounded even worse than Hell or Hel. "If you release Athena's soul, she'll remember the horrors of the soul plane and be eternally indebted to you for rescuing her. That would be the worst torture imaginable for someone so arrogant."

"Absolutely!" Thanatos shivered with delight. "But I also do not want to be present when she discovers this, for she'd likely try to punish me in some terrible way."

"Undoubtedly." Artemis laughed. "I will witness her reincarnation firsthand so one of us can revel in her humiliation."

"Oh, would you do that for me?" Thanatos clapped his hands together with delight.

"Of course, my dear," Artemis said.

Shraya nickered gently. "Cain, you are clever for a mortal."

I didn't want to ruin the moment, so I simply nodded at her and turned to Thanatos. "How do we free the souls?"

He flinched as if awaking from a pleasant dream. "The magic bound to the sword is dangerous to break all at once, considering the number of souls Mars reaped with it." He touched the sleeve of my cloak. "I crafted these garments and other tools to make it possible for a mortal to do the duties I left behind. The magic of the soul catcher is based on the magic I used in Soultaker."

I hadn't even made the connection before, but it seemed painfully obvious now. "So, I just need to dip the sword in the river, and it'll free the souls?"

He shook his head. "First, you must put the blood of the killer on the tip of Soultaker's blade. Once done, summon the soul you wish to free. Dip the sword in River Styx and then drive it through the heart of the soul, killing the temporary body. This will free the soul. Since you are in Purgatory, the soul will already be ready for collection, provided it is bound for Hell, Heaven, or Hades.

"What about souls that belong to other pantheons, like the Norse?"

"I believe their respective gods will come collect them once you free them." Thanatos shrugged. "I cannot say for sure."

"And outsider souls?"

He frowned. "They should be collected by their death gods, but I have no idea."

I was so excited to finally have an answer that I had to resist the urge to leave right then and there. "Thank you. If you'd like, I can make a video of Athena's resurrection so you can relish that Kodak moment for all eternity."

Thanatos clapped his hands joyously. "That would be beautiful beyond words, mortal!"

"Great." I bowed toward him, Artemis, and Shraya. "This has been an honor. I will bring back a video once I have it." I summoned Mortis with a thought. Moments later, he galloped into view.

Shraya neighed and reared on hind legs. "Your steed is infected!"

Without another word, she charged Mortis, horn lowered, and impaled him right in the chest.

Mortis shrieked and collapsed in a heap.

"What the fuck?" I raced toward Mortis. "I need him!"

"He is infected!" Shraya put a hoof on his neck, keeping the wounded Mortis pinned. "He bears the mark of an Elder Thing."

"You brought a creature of the Elder Things here?" Artemis's bow appeared in her hand. "What betrayal is this?"

"It's not a fucking betrayal!" I leapt in the way of the nocked arrow. "All the horsemen and their horses are infected. I'm trying to find a cure."

"The only cure is death, I'm afraid." Shraya neighed and other unicorns formed a circle around us.

I turned to Thanatos. "Would you let them kill Mortis even though he could probably be cured?"

Thanatos held up a hand. "Shraya, there must be another way."

"What about unicorn blood?" I pointed vaguely at the herd. "Maybe that would kill the mind worm."

"I'm afraid it would have no effect for the infection is not the same as a disease." Shraya looked down at Mortis. "It is a parasite that cannot live in a dead host."

"How do you even know he's infected?" I asked.

"I can smell them." Shraya's nostrils flared.

"Just let me take Mortis and leave!" I knelt next to him and examined the gory wound. "He's been resisting the worm all this time just to do his job and now you attempt to murder him on sight?"

Mortis whickered and bobbed his head. For the first time in a while, he seemed to be looking at me as he had before the worm took his mind. Just as with War, the pain seemed to temporarily wrest control of his mind away from the worm.

Shraya removed her hoof. "Very well. Take him and leave this instant. I won't risk my herd being infected. I've worked too long and hard to increase our numbers only to have them fall prey to an Elder Thing."

I didn't know if the worm could even spread to others, but there was no point in arguing about it. We needed to get the Hel out of here before she changed her mind.

Artemis lowered her bow. "Do not bring him back here, Cain."

I nodded. "Why would I? You tried to kill him without even a warning."

Mortis rose, blood pouring from the wound in his chest. Artemis, Thanatos, and Shraya stepped back from him. I considered asking one of them to heal him, but that seemed unlikely.

I grimaced. "Are you okay?"

Mortis bobbed a nod but staggered as he tried to take a step. His supernatural resistance to injury hadn't stood a chance against a unicorn horn.

I gingerly climbed onto his back and turned to Artemis. "Ask Zeus and especially Mars to meet me on the shores of the Styx with Athena's and Layla's bodies, please."

She nodded. "I will do so the moment you are gone."

I patted Mortis's neck. "Let's go to the Styx."

He began trotting, but his gait was uneven, and he staggered side to side. I wondered if he could even get us there or if he'd die first. Then again, he was a supernatural horse. Maybe he just needed time to heal. Unfortunately, we didn't have the luxury of waiting for him to heal here.

Mortis neighed, and foam-flecked blood sprayed from his nostrils. He lowered his head and charged forward, grunting in pain but pushing through it. The divine realm flattened, and we entered Limbo. Purgatory unfolded a moment later. With a final bellow of pain, Mortis's legs gave out. I leapt, hit the ground, and rolled as he plowed through the grass and came to a stop at the river's edge.

I sprang to my feet and rushed to his side. "Mortis!"

Sides heaving, he whickered gently and regarded me with his pale eyes. The blood around the wound was already congealing and it looked like he'd soon be on the mend. I knew he didn't like me, but I knelt and put a hand on his neck.

"I'm sorry. I didn't even see that coming."

He whickered again.

There was nothing I could do for him except let his supernatural healing do its job, so I wandered out to the water's edge. Neither Charon nor his boat were at the dock. I imagined he was probably still with Agatha the witch and her coven. I instantly regretted the mental image that conjured and tried to think about something else, but it was a hard image to shake.

The hairs on the back of my neck prickled. I spun and saw...nothing. The wards tattooed on my body seldom gave me false alarms, so I settled into a defensive stance and looked around, drawing my staff so I could look through the true sight scope. I flipped it open and examined the surrounding area. Aside from Mortis, there was nothing and no one.

Then I noticed a thin glowing trail leading away from Mortis. I followed the trail through the grass. It led straight to my feet. Horror surged through me as I realized what it was. Something cold touched the bare skin of my neck. I snatched at it. My hand found something thin and slimy. It nearly slipped through my fingers, but I managed to jerk it off my skin and threw it to the dock.

The creature was long, flat like a tapeworm, and sickly white. It slithered toward me, quick as a snake, and leapt. I caught it midair just inches from my face. It hissed, snapping an orifice of needle-like teeth. Spines rose from its skin, glistening with milky liquid. If not for the cloak's protections, they would've pierced my skin and injected whatever it was into my hands.

Despite the spines, the worm was so slick that my bony fingers couldn't maintain a grasp. I couldn't kill the thing with my bright-blade without severing my hand, so I did the only thing I could and threw the worm into the river. It screeched and hissed.

The dark soul remnants swirled around it, dragging it under the surface. Moments later, it floated to the top, limp, lifeless, drowned. I watched as it drifted away, a speck of debris in the massive body of water.

As if I didn't have enough things to worry about, now I had to worry about mind-controlling worms finding me when I least expected them. I looked through my scope and examined Mortis. It seemed the worm that had infected him had tried to find a new host. Death's horse was free—but for how long? If Nyar had infected him and the others once, what was to stop him from doing it again?

A bolt of lightning struck a distant hill. Zeus and Mars appeared amid a puff of smoke. Light blurred across the hills and Hermes joined them. Artemis on her stag bounded into view from a different direction. An instant later, Mars and Zeus stood next to me, Hermes holding onto their arms. Mars had Athena's body slung over one shoulder and Layla's over the other. They watched Artemis approach, eyes narrowed.

Mars growled deep in his throat. "Why is she here?"

"I don't know." Zeus continued watching her. "But she is vital to the safety of our realms, so be nice."

Mars grunted. "I'm aware."

I scoffed. "Wow, Olympian politics are so...normal."

Zeus turned to me and raised an eyebrow. "Well?"

I wanted to be snarky, but figured it was best not to antagonize them. "I found out how to release the souls, but I need ingredients."

The king of the gods towered over me and spoke in a booming voice. "What do you need, mortal?"

"The blood of the killer." I looked pointedly at Mars. "That would be you."

Artemis climbed off her stag and joined us in the middle of the conversation.

Mars scoffed. "I didn't kill Athena."

"No, but I'll need your blood to free Layla." I nodded toward the sword on his back. "Prick yourself, please."

Mars dropped Layla's body roughly to the ground, then set Athena's gently to the other side. "No."

Zeus turned to Hermes. "Fetch the blood of the elf who killed Athena. If the eagle is eating her liver, there should be plenty."

Artemis snorted with repressed laughter. "An elf killed the mighty Athena?"

Mars bared his teeth. "Hold your tongue, you—"

Zeus put up a hand to silence Mars. "It was done through trickery and deceit."

Hermes gave me an amused look. "Have you truly discovered a way to free the souls, or is this just an attempt to make Mars cut himself?"

"This is straight from Thanatos," I said.

"Ah, Thanatos, the original emo god." Hermes laughed. "I'm surprised he helped you. Athena was never kind to him."

Mars scowled. "Where did you find the little weak thing?"

"In Hel." I didn't know if they could tell I was lying, but it was best to keep Thanatos's current activities a secret, especially if they took pleasure in bullying him.

Artemis gave me a nod of approval and turned to them.

"Hel?" Zeus looked aghast. "Why would anyone want to visit some Norse dirt hole?"

Hermes scoffed. "The Norse are filthy enough, but Hel is a mud pit."

I couldn't exactly disagree with his assessment of Hel, but I remained silent.

"Hermes, bring us the blood." Zeus snapped his fingers and lightning crackled between them. "There's no time to waste."

Hermes zipped away without another word.

Mortis staggered to his feet and nibbled at the grass. The wound on his chest was healing at a steady pace, the sunken flesh and bone knitting together. I walked away from the others and patted his neck. "How are you feeling?"

He whickered.

Artemis joined me and flicked her fingers. Everything went silent around us, leading me to believe she'd just blocked sound so we could talk freely. "At least he is healing."

"No thanks to Shraya." I nodded toward the water. "The mind worm came out of Mortis, and I threw it in the river where it died."

Her eyebrows rose. "He is free of the Elder Things?"

I nodded. "For now."

Mortis nuzzled my face and snorted.

I stared at him in puzzlement. "Was that gratitude?"

Mortis bobbed his head and whickered again.

"I thought you didn't like me."

Mortis stomped a hoof and made more horse noises.

"He is grateful, and duty bound." Artemis smiled. "You have made a new friend, Cain."

"Wonderful." I patted Mortis on the neck, then turned and went back to Zeus and Mars who were staring into the distance and conversing quietly.

"What's taking him so long?" Mars said.

Zeus scowled and shook his head.

Wings flapped and Lucifer landed nearby, a wide grin on his face. "Ah, I should have known it."

"Known what?" I looked around to see if others might be joining this ever-growing party. "How did you know I was here?"

"I always have eyes on this place, Cain." He brushed off the lapel of his violet suit and regarded the two gods standing behind me. "What glorious reason brings the Greeks to our humble Purgatory?"

I glanced over at Artemis who was petting Mortis and talking to him. "I found Thanatos and he told me how to free souls."

Lucifer gasped. He clapped his hands together. "How delightful!"

Wind rushed past and Hermes appeared before Zeus.

"What took you so long?" Zeus thundered.

"We have a problem." Hermes held out his hands apologetically. "The elf isn't on the rock anymore. She's gone. Rain has long since washed away her blood."

Lightning crackled in Zeus's eyes. "She's gone?"

"Someone must have freed her." Hermes backed up a step. "She was there a few weeks ago."

"Impossible!" Mars roared. "Nothing could free her from those chains except a god."

"That's not entirely true," Hermes said. "A demigod could do it."

A sneaking suspicion creeped over me. What if one of the gods had moved Aura Beta? What if one of them infected by Nyarlathotep?

37

I raised my staff and peered through the scope at Hermes using the thermal setting. His body heat was off the charts, probably due to an insane metabolism, but there was no sliver of coolness in his brain or elsewhere. Zeus, Mars, and Artemis were clean as well. I turned the scope on Lucifer and found him normal too.

Lucifer backed up a step when I swung the staff toward him. "What are you doing, Cain?"

"Looking for worms."

"Worms?" He wrinkled his nose. "How revolting."

"I'll tell you more later." I walked over to Mortis. "Can you take me somewhere?"

He bobbed a nod.

I swung into the saddle. "I'll be back." Zeus and the others were too busy arguing to pay attention to little old me, so I urged Mortis toward what I hoped was a solution to the dilemma. It took little more than five minutes and a very heated argument to get what I wanted, and then I returned.

Mars was bellowing at Hermes that they needed to mount a search party while Zeus looked ready to unleash a lightning bolt at Hermes's face.

I drew Soultaker and summoned Athena's soul. She appeared, her face screwed up in furious insanity as it had been the last time, her body surrounded by a greenly glowing aura. I put a speck of blood on Soultaker and dipped it into the Styx, then drove it into Athena's chest. She threw back her head and screamed.

Zeus and Mars stopped arguing and stared in open-mouthed horror at the mortally injured ghost. The green aura around Athena's body melted, revealing a brightly illuminated soul. With a final scream, the soul flashed toward Athena's body and was sucked inside.

"You got the blood?" Mars stared in disbelief. "From where?"

"When you beat Aura, she bled all over the sidewalk." I shrugged. "I saved some." It was a necessary lie.

A tortured shriek tore from Athena's throat. She jerked upright, eyes blazing with insanity, and lunged at Mars. His eyes flared in surprise as she slammed into him, and the pair tumbled through the grass.

Lucifer shivered and grinned with delight. "Oh, my. This is even better than I'd hoped it would be."

"Athena, stop!" Mars flailed uselessly as Athena, a mad grin on her face, twisted in front of him and gripped his neck in her powerful hands. She kneed him mercilessly in the crotch several times in a row. Mars howled in pain.

Hermes winced and shielded his eyes as Athena pummeled Mars in the balls three more times then slammed him face-first to the ground. Her fingernails raked down the side of his face, ripping skin.

A bolt of lightning caught her in the chest, and Athena rolled backward, smoke drifting from her leather armor. Zeus slammed her with a massive volley of lightning and Athena finally went down in a heap, groaning weakly.

"What in my name is wrong with her, mortal?" Zeus spun on me, energy crackling across his skin. "What did you do to her?"

I faced him calmly, refusing to cower, for nothing, not even the Death cloak could save me from his wrath. "She has been trapped in a living hell, fighting, killing, and dying every day. It will take some time for her to recover from the trauma."

Zeus hefted Mars to his feet, but the god of war was still nursing his crotch. "Pull yourself together, man!"

Eyes watering in pain, Mars limped over to Athena and booted her in the ribs. "Merciless bitch!"

"Gather her and let us go." Zeus turned to Hermes. "Now!"

Hermes looked reluctantly at the groaning goddess, then picked her up and zipped away.

I stepped in front of the remaining gods. "Mars, I need your blood to revive Layla."

He spat on the ground. "You have ruined Athena! You will get my blood when the earth freezes over."

"Um, that's Hell freezes over, Mars." Lucifer tutted. "And you should give the man what he's owed. You had a bargain, after all."

"I never promised him my blood. I only killed the woman for incentive. Now we have what we want. He can get out of my way or die."

Lucifer stepped next to me, his eyes glowing dangerously. "Mars, you will give the man your blood, or I will—"

"Do what?" Mars jabbed Lucifer in the chest. "You're not even a god."

Lucifer's hand moved so fast it was a blur. He gripped Mars's finger and viciously yanked it. The bone snapped with a sickening sound. "I fought battles in Heaven and defended my throne in Hell, you braindead twit. You've done nothing but murder mortals during your insignificant life. Don't you dare tell me I'm not a god."

Zeus gripped Mars and raised a fist. "I will have a discussion with you about this later, Lucifer." Lightning flashed and he and Mars vanished.

"No!" I shouted. "Give me the blood I earned, you fucking assholes!"

"That's the spirit, Cain!" Lucifer chuckled. "Oh, that felt good. I haven't fought a Greek god in far too long."

"Get me to Olympus, Lucifer!" I gripped Soultaker so tightly my knuckles cracked. "I'm going to murder Mars myself!"

"No need." Lucifer inspected a fingernail, then wiped his finger on the flat of the blade, leaving a red streak. "Athena scratched the poor chap rather hard across the neck." He held up his hand to show it was smeared with blood. "So, I took a bit for you."

I gripped Lucifer in a fierce hug for an instant, then released him, completely taken aback by my strange behavior. "What the fuck? I don't know why I did that."

Lucifer patted my shoulder gently. "Be grateful for such feelings, Cain. They are rare jewels indeed."

I cleared my throat and walked toward the river. "Sure, they are." I summoned Layla's ghost from the sword. She sprang into existence, scowling and clenching her fists. I blew out a breath since I knew what was coming once I freed her soul.

"Protect your crotch, Cain." Lucifer grinned brightly.

I gave a little more thought to what was about to happen and reached for the mortal coil in my utility belt. Unfortunately, it was back at Fitz's securing Pestilence and Famine, so I settled for magically enhanced zip-ties. I approached Layla's physical body and secured her wrists to her ankles. She was no small thing, tall and muscular, so it was hard enough tying her up when she was dead, much less alive and murderous.

Once that was done, I dipped the sword into the river and plunged it into the ghost's chest. Layla's ghost didn't scream or cry out, but silently drifted into the body. She jerked to life with a gasp, shivering violently. Her eyes locked onto mine.

"Cain," she said in a ragged voice. "Cain."

I nodded and knelt next to her, tensed in case she tried to bite my face off. "I'm here and you're alive again."

Layla nodded calmly. "I knew it. Knew you'd get me out." Sweat glistened on her skin. "Okay."

She wasn't making much sense, but her response was a million times better than Athena's. "Do you feel okay?"

She swallowed hard and shook her head. "Hurts."

"What hurts?"

Layla closed her eyes and tears trickled down her cheeks. "Life."

"Poor dear." Lucifer sighed and knelt next to her. "Life is pain. Anyone who says differently is selling you something."

I touched the zip ties on Layla's wrists. "I'm going to release you, okay?"

She nodded dully.

Once I released the zip ties, Layla rose to her feet and looked around. She looked as disoriented as an addict emerging from an opium den after a weeklong binge. I took her hand. "Layla, do you remember what happened?"

"Yes." She took a deep breath and straightened her shoulders. "Can we go home?"

"To your house?" I still didn't know where she lived and felt a little excited at the prospect of finding out despite the circumstances.

She shook her head and touched my chest. "Home."

I flinched.

Lucifer laughed. "Oh, Cain, how sweet this is."

I glared at him. "My house is not her home."

"She apparently doesn't agree with you." He patted my back. "Why don't you lovebirds go home, and we can catch up later?"

"Don't tell anyone I hugged you." I gave him a dangerous look that made absolutely no impact on his grin. "I mean it."

Lucifer smirked. "I'll think about it."

I sighed, knowing full well that everyone was about to know I hugged the damned Devil. I led Layla to Mortis who looked fully recovered, and I helped her into the saddle. I climbed on behind her and gripped the reins. "Mortis, home."

We arrived at the perimeter of Sanctuary moments later. I led us past the wards and took Layla into the house.

Hannah and Shae leapt up from the couch, mouths agape. Aura rose from the couch, a concerned look on her face as she studied Layla's emotionless face.

"It worked?" Aura said.

I nodded. "Your blood worked. You might not have killed Athena, but you and Aura Beta are identical in almost every way that matters."

Aura scowled. "I can't believe you convinced me to help you bring Athena back to life. That bitch cursed my entire bloodline!"

"Yeah, but the curse is gone now." I sighed and looked at Layla. "The cost of killing Athena was too high."

"But Layla's back." Aura raised her eyebrows. "Isn't that your happy ending?"

I shook my head. "I don't think she came back the same."

"Layla?" Hannah leaned into Layla's face and snapped her fingers. "Are you in there?"

Layla's hand blurred and caught Hannah's hand. "Yes, girl." Her voice was a shadow of its normal self, but it was enough to make Hannah smile.

"I hate to admit it, but I'm glad you're back." Hannah kissed Layla on the cheek. "Cain's miserable without you around to torment him."

Shae smiled. "It's been rough."

Layla turned toward me. "Sleep."

"Yeah." I shooed the others away and took Layla into my bedroom. After closing the door, I took her hands. "How are you so calm? You just came from a living hellscape. You had to fight and die repeatedly."

"It was bad, but nothing like my early life." Layla sighed, as if releasing a great weight. "My wings were cut off, Cain. I was tortured daily. This was bad, but not the worst." She gently kissed my cheek, then disrobed and climbed under the bed covers.

I sat next to her and stroked her hair. "Welcome back, Layla."

She snored gently, already asleep.

I lay down next to her and sighed. Layla hadn't reincarnated with the same homicidal rage that Athena had, but her explanation made sense. Even so, I couldn't imagine what could possibly be worse than the unliving hell during her time in the sword.

I pulled out my phone and checked several texts that I'd missed while in the divine realm. Two were from Fitz. It seemed he had some promising results for purging the mind worms. I went back into the den and closed the bedroom door behind me.

Hannah and the others stood just outside studying me as if my expression might offer a clue as to Layla's condition.

I spoke before they could barrage me with questions. "Being trapped in the sword was like being in Hell for all this time. She mindlessly fought, killed, and probably died almost every day. Now that she's back in her body, it'll probably take some time to readjust to living, so leave her alone for now." I headed toward the front door. "I've got another matter to attend to."

"Did you figure out how to fix Garrick?" Hannah said.

I shook my head. "No, but Fitz might have some answers."

Aura touched my hand. "Cain, I'm sorry. I thought things would be okay with Layla back."

I scoffed. "Death is traumatic enough. Having your soul trapped inside an enchanted sword is something she might never recover from." I was also worried about something else. What if Aura Prime's blood wasn't exactly the same as Aura Beta's? It might have been enough to bring back Athena, but what if the magical composition was off just enough to cause side effects? Unfortunately, I didn't have time to think about it. There were far more pressing issues to fix before time ran out.

I went outside and found Mortis waiting on me. He took me to Fitz's backyard. I went into the root cellar and found the witch doctor studying a pale worm in a mason jar. The creature struck against the side of the jar angrily.

Fitz looked up. "Cain, I wasn't sure when you'd return."

I looked at the worm. "You did it? You freed Pestilence and Famine?"

"Pestilence is free." He tapped a scalpel on a jar and the worm flinched back. "As you suspected from your battle with War, intense pain is the key. I concocted various potions to cause her pain, and finally found that intense, stabbing pains work the best." He held up a syringe filled with glowing blue liquid. "This potion seems to do the trick."

It seemed when Shraya stabbed Mortis, she'd unwittingly freed him from his worm. "Why stabbing pains?"

He tapped the jar with the creature. "The worm uses its spines to penetrate the brain and inject various chemical cocktails to induce control. When intense pain occurs, it causes a flood of electrical current across the brain cells. The resulting endorphins somehow counteract the mind control chemicals of the worm. It seems stabbing pains cause higher surges of endorphins."

"What if we just injected someone with endorphins?"

He shook his head. "They must be released directly in the brain to have any effect."

"But you're saying endorphins are what do the trick?"

Fitz swished pursed his lips. "I think it's a combination of endorphins and other neurotransmitters that overcome the worm's chemicals, but I've barely cracked the surface. I had to subject Pestilence to extreme pain before the worm crawled out of her ear. Even then, it attacked me before I was able to trap it in a jar."

"Same thing happened to the worm in Mortis's head." I blew out a breath. "Do you plan to kill that thing? The last thing I need is you getting infected."

"I'd love to study it alive, but I'm afraid it's too risky." He shuddered. "One prick from those spines might sedate me for all I know, and then it would make itself at home in my brain."

"Yep." I cast a sigil and a pair of invisible shields formed inside the jar on either side of the worm. I willed them together and they sandwiched the nasty thing. It shrieked as its spines shattered and its body squished into paste. When I dispelled the shields, there was nothing left but pale ichor beneath the jar.

"Well, it's not much to study, but it's something." Fitz raised the jar and scraped the remains into a petri dish.

I turned to Pestilence who was slumped over. "Is she sleeping?"

He nodded. "She passed out after the worm emerged. I was waiting to see if it did any catastrophic brain damage when it exited."

"Probably." I tugged on the mortal coil. "But once I remove this, she should heal."

"Ah, yes." Fitz nodded. "Perhaps we should test that theory before I awaken Famine and try to force the worm out of her."

"Yeah, maybe so." I just hoped Pestilence wasn't in a murderous mood when I freed her. I knelt next to her. A trail of dried blood streaked from her ear and down her cheek. A steady stream of drool trickled from her mouth and puddled on the floor. "Wow that thing did a number on her."

"Perhaps there are gentler ways to remove these worms, but I'd need multiple subjects to experiment with." Fitz shook his head. "And I really don't have the time to do it anyway."

The ramifications of mind-control worms were far more dire than I wanted to even think about. If Nyar could infect powerful deities, what stopped him from controlling gods? There wasn't a lot that terrified me, but having my free will stripped away by one of these worms was high on my fear factor list. My brief encounter with Nyar proved that he'd known of me for quite some time and wanted me to nurture the seed—whatever that meant.

If I was important to him, why hadn't he infected me with one of these worms? I suspected the answer to that question was very important, indeed. Perhaps there was a price to subjugating a mind. It might make someone less effective at their job if their brain was altered. Maybe that was why Garrick hadn't been infected. Death was instrumental in bringing about the apocalypse while Pestilence, Famine, and War were just along for the ride.

There were too many questions and not nearly enough facts to fill in the blanks. I'd have to be content with freeing the other horsemen for now and just be done with it.

A few slaps to the cheek pulled Pestilence from her stupor. She looked up at me groggily and mumbled something incoherent.

"What's your name?" I said.

"Nugh." She stared at me blankly, head lolling.

"Definitely some catastrophic brain damage." Fitz snapped his fingers in front of her face, but she didn't even flinch. "I just hope it's not permanent."

38

I slid the mortal coil off Pestilence and tightened the slack to keep Famine tied up. Looping my arms under hers, I dragged Pestilence to the side and hoped that her supernatural regeneration would kick in. If it couldn't heal her brain, then it seemed the apocalypse wasn't likely to happen anytime soon with a mentally impaired horseman. Mortis seemed to have recovered quickly, but that didn't guarantee the riders would.

Fitz backed up closer to the stairs, apparently preparing to run if Pestilence regained consciousness and wasn't in a friendly mood. But he needn't have worried, it seemed, because she lay on the floor, gazing blankly, drool trickling from the corner of her mouth.

We continued observing her for nearly half an hour, but there were no visible changes. I blew out a sigh. "Maybe I should take her to Lucifer and see if an angel can heal her, or at the very least, put her in a nursing home for immortals."

"Perhaps." Fitz grimaced. "Just don't tell them I'm the one who brain-damaged one of the horsemen of the apocalypse. I'm not even a Christian."

"I'll tell them she fell off her horse."

He chuckled. "Somehow, I don't think they'll believe that."

I checked the death locater and saw I was running behind on reaping since I'd forgotten to pause death. "Crap. I've got to collect some souls. I'll be back in a while."

Fitz pursed his lips. "I certainly hope Pestilence doesn't recuperate and proceed to tear me limb from limb."

"Maybe I should take her with me. Purgatory might be a safer spot to keep her."

Fitz nodded emphatically. "I would certainly feel safer."

I hefted Pestilence's beefy frame and carried her upstairs where I slung her behind Mortis's saddle.

Fitz handed me a small plastic case. "Take these pain potions. I'm not certain if they'll work on War unless he's been compromised by the mortal coil, but it's worth a try if he comes after you." He glanced at Pestilence. "If she heals, then we can proceed with Famine."

I tucked the case into my utility belt. "Sounds good." I mounted Mortis and directed him to Purgatory. We emerged from Limbo and arrived at the shores of the Styx. Pestilence moaned and lurched, flopping off Mortis's back and onto the ground. Flailing like a dying fish, she screamed incoherently for several seconds and then went still.

"I hope that's a good sign," I muttered to myself.

The brain-damaged horseman, however, remained deathly still, even when I got off the horse and nudged her in the ribs with a Death boot. I picked her up and set her on the dock. Charon wasn't around to keep an eye on her, but deaths were piling up in the mortal world and I couldn't stay here indefinitely.

I blew out a breath and nudged Mortis forward. "Let's do our job."

He whickered in agreement and galloped onward.

By the time I reaped seven souls and returned to the Styx, an hour had passed. Pestilence lay motionless on her side facing away from me. Fearing the worst, I hopped off Mortis and put a finger to her neck to check for a pulse. She flinched and leapt upright, eyes wide with fear. She blinked. Frowned. "Death?"

I still wore the cowl, so only my skull face showed. "Yes. How are you feeling?"

"My head aches as if run through with a sword, but I am alive." She flexed her fingers and shook her head. "The whispering is gone from my thoughts, and I seem to have full control again." Pestilence scowled. "What happened to me?"

I lowered the cowl and revealed my flesh face. "You, Famine, and War were somehow infected with a mind worm. We were able to get it out of you, but it damaged your brain. Do you remember what happened?"

Her gaze went distant. "I remember chasing you. I remember plotting about how to make you ride with us and bring about the end days. But there are gaps—missing time that I can't recall."

"That could be due to the brain damage, or it might be because Nyar's worm made you forget." I shrugged. "At least you're back and you don't seem hell-bent on hunting me down."

"I would never willingly overstep my bounds to bring about the end days!" Pestilence clenched her fists. "Tell me what I must know to make this right."

I filled her in on all the details I knew. She remembered helping bind Garrick's mind when he was in his earthly apartment, and she recalled other tidbits, including me capturing her and Famine.

"How dare an outsider god interfere with us!" Pestilence looked ready to rip something apart with her bare hands. "Our horses are also infected? My dear Ruin has a worm in her brain?"

I assumed Ruin was the name of her horse. "Yes. Can you summon her?"

Pestilence summoned her bow and held it aloft. "I can sense her. She feels my calling, but resists."

"We might have to go to her." I mounted Mortis. "The control of the worm is powerful."

A white horse folded into existence nearby, its two-dimensional form turning sideways and filling out to full three-dimensional proportions. Ruin bucked wildly, neighing and shrieking as if being torn apart from the inside out. Pestilence gripped the reins and managed to calm the horse. I took out the container with the syringes Fitz had given me and readied one.

"Will that remove the worm?" Pestilence said.

"I hope so. Just be ready to kill it." I took the protective cover off the end of the needle. "The last thing we need is one of those worms running loose." I jabbed Ruin and injected her with the potion.

She reared up, jerking the reins from Pestilence's grip, bucking and twisting like a wild bronco in a rodeo. The sounds of pain she made sounded more like a dying human baby than a horse. At long last she stopped bucking, staggered, and collapsed to the ground. Blood spurted from an ear and the worm crawled out.

An arrow sang through the air, penetrating the worm and spearing it to the ground. It hissed and shrieked. Pestilence nocked another arrow in her silver bow and ran over to the squirming worm. She stomped it beneath her armored boot, and it went quiet.

Ruin bellowed and climbed unsteadily to her feet. Pestilence stroked the horse's neck and cooed to her. "Are you okay, my precious?"

The horse whickered and bobbed her head. Like Mortis, it seemed she'd have a quick recovery. I wondered if the mortal coil had contributed to Pestilence's long recovery. With the two of us holding Famine, we could probably test that theory by injecting her without the mortal coil touching her.

I mounted Mortis. "We need to free Famine and then hunt down War. Once you're all back to normal, can you remove the curse from Garrick?"

Pestilence nodded. "Yes. The three of us will need to untangle the threads holding his mind hostage." She patted Ruin. "I'm not sure she's recovered enough to be ridden."

"Mortis can take us."

Pestilence vaulted onto Mortis's back behind me. "Then let us go. Ruin will follow when she's ready."

The other horse neighed and bobbed its head.

Mortis took us back to Fitz's place. The root cellar was locked, so I knocked on the back door.

Fitz answered with a half-empty bottle of bourbon in one hand. He glanced from Pestilence to me and nodded. "She recovered?"

"I did." Pestilence gripped his forearm. "You have done the kingdom of God a service. May he grant you favor."

Fitz winced. "I'm perfectly fine if he never notices me." He flashed a smile. "Safer that way."

Pestilence frowned. "Perhaps you are right. When divinity shines upon a mortal, trouble soon follows."

"That's for damn sure." I nodded toward the cellar. "We're going to try something different with Famine. Can you let us in?"

Fitz took another gulp from the bottle and set it on a counter inside the house, then stepped out back and unlocked the cellar door. "Just try not to destroy my shop, okay?"

"We'll do you one better and take her back to Purgatory with us."

Fitz sighed with relief. "Thank the gods for that."

Keeping Famine secured in the mortal coil, I carried her upstairs. A black hearse carriage appeared behind Mortis. I loaded Famine onto the bench inside, then Pestilence and I sat across from her. Mortis galloped forward, taking us back through Limbo to Purgatory.

"How were you able to secure us with such flimsy looking rope?" Pestilence said as we disembarked the carriage.

"It's magic." I decided not to tell her about the mortal coil just in case. "Once I untie her, we'll have to hold her down while I inject the potion." I unwrapped the mortal coil, leaving a strand touching Famine's wrist and laid the deity on her back. Pestilence sat on her legs, pinning them beneath her. I put my knees on Famine's shoulders and hoped it'd be enough to keep her down.

I inserted the needle into her neck and put a thumb on the plunger. Her skin was so thin and sickly that I had to be careful that the needle didn't poke out the other side.

Then I removed the last strand of mortal coil from her hand. Famine groaned. Her eyes flicked open and she looked up at me with a bafflement followed by anger. I depressed the plunger. Famine's back arched and she screamed in agony. Pestilence and I held her down easily despite her flailing.

Blood trickled from her right ear and the spiny worm crawled out. Pestilence gripped it with an armored glove and crushed it before it got far. Famine went still, eyes wide and staring blankly up at the purgatorial sky. Moments later, she gasped and blinked. Sat up and looked at us.

"I'm free," she murmured.

Pestilence nodded. "You are free."

"Where is Famish?" she said.

"You must call him so we can heal him," Pestilence said.

"Famish?" I grunted. "I thought your horse would be named Starvin' Marvin."

The pair stared blankly at me for a moment, then resumed talking as if I weren't there. Moments later, Famish galloped onto the scene, bucking and fighting the mind worm the same way Ruin had. Once Famine calmed the horse, I injected the potion, and we killed the worm when it emerged. Now we had one final battle to fight, and I wasn't looking forward to it.

I gathered the others once Famish recovered and was ready to ride. "Where can we find War?"

"I don't know." Pestilence shook her head slowly. "We have been all over the world fomenting conflict, unleashing plagues. Each of us had our own tasks to accomplish. All I know is that War was working on something devastating."

"Lovely." I turned to Famine. "Do you have any idea what he was doing?"

"I was too busy starving millions." Famine sighed with contentment. "I have not enjoyed such widespread hunger in ages, but it was all outside the grand plan, thanks to Nyar's mind worms."

"It was wrong, but it was also glorious." Pestilence rubbed Famine's shoulder. "I only wish it had been part of the plan. Now I'm afraid we have upset the balance, making it impossible to tip fate back where it should be."

"How can you enjoy spreading death and destruction?" I shook my head. "The worldwide plague you unleashed is killing millions and nearly destroyed Fate's loom."

Pestilence's eyes brightened. "Ah, yes. Perhaps Fate can discover War's whereabouts by studying the threads on her loom."

Famine looked at me pointedly. "We are proud of our jobs, Death. If we did nothing, the mortals would stagnate and wither on the vine."

"The trick is sowing just enough chaos that it promotes growth and not regression." Pestilence stroked the neck of her horse. "Bad times create strong people. Strong people create good times. Good times create weak people. Weak people create bad times. The cycle continues unabated, each time forcing the mortals to become better while purging the chaff. I'm afraid our actions while controlled by Nyar may bring about regression."

"Once we cure War, we can start setting things right," I said. "Make a cure for the plague and find a way to restore peace and order for a recovery."

Pestilence offered a curt nod. "Agreed. We will ensure the strong are able to lead a recovery. If the weak-minded remain in control, they will undoubtedly plunge the world into a regressive state." Pestilence raised her sword. "Fate we summon thee!"

I blinked. "You can summon her just like that?"

Pestilence nodded. "If she wishes, she can come. I suspect she'll hurry here once she realizes I am the one summoning her."

A few feet away, the air glazed over like fog on a window and unraveled as if someone tugged on a thread. Ithia stepped through the breach and the threads wove themselves together, stitching the hole closed.

"Finally, the tapestry is starting to heal!" She huffed and glared at Famine and Pestilence. "What possessed you to curse Garrick and initiate the end days? Do you know how hard it's been keeping fate from unraveling altogether?"

"An outsider god infected our minds," Famine said. "We ride now to find War and fix him, but we needed your help."

"You wish me to seek him out on the loom." Fate nodded. "Very well." She spread her hands and an intricate web spread out between them. Concentrating on a section of web, she shifted it to the side and eventually came to a section where the threads were shaded crimson and looked as if they'd been hacked off, leaving a gap in the web.

Fate traced a finger on the web. "This is the near future."

"That is an extremely bloody event," Pestilence said.

"Thousands are about to die." Fate studied it a moment. "There will be a major attack against a city. I can't see much more than that." She stopped at a kink in the thread. "This indicates a disruption in fate, an event outside the plan."

"Does this grand plan mean people's lives are on rails and headed for an inevitable conclusion?"

Ithia shook her head. "These are calculations based on decisions. There are agents who nudge things to keep them in line with the architect's grand plan, but people arrive at these decisions mostly on their own." She sighed. "People are predictable."

I studied the kinks but had no idea how they helped us. "So how do we find War?"

Ithia traced a finger over the kinks in the thread. "Within the next hour, this kink will happen. Judging by the severity, I'm almost certain War will be the one to cause it. I keep seeing glimpses of a warehouse as I trace the thread, but the event is still too far out to give me a clear picture."

"You were able to track me when I was out and about." I gave her an expectant look. "Why can't you do that for War?"

"Because his current actions aren't causing massive ripples like yours were." Ithia studied adjacent threads. "The people represented by these threads are from all over the world. I sense Australians, Russians, South Africans, Americans, and even Icelanders. If they were all from one country, I could probably narrow down the location. It seems they were chosen so the connections to his plans wouldn't be obvious."

I studied the threads. "Can you see names?"

"Yes, but that doesn't do much good." Her fingers moved nimbly from thread to thread, gaze distant as she peered through the lens of fate itself. "I am normally forbidden from doing this, but the circumstances are extraordinary." She flinched and paused. "I just glimpsed Red Square in Moscow." Her eyes flared. "The Kremlin is exploding and collapsing."

Pestilence licked her lips. "What else do you see?"

Famine leaned closer. "People starving, I hope?"

"Shush and let me concentrate!" Fate scoffed and began tracing the thread again. Her brow furrowed. "I see people dressed in military uniforms with Ukrainian flags embroidered on the shoulders."

"Ah." Pestilence nodded knowingly. "They wish to create a regional conflict between Russia and Ukraine. Tensions are already high between the two countries. This is likely to explode into full-fledged war."

Famine moaned. "A war to end all wars."

At that moment I realized that finding War was no longer just about saving Garrick and finally getting me out of the soul reaping business. It was about saving Gaia from a cataclysm.

39

I blinked. "You're telling me that War is about to singlehandedly bring about the apocalypse if he goes through with this?"

Pestilence nodded. "It's quite possible."

"Wonderful." I blew out a breath. "Now if only we could find War before this shit show breaks out." Unfortunately, at this point there was nothing we could do but hope Fate had a moment of clairvoyance that led us straight to him. I examined the kink in the thread. "Does the kink represent a fate-altering event?"

Ithia nodded. "In this case, an action from a powerful supernatural agent, perhaps the moment War delivers weapons of mass destruction to the conspirators."

I pointed to the cut threads. "How far out are all those deaths?"

"About three hours from now." Ithia's fingers stopped at the bloody ends. "Oh, no."

"What is it?" I asked.

"Everything past this point is black." She ran her fingers over adjacent threads and others that crossed close to the cut ones. "Earlier I was able to catch glimpses of events beyond this point, but everything is going black, even the uncut threads!"

"That can mean only one thing," Pestilence said grimly. "Fate will be broken by whatever War has planned. Billions of mortals will die."

Ithia frantically pulled the tapestry, scrolling past the bloody hole of cut threads and reached a spot where she could go no further as all the threads simply ended. They didn't look cut so much as they seemed to fade out of existence. Beyond that, only a few threads remained. "Pestilence is right. The plan will be broken, and billions will die over the next few weeks." She scrolled back to the bloody hole and gasped. The threads near the hole were shading crimson, some of them snapping right before our eyes.

"Well, shit." I blew out a breath. "You'd better get us a location fast or there won't be too many tomorrows to come."

Ithia touched the tainted threads. "I can't see anything useful. All I know is that Red Square is the epicenter for the breaking of the loom."

Something occurred to me—something that might help us narrow down War's location. I pulled out the Death manual and flicked through until I reached the section that I needed. The Death beacon was tied to the loom, thus giving it advanced information about who was going to die. I found the setting I was looking for and traced a finger along the top of the device.

White blips traveled across the map at double time, turning green at their final destinations. The beacon could calculate the deaths of everyone within the next twenty-four hours. According to the manual, it wasn't exact, but it was close enough. Six hours from now, the center of Moscow was going to be filled with green blips.

I continued moving my finger across the edge, looking for the maximum peek into the future. I found it eighteen hours away—Ukraine and Russia were covered in green blips. There was no other way to achieve such mass destruction except with nuclear weapons. Death didn't typically collect the souls of those who died in battle, but the vast majority of deaths in a nuclear war would be non-combatant civilians.

I backed up the timeline, scanning Moscow for deaths within the next hour. I found three scattered around the inside perimeter.

"What are you looking for?" Pestilence said.

"Deaths around the time of the kink in the timeline." I zoomed in on one that was closest to Red Square. "Weapons deals almost never go down without some violence and bloodshed, especially if War is involved." I zoomed in on the map and discovered the green blip was inside an apartment building.

"That doesn't seem a likely place for the deal to go down." Pestilence turned to Fate. "It's a warehouse, yes?"

Fate nodded. "I've caught several glimpses of the same warehouse, but there's nothing identifiable about it.

I examined the locations of the other two deaths, and neither were anywhere near a warehouse. It seemed my bright idea was going nowhere. "Ithia, can you share what you see?"

"Not without a medium, I'm afraid." She looked up from the threads. "Why?"

I stood next to her. "When you glimpse something, can you also hear and smell things?"

Ithia nodded slowly. "Yes, why?"

"I want you to close your eyes, listen, and smell when you get the next glimpse."

"Sometimes they pass too quickly for me to sense anything like that." She sighed. "That's why I call them glimpses."

"The moment passes, but it'll still activate your senses." I touched her forehead. "I'm going to give you a memory sigil that'll help hold onto the glimpses for a few extra seconds."

Ithia frowned. Nodded. "You may proceed."

I traced the sigil and powered it. "Now, keep looking."

Famine seemed intrigued. "You are a human wizard?"

"I use magic, but I'm not a wizard." I put a finger to my lips. "Let's be quiet and let Ithia concentrate."

The others nodded and grew silent.

Ithia continued tracing threads, a look of frustration mounting on her face. "That's not it. No, that isn't either." She huffed. "All I see now are adjacent events."

"Describe everything you see and hear."

"People walking. Screams." Her nostrils flared. "It smells dank."

"What do you hear?"

Her forehead pinched. "Traffic. People talking. Water. A distant siren."

"Go to the next one," I said.

"Same thing. Traffic, talking, flowing water."

"Try another one."

Ithia's fingers found another thread next to the kinked one. "It's almost identical. Smells like food this time."

"Now try the one with the kink in it."

She traced her fingers along it, face straining like someone trying to enhance their senses through willpower alone, or possibly someone who'd just eaten ogre cuisine for the first time and had to rush to the bathroom. A soft gasp escaped her lips. "Finally, I see it again."

I touched the sigil on her forehead and sent more power into it. "You know the routine. Tell me everything you sensed."

"Only a few people talking. It smells like food." Her head tilted. "I hear water and there's a really strange boat through the window."

"A boat? Small or large?"

"It looks like a pirate ship and there's a giant man standing on it."

Pestilence snapped her fingers and spoke in Russian. "Peter the Great's monument on the Moscow river!"

I nodded. "That's it. They're in a building on the Moscow River." I checked a map of the area on my phone and found the monument. There was a park without buildings on one side of the river near the statue. But opposite that were four buildings all of which sat right on the river and had restaurants nearby. Only one of them was large enough to be considered a warehouse.

"Found something?" Pestilence said.

I nodded. "I think we've got the location." I whistled and Mortis trotted over. "Let's go catch War before he blows up the world."

The other horsemen hopped on their steeds, and we took off for Russia. We crossed through folded Limbo and reached Moscow moments later. Historic buildings along the river popped up like props for a theatre production. Peter's monument appeared on a small island in the middle of the water.

The first thing that caught my attention was the missile battery on the roof of the building. The second thing I noticed was the men loading it with large, guided missiles. Despite it being out in the open, none of the passing pedestrians or military police seemed remotely aware of it.

Pestilence halted her horse. "War is hiding the weapon with glamour."

Famine gasped. "That's against the rules. It's no wonder he'll cause a kink in the timeline."

"War, like us, is an instrument of fate." Pestilence shook her head. "That worm in his mind is causing him to defy his duty. That is what will cause the kink."

"Well, whatever causes the kink, we need to stop it." I directed Mortis toward the building. "It doesn't look like we have much time before they'll have that thing loaded." Mortis had proven he could run up the side of a building, and that seemed like the quickest route to nipping this in the bud.

Mortis took a few steps forward, then stopped and turned in place. I urged him on, but he whickered and shook his head.

Pestilence held up a hand. "There is something protecting the building. I believe it is warded to prevent our horses from getting too close."

I hopped off Mortis and took a few steps. Nothing stopped me.

"Those are American missiles being loaded by men in Ukrainian uniforms." Pestilence frowned. "It's no wonder this event breaks the world."

"People posing as Ukrainian insurgents firing American weapons at the Kremlin seems like the perfect way to trigger an international incident." I jogged toward the building and shoved against the metal door on the side. Naturally, it was locked. I summoned my bright-blade and slashed through the latch, then kicked it open.

The inside was wide open with exposed metal beams and a concrete floor. Sections looked as if they'd once been rooms but had been demolished down to the bare bones. The place smelled dank, like stagnant water. A large hole blasted in the middle of the floor seemed to be the source of the odor.

Pestilence looked up at a hole cut into the concrete ceiling. A large hoist hook dangled just on the other side. She walked over to the hole in the floor and grunted. "It appears the weapon was brought in by the river and then smuggled in here."

I stepped beside her and peered over the edge. Water filled the bottom half of the hole. A tunnel bored into the wall led to the river, but the end was covered with wooden planks, blocking a clear view outside. The pool was large enough to hold a sizable boat capable of carrying cargo like a missile battery.

"You two were working with War all this time and you didn't know about this plot?"

"We were on missions of our own," Famine said. "Although I'm having trouble remembering exactly what they were."

Even if they had been in on the plan, the removal of the worms had probably damaged their memories and caused memory loss. That, and Nyar had made them carry out his plans separately from each other. I'd thought Cthulhu was clever, but Nyar made him look like an amateur by comparison.

A door at the far end of the space opened and War stepped through, a smile spreading across his face when he saw Pestilence and Famine. "I see you finally caught the troublesome one. Has he agreed to ride with us?"

I decided to play along, draw him closer, and snare him so we could inject him with the potion. "They got me."

Famine, however, had other plans. "We are free of Nyar's bonds, War, and have come to free you as well."

His eyes flared. "What?"

"Why would you tell him that?" Pestilence shouted. "All we had to do was lure him over and be done with this mess."

Famine frowned. "I didn't think of that."

War drew his great red sword and rammed it to the floor. "Famine never was good at strategy. Nyar, however, is a supreme master of it."

"You're just saying that because he's controlling you," I said, trying to keep him talking so I could find a way to get closer before he made a run for it. "Are you too weak to resist him?"

The water in the pool bubbled and boiled. Slick-skinned creatures swarmed the surface, humanoids with frog legs, angler fish hybrids, and several other varieties of deep ones. They swarmed up the sides of the holes and leapt up in front of us. Water sprayed into the air as a giant pale worm burst from below. Its mouth peeled open in layers, revealing rows of sharp teeth and tentacles. It screeched, spraying salty water and pale goo across the floor.

There were plenty of deep ones to deal with as it was, but a freaking dhole took things up to a whole new level.

Pestilence drew her bow and aimed the flaming tip at the deep ones. "War, look within yourself and realize that you are being manipulated. Fight Nyar's control that we might help you."

War whipped his sword through the air. "I'm afraid that war has already been lost."

"Is that you Nyar?" I shouted above the croaks, grunts, and animalistic noises of the deep ones. "Do you really want the world to end?"

"Yes, Cain, it's me." War's voice changed slightly, becoming so guttural it almost sounded as if he were choking on tentacles. "This world must reach an end so it may begin anew."

"How are your worms strong enough to control deities like War?" I said, trying to stall.

"A good question," Nyar replied through War. "One that I will provide no answer to."

I changed subjects, hoping to elicit a response. "What's the seed you want me to nurture?"

"Cain, even though this world is about to meet its end, you will still be very useful. You must go now and survive what is to come, for my plan will have great need of you in the years ahead."

He glanced up and I realized that Nyar was the one stalling, not me. The kink in the timeline was minutes away, meaning the instant that missile battery was operational, he'd use it to trigger the apocalypse. There was no way in hell we were fighting our way through this small army before the launcher was ready. I needed to get back outside and find another way to the top of the building.

I couldn't fool Nyar by pretending to give up and leave. That would be too obvious, and he'd simply put more deep ones on the roof to guard the insurgents. I also couldn't run outside and have Mortis run me up the side of the building thanks to the protective wards.

The ground rumbled. The concrete heaved up behind us and another dhole burst to the surface. Its tentacles wrapped around Famine. She struggled to break the monster's hold, but it was too strong. Pestilence charged the beast, firing a flurry of arrows. The deep ones swarmed toward us, forcing us toward the newly made pit where the second dhole waited, maw quivering in anticipation.

"Take a seat and relax." Nyar whirled War's sword. "I will release you unharmed shortly."

Oddly enough, I trusted that Nyar would release me as he said. He seemed to need me for some nefarious purpose I had yet to figure out. Even so, I didn't like the idea of falling into the slimy grasp of deep ones. Smelling fish breath up close wasn't the way I wanted to spend the next few hours of my life.

Unfortunately, this was an impossible fight to win even with the supernatural strength of Death's vestments and the help of Pestilence and Famine. We three horseless horsemen might be able to overcome this small army under normal circumstances, but the wards around this place were also sapping our strength. At best, all could hope for was to run in circles and stay out of the grasp of the deep ones.

As it turned out, that was the only path that might take me to victory.

An outside observer might look on the situation as completely hopeless. Swarms of deep ones, a pair of giant worms, and a mind-controlled god of war, all standing in my way. Under normal circumstances, they'd be correct. I had an ace up my sleeve, but it was a razor sharp, quadruple-edged card that would, no doubt, make me regret having ever used it. Unfortunately, to stop this madness, I had little choice.

I considered giving Nyar another warning, imploring him to cease and desist, but it was obvious that no threat could dissuade him from using War as a puppet to kick off the apocalypse with fireworks. I was going to have to use Soultaker right in the middle of Moscow and pray that I could keep the army under control long enough to stop Nyar while also not leaving a swath of utter destruction in my wake.

One thing was guaranteed. This would not end well.

40

I slipped on the ring I'd taken from Aura Beta and prayed it worked inside the wards. My vision split and the warehouse appeared. I would have breathed a sigh of relief, but what I was about to do would be like using a sledgehammer to swat a fly.

I willed myself to switch to the warehouse just as a horde of deep ones swarmed my position. They piled onto each other, those behind them shoving and pushing, apparently unaware that the prey had slipped through the clutches at the last instant. That was when I realized that there was another way out of this mess that didn't require nuking downtown Moscow with an army of the dead.

Keeping focused on the building in Moscow, I willed myself to move toward the door behind War. He watched the deep ones swarming my previous position, unaware that my body was somewhere far, far away. I continued past him and to the stairs. Waves of dizziness passed over me and I staggered. Just as before, using the ring like this for too long was giving me a headache and causing disorientation. It felt as if my brain were being stabbed by tiny needles.

I could take off the ring and recover in the warehouse, but that would take precious moments the world didn't have. The insurgents on the roof would launch the missiles the instant they were loaded. All they had to do was launch a couple of them and that would probably be enough to set in motion the cascade of events leading to the end days.

There were only two options available to me.

Option One: I step back through to Moscow, take off the ring, and sneak my way upstairs. There was a good chance I could make it most of the way before War spotted me. By then, it'd be too late for him to stop me from killing his squad of insurgents. The downside to the plan was then I'd have to fight War and it was likely he'd find a way to launch the missiles with the help of the deep ones or the dholes.

Option Two was already better, so I just went with it. I willed myself back through to Moscow and took off the ring. I was already standing directly behind War. He was completely under the control of Nyar, and I hoped that didn't make what I was about to do a stupid decision.

There was no more time to think, so I reached into my utility belt, grabbed a syringe, and slammed it directly into War's neck. He flinched so quickly that I didn't have time to depress the injector. War spun, the syringe jutting from his neck. His sword blurred toward my neck. I ghostwalked behind him and slammed the palm of my hand against the plunger.

War stiffened and shrieked in Nyar's guttural voice. I booted him headlong down in the mass of deep ones, then spun and ran upstairs, drawing my staff and activating the brightblade. The metal door at the top was locked from the other side. I slashed the hinges on one side and the latch on the other, then used all of my Death strength to rip the door out of the way. It clanged its way downstairs, slamming into pursuing deep ones and sending them tumbling over the sides.

I stepped onto the roof. Gunfire exploded. Bullets pinged off the brick wall. I spotted the nearest gunner and ghostwalked five feet to my left since I didn't have the range to make it behind him. His eyes flared. I dashed forward, slid, and slashed off his legs as I passed by. He screamed and the rifle clattered to the roof.

I rolled, switched the staff to longshot mode and aimed at a gunman across the roof. His head exploded as the kinetic magic ripped through his cranium. I aimed at his buddy next to him and took him out before he knew what was happening. My dueling wands would have been ideal for the situation, but I didn't have them on me.

The remaining insurgents took cover behind the missile battery and the metal frame of the hoist that had been used to lift it to the roof. The hook was still attached to the launcher by a metal loop on the top since they apparently hadn't taken the time to disconnect it in their haste to load the missiles. The gunmen raised their rifles over the side of the hoist frame, firing blindly at my position.

Bullets pinged off the Death cloak and one struck the cowl. It was like being hit in the head with a rubber mallet. My vision swam for an instant. I rolled behind a metal duct and shook my head as if that would help me recover my senses faster.

"How in the hell do they see me?" The Death cloak should have hidden me, but the bullets pinging all around told me otherwise. It probably had something to do with the wards protecting the building. They prevented Mortis from running up it and also apparently made me visible even to mortals.

On the upside, their attacks had enabled me to return fire. Still, it would have been much simpler to invisibly make my way to the missile battery and disable it.

At least the protective properties of the cloak still worked, or they would have blown off my head. The cloak might keep me from being riddled with bullets, but there was no way I could wade through a hail of gunfire to reach the targets. I spotted a stack of crates to the left that were just within range of ghostwalking. Doing it while prone on the ground wasn't as easy as standing up. I concentrated on where I wanted to go, then rolled toward it.

I blipped into position behind the crates and took a second to reassess the situation. The insurgents were still firing on my old position just a few feet away. I peeked around the left corner of the crates and saw one of the insurgents making a run for a laptop connected by a cable to the battery. It didn't take a missile scientist to realize pressing a few keys on the keyboard would launch the missiles.

We were some distance away from Red Square and the intended targets, but that didn't matter to guided missiles. The coordinates were probably already programmed in via the laptop and launching the missiles would send each of them to their targets. It was hard to tell from this angle, but it looked like the battery was fully loaded with twelve missiles.

There was no other cover between me and their position, meaning no way for me to sneak my way around behind them, not even with ghostwalking. I'd worked my way into a bad spot, and I didn't see how I was going to get out of it.

Gurgling voices echoed from the stairwell leading back down into the building and then deep ones exploded through the doorway and onto the roof. The insurgents shouted in panicked voices. They obviously hadn't known about the supernatural when War came to them with an opportunity to start World War Three, and the deep ones were their surprise introduction to eldritch horrors.

Thinking the deep ones were a new threat, the insurgents unleashed a hail of gunfire at them. Their unsuspecting allies roared in surprise.

I used the opportunity to look for an opening that would allow me to take out the missile battery. The easiest choice presented itself almost at once. I took aim with the staff and fired a shot at the cable connecting the console to the launcher. Sparks flew and the lights on the console went dead.

"Easy, peasy." I would've patted myself on the back, but there were about twenty deep ones and gunslinging insurgents between me and freedom.

One of the gunmen raced for the missiles and tore a panel off the side of the battery. He frantically flicked a row of switches an instant before I blew off the top of his skull with another shot. The battery hummed to life. Flames flickered as the missiles prepared to fire.

Firing at the missile battery would do nothing. The launch sequence was already started, and I couldn't prevent all those missiles from taking flight in the next few seconds. Shooting one of them in the nose would presumably ignite the payload and destroy the rest of them in the process, but there was no guarantee that would work.

One insurgent was firing on my position while the others unloaded on the deep ones. Those odds were good enough for me to risk doing the only thing I could do. I ran toward the missile battery, bullets slamming into the cloak. I staggered and winced with every blow.

Thankfully, the lone person firing on me was in full spray and pray mode, missing at least seventy percent of his shots. The gunfire ceased as he paused to reload. I took that instant of reprieve and ghostwalked closer to the battery just as the missiles in the launcher roared to life with full ignition. I slammed the button on the hoist controls. The hook yanked the battery sideways, dragging it over the hole in the roof. I turned on the brightblade and slashed the cable.

The battery plummeted just as the missiles launched.

Explosions rocked the building. The roof crumbled at the edges and the entire structure shook. I had about ten seconds before the entire place fell apart beneath me. Gunfire abruptly stopped as the insurgents screamed and fell into the abyss opening beneath their feet. Deep ones howled and gurgled. I ran toward the back section of the roof. There was no fire escape, no stairwell that could get me safely down five stories and to the ground.

Even if there were, the building would fall apart before I could descend stairs or a ladder. I didn't even have time to reach into my utility belt, grab the ring, and slip it on so I could transition to the warehouse.

So, I did the only thing I could and took a leap of faith. Faith that the vestments of Death might keep me from pancaking on the road far below. Faith that maybe I could survive with a few dozen broken bones if I didn't die on impact. Faith that maybe if I jumped far enough, I could reach the building across the road and grab a ledge.

Smoke engulfed me as I reached the edge of the roof. I gave it everything I had and jumped, flailing my legs and arms like a long jumper in the vain hope that it would be good enough to cross the gulf between this building and the next. Unfortunately, the roof gave out right when I jumped.

I dropped like a lead balloon.

My crotch slammed into something. I grunted in pain and doubled over, finding Mortis's mane in my face. He neighed as if amused while we flew at frightening speed toward the brick wall of the building across the road. The building abruptly folded like a deck of cards and we crashed to earth in the blackness of Limbo.

Mortis stumbled and fell. I flew off his back and rolled across the obsidian terrain, coming to a halt through no effort of my own. My body ached right down to the bones. Then again, I was nothing but bones while wearing the cloak, so maybe my flesh had avoided the worst of it.

I climbed to my feet while Mortis did the same. He stumbled, apparently still not a hundred percent recovered from Shraya's horn. I walked over to him and patted his neck. "Nice save."

He whickered and nuzzled my hair.

"Does this mean you don't really hate me? That it was just the worm talking before?"

He snorted black mist my face then wagged his head in the direction of his back. I took the hint and climbed on.

"How did you get to me on the building?"

He galloped forward and Moscow popped into existence around us again. Mortis stood on a building neighboring a smoking pile of rubble. He stomped his foot then bobbed his head toward the destroyed building.

Screaming people below scattered in all directions as the rest of the building collapsed. Others watched in horror from a safe distance while others freed people from the rubble. A man cried out in terror as he uncovered a deep one. A dhole burst from the ground and shrieked. People scattered and fled, their cries echoing through the streets.

I understood what Mortis was trying to tell me. "The explosion destroyed the walls that were warded, allowing you to leap across to the roof."

He bobbed a nod.

More deep ones emerged from the rubble. The dhole gripped giant pieces of concrete in its mouth and hurled them away, slamming them into nearby buildings as it cleared the water-filled crater that had once been hidden in the building. Deep ones dove into the water, and the dhole vanished beneath the surface once more.

I counted at least a dozen people recording everything with their phones.

"This is a real fucking mess." It wouldn't be long before the internet was awash with copies of the videos. I just wondered if the nubs would believe they were real. Then again, it wasn't my problem.

Anxiety wormed through my insides as I looked for any sign of the horsemen. If I'd blown them up, then Garrick would be comatose for the rest of his life, and I'd be stuck with the mantle of Death unless I found someone to take the thankless job from me. I could probably just abandon the job, but it wouldn't look good on my resume, and I really didn't want to deal with another zombie uprising anytime soon.

The horsemen might be tough, but I saw no sign they'd survived the missile explosions. It seemed I'd well and truly fucked myself.

41

The hairs on the back of my neck prickled. I spun around as Famine and Pestilence folded into being behind me. They didn't look any the worse for wear.

I frowned. "How'd you make it out?"

"When you injected War with the potion, the dholes and deep ones went crazy." Pestilence pursed her lips. "I think ripping them from Nyar's control must have hurt them. The dholes released us, and we were able to gather War and exit the building."

I scowled. "You mean, you left me in there fighting an army all by myself?"

"You did well." Famine grinned, revealing meth-head teeth. "Masterful moves from a mortal, I must say."

"Very impressive." Pestilence tilted her head slightly. "You see, we have been in our roles since the beginning. We were created for our sole purposes and not bequeathed powers by a god like Thanatos. We have always looked down at Death, thinking of him as an errand boy rather than a true incarnation of purpose. A mere shadow compared to Thanatos."

Famine nodded. "We were mistaken. Though you are not Garrick, you have proven that in the right hands, Death is most formidable."

"Well, you can take this job and shove it. I ain't working here no more if I have a choice." I blew out a breath. "Where's War? I want you to revive Garrick so I can get out of this cloak ASAP."

"He's in Purgatory recuperating." Pestilence smiled. "The havoc unleashed today was glorious. I am curious if our intervention was enough to avoid the kink in fate, or if we have only delayed it."

I really didn't care. I just wanted to go home and watch a movie with Hannah and Shae, then go to sleep in my own bed. "Mortis, take me to Garrick, please." I turned to the others. "Join me and bring War."

Mortis puffed black vapors from his nose and gave Famine and Pestilence a look before leaping from the building and taking us to the desired destination. I hopped off Mortis and waited in the front yard of Garrick's house. Moments later, the other three horsemen appeared. War looked a bit unsteady in the saddle. He averted his gaze when he saw me, eyes to the ground. He was a powerful being, accustomed to manipulating the bloodlust of men. Thanks to Nyar, he now knew what being on the receiving end was like.

"Ready to do this?" I said.

The others nodded and climbed off their horses.

War approached me. "Cain, I am truly sorry for my actions."

I waved him off. "They weren't your actions. If you want to pay me back, find out how in the hell Nyar was able to infect you with his worms. If he can control you, what's to stop him from controlling other gods?"

War nodded enthusiastically. "It will not happen again."

"Good." I went inside.

Yuki ran from upstairs, a rapier in hand. She flinched when she saw us. "Why did you bring the enemy into my home, Cain?"

"They were being controlled by an Elder Thing." I sighed loudly. "Look, can I explain later? I just want Garrick back on his feet so I can get on with my day."

She bared her teeth. "How do I know you're not being controlled?"

I held out my hands. "I've got no strings to hold me down. To make me fret, to make me frown."

Yuki bared her teeth harder, but she lowered the sword. "Then help Garrick and get out of my home."

The three horsemen went into the bedroom and finished their business in a matter of minutes. Then they apologized to Yuki and left because she looked as if she wanted to beat them all to a pulp.

Garrick yawned and woke up a little later. He sat up and saw me at the foot of his bed. Yuki peppered him with kisses and asked if he was okay.

Garrick groaned. "They got me, didn't they?"

I'd taken off the cloak and was just plain old me. I nodded. "Yup. I hope you're well rested, because I'm done reaping souls."

"Aren't you even going to tell me what happened?" he said.

"Later." I headed for the door. "Hell, I don't even know what time it is in my time zone right now. If it's not too late, you can find me at Voltaire's. I need a drink."

Yuki nodded. "Cain, thank you."

"Any time." I stepped through the door and paused. "I don't mean that literally. Find someone else next time, okay?" Then I went downstairs and outside.

Mortis looked up from grazing and whickered.

"Can you give me a lift home, please?"

He bobbed a nod and turned so I could climb into the saddle. Then he fast traveled to the edge of Sanctuary. I dismounted and patted his neck. "I'll walk from here."

Mortis nudged my shoulder, snorted, then folded away into Limbo.

The sky was pink with the rising sun. I hoped this meant Gaia had survived another crisis, but I was too tired to worry about it. I walked to the church and went inside. The girls were still asleep, so I went into my room and dropped onto the bed, too tired to take a shower. Layla wasn't there. I'd been gone a while, so it was likely she'd gone to wherever she lived in the meantime.

· · ·

I WOKE UP AT NOON, but the girls weren't there. A quick check of my phone told me it was a school day. I made a sandwich and savored the crunch of lettuce, the tang of homegrown tomatoes, and the sting of spicy mustard on my tongue. It was beyond amazing to have things back to normal.

There were obviously plenty of loose ends to worry about. Aura Beta was free from Prometheus's rock. Nyar was proving to be a bigger threat than Cthulhu had ever dreamed of being. There was no telling if Layla and Athena would recover from their time in Soultaker.

And then there were the big items.

I now had a way to free most of the souls in Soultaker. Mars had slain the majority of them, and I had his blood. I assumed by freeing souls with no bodies to inhabit that they would go to their respective afterlives. It was something I needed to think about long and hard before doing it.

Souls released from Soultaker would be even more insane than the souls I'd freed from the zombies. It wasn't something I even had to do, but keeping souls trapped in such a place was a fate worse than Hell, Hel, or Hades. I'd want to be freed if I were trapped in such a place. Having experienced at least two of the underworlds on that list, I could safely speak from experience that anything was better than the hellscape inside Soultaker.

It was still hard to believe everything I'd done over the span of the last couple of weeks. I'd stopped a zombie apocalypse, led a Norse uprising in Hel, captured and cured three horsemen of the apocalypse, and stopped a small group of insurgents from unleashing Armageddon. I had a lot to think about. I really didn't want Aura Beta free to wreak havoc again, so she was high on my priority list.

But that could wait. It was time to rest, relax, and most importantly, enjoy a mangorita.

EPILOGUE

I drove the rental car down the winding roads of the Pacific Coast Highway, passing mansions precariously perched atop the cliffs facing the ocean. I parked at a scenic overview and grabbed a backpack from the passenger seat. A short hike took me to the towering black walls of my destination.

The dark gray mansion was built in a contemporary style—all rectangles and cubes with huge windows facing the road and the ocean. It rose like a jumble of building blocks from behind the high walls protecting its secrets.

It was high time those secrets were brought to life, and time for the homeowner meet his demise.

I was no longer Death, no longer bound by the strict rules governing the deity. Now I was just little old Cain, master of my own destiny. I peered through the true sight scope at the wall. It was covered in glowing runes and sigils—a strange mix of magics that would confound most wizards.

Oblivion Guard training offered many ways of bypassing even the toughest of wards. Unfortunately, many of those ways utilized enchanted objects that I no longer had at my disposal. I'd have to rely on my deep knowledge of encrypted sigils to untie the protections guarding this place.

I started toward the wall then paused. The ground was rocky up until it reached the base of the wall where rows of scrub brush had been planted in sandy soil. The landscaping caught my attention because it seemed unnecessary. Then again, rich people did strange things.

The true sight scope indicated nothing wrong with the sand, nor did it indicate any explosives or traps were hidden there. There was no such thing as being too cautious, so I continued to be suspicious of the sand, stopping right at the edge of it, kneeling, and inspecting it.

"Cain, don't."

Normally, my brightblade would have been out in an instant, but I'd expected something like this might happen. I turned and faced Ithia. "Why not?"

"Because you discovered Alistair during your time as Death." She sighed. "You weren't supposed to ever be Death. Fate was subverted and nearly broken. If you remove Alistair from the tapestry, the ripple effects will threaten everything all over again."

"You're telling me that a strange twist of fate means I can't end that monster?" I scowled. "He's murdering kids and turning them into his own personal zombie army!"

"Be that as it may, you have insider information that you shouldn't have. You cannot take action, or you'll risk destroying the loom again."

"Visitors? What a surprise!" Alistair stood atop the roof of his house, peering down at us with his special glasses. "Would you like to come in for drinks and entertainment?"

My brightblade sizzled to life in my hand. "How about a home cooked meal of necromancer?"

He laughed. "I recognize you, Cain Sthyldor."

I froze. "How in Hel do you know my name?"

"Come inside for refreshments and I'll tell you all about it." He looked at Ithia. "And that lovely deity may come as well."

Ithia growled and waved a hand. The world around us froze. "Cain, leave now. Your presence here is damaging fate already!"

"No." I swung the brightblade. "I'm going to end that sick fucker."

"You do, and everything you did to help Death will be for nothing!" She slapped me so hard I saw stars.

I rubbed my jaw. Without the protections of the Death cloak, that shit hurt. "What's your problem, Fate? Will taking out one demented, murdering pervert really cause that much damage or is there another reason you're protecting him?"

Ithia jabbed a finger in my face. "Don't make me remove you myself, Cain."

"Won't you be the one fucking with fate then?"

She shook her head. "No, I'll be doing my job and protecting it. Trust me when I say that this will devastate the timeline."

I pointed my brightblade at Alistair. "Let's fuck around and find out."

"There is no finding out, Cain, because I already know!"

"Instead of taking that chance, you could trust me." A man in a blue cloak stood to my other side, an hourglass in his hand.

"Gods be damned, you people just love to show up and spoil a good time." I scoffed. "Chronos, I presume? Where were you when the other horsemen were trying to start Armageddon?"

"I have been tracking and repairing fractures in the timeline." He lowered his hood. "Death, Fate, and Time have a special synergy that keeps mortal affairs running smoothly. Unfortunately, this latest crisis unleashed a storm of alternate timelines. Not all of them will survive, but those that continue to exist may wreak havoc with Prime."

"Wonderful." I threw up my hands. "I'm not Death anymore, so why don't you run along with Fate and fix things?"

"Because you're about to cause another fracture, Cain." He folded his arms over his chest. "Please, for the love of all that's holy, leave this alone and go home. You've earned the rest."

I paced back and forth, occasionally glancing up at Alistair's frozen smirk. As much as I wanted to kill the prick, ignoring the warnings of the guy whose job it was to manage time was foolish. I turned to Chronos. "Can't you just go back in time and fix things?"

He shook his head. "There is no such thing as true time travel, Cain. I can look into the past and sometimes into the future, but there are no second chances, no mulligans. We have to get everything right in the present or deal with the consequences."

I threw up my hands. "Great. So now we've got more than just Alpha and Beta dimensions to deal with?"

"I suggest you pay a visit to Beta if you want to see what Prime might look like if our timeline continues to take damage." He sighed. "And yes, I'm still tracking the new timelines to see which survive."

I banished my staff and headed back toward my car. "Fine."

Chronos paced alongside me. "While you're here, there's a place you might like to visit."

I raised an eyebrow. "Are you a part-time travel guide too?"

"I hear you like mangoritas."

I stopped walking. "You've got my attention."

He motioned toward the rental car. "I'll show you where to go."

"I'm coming too." Ithia hurried after us. "Alistair will resume real time in thirty seconds."

Chronos nodded. "Good. Hopefully this visit didn't do too much harm." His gaze went distant. "I already feel two more timelines forming from this juncture, but let's hope they wither and die."

I slapped the roof of the car. "You mentioned mangoritas."

He blinked from his reverie. "Yep. A great little place down on the beach makes them."

I stared at the dark specter of Alistair's mansion. I wasn't finished with him, not by a long shot.

Ithia blinked. "Garrick will join us shortly."

I blew out a breath. "Gods be damned. Never thought I'd be having mangoritas with Fate, Time, and Death."

"Neither did we realize your importance, Cain." Chronos climbed into the passenger seat of the rental. "There's a lot to talk about."

"Indeed." Ithia frowned. "I wanted shotgun."

Chronos grinned. "Guess your timing was off."

I groaned. "I'll be you're just full of time puns, aren't you?"

"You can't imagine." Ithia climbed into the backseat.

"I do enjoy them from time to time." Chronos smirked.

I got into the driver's seat and started the car. *Fate, Time, and regular old Cain walk into a bar.* I was sure there was a joke in there somewhere. Maybe tonight was the night to find out what it was.

BOOKS BY JOHN CORWIN

Join the Overworld Conclave for all the news, memes and tentacles you could ever desire!

https://www.facebook.com/groups/overworldconclave

Or get your tentacles via email: www.johncorwin.net

Fan page: https://www.facebook.com/johncorwinauthor

CHRONICLES OF CAIN

To Kill a Unicorn

Enter Oblivion

Throne of Lies

At The Forest of Madness

The Dead Never Die

Shadow of Cthulhu

Cabal of Chaos

Monster Squad

THE OVERWORLD CHRONICLES

Sweet Blood of Mine

Dark Light of Mine

Fallen Angel of Mine

Dread Nemesis of Mine

Twisted Sister of Mine

Dearest Mother of Mine

Infernal Father of Mine

Sinister Seraphim of Mine

Wicked War of Mine

Dire Destiny of Ours

Aetherial Annihilation

Baleful Betrayal

Ominous Odyssey

Insidious Insurrection

Utopia Undone

Overworld Apocalypse

Apocryphan Rising

Soul Storm

Devil's Due

Overworld Ascension

Assignment Zero (An Elyssa Short Story)

OVERWORLD UNDERGROUND

Soul Seer

Demonicus

Infernal Blade

OVERWORLD ARCANUM

Conrad Edison and the Living Curse

Conrad Edison and the Anchored World

Conrad Edison and the Broken Relic

Conrad Edison and the Infernal Design

Conrad Edison and the First Power

STAND ALONE NOVELS

Mars Rising

No Darker Fate

The Next Thing I Knew

Outsourced

ABOUT THE AUTHOR

John Corwin is the bestselling author of the Overworld Chronicles and Chronicles of Cain. He enjoys long walks on the beach and is a firm believer in puppies and kittens.

After years of getting into trouble thanks to his overactive imagination, John abandoned his male modeling career to write books.

He resides in Atlanta.

Join the Overworld Conclave for all the news, memes and tentacles you could ever desire!
https://www.facebook.com/groups/overworldconclave
Or get your tentacles via email: www.johncorwin.net
Fan page: https://www.facebook.com/johncorwinauthor
Website: http://www.johncorwin.net
Twitter: http://twitter.com/#!/John_Corwin